GALACTIC HOT DOGS™
THE WIENER STRIKES BACK
BOOK 2

By MAX BRALLIER
Illustrated by RACHEL MAGUIRE & NICHOLE KELLEY

CREATED BY MAX BRALLIER

ALADDIN
New York   London   Toronto   Sydney   New Delhi

🪔
ALADDIN
An imprint of Simon & Schuster Children's Publishing Division
1230 Avenue of the Americas, New York, NY 10020
First Aladdin paper-over-board edition May 2016
Copyright © 2016 by Sandbox Networks, Inc.
Cover art by Vivienne To
All rights reserved, including the right of reproduction in whole or in part in any form.
ALADDIN is a trademark of Simon & Schuster, Inc., and related logo is a registered trademark of Simon & Schuster, Inc.
For information about special discounts for bulk purchases, please contact Simon & Schuster Special Sales at 1-866-506-1949 or business@simonandschuster.com.
The Simon & Schuster Speakers Bureau can bring authors to your live event. For more information or to book an event contact the Simon & Schuster Speakers Bureau at 1-866-248-3049 or visit our website at www.simonspeakers.com.
Designed by Rachel Maguire, Nichole Kelley, and Dan Potash
The text of this book was set in Good Dog.
Manufactured in the United States of America 0316 FFG
10 9 8 7 6 5 4 3 2 1
Library of Congress Control Number 2015952897
ISBN 978-1-4814-2496-7 (POB)
ISBN 978-1-4814-2497-4 (eBook)

For my dad. The best any kid could ask for.
I love you.

—M. B.

To my trifecta!

—R. M.

PROLOGUE

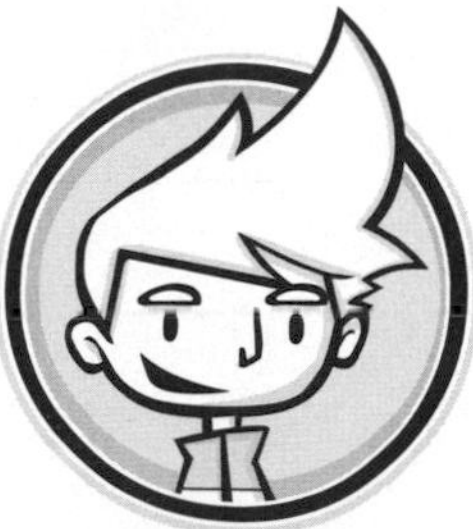

I'm Cosmoe the Earth-Boy . . . and I used to just be a regular orphan kid from Planet Earth. But then I kinda became a galactic hero!

I even have a sort of superpower: the elastic blobby creature named Goober. Goober is attached to my wrist—*always*. And he can transform into pretty much *anything*.

In space, Goober and my best buddy, Big Humphree, and I spent our days selling hot dogs from the side of our flying food truck, the *Neon Wiener*. We had a robot butler named F.R.E.D., we were videogame masters—life was perfecto! But then we met Princess Dagger. And that's when all the trouble started . . .

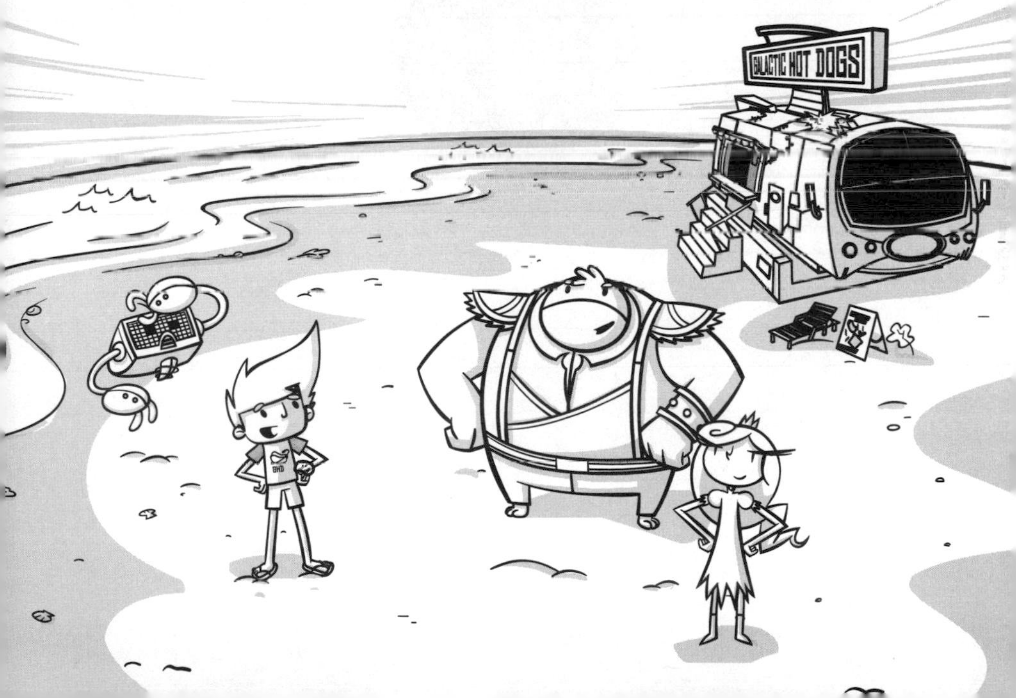
GALACTIC HOT DOGS

THE WHAT IS IN TOWN?!?

1

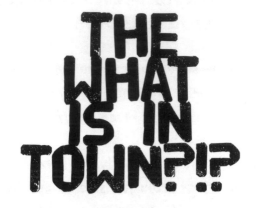

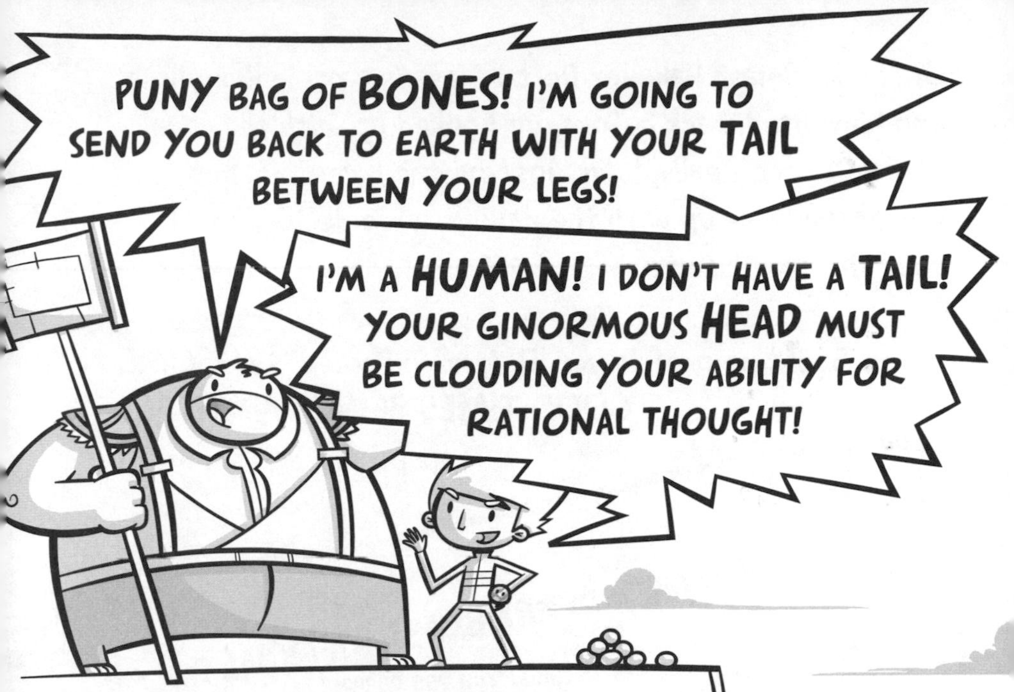
PUNY BAG OF BONES! I'M GOING TO SEND YOU BACK TO EARTH WITH YOUR TAIL BETWEEN YOUR LEGS!
I'M A HUMAN! I DON'T HAVE A TAIL! YOUR GINORMOUS HEAD MUST BE CLOUDING YOUR ABILITY FOR RATIONAL THOUGHT!

Grinning, I look down to Dagger. "How did we sound? Silver Surfer cool?"

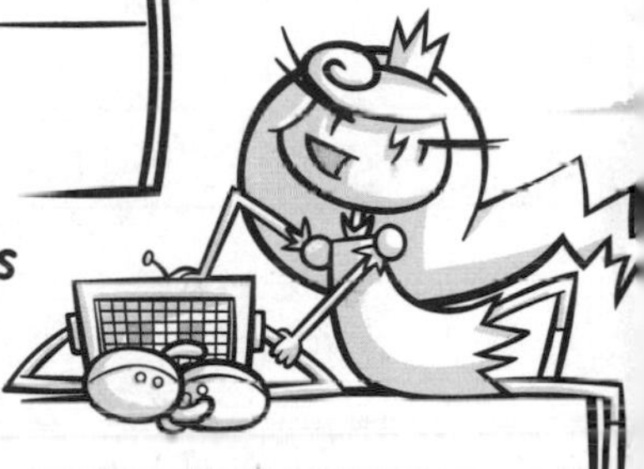

"Ehh . . . decent trash talk," the princess says. "But you two can do better."

Humphree slaps me on the back. "We just have to keep at it, short pants! We'll be trash-talk masters in no time."

"All right, you fools," Dagger says. "Enough chitchat . . ."

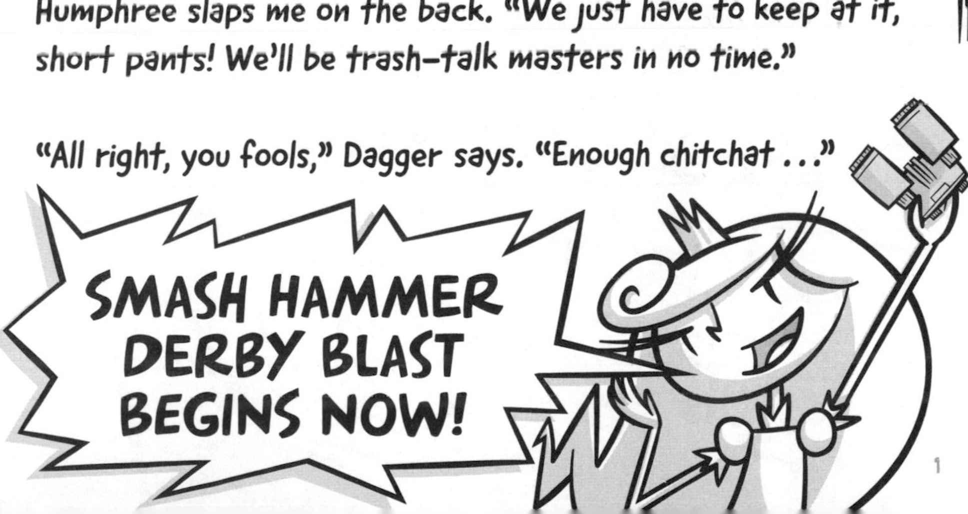
SMASH HAMMER DERBY BLAST BEGINS NOW!

OK, so ... Smash Hammer Derby Blast is a game Humphree and I invented, back before we hooked up with the royal rascal Dagger. Really, I did most of the inventing, but Humphree came up with the name, so we decided we'd split the credit and profits 50/50.

Sadly, no profits yet. Unless you count AWESOME GOOD TIMES BEING HAD BY ALL as profit. Which I do. :)

SMASH HAMMER DERBY BLAST—OFFICIAL RULES
and Princess Dagger!

1. COSMOE AND HUMPHREE ᵛ TAKE TURNS SMACKING SLUDGE-SPHERES.

2. IF A SLUDGE-SPHERE HITS SOMETHING FUNKY, LIKE A HOLO-BOARD OR A BOMB TREE, THE BATTER'S SCORE MULTIPLIES.

3. GAME ENDS AFTER ALL BATTERS HAVE HIT TEN SLUDGE-SPHERES. BATTER WITH HIGH SCORE WINS.

4. HUMPHREE MUST APPLY DEODORANT PRIOR TO EVERY AT-BAT.

5. THE LOSER MUST WEAR THE **BOOT OF DISHONOR** TO DINNER.

Boot of DISHONOR!!

When Humphree bats, he uses a sledgehammer made of Xanulite, this crazy rare metal from the moon of Qaanab out in Andromeda 14. I begged him to take me there so I could get a sword or an axe or at least a pair of pliers or something, but Humps said he barely made it off the moon alive.

But none of that's so important right now, 'cause I'm up to bat first.

G, IF WE LOSE, I HAVE TO CLEAN THE BATHROOM FOR A WEEK. AND *YOU* KNOW WHAT THAT MEANS.

THIS HAND.
YOUR HEAD.
IN HUMPHREE'S TOILET.

As you can see, the stakes are high. But that's OK, 'cause I'm going to SHUT. THIS. PLACE. **DOWN!**

With a flick of my wrist, Goober's rubbery body transmutes into a big ol' Earth-style baseball bat. I squeeze the mushy Sludge-Sphere, toss it into the air, and ...

3

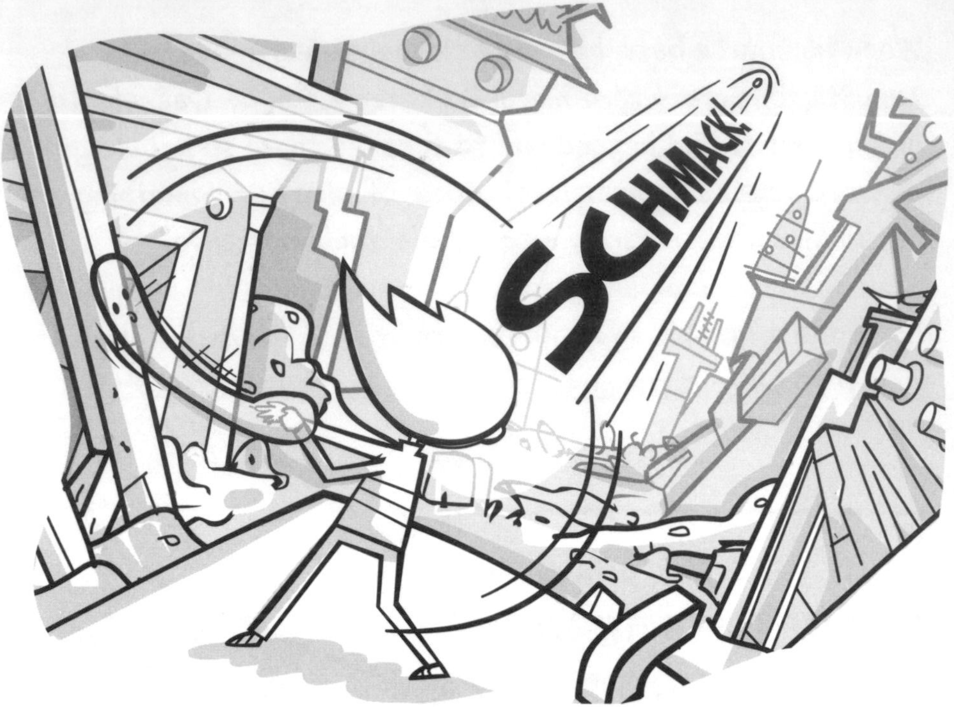
SCHMACK!

"Holy milk-producing domesticated ungulates!" I exclaim. "I **HAMMERED** that thing!"

Our robot butler, F.R.E.D., is linked to the Sludge-Spheres, so he instantly reports back on my home run blast.

"CONTACT MADE. POINT TOTAL: 1658," F.R.E.D. says.

"That's a fatty four-bagger moonshot! What did I hit?"

"AN AMARUUK CREATURE," F.R.E.D. says.

"Did you say Amaruuk?" I yelp, not even hiding the total terror in my voice. "OK, THAT'S IT. GAME OVER! SHUT IT DOWN."

So, here's the deal with Amaruuks: they're mean. Actually, worse than mean: brutal and cruel and just generally super-unpleasant. If you hit an Amaruuk with a Sludge-Sphere, there's a good chance that Amaruuk will come yank your ears off.

"Whoa jelly!" Humphree exclaims. "Toys away! Not tangling with any Amaruuks. Now, mates, you get the *Wiener* into food-truck mode while I head out to find some spare thermal cells for the grill."

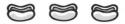

The sun is beating down like a firestorm. This desert planet we're on, Arahas, is hotter than spicy mustard.

Switching the *Neon Wiener* from flying mode to hot-dog-selling mode takes some work. But we keep the radio blasting, and pretty soon Galactic Hot Dogs is . . .

GALACTIC HOT DOGS
OPEN FOR BUSINESS!

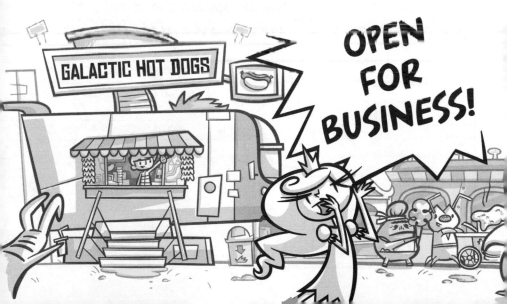

Unfortunately, our first patron has no interest in eating . . .

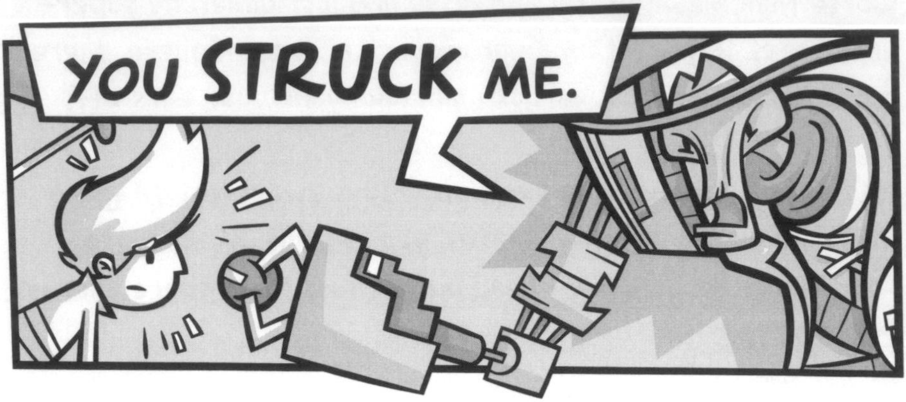
YOU STRUCK ME.

Oh no. It's the Amaruuk.

I smile real wide and flash my not-so-pearly yellows and do my best to look sweet and innocent. "Someone struck you?" I say. "How awful! That is an outrage! I'm sure whoever hit you, though—they're probably super-sorry about it. Really sorry. But it wasn't me! Totally not me."

The Amaruuk holds up the Sludge-Sphere and growls, "It says here **PROPERTY OF GALACTIC HOT DOGS.**"

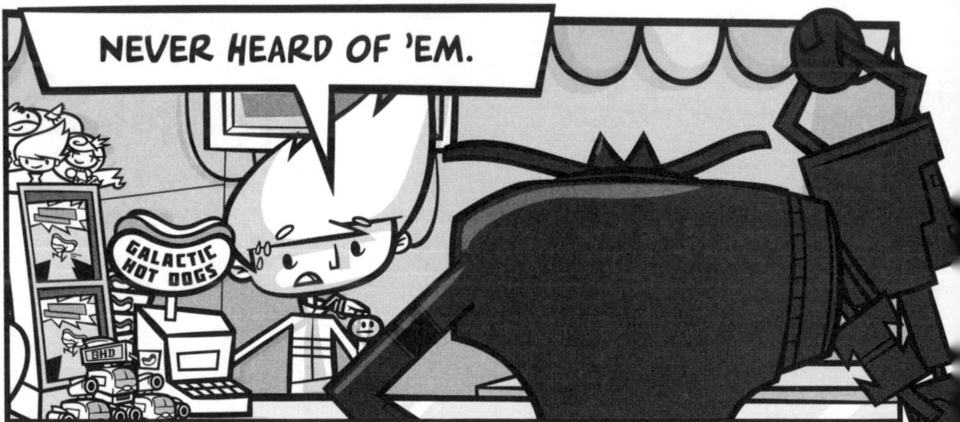
NEVER HEARD OF 'EM.
GALACTIC HOT DOGS
GHD

This Amaruuk has a crazy complex mechanical arm, and it makes a clinking, jinking noise as he shoves the Sludge-Sphere into my face. “Hit me with another of these, and I’ll shove it up your tiny human nostril. Understand?”

Before I can say “Yes, sir. I understand, sir. I’m sorry, sir,” Princess Dagger shouts out, “Buddy! Your arm is awesome!”

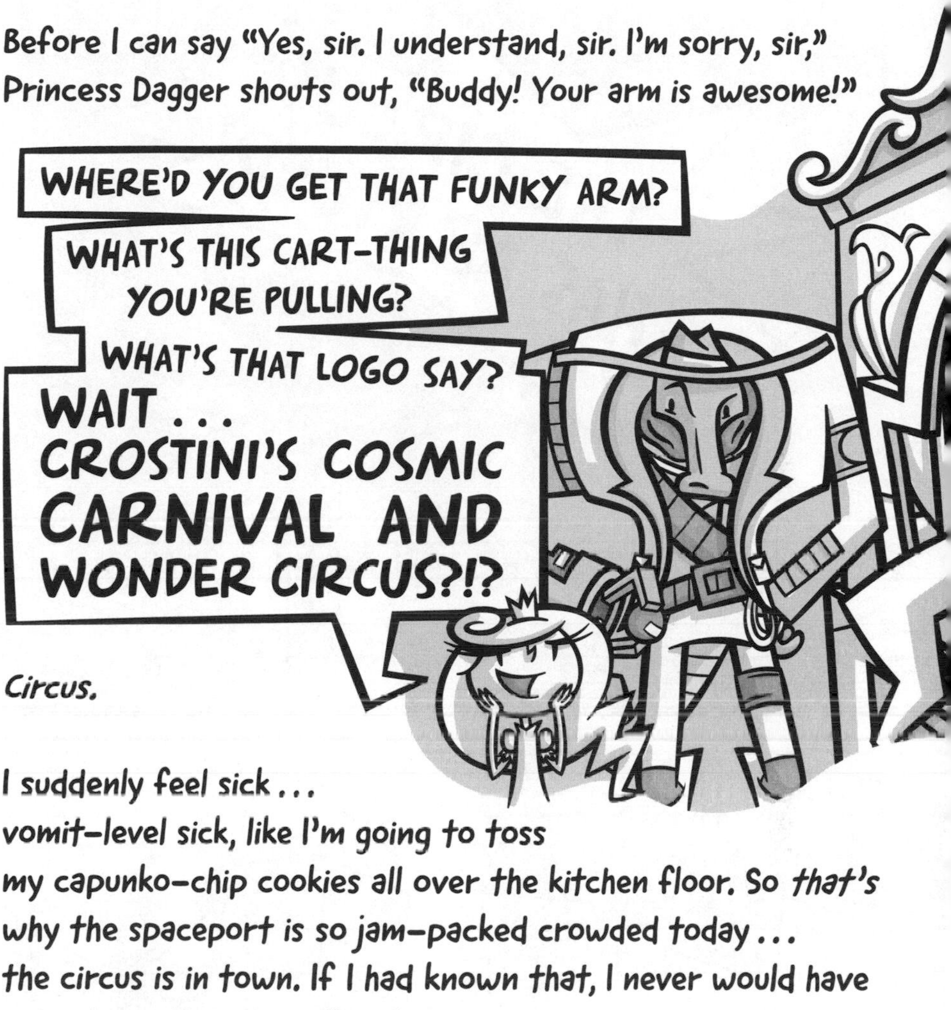
WHERE’D YOU GET THAT FUNKY ARM?
WHAT’S THIS CART-THING YOU’RE PULLING?
WHAT’S THAT LOGO SAY?
WAIT . . . CROSTINI’S COSMIC CARNIVAL AND WONDER CIRCUS?!?

Circus.

I suddenly feel sick . . .
vomit-level sick, like I’m going to toss
my capunko-chip cookies all over the kitchen floor. So *that’s* why the spaceport is so jam-packed crowded today . . .
the circus is in town. If I had known that, I never would have come here. Not in a million light-years . . .

Just then the screeching of rusty air brakes sounds through the port. I look to the sky, just in time to see it . . .

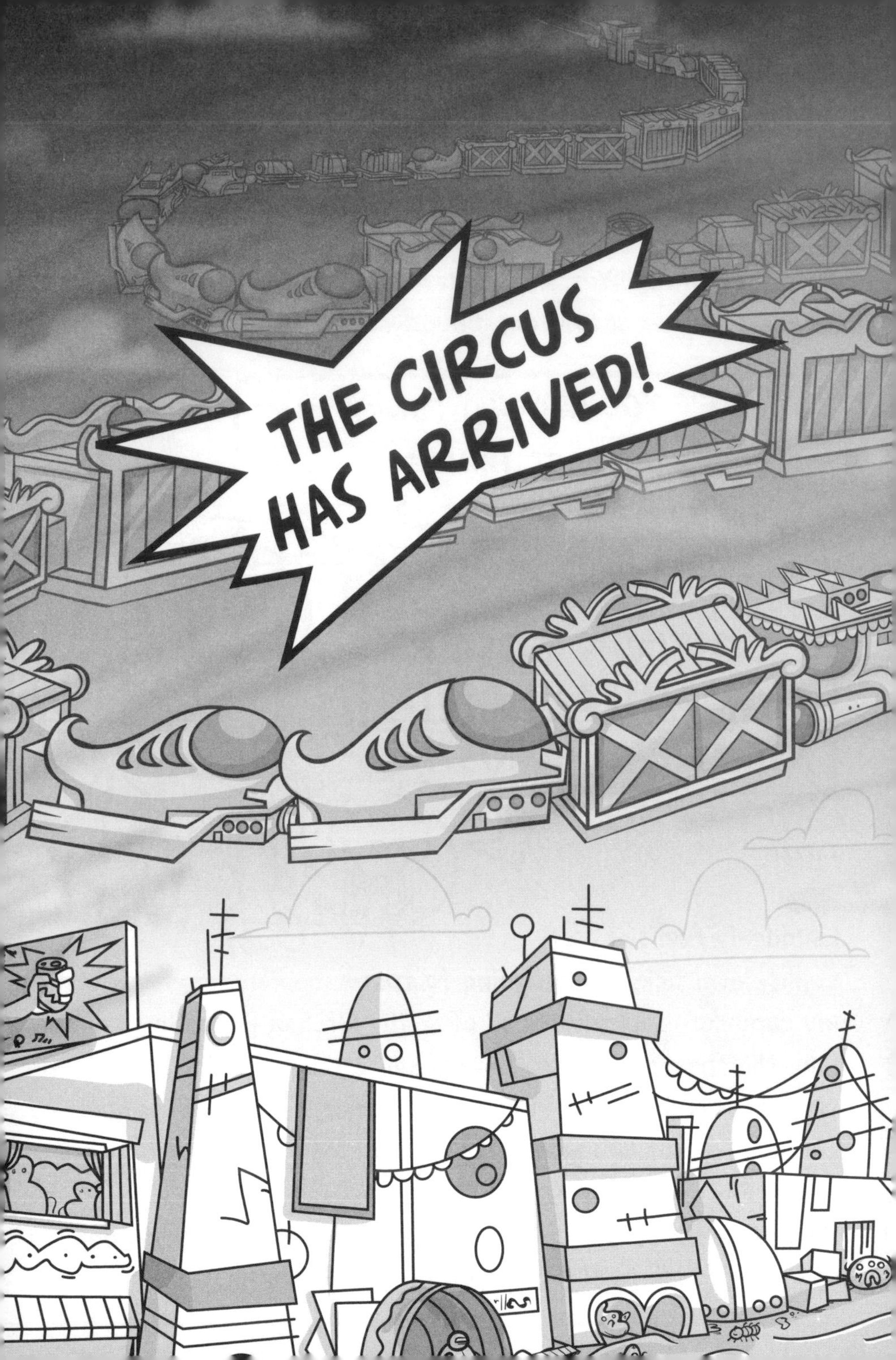
THE CIRCUS
HAS ARRIVED!

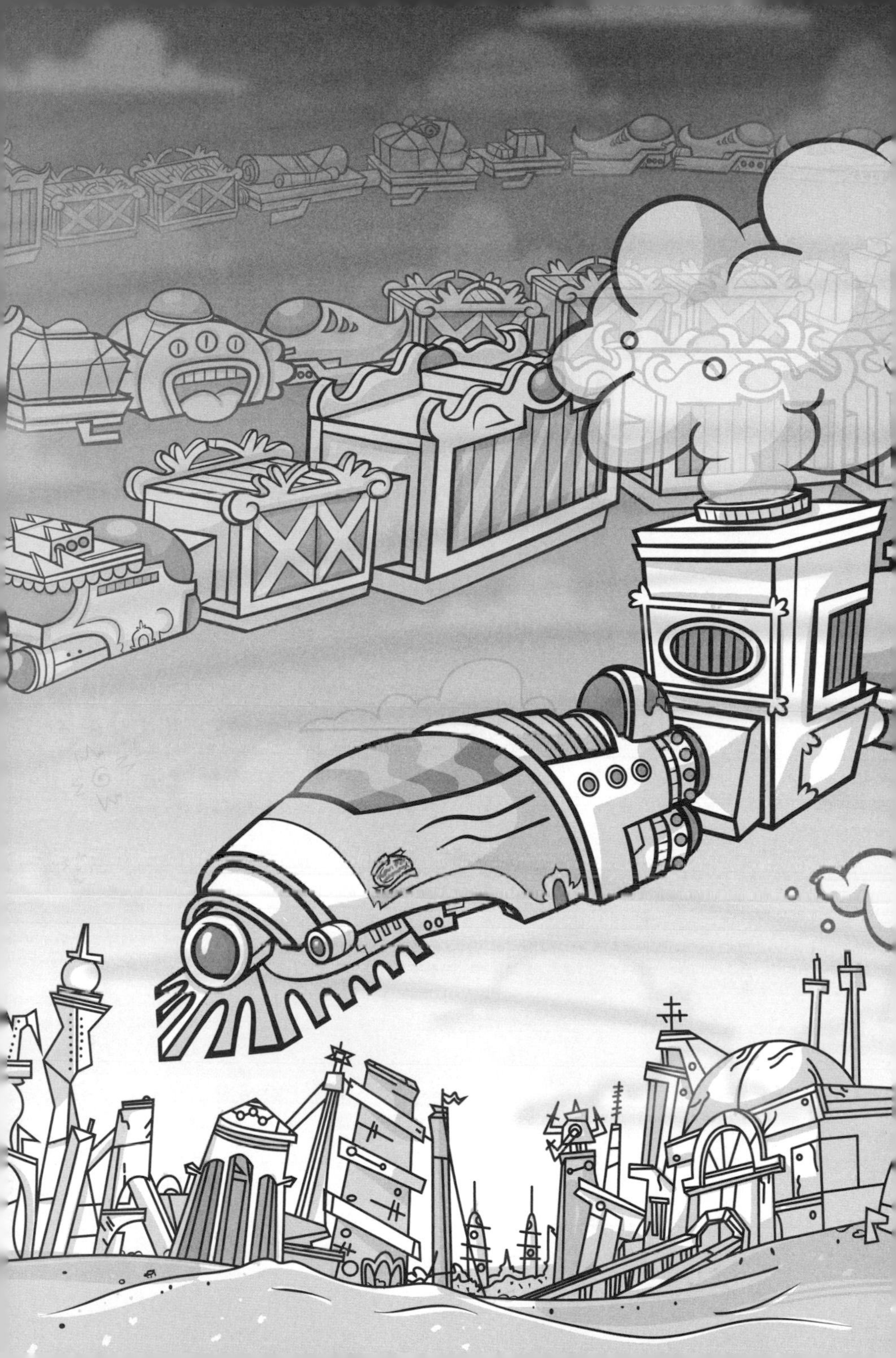

SHOWDOWN ON THE STREETS OF ARAHAS

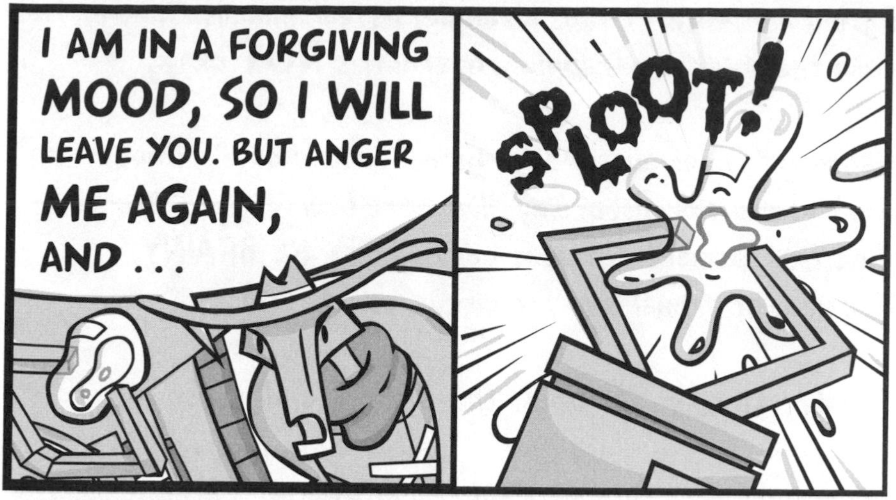
I AM IN A FORGIVING MOOD, SO I WILL LEAVE YOU. BUT ANGER ME AGAIN, AND . . .
SPLOOT!

With that, the Amaruuk strides away, pulling a hover-cart behind him. Dagger looks at me, confused. "I don't get it. If he's with the circus, and the circus is just landing, how come he's already here?"

"He's a circus wrangler . . ." I say. I still feel weak and light-headed. "Wranglers, um—they scout ahead to collect local animals for the show. See, like he's doing now."

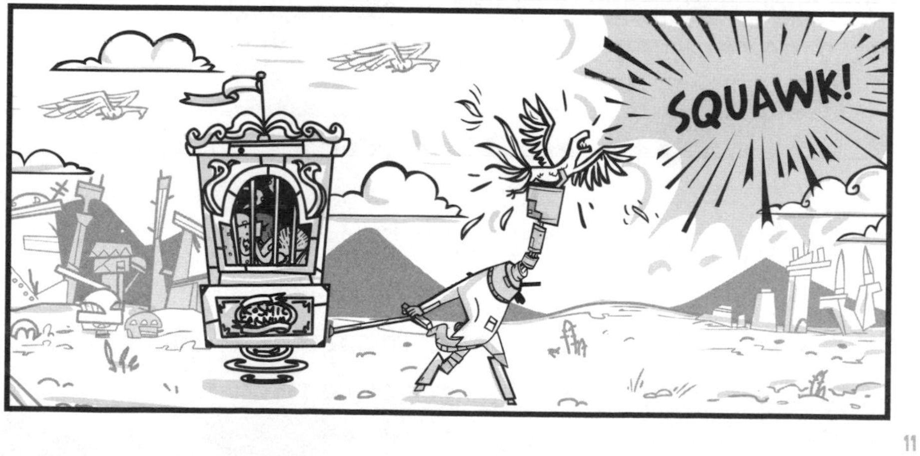
SQUAWK!

I grind my teeth. "Circus wranglers steal animals. They just take them with no frappin' regard! It's **NOT** okay..."

Dagger rolls her eyes. "Your moral code is doofy, 'Moe. Animals are animals, brainy aliens are brainy aliens! Brainy guys get special treatment cause **THEY'RE BRAINY.** If a regular animal is in the circus, so what?!"

"Look, just trust me, Dags. The circus is bad news..."

When Humphree returns a few minutes later, I practically pounce on him...

HUMPHREE! THE CIRCUS IS IN TOWN. YOU HEAR ME? **THE CIRCUS.**

I KNOW.

"You know?! Wait, you knew all along, didn't you?" I shriek. "Why didn't you tell me?!"

"'Cause you hate the circus," he says with a shrug.

"That's right! I **HATE** THE CIRCUS. So why are we here?"

"We're broke, Cosmoe! We got zero spaceos. We need to sell wieners. And right now, this is the place to do it."

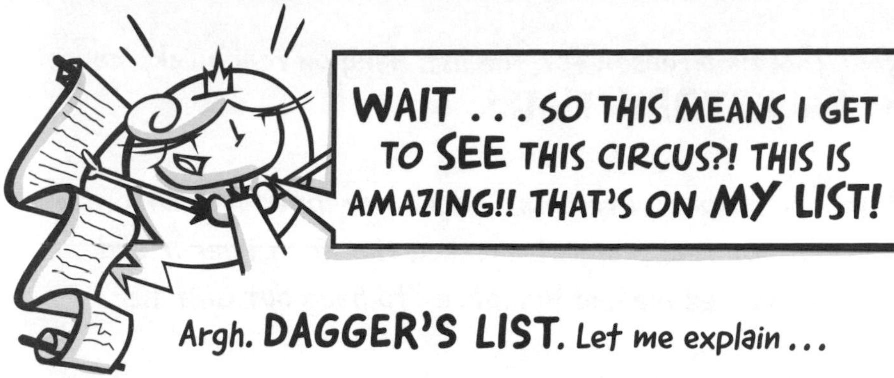
WAIT . . . SO THIS MEANS I GET TO SEE THIS CIRCUS?! THIS IS AMAZING!! THAT'S ON MY LIST!

Argh. **DAGGER'S LIST.** Let me explain . . .

A few days ago, Princess Dagger started this list called **PRINCESS DAGGER'S AWESOME ADVENTURE GOALS,** and it's full of thrilling, death-defying, and adventurous junk she wants to do.

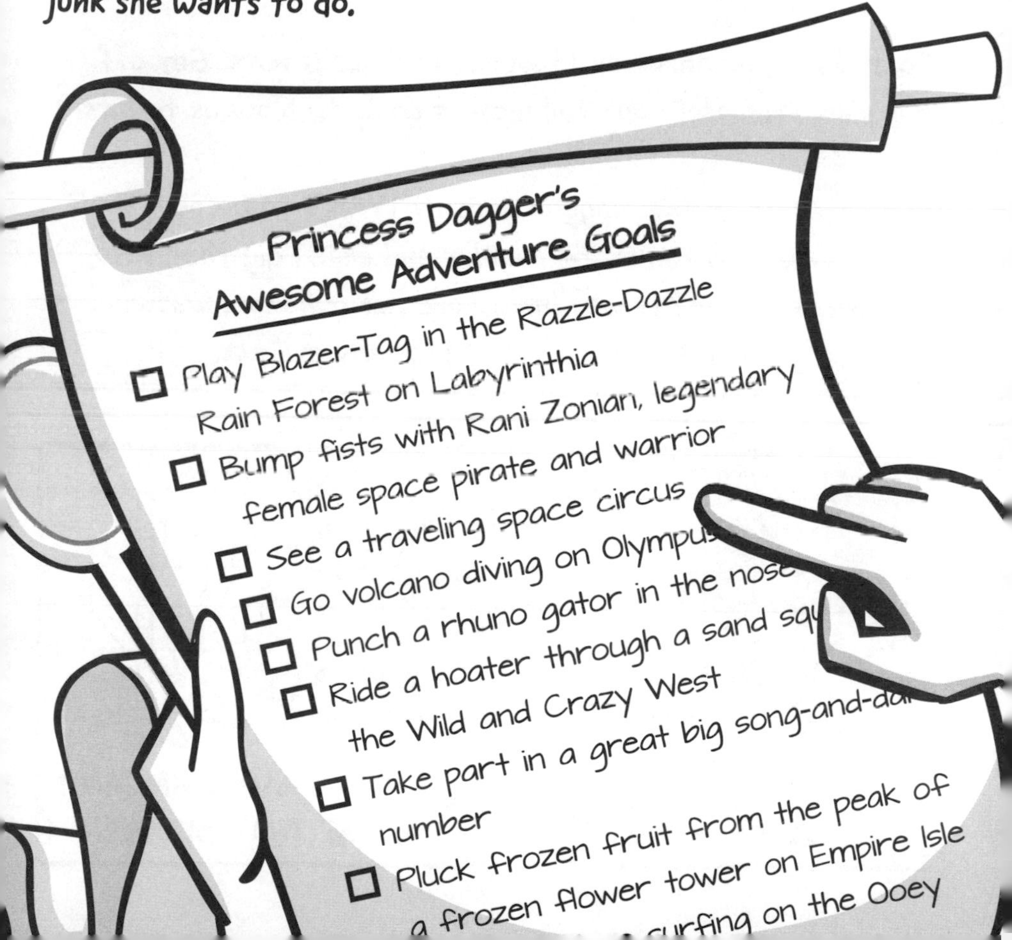
Princess Dagger's
Awesome Adventure Goals
☐ Play Blazer-Tag in the Razzle-Dazzle Rain Forest on Labyrinthia
☐ Bump fists with Rani Zonian, legendary female space pirate and warrior
☐ See a traveling space circus
☐ Go volcano diving on Olympu
☐ Punch a rhuno gator in the nos
☐ Ride a hoater through a sand sq
the Wild and Crazy West
☐ Take part in a great big song-and-
number
☐ Pluck frozen fruit from the peak of a frozen flower tower on Empire Isle
surfing on the Ooey

Now, there's a reason for the list. Hang on real quick, 'cause it's **BACKSTORY TIME!**

A little while back, Princess Dagger kidnapped herself onto our ship. For real, she just hijacked the *Neon Wiener* and basically forced me and Humphree to hang out with her.

See, Dagger is evil with a capital **E** (also a capital *V, I, L*). She's <u>THAT</u> **EVIL.** She has evil genes! There's evil in her blood, inherited from her evil mom. Her mom is Evil Queen Dagger. She rules the galaxy with an evil iron fist.

So at first Humphree and I were like "This is nuts. Get off our ship, Princess! Your evil mom is going to blow us to bits!"

But here's the thing: Dagger doesn't <u>**WANT**</u> to be evil. She's trying way hard to just be regular and chill. I dig that. Also, her life before us? It was lamesville. Her evil mom was always tying to get her to do stuff in a properly evil way.

WHEN I SAID CLEAN *YOUR* ROOM, I MEANT DO IT **EVILLY!**

I DON'T EVEN KNOW WHAT THAT MEANS!

Princess Dagger begged us to let her stay on board the *Neon Wiener.* Humphree thought it was risky. But like I told him, deep down in my hot-dog-filled gut, I think everyone has the right to choose **NOT** to be evil and to choose to chill out with buddies.

So we let the princess stay. Her mom, the evil queen, was not pleased and was all like ...

I'LL GET YOU, COSMOE!

Anyway, that's how we hooked up with Princess Dagger. And that's why I understand her **AWESOME ADVENTURE GOALS** list. I get that she wants to see the galaxy and do all the crazy stuff she never could have done while she was stuck under her evil queen mom's evil thumb.

I'm supportive of all adventure goals! That is, all adventures **NOT** involving the circus ...

"Tell you what, Princess," Humphree says. "Someday I'll take you to the circus—**WITHOUT COSMOE, BECAUSE COSMOE CAN'T HANDLE THE CIRCUS.** But for now, we need to make some cash. So . . . is the mustard done?"

"You tell me!" Dags says proudly. She dips a spoon into a giant vat of mustard and scoops it into Humphree's mouth. And then—

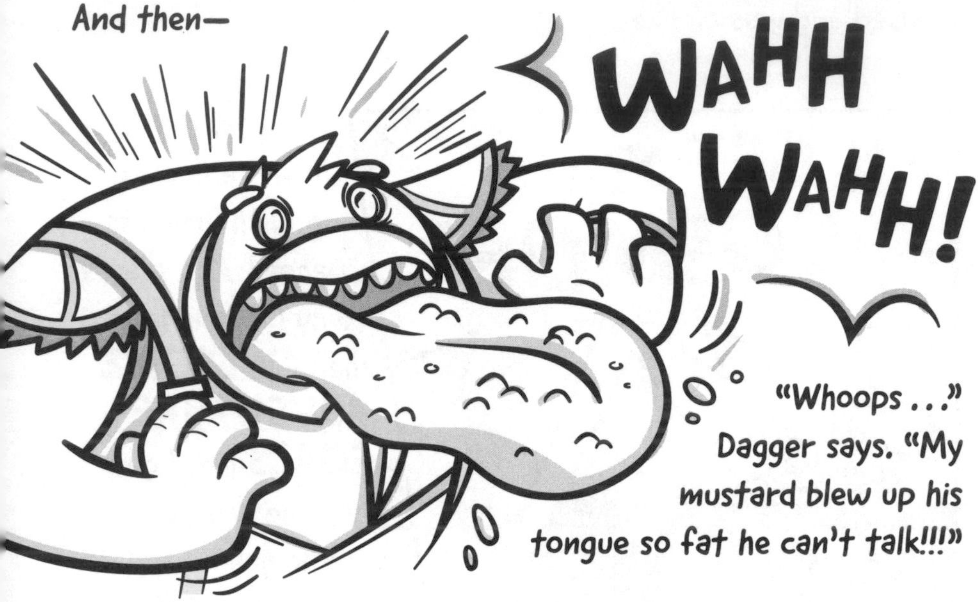
WAHH WAHH!

"Whoops . . ." Dagger says. "My mustard blew up his tongue so fat he can't talk!!!"

Suddenly, Humps is barreling through the spaceport! "He needs water!" I say. "Dags, c'mon. F.R.E.D., you're in charge!

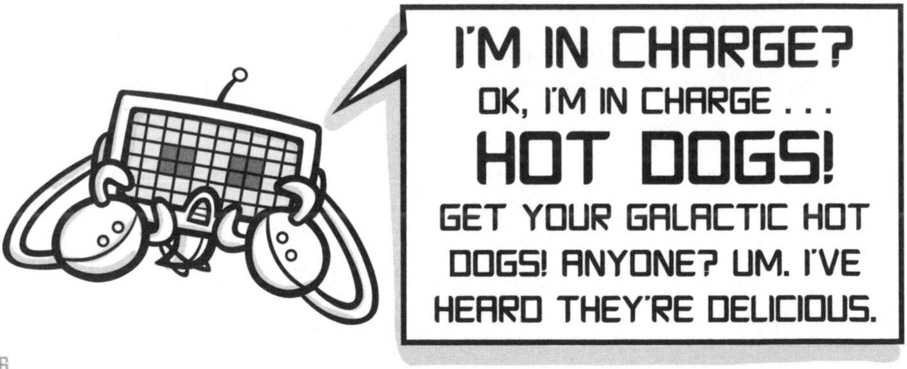
I'M IN CHARGE?
OK, I'M IN CHARGE . . .
HOT DOGS!
GET YOUR GALACTIC HOT DOGS! ANYONE? UM. I'VE HEARD THEY'RE DELICIOUS.

In a flash, I'm chasing my thirsty buddy through the crowd. The streets are thick with aliens all abuzz about the just-landed circus.

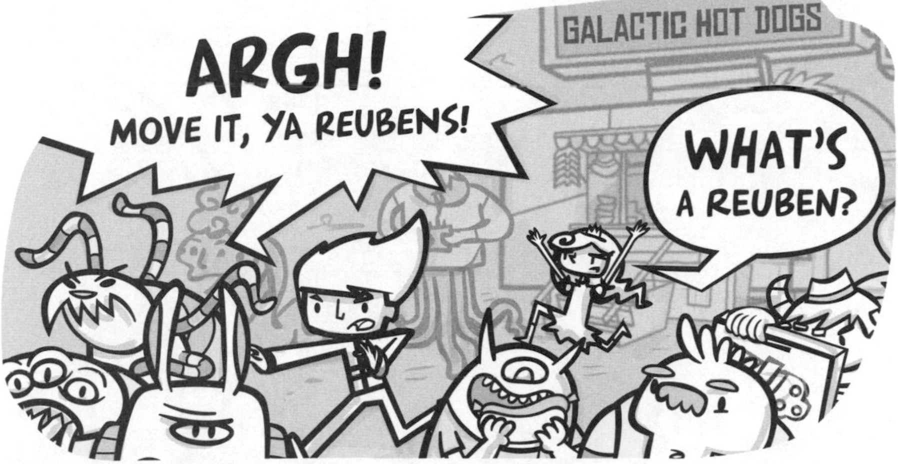
GALACTIC HOT DOGS
ARGH!
MOVE IT, YA REUBENS!
WHAT'S A REUBEN?

"Dimwits who go to the circus looking to lose their money!" I shout, nearly plowing into a zapple cart. "Circus workers call them reubens."

"Cosmoe, if you hate the circus," Dagger shouts, "how come you know so much about it?!"

"YEEEE-ARGHHH!"

A screeching squeal silences Dagger. I know that sound—it's the unmistakable howl of the Bronkle. It's Humphree: in pain, in trouble.

The princess and I race around the corner, and there, directly in front of us—

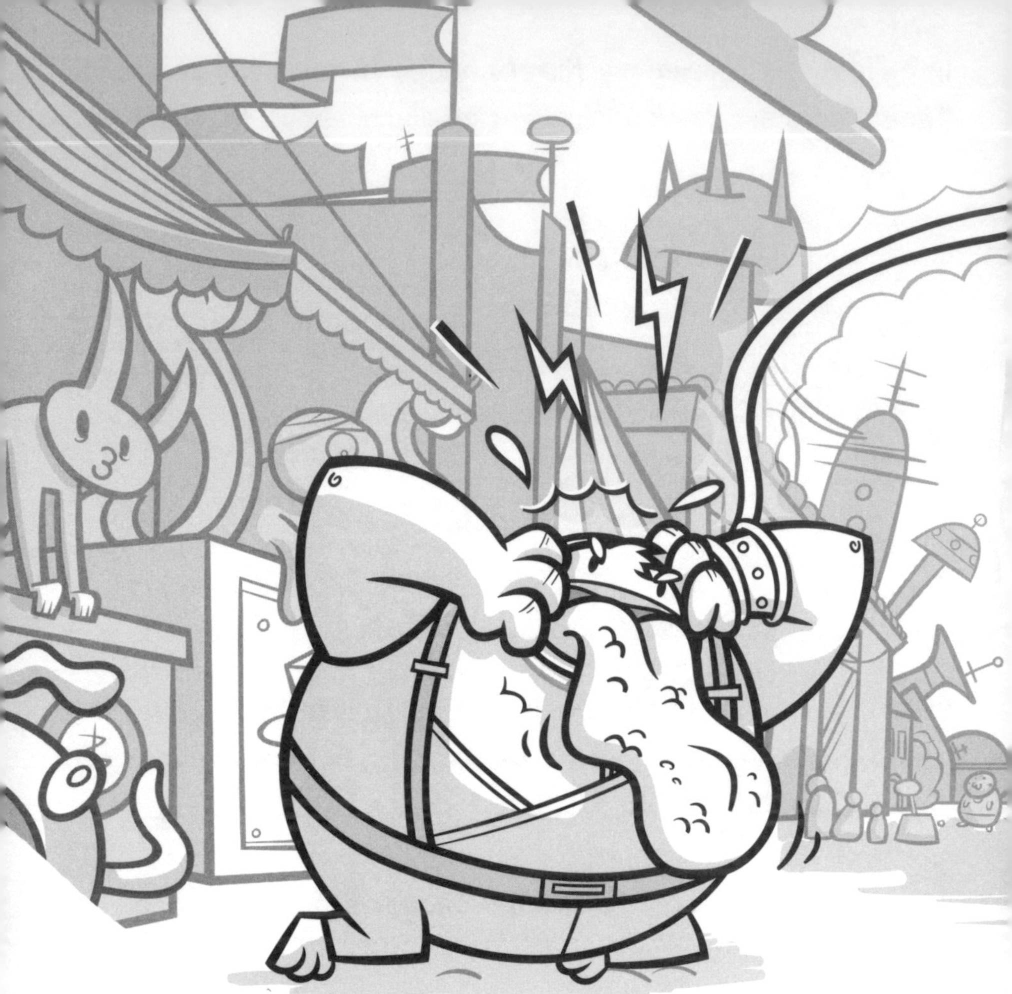

"Yo!" I bark. "What the smudge?! Release my buddy."

The Amaruuk wrangler turns his head. His eyes narrow. "Your 'buddy' does not speak," he growls. "A creature that does not speak has a small brain. Creatures with small brains will join the circus."

"He's got a regular brain! It's actually a pretty decent brain! Does smart stuff sometimes!" I shout back.

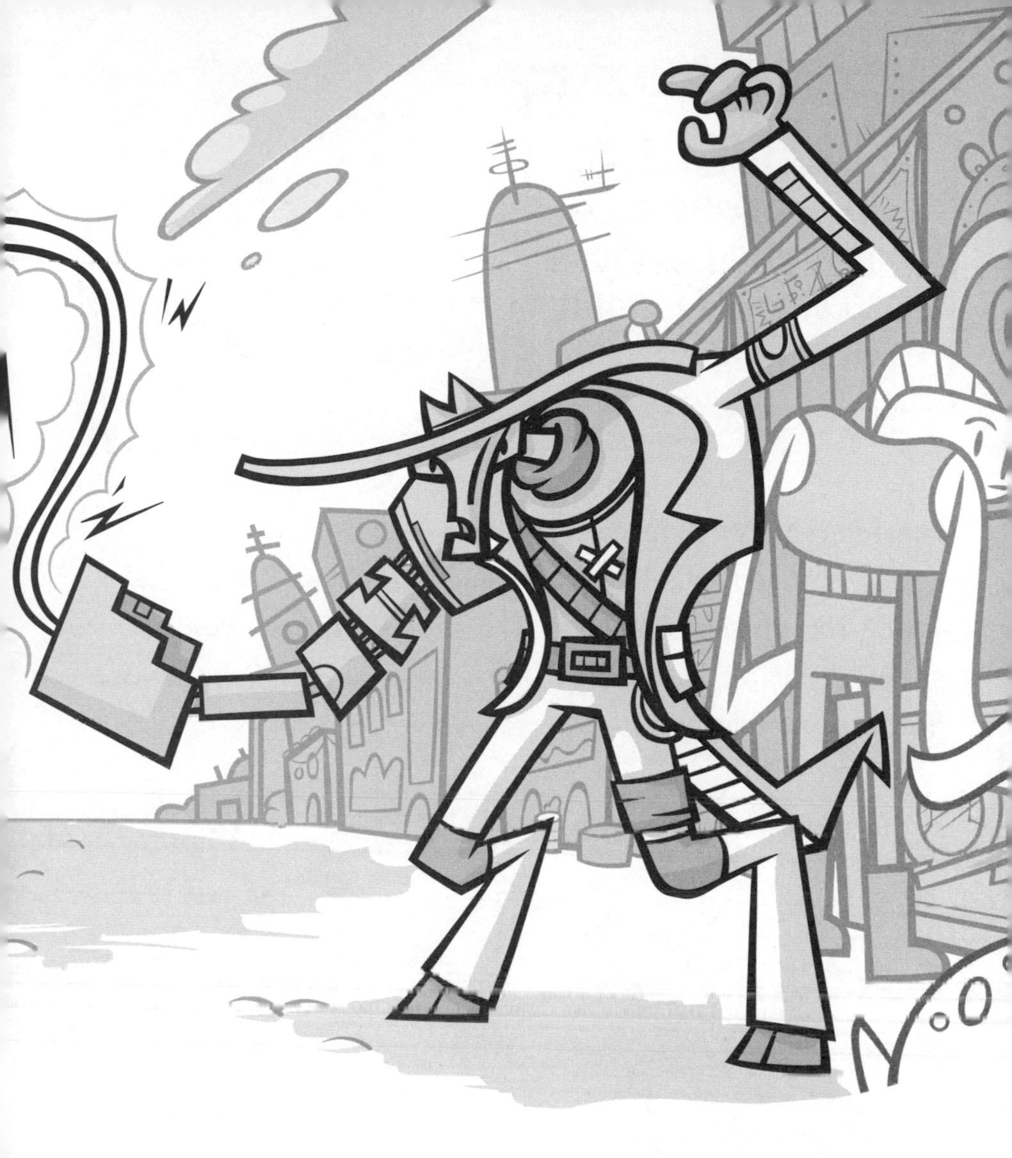

Suddenly—**KRAK!**—Humphree swings his beefy fist up into the wrangler's mechanical arm. The lasso releases and the wrangler staggers back. Humphree rises, nostrils flaring.

There's about to be a big boy rumble on the streets of Arahas—but a rich voice bellows out and stops everything . . .

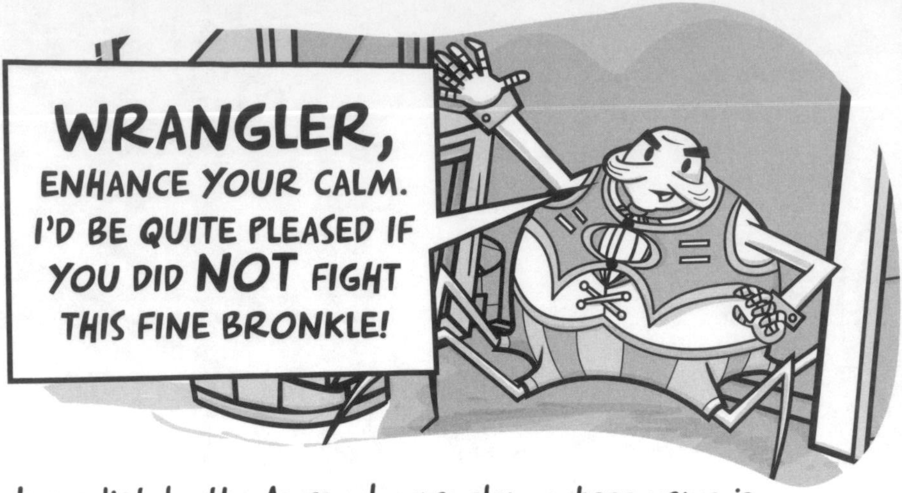
WRANGLER, ENHANCE YOUR CALM. I'D BE QUITE PLEASED IF YOU DID NOT FIGHT THIS FINE BRONKLE!

Immediately, the Amaruuk wrangler—whose name is apparently just **WRANGLER**—lowers his arm. "Now, shake feet," this strange new creature says. Humphree doesn't shake. He simply marches to a trough of water for the local hoaters and inhales liquid. . . .

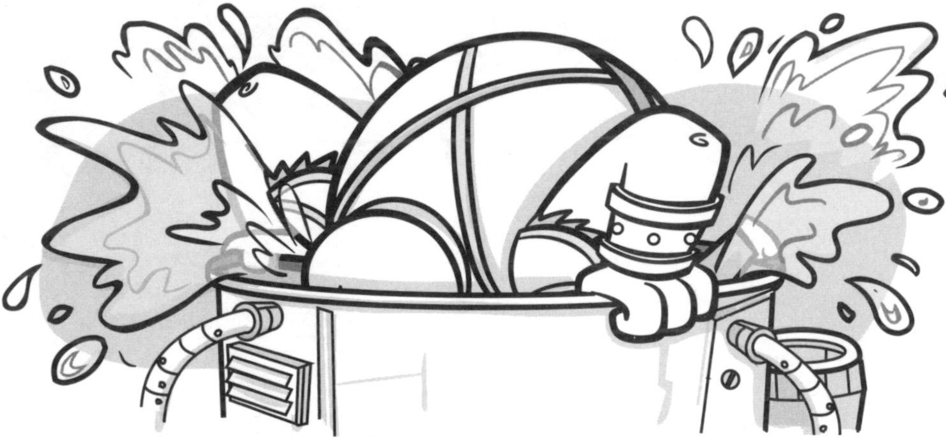

This odd creature scuttles toward me and proclaims in a booming voice, "I am Looper Crostini, owner and ringmaster of **CROSTINI'S COSMIC CARNIVAL AND WONDER CIRCUS**. I apologize for this conflict. I despise fighting! I crave cheerfulness and deliver delights!"

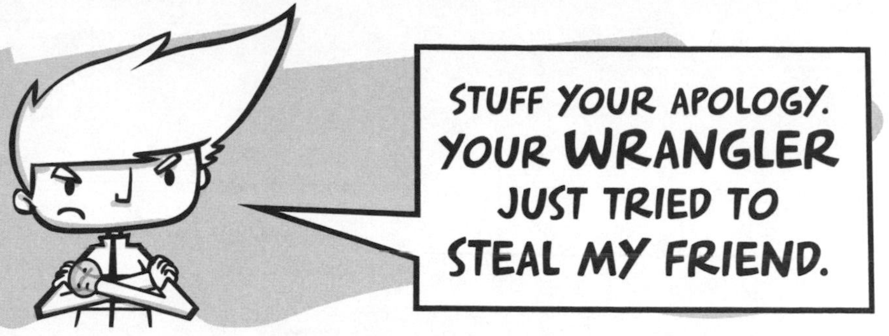
STUFF YOUR APOLOGY. YOUR WRANGLER JUST TRIED TO STEAL MY FRIEND.

Looper Crostini smiles and spreads his arms. "We collect creatures for the circus, yes, but they are the best-treated beings in the galaxy! We meant no harm. We meant less than harm! Please, let me make it up to you."

Before I can tell him to make like a halley hornet and buzz off, Princess Dagger blurts out, "THREE TICKETS TO THE CIRCUS! That's how you'll make it up to us!"

Humphree staggers over. "Tickets, meat'r. Hand 'em over."

Looper Crostini suddenly spins, twirling around like some whacked-out ballerina until he's again facing us, staring directly into my eyes . . .

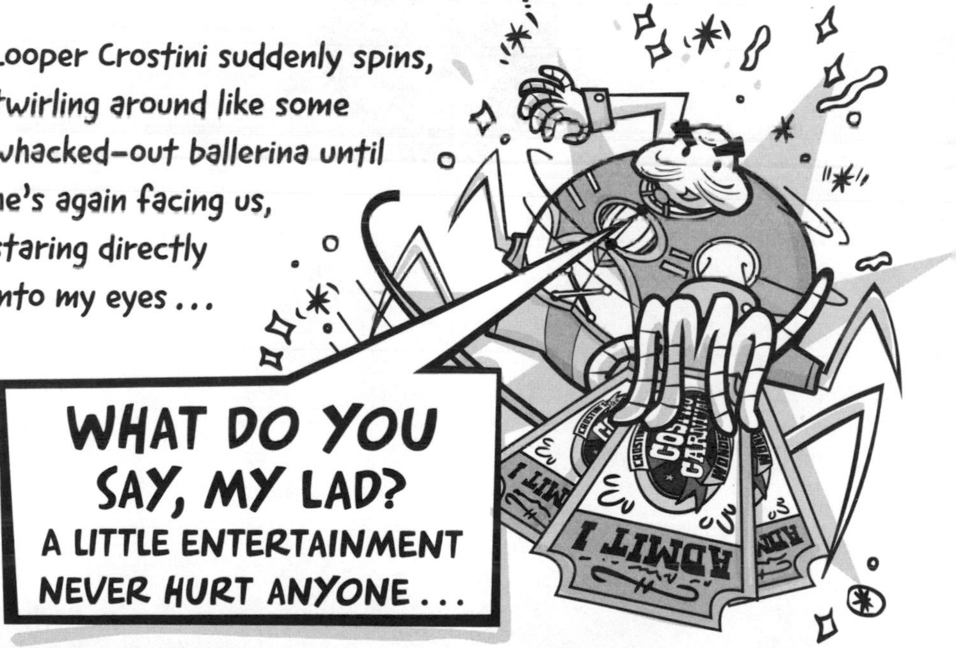
WHAT DO YOU SAY, MY LAD?
A LITTLE ENTERTAINMENT NEVER HURT ANYONE . . .

THE BIG SHOW

"We don't need no stinkin' tickets!" I say, stomping away.

"Cosmoe, wait!" Dagger says, chasing me down and grabbing my wrist. "I faced my mom. My fear. 'Cause **YOU** told me I could. Now, I don't know why you're mad at the circus or in a fight with the circus or whatever, but—"

"So go!" I say. "You and Humps go have fun without me. I don't care. Couldn't care less. Care level: <u>ZERO</u>."

"No. I want to go with my best friend. You, Cosmoe."

I sigh. Dagger's right. She's my friend. And for friends, sometimes you do stuff that makes you uncomfy. Sometimes you even face your deepest, darkest fears . . .

But still . . . I won't.
I can't.

But then I hear the music. The calliope. The steam-powered circus horn echoes across the spaceport. It's strange, even on this crummy planet, one hundred light-years from Earth, the circus still sounds like the circus. Like home. Finally, I swallow hard and say . . .

CIRCUS TODAY

OK. WE'LL GO SEE THE SHOW . . .

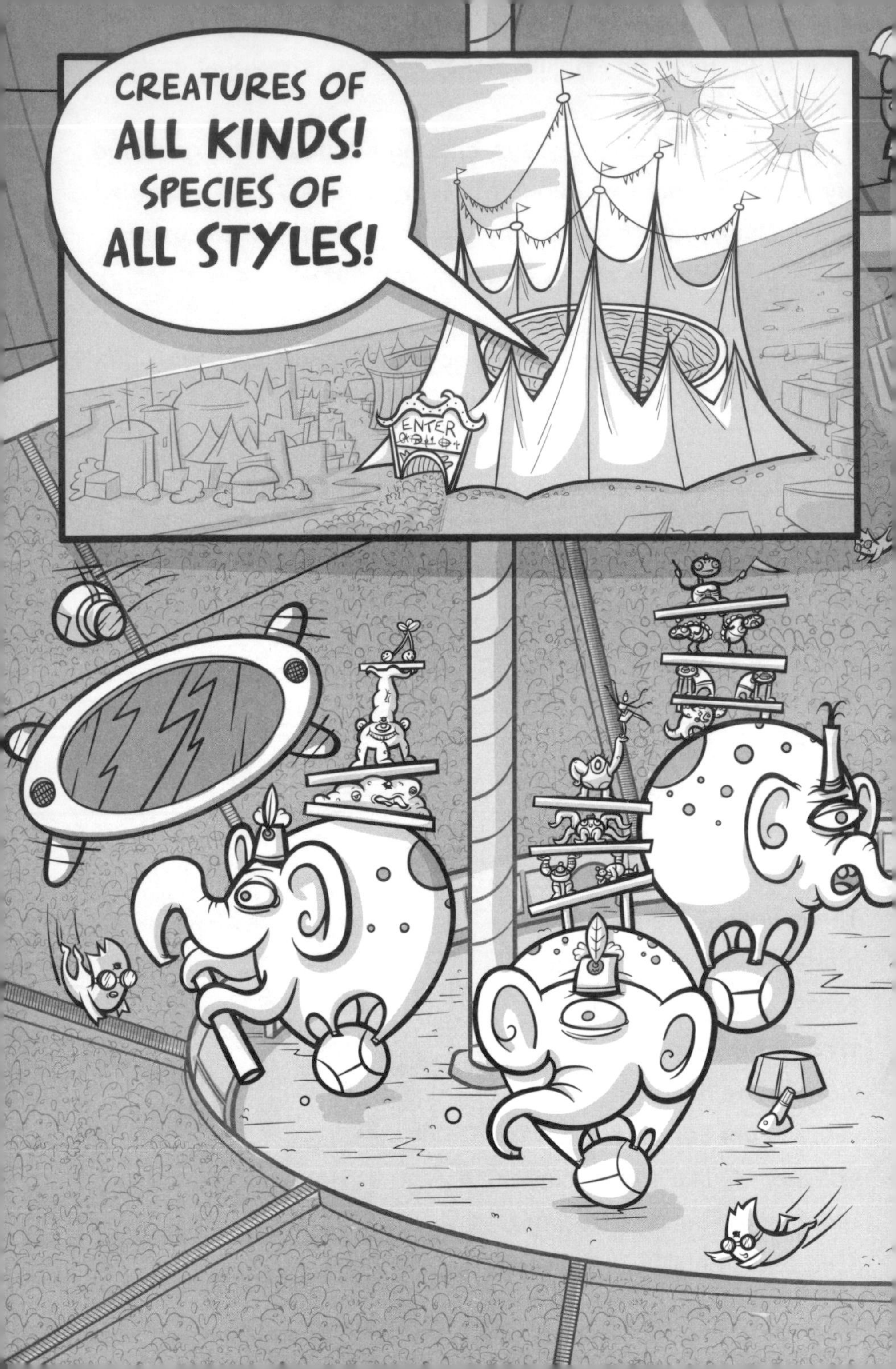
CREATURES OF ALL KINDS! SPECIES OF ALL STYLES!
ENTER

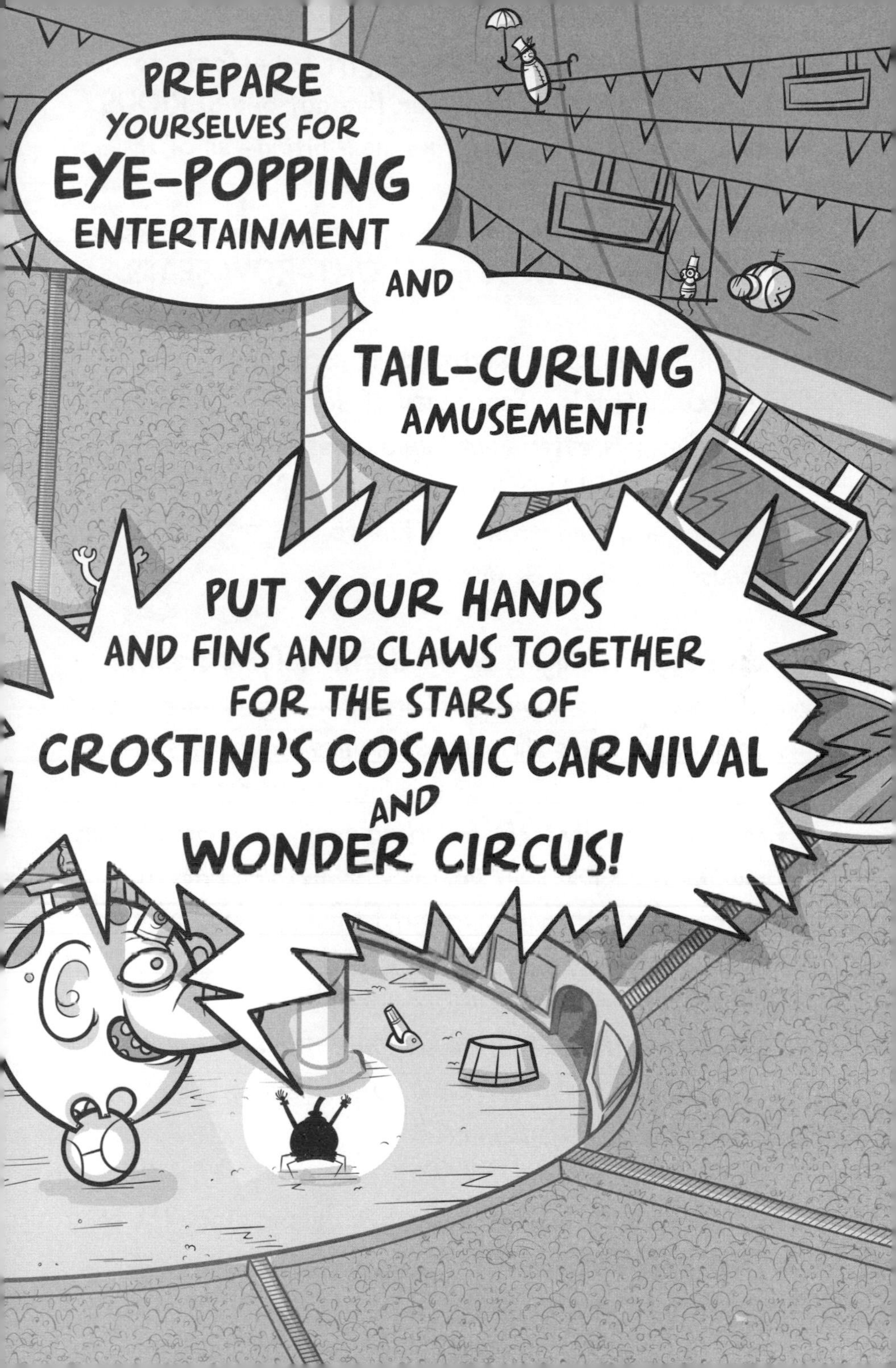
PREPARE YOURSELVES FOR EYE-POPPING ENTERTAINMENT
AND
TAIL-CURLING AMUSEMENT!
PUT YOUR HANDS AND FINS AND CLAWS TOGETHER FOR THE STARS OF CROSTINI'S COSMIC CARNIVAL AND WONDER CIRCUS!

So I did it. I'm at the circus. And despite my efforts to remain calm as a cosmic cucumber, I've got one **SERIOUS** case of the freak-outs. Sweating, nail-biting—all of it.

At least my buds are enjoying themselves. Thanks to Looper Crostini's generosity, we've got **FRONT-ROW SEATS.**

Humps is mainly into the gastronomic aspect of the circus. (That's a fancy way of saying food.) So far, he's eaten four hamburzles, a mess of frozen flicktails, and two boxes of Krack-Smackers. I'm waiting for him to burp 'cause it's gonna be nuclear . . .

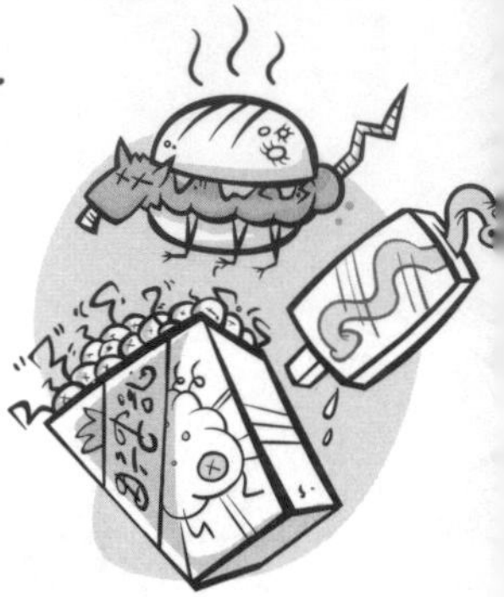

Princess Dagger is digging all the death-defying drama. Every time some high-wire performer nearly plummets to a splattery death, Dags shrieks and giggles and cheers.

At first I was totally **100%** hating every moment of this. But now, as the show rolls on, I feel something I haven't felt in years. I can't believe it, but I think I'm kind of even starting to enjoy myself . . .

And when a mini hover-car cruises into the arena and like two hundred clown-bots tumble out, I smile so wide I think my face just might break in half!

Finally, I just sit back and sip Sugar Soda and enjoy the show. And what a show it is . . .

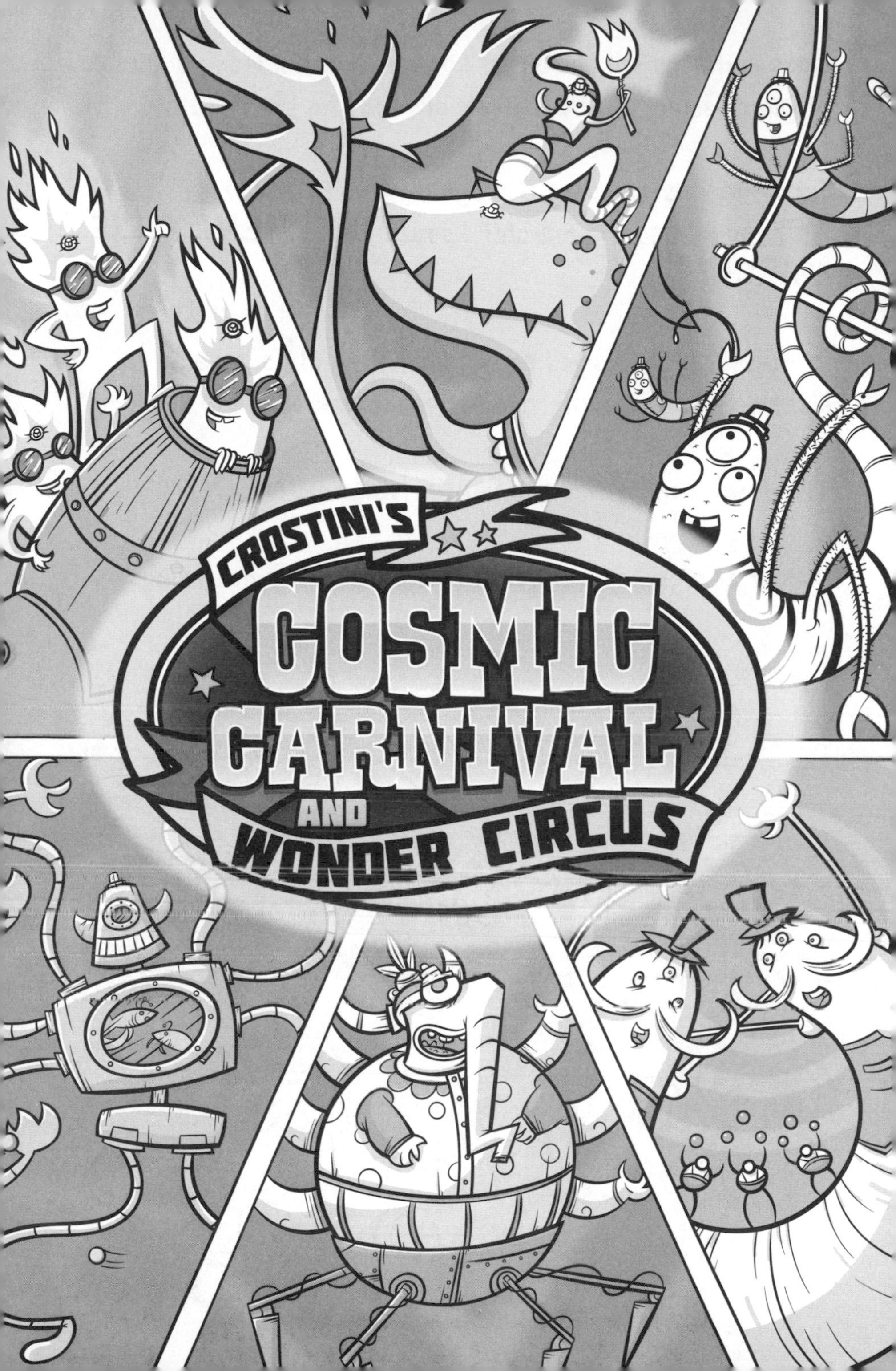
CROSTINI'S
COSMIC
CARNIVAL
AND
WONDER CIRCUS

Oohs and aahs fill the air as Looper Crostini leads a long row of giant-sized, exotic animals around the stadium.

Excitement is pumping through me and I can barely sit still. "It's the menagerie march!" I say. **"THE MENAGERIE MARCH!"**

Princess Dagger's eyes are wide. "I haven't seen anything like this since my mom tried to make her own zoo."

"Wait, your mom tried to **MAKE HER OWN ZOO?"**

Dagger shrugs. "She's weird. And evil. That's her thing."

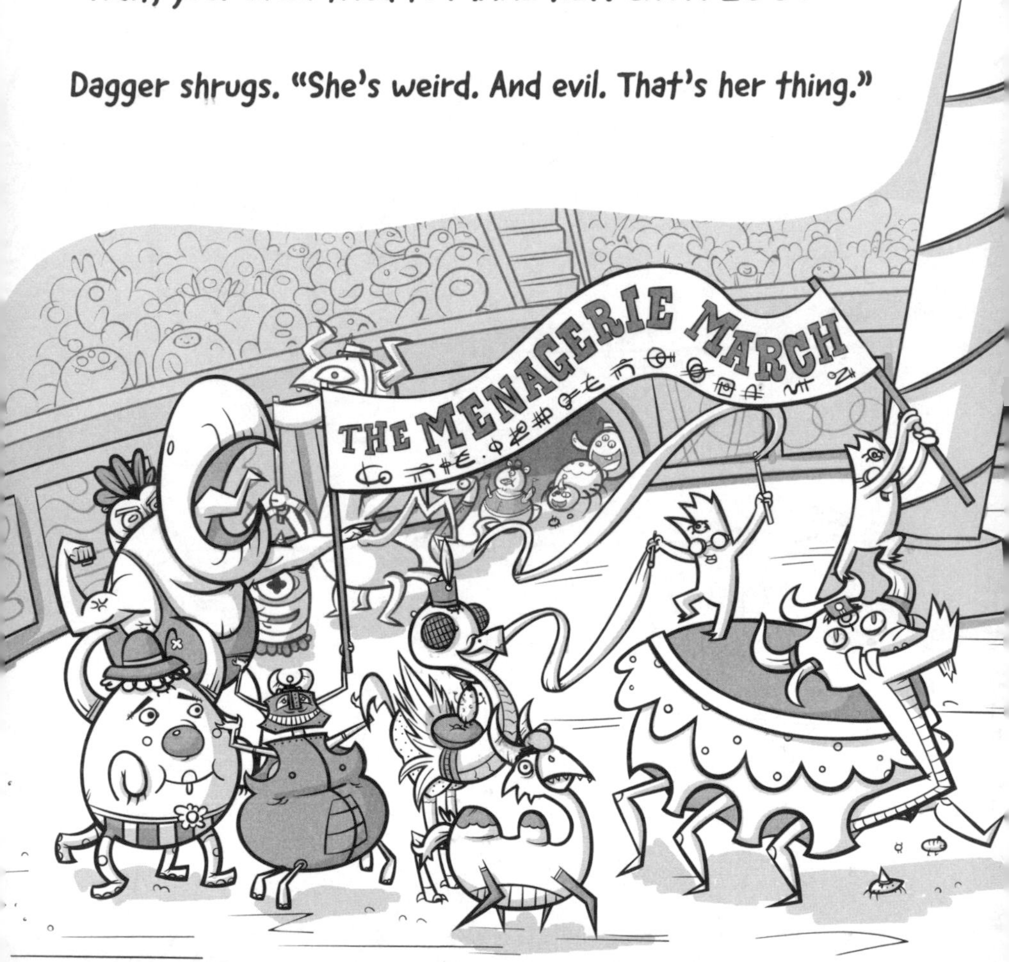
THE MENAGERIE MARCH

I'm watching a horned dreybuck shuffle along when a shiny glint catches my eye. Leaning forward, squinting, I see that there's a glistening gizmo attached to the dreybuck's head.

I realize there are gizmos attached to the heads of *all* the creatures. I elbow Humphree. "Yo, what's that electronic junk on the animals' heads? You see those?"

But before Humps can give it any thought, someone screams the word.

THE. WORD.

The LAST word

you EVER want

to hear ANYONE yell

on desert planet Arahas . . .

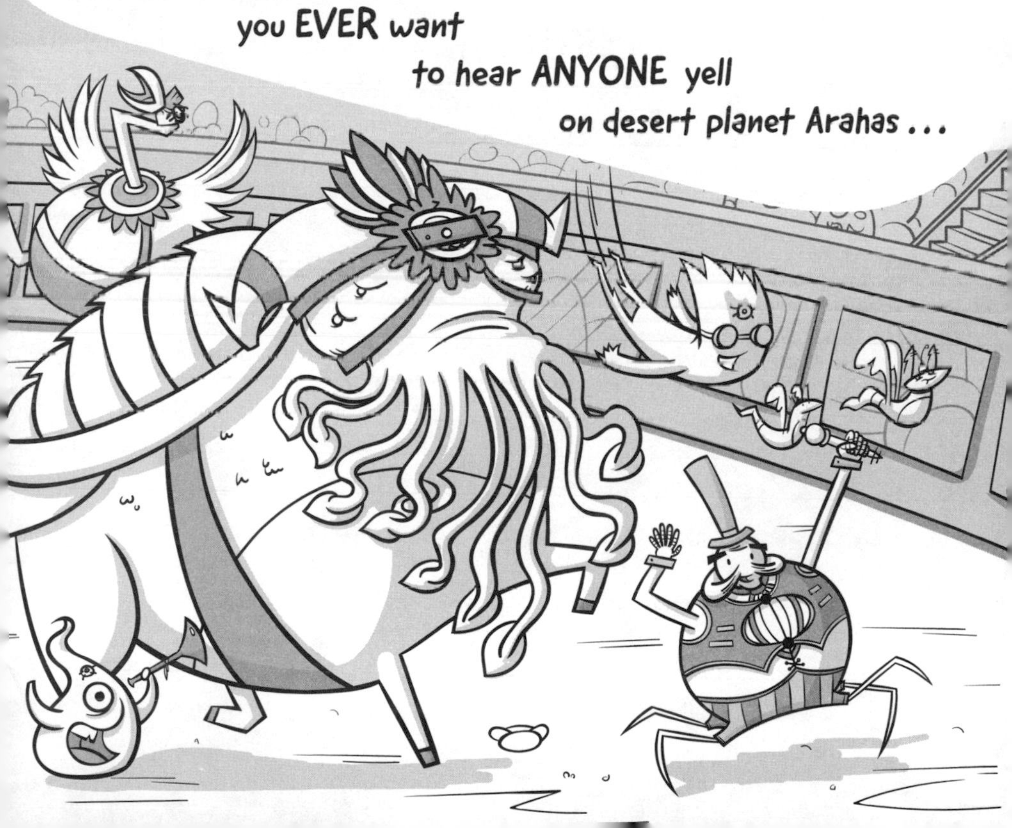

"SANDSTORM!"

Sandstorms on Arahas will straight-up END you. They come hard and fast and swallow cities and spaceports whole.

Screams explode around us! Aliens scramble over each other, racing for the exits. It's chaos!

I leap from my seat and race up to the very top row of the stands. But looking out at the desert wasteland beyond the spaceport, I see that this is no sandstorm.

This is worse. This is a **SKORLAX**.

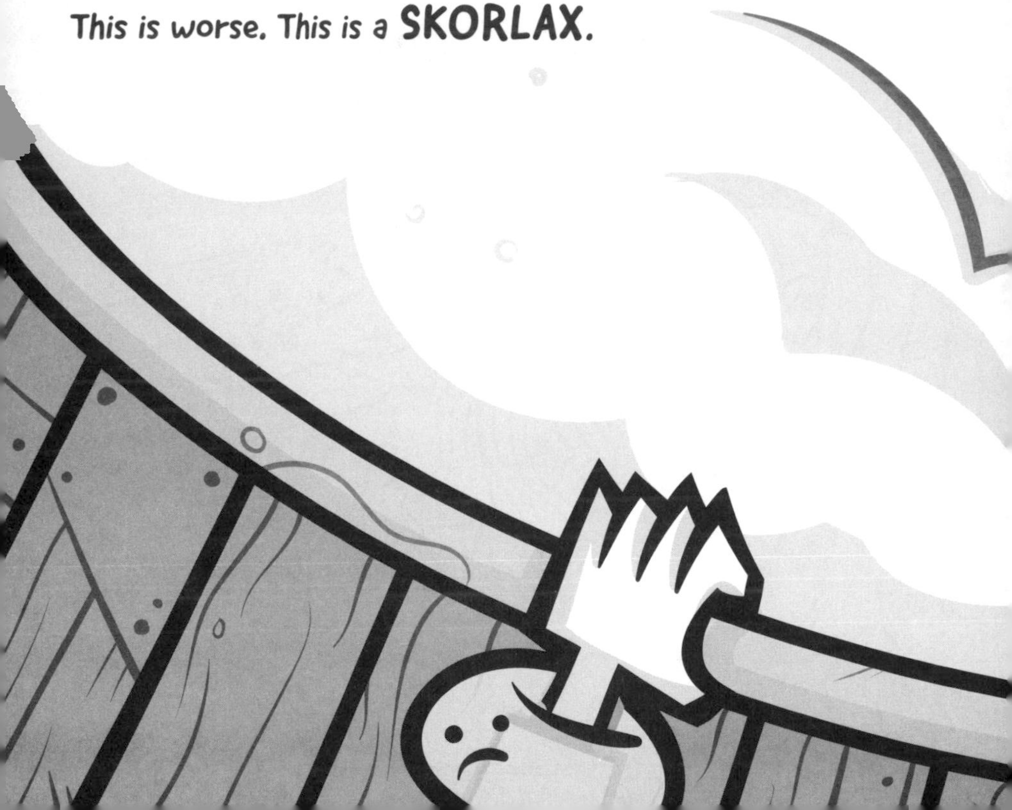

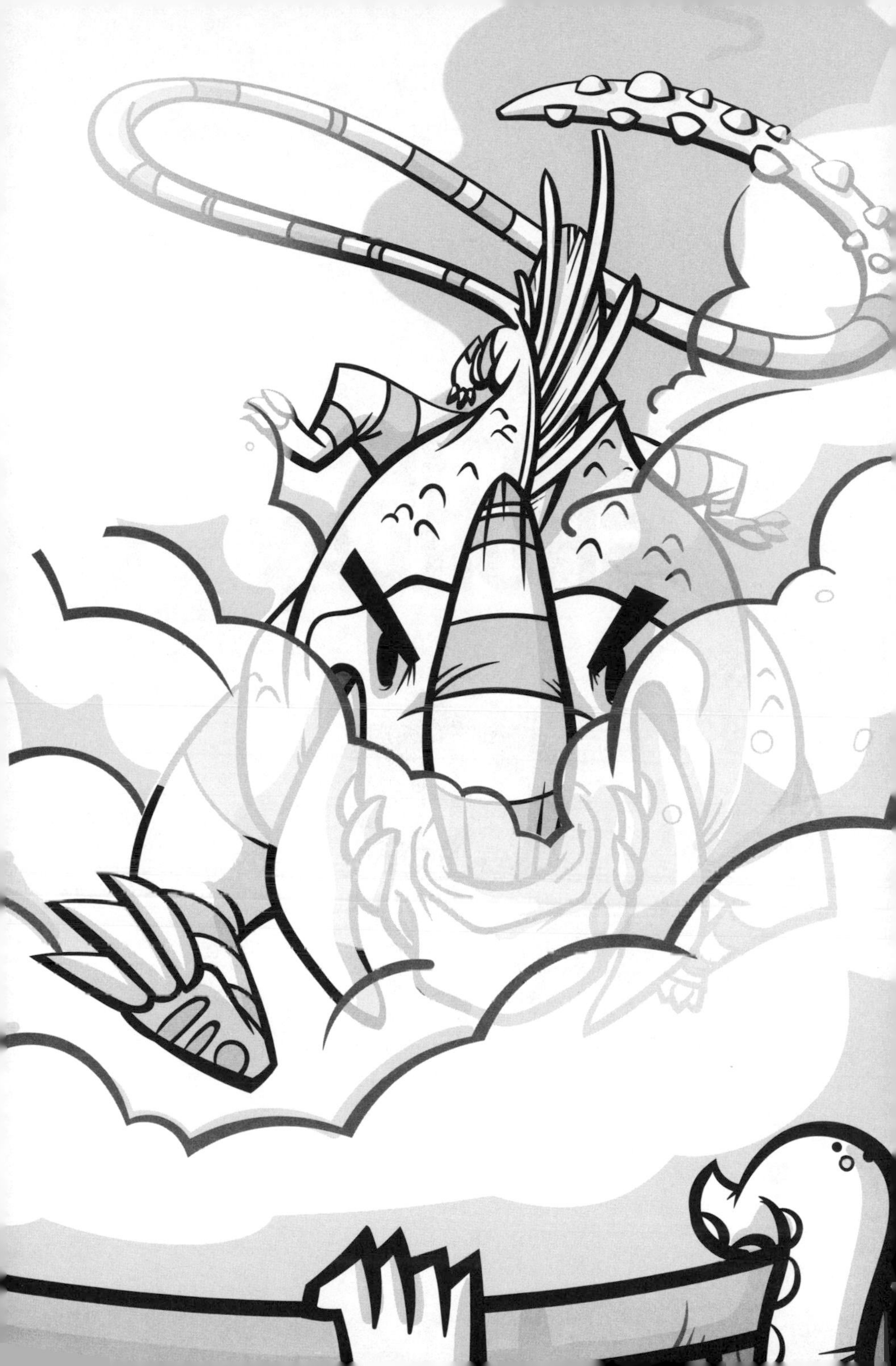

THE SKORLAX

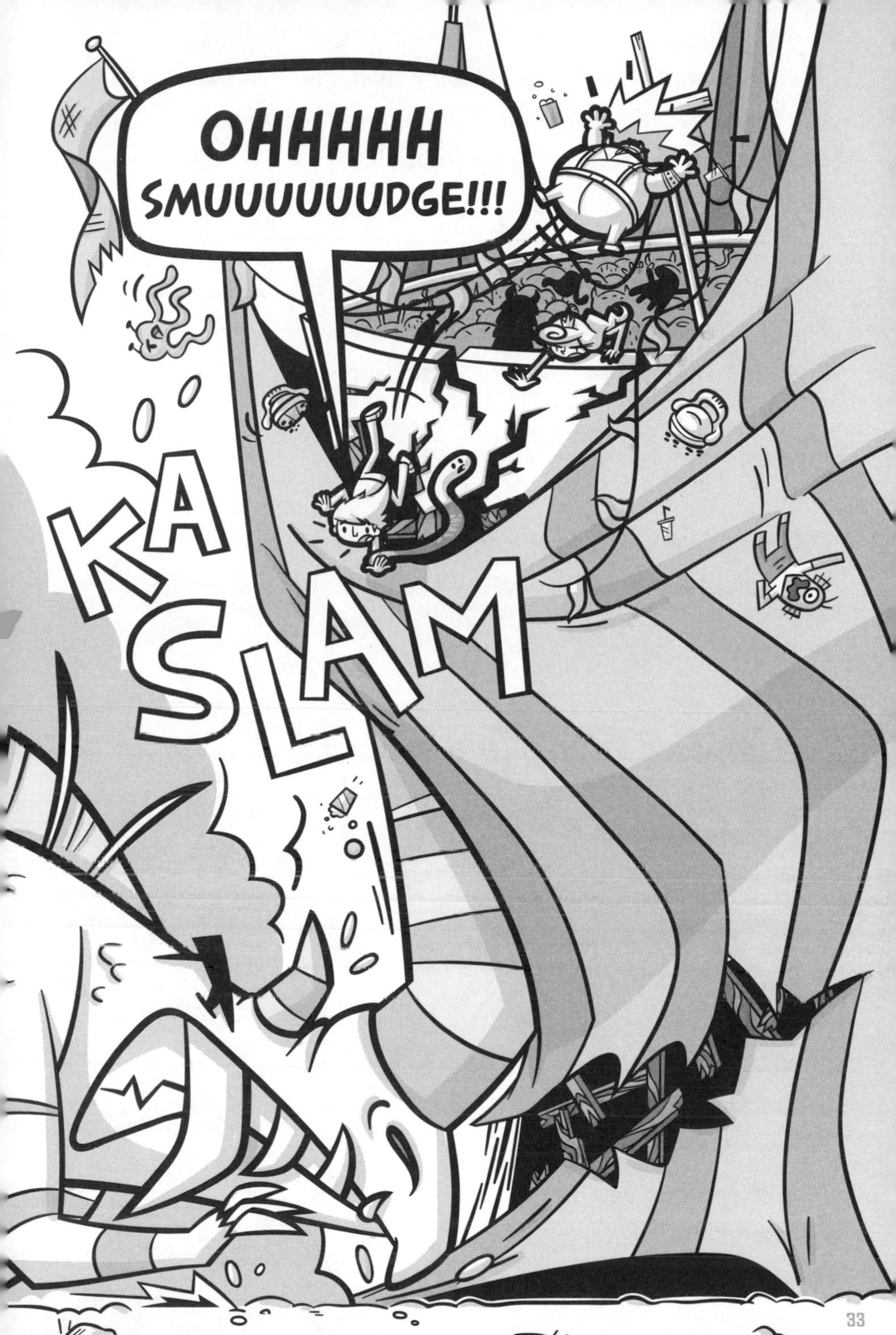
OHHHHH SMUUUUUUUDGE!!!
KA
SLAM

The skorlax shatters the stadium wall, and the impact hurls me over the side. I plummet, bouncing off the monster, then crashing to the sandy soil beyond the stadium. "Ugh," I groan. "I think I broke my butt . . ."

But there's no time to worry about my busted behind—the skorlax is halfway inside the stadium! In moments, the monster will devour everyone and everything!

I need to get this beast's attention.

OK, look, I know I play it cool. Really, though, I'm fairly *not*-talented. But there are a few things I can do well:

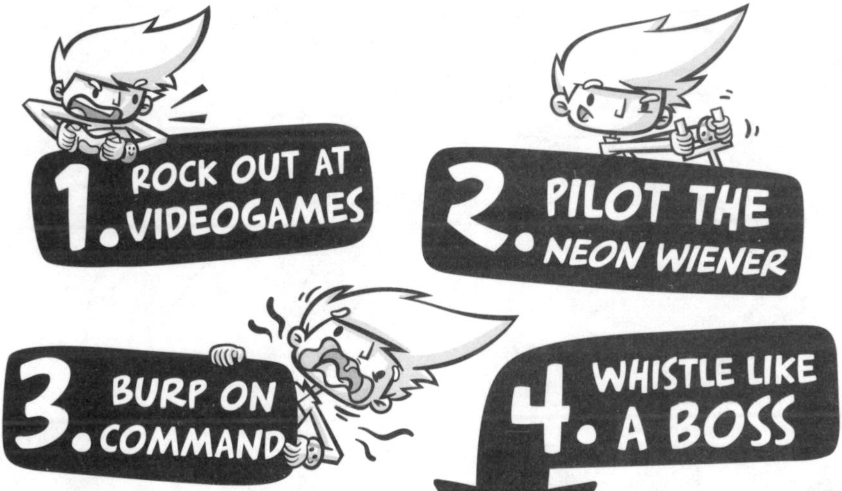
1. ROCK OUT AT VIDEOGAMES
2. PILOT THE NEON WIENER
3. BURP ON COMMAND
4. WHISTLE LIKE A BOSS

I know, whistle . . . Weird thing to be good at, right? But someone taught me long ago, and I'm about to see if I still remember how . . .

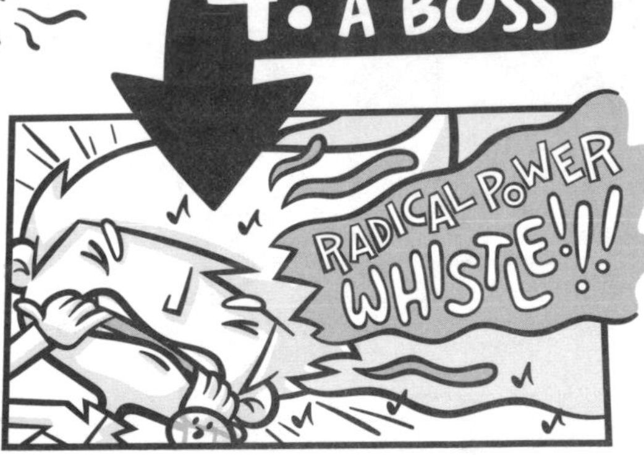
RADICAL POWER WHISTLE!!!

The piercing shriek gets the great beast's attention. Bleachers break as the skorlax steps back. Its massive head swings toward me, splashing me with great globs of green saliva. More saliva drips from the monster's shark-fin-sized fangs.

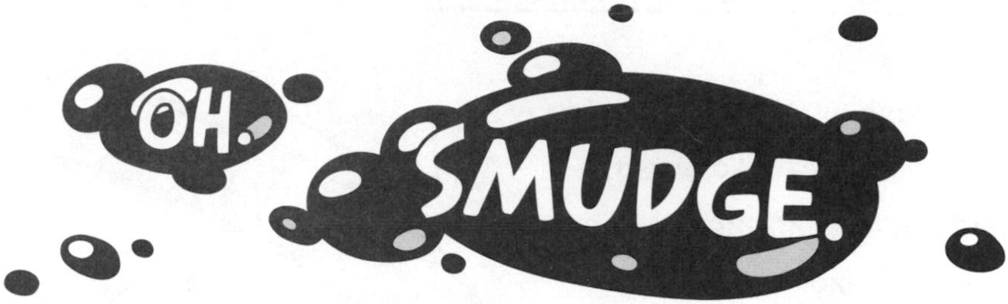
OH.
SMUDGE.

I didn't really think out this plan beyond "get big monster's attention."

I forgot that the logical follow-up to that is "get eaten by big monster."

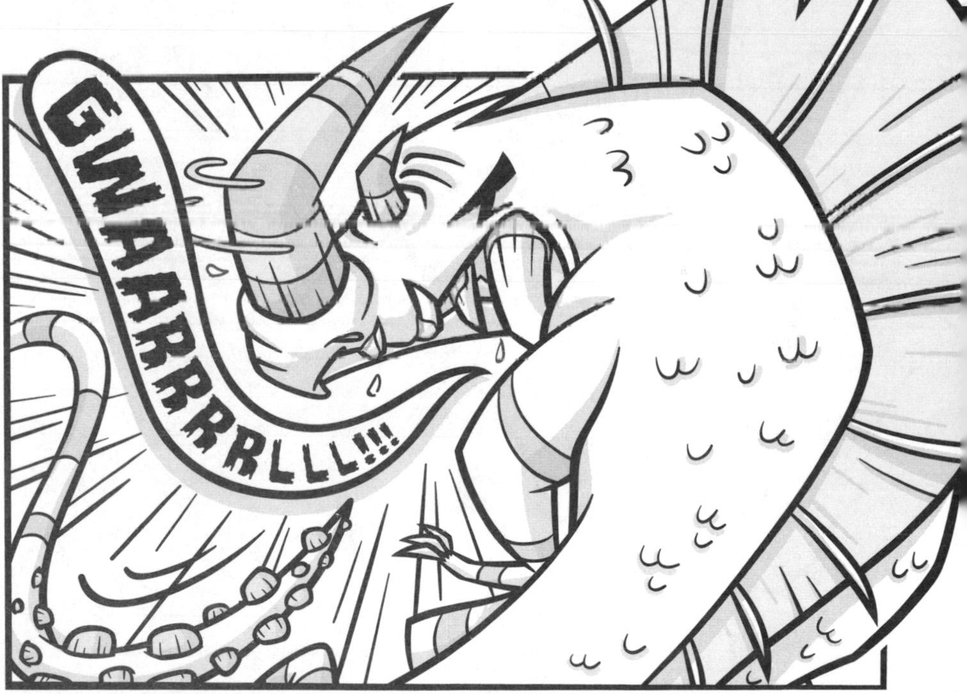
GWAARRRRRLLLL!!!

The skorlax's tail whips through the stadium wall! Hunks and chunks of junk soar my way!

I drop to one knee like Superman preparing for liftoff, and I holler, "Goober shield!"

In a flash my rubbery buddy is morphing, transforming, and enveloping me in elastic armor.

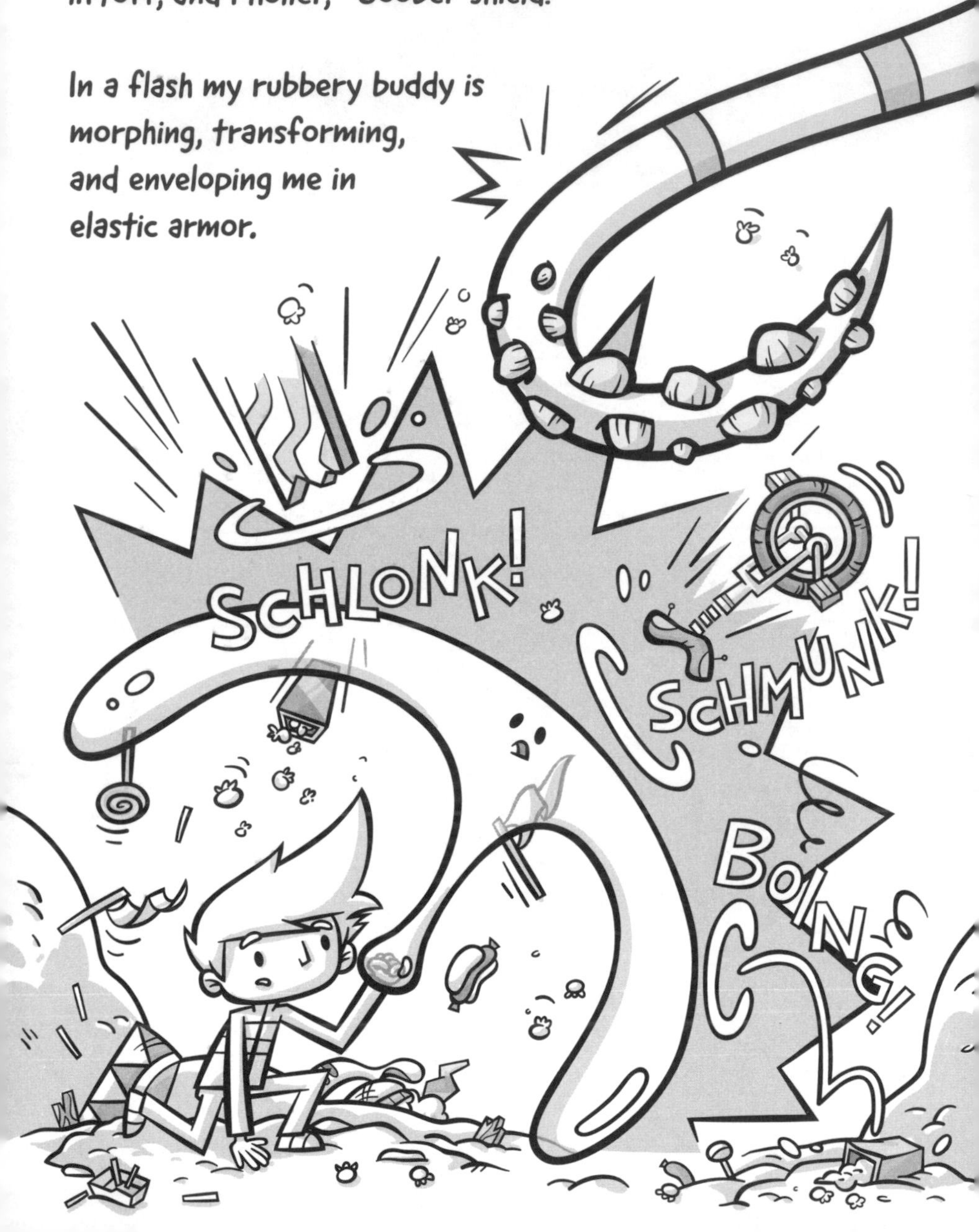
SCHLONK!
SCHMUNK!
BOING!

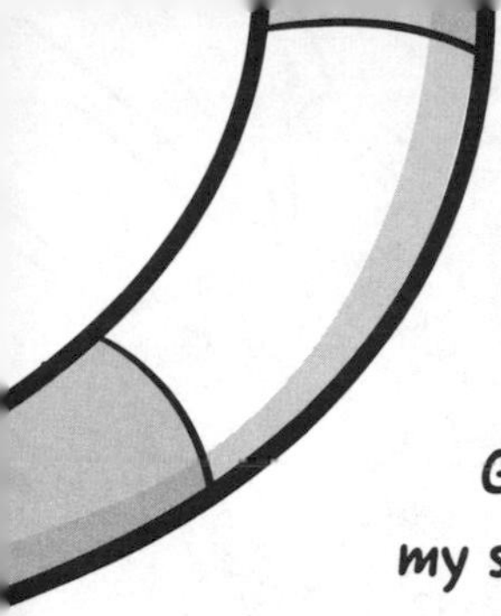

When the busted-bleacher barrage subsides, Goober snaps back to my wrist. The skorlax's eyes narrow. This monster is fuming—it didn't know I had Goober up my sleeve (well, technically on my sleeve).

A single hover-seat tumbles down and knocks me in the noggin. That's when it hits me. Literally.

A memory is knocked loose—shaken free from the deep dark spot in the back of my brain where I kept it buried—and I now know EXACTLY what to do.

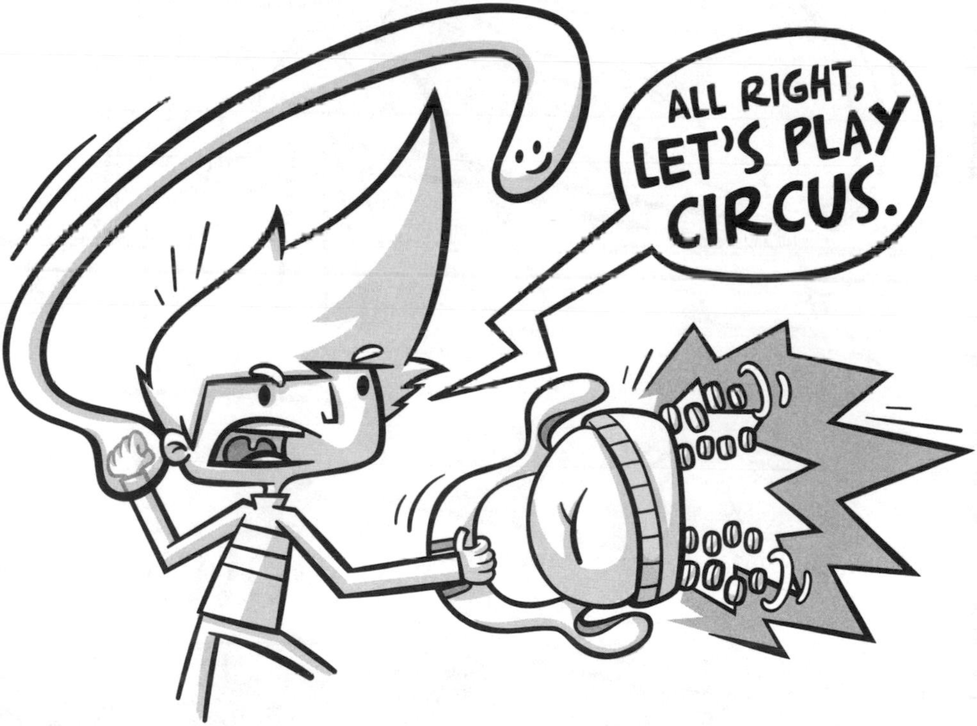
ALL RIGHT, LET'S PLAY CIRCUS.

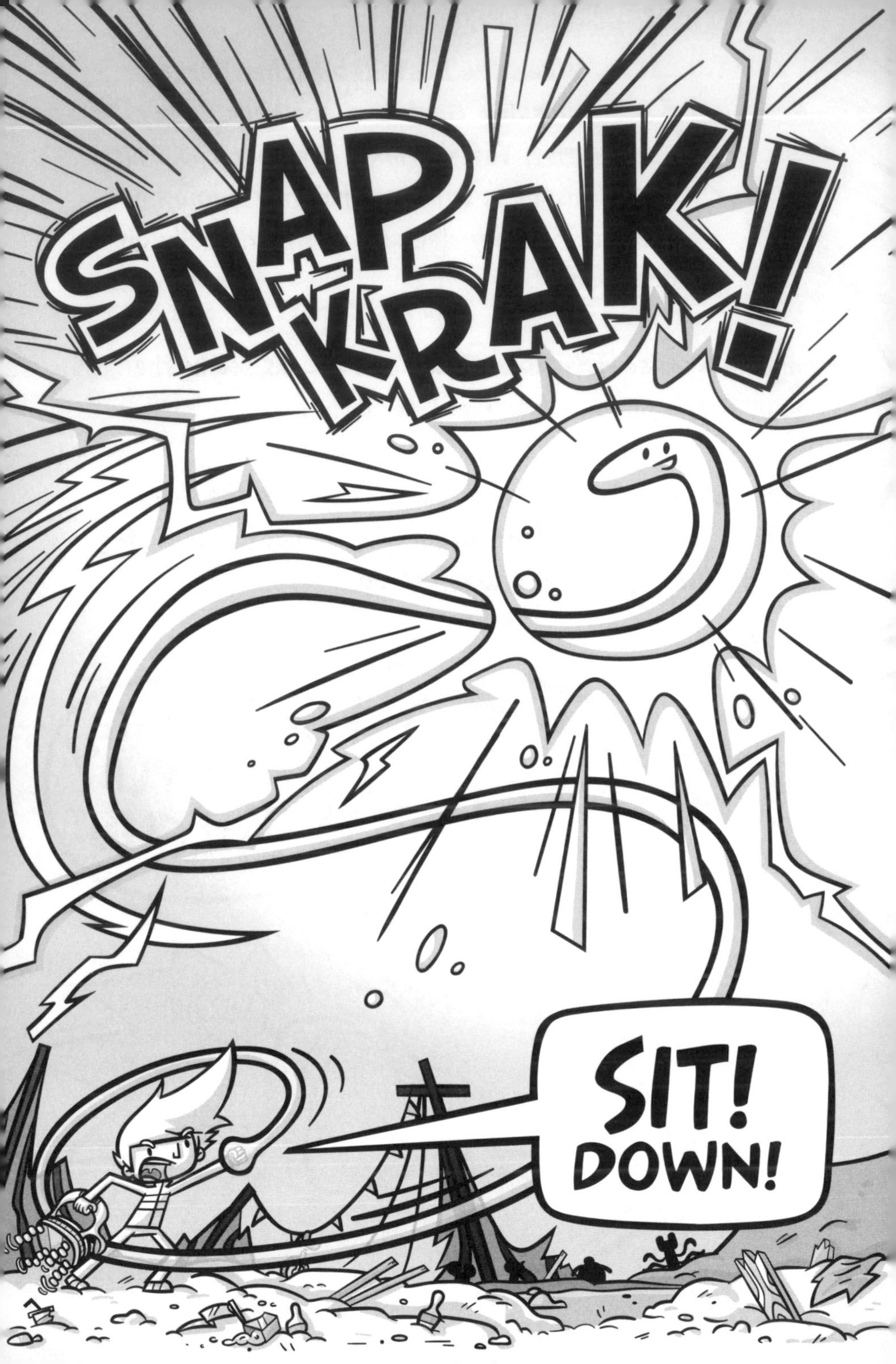
SNAP KRAK!
SIT! DOWN!

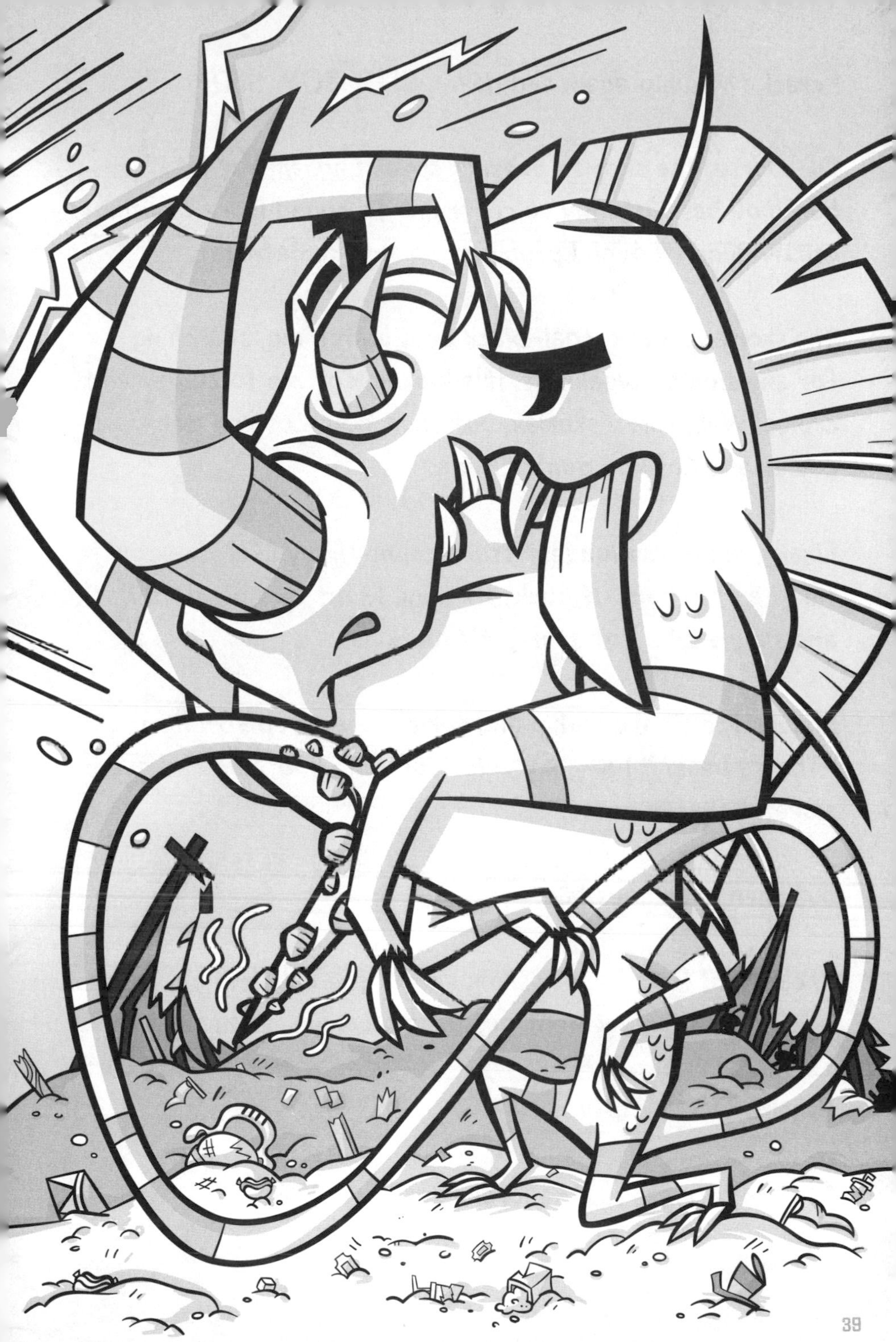

I crack the whip again and holler, **"SIT, BOY. SIT!"**

Of course, the skorlax doesn't speak English, but I put a bunch of bass into my voice, trying to sound like a bruising grizzly dude (though I prob just sound like Batman).

The skorlax's dark, coal-black eyes watch me, searching for any sign of weakness. It's looking for me to cower and cringe. Well, sorry skorlax, but right now Cosmoe don't cower and Cosmoe don't cringe.

Finally, after the longest stare down of my life, the monster takes a step back. It tucks its huge front legs beneath itself and slowly sits. Hot stuff, it's working!

I lower the Goober whip and take a slow step forward. "Thatta beast," I say, my voice soft and soothing and even sweet. "Thatta beast."

But then it all goes bad.

I hear hard footsteps rushing across the rubble. I catch a quick flash of movement out of the corner of my eye.

I shout, **"NO! DON'T!"**

But it's too late . . . The wrangler is attacking . . .

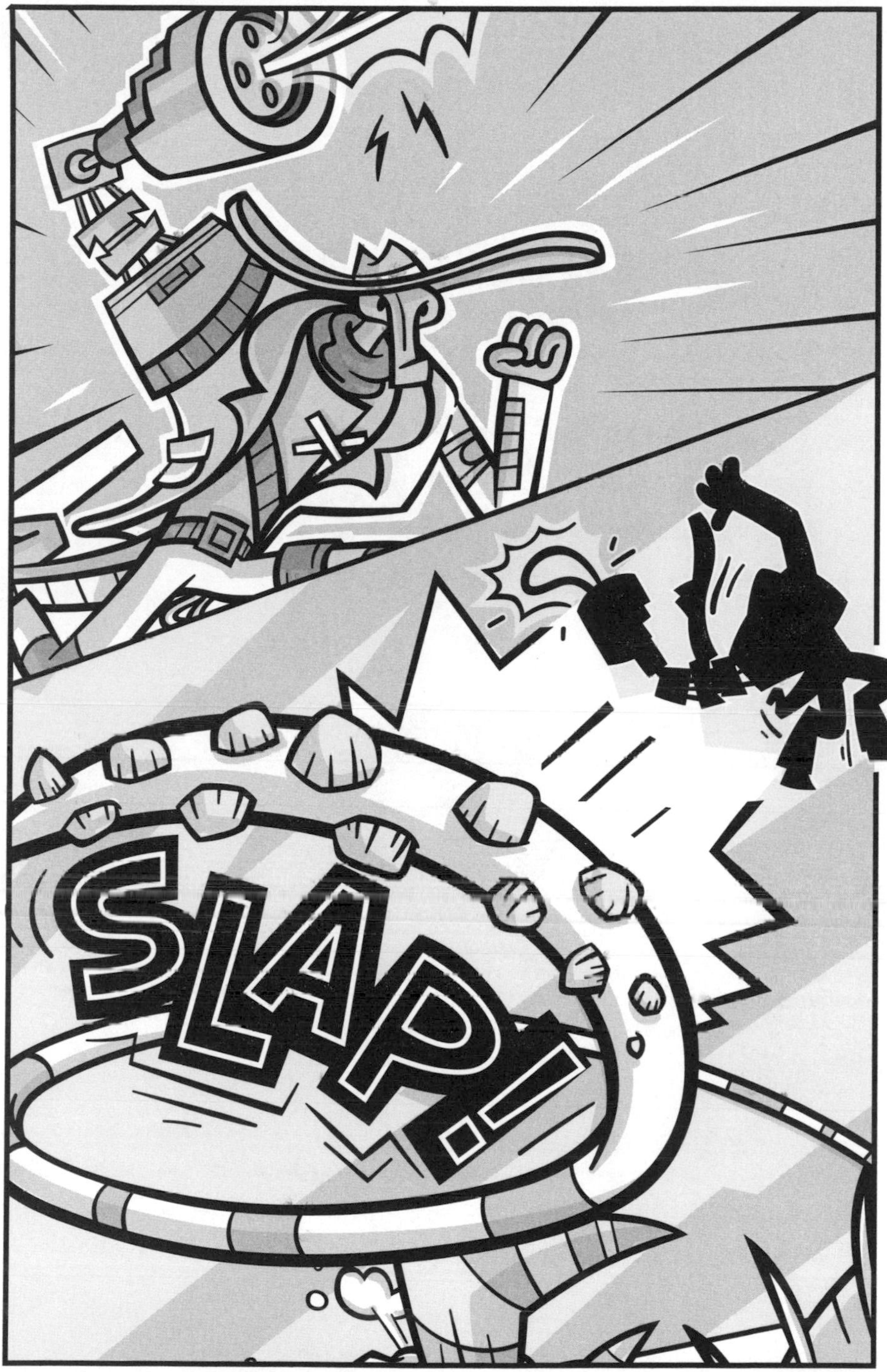
SLAP!!

COSMOE THE MONSTER-TAMER

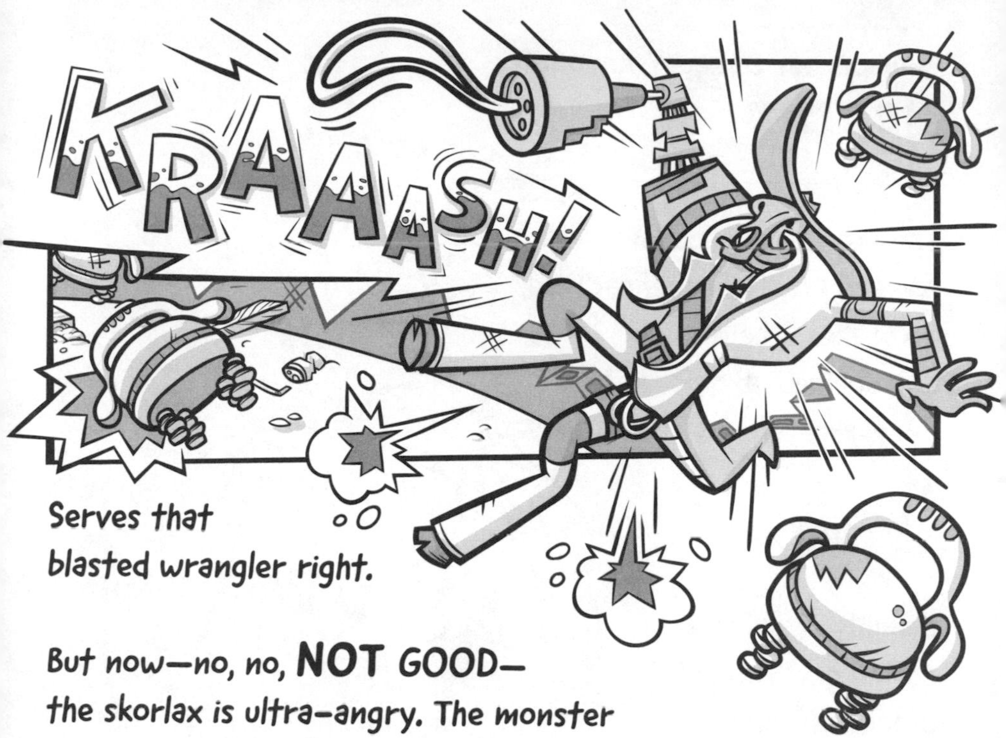
KRAAASH!

Serves that
blasted wrangler right.

But now—no, no, **NOT** GOOD—
the skorlax is ultra-angry. The monster
roars and turns, about to charge back into the stadium.

I try whistling again.

Nope.

I scream "HALT, STOP, come back, please, I'M BEGGING YA!"

Nada.

Finally, one last time, holding my breath as my heart
pounds, I crack the Goober whip. And the ferocious,
growling skorlax turns.

And it comes right for me . . .

"Humphree? Dagger? Anyone?

HELP!"

The skorlax is barreling toward me, full-on, headlong, no brakes. The ground shakes and quakes—and so do I. I'm terror struck!

I do nothing.

I simply stand there as the great beast plows into me . . .

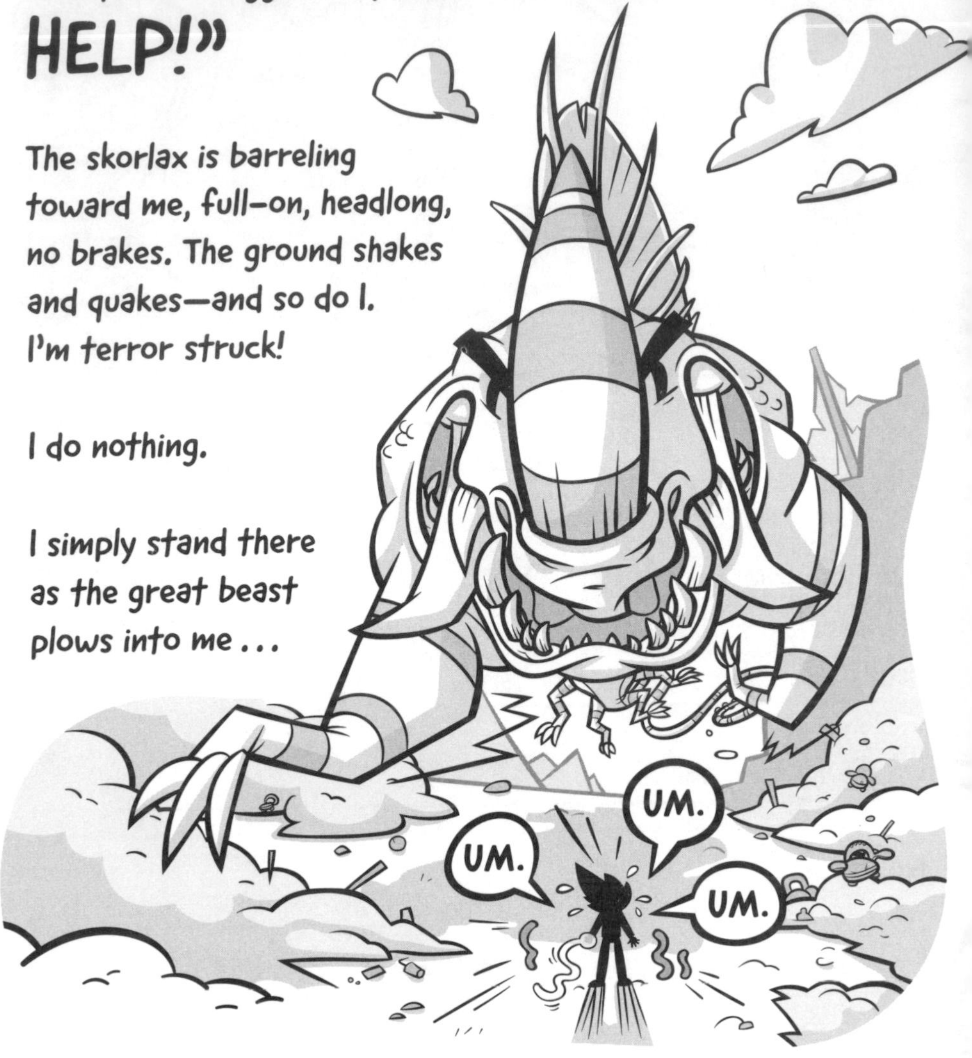
UM.
UM.
UM.

BA-BAMM! One massive monster paw hits me, and I'm dragged and trampled beneath the beast. I taste dirt and sand. I see flashes of sky, and then ground, and then monster hide. I'm gonna be squashed—turned to paste.

My arms are flailing, Goober is flying, and then . . .

We stop! And I'm still **ALIVE!**
Not squashed or turned to paste!

I manage to squeak out from beneath the beast. I'm confused.
Shouldn't I have been, like, eaten? Like inside the skorlax's
belly, right now?? What went wrong? I mean—actually—
WHAT WENT RIGHT?

And then I see ... I **<u>WON THE BATTLE!</u>** Sorta ...

The skorlax is all tangled up in Goob! The monster is flat on
its back, and Goober is wrapped around its hind legs.

Now's my chance! I dash up and across the skorlax's soft
stomach using Goober like a giant cowboy lasso, tying the
monster's legs together, until ...

I leap down and collapse against the side of the upside-down skorlax. I just wrestled a colossally colossal monster to the ground on steamy Arahas! I'm soaked in sweat, swimming in my undies!

All around me, aliens are crawling from the wreckage. A few winged aliens push their way through the crumbled stands, then burst upward, into the air—eager to escape.

I spot my compadres coming through the hole in the stadium wall.

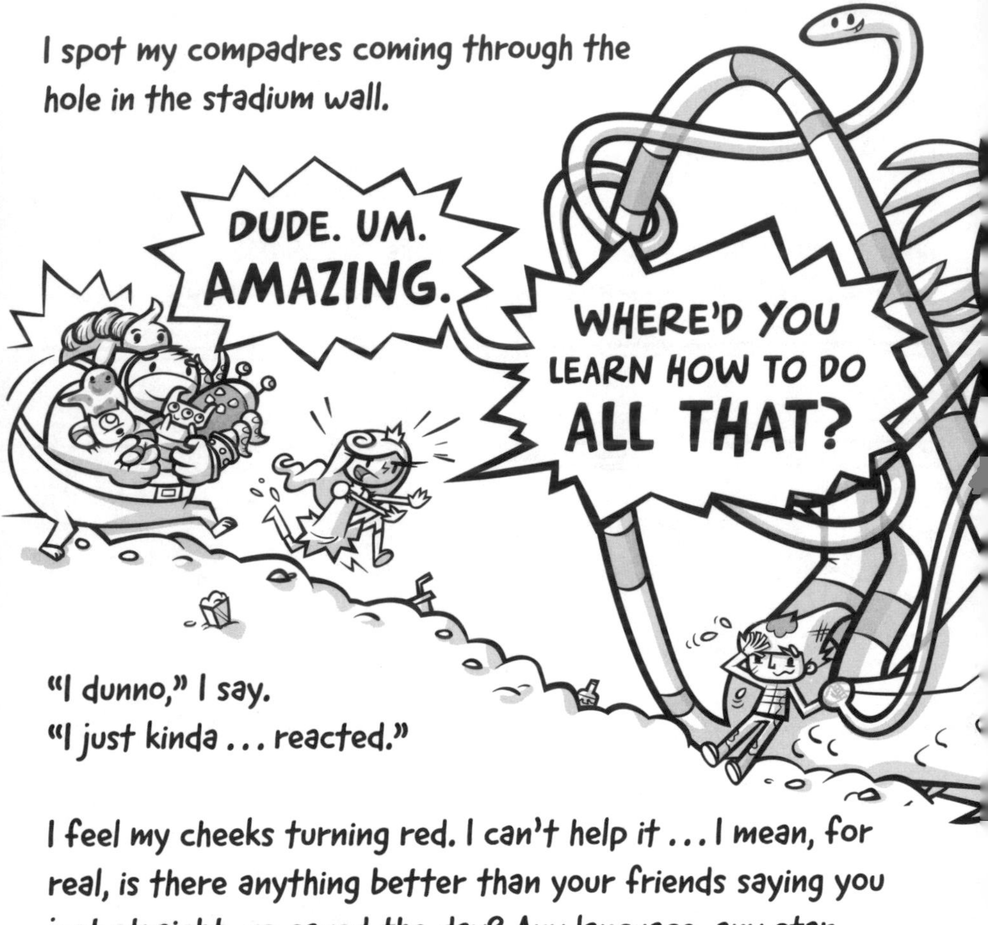
DUDE. UM. AMAZING.
WHERE'D YOU LEARN HOW TO DO ALL THAT?

"I dunno," I say.
"I just kinda . . . reacted."

I feel my cheeks turning red. I can't help it . . . I mean, for real, is there anything better than your friends saying you just straight-up saved the day? Any language, any star system—that's righteous!

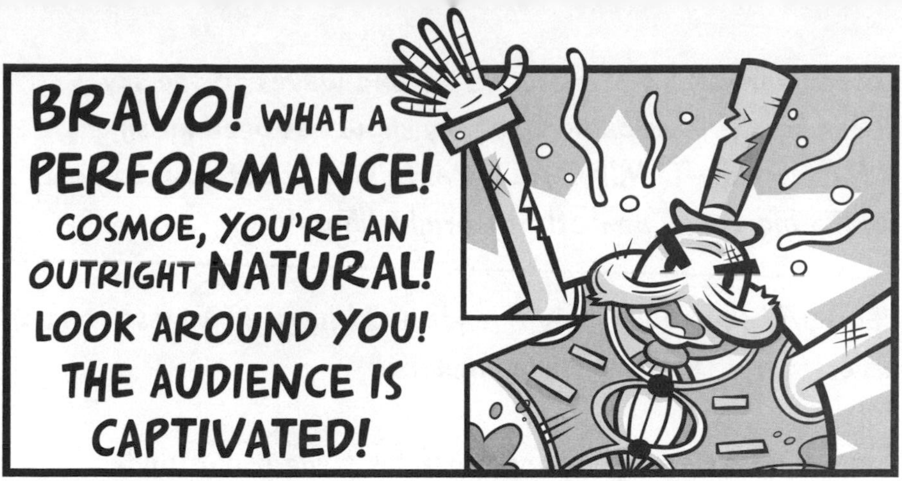
BRAVO! WHAT A PERFORMANCE! COSMOE, YOU'RE AN OUTRIGHT NATURAL! LOOK AROUND YOU! THE AUDIENCE IS CAPTIVATED!

"They're captivated because I saved them. And that would have been a lot easier if your nutcase wrangler hadn't done something dumb," I say.

At that moment, the wrangler casually tosses aside a frizzle-fried furble and steps from the debris.

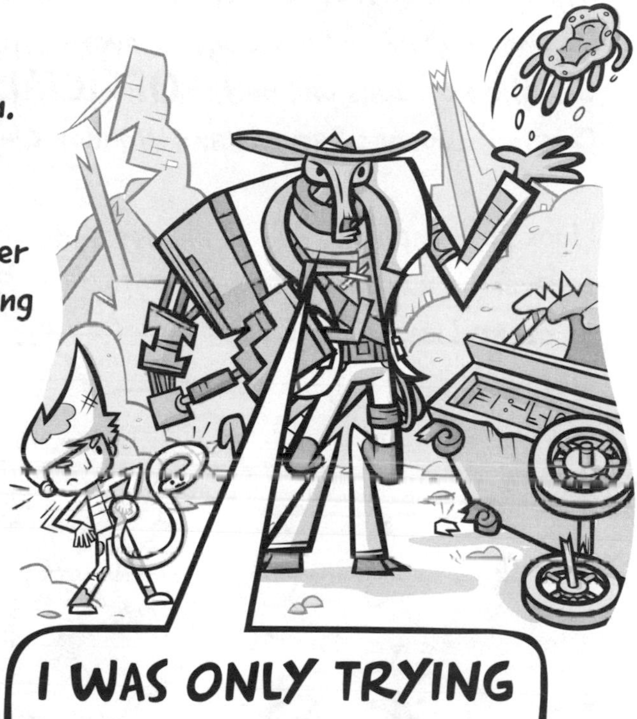
I WAS ONLY TRYING TO PROTECT THE AUDIENCE.

"Wrangler," Looper says, "please restrain this skorlax. The boy and I have more important matters to discuss. Because . . ."

Looper throws his arm around me and waves to the sky. "I can see it! A vision of what my show has been missing! A **MONSTER-TAMING ACT!** I'm talking about you, Cosmoe, on the big stage, beneath the bright lights!"

"Sorry," I say coolly, "My friends and I have a business to run. Galactic Hot Dogs. We sling wieners."

Looper thinks for a moment, then his smile grows wider. "Then I shall improve my offer! All three of you will join us, and you can sell hot dogs at every stop on the circuit! Galactic Hot Dogs will be the **OFFICIAL** hot dog of Crostini's Cosmic Carnival and Wonder Circus!"

I look to Humphree. He will always and forever be a money-hungry pirate at heart. I know **EXACTLY** what he's thinking . . .

"I don't want to spend all my time inside a crummy circus car," Princess Dagger groans. "I want to see the stars!"

"See the stars?" Looper chuckles. "My dear, you'll see the entire galaxy! The circus circuit runs from the Dark Kingdom to the Wild and Crazy West! You'll see it all!"

Princess Dagger's eyes light up like fireworks over Endor. **"MY LIST!"** she exclaims. "I'd be checking off stuff up, down, right, and left!"

Dags is practically shaking with excitement—like someone pumped her full of electro-volts. And Humphree's staring at me with those money-struck eyes.

Okay, fine, whatever, I get it. Humphree and Princess are on board with getting on board. But they don't understand. I just can't . . .

Turning away, I hang my head. I see my reflection in a puddle of skorlax saliva at my feet. My face is smeared with soot. My hair is slick with sweat. My shirt is a torn, baggy mess, and my sneakers and pants are covered ankle high in muddy spit-sand.

I barely recognize myself. It's like, it's not me I'm looking at. It's like I'm looking at someone else entirely.

And I know who that someone is . . .

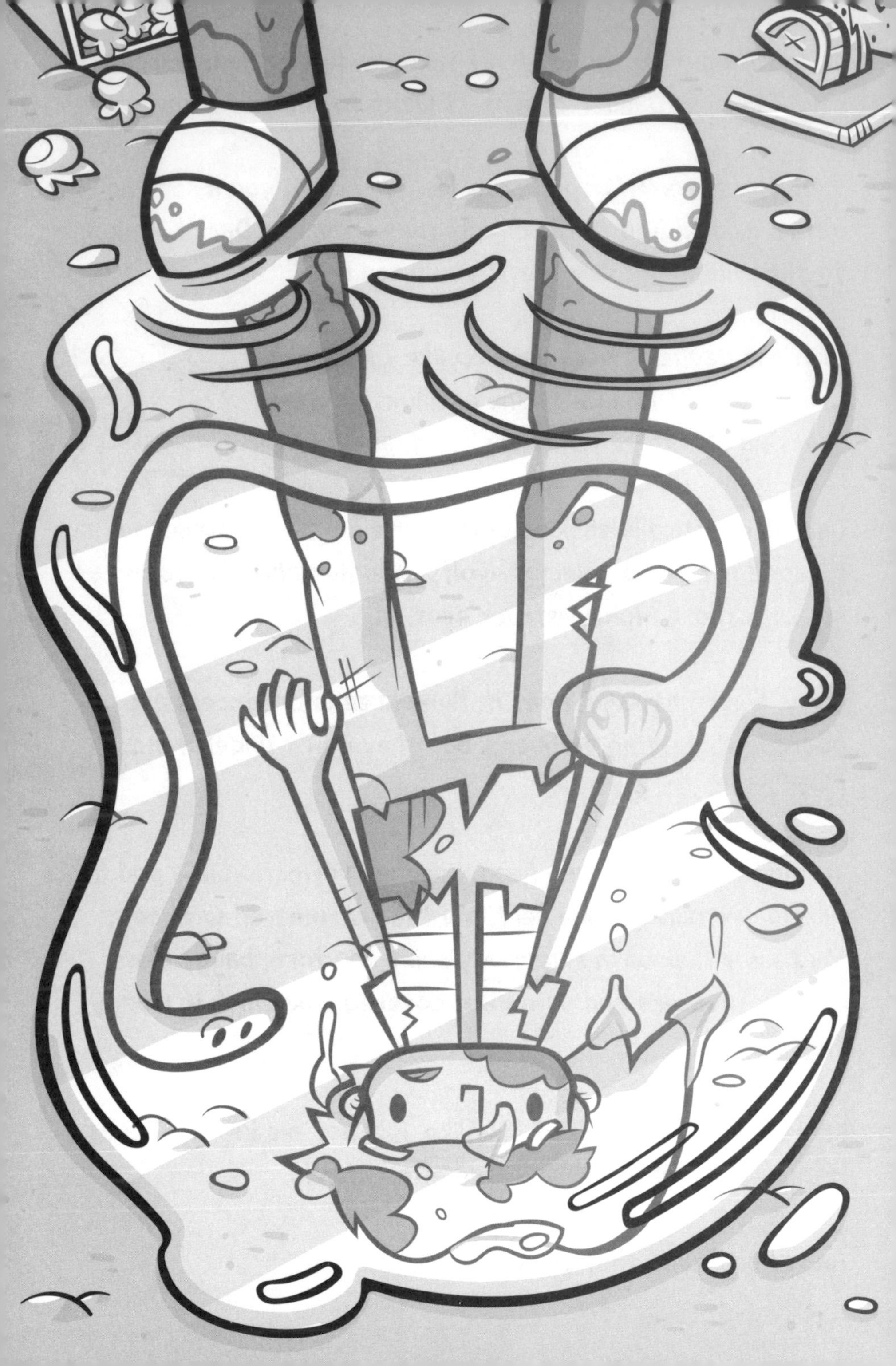

Seeing that image in the puddle, my heart just about stops. I feel something tugging at me. And for a second I'm like "OH SMUDGE, THE SKORLAX IS BACK, AND HE'S TUGGING AT ME WITH HIS TEETH!"

But then I realize "Cosmoe, you're kind of dumb—you're being emotionally tugged at." Memories, buried deep inside, are yanking on the ol' heartstrings.

And it all feels right.

It feels like I'm supposed to be here. As I stare down at my reflection, I see the past and the present and the future all colliding like neutron stars.

It's like ...
It's like this is my destiny ...

Goober snaps back to my wrist. I wipe the crud from my face, run my hand through my hair, and turn to Humphree and Dagger.

BUDS, WE ARE **FRAPPIN'** JOINING THE **SPACE** CIRCUS.

ALL ABOARD!

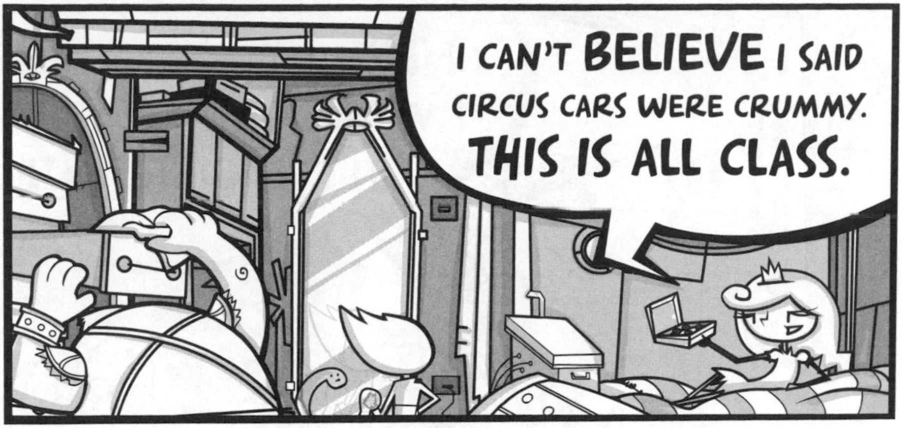
I CAN'T BELIEVE I SAID CIRCUS CARS WERE CRUMMY. THIS IS ALL CLASS.

Looper Crostini's roust-a-bots loaded the *Neon Wiener* into a spare car for storage, and just after sunset, the train blasted off into space. Now we're chilling inside our own private car, hanging like some VIPs.

Dagger's kicked back on a plasma bed, absolutely housing some stinky snack. "Cosmoe, you gotta try this candy! When you bite into it, scrumptious jelly oozes out!"

"Uh, Princess?" Humphree says. "That's not oozing jelly. That's bug guts. You're eating chocolate-covered bugs."

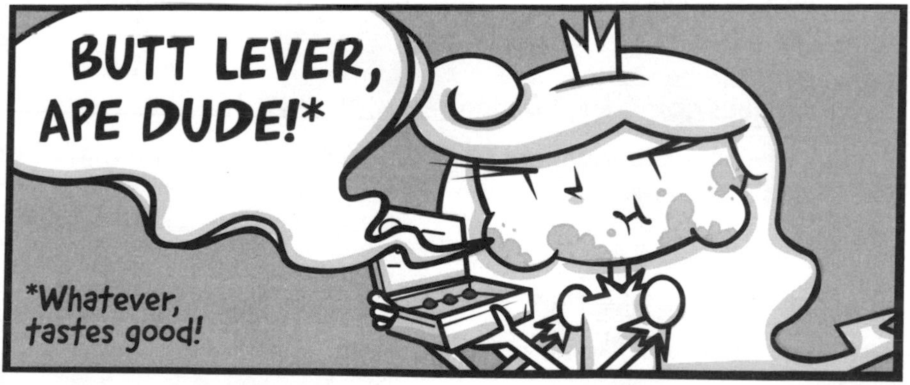
BUTT LEVER, APE DUDE!*
*Whatever, tastes good!

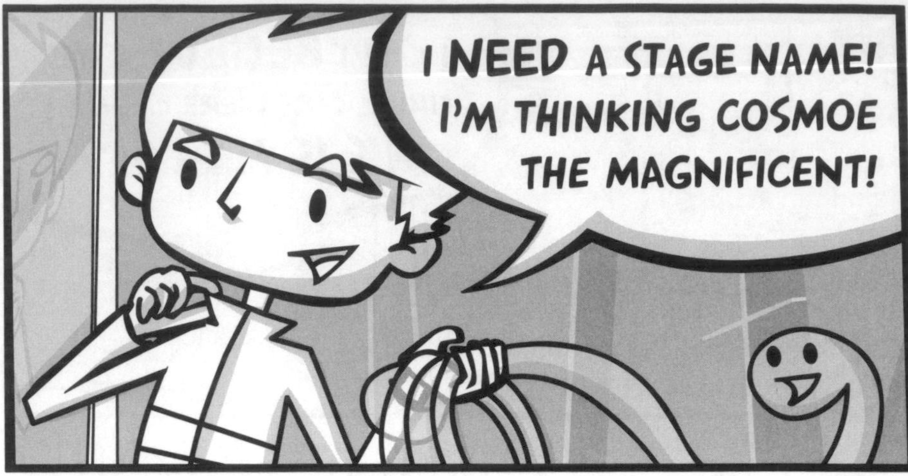
I NEED A STAGE NAME! I'M THINKING COSMOE THE MAGNIFICENT!

"Eh, but you're not really THAT magnificent," Dagger says. "How about Cosmoe the Mildly Magnificent?"

"Or Cosmoe the Kinda Decent?" Humphree chimes in.

I roll my eyes and go back to looking-awesome practice (not that I need much practice). But suddenly I feel my buds boring holes in me with their alien eyeballs.

I spin around. "What?! What's up?! Why are you giving me weirdo stares?!"

"Serious question time," Dagger says. "When the skorlax attacked—how did you know how to do all that taming stuff?"

"I never saw you like that, short pants," Humphree adds, wrinkling his brow like he's studying me.

Emotional smudge. I knew they couldn't just let me be. I knew they'd ask questions.

The room is silent except for the soft, steady hum of the engines propelling the train through the Milky Way.

"Look," I say finally. "It's just that . . . once I tell you, it's going to change stuff, and—**ARGH!** Fine, here's the deal: Yes, I've been to the circus before. Yes, I know a little about the circus. But it's not something I like to talk about or even let myself think about. OK?"

Dagger opens her mouth, but Humphree stops her. "We all got pasts, short pants," he says, "And we don't all necessarily like 'em. That's life. You keep your stuff to yourself as long as you like."

Just then there's a—

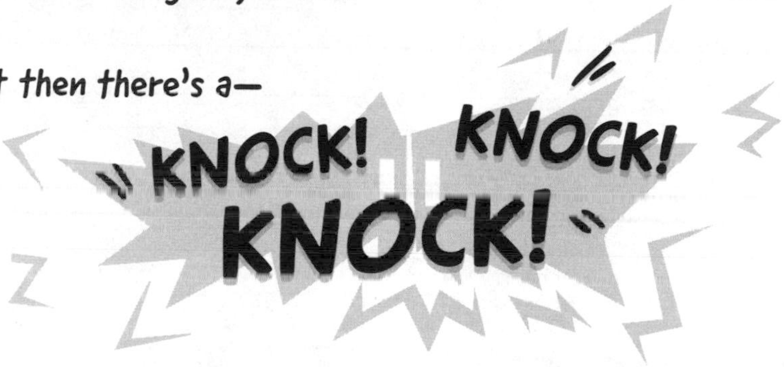
KNOCK!
KNOCK!
KNOCK!

The door opens with a whoosh, revealing a grinning Crostini in a shiny spacey tuxedo. "Please join me for a tour of the train followed by dinner in my private car. I will not take 'We're not hungry right now' for an answer!"

So we agree. And we discover just how amazing this circus is.

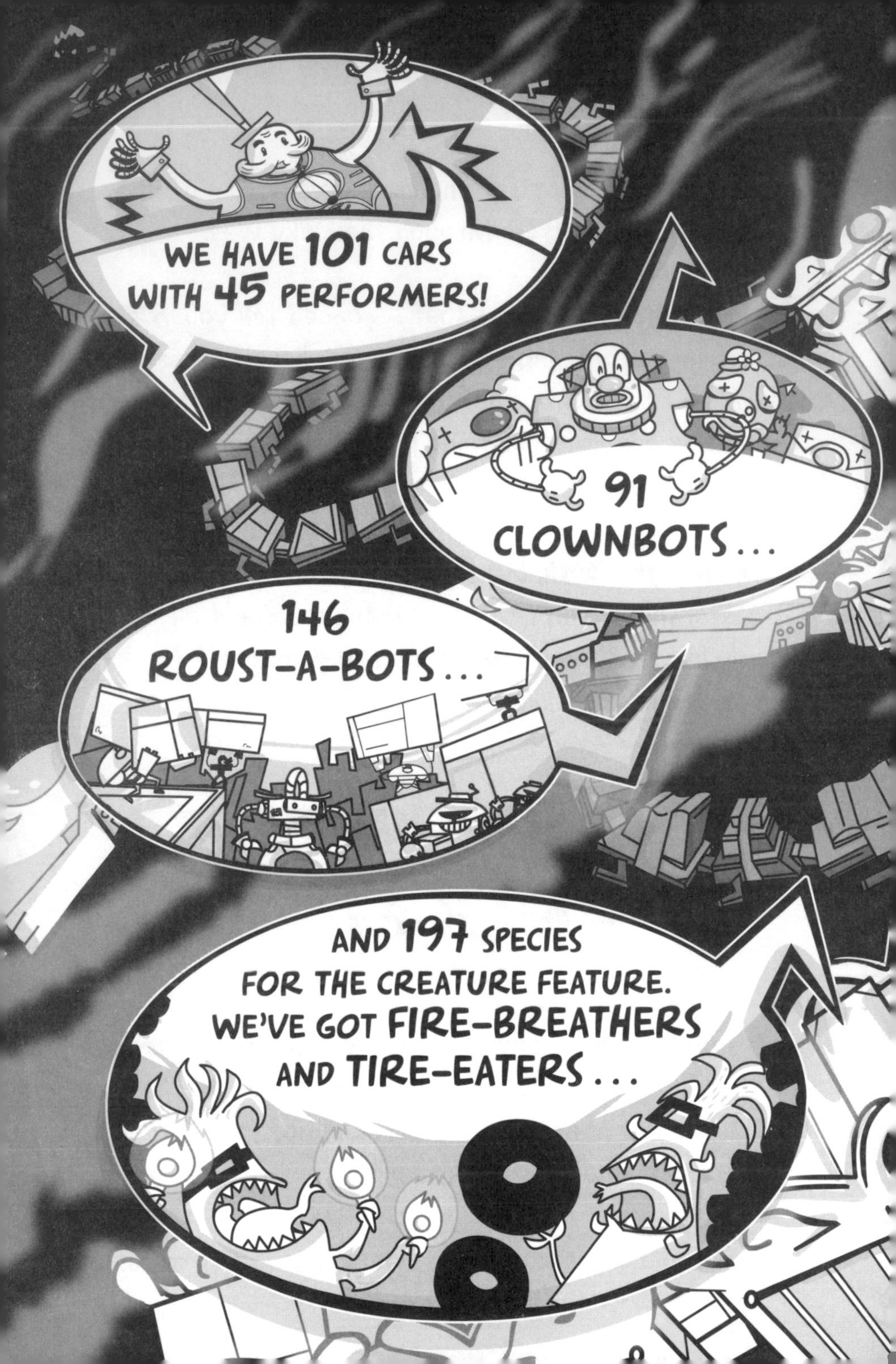
WE HAVE 101 CARS WITH 45 PERFORMERS!
91 CLOWNBOTS . . .
146 ROUST-A-BOTS . . .
AND 197 SPECIES FOR THE CREATURE FEATURE. WE'VE GOT FIRE-BREATHERS AND TIRE-EATERS . . .

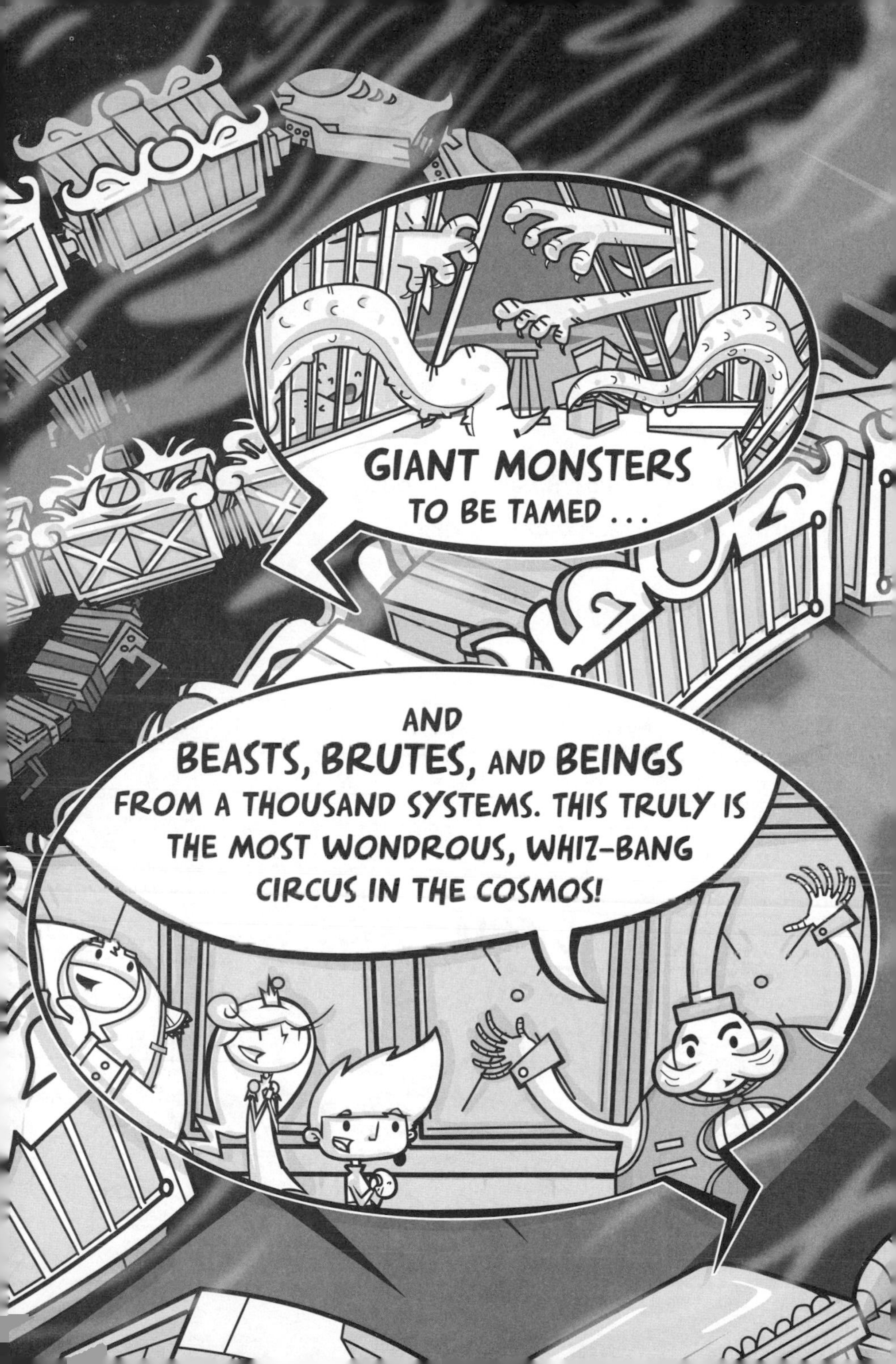
GIANT MONSTERS
TO BE TAMED . . .
AND
BEASTS, BRUTES, AND BEINGS
FROM A THOUSAND SYSTEMS. THIS TRULY IS
THE MOST WONDROUS, WHIZ-BANG
CIRCUS IN THE COSMOS!

After walking the entire length of the train, we follow Looper down a dimly lit hall to a fancy-pants door, covered in diamonds from the rings of Saturn Six.

"I hope you brought your appetites," Looper Crostini says. The door whooshes open, and servants greet us with platters of piping-hot food. We're shown to our seats.

"I FEEL LIKE THE KING OF ENGLAND!" I say.

"England?" Mr. Crostini asks curiously. An alien servant is pouring him a green bubbling drink.

"Oh, it's—um—it's where James Bond comes from."

"I do not know this James Bond," Mr. Crostini says. "Please, you must introduce me."

"Ha," I say, jamming a soup wad into my mouth. "Sure thing."

Servants come and go from tiny entrances on either side of one hugely huge metal door at the rear of the room. It looks like it's made from Ionic Iron. "That's one impressive door," I say. "What are you hiding back there? A hangout room?!"

Mr. Crostini slurps on spider spaghetti (yes, it's as gnarly as it sounds), then says, "My private quarters."

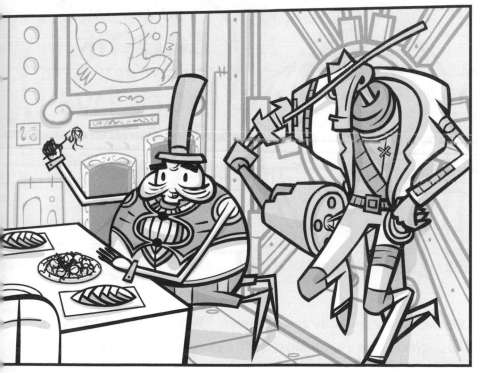

I lean in, getting all buddy-buddy. "Fancy guy like you, I bet you've got a holo-TV and all sorts of cool junk. Can I see?"

"Cosmoe, my boy," Mr. Crostini says, narrowing his eyes, "must I define the word 'PRIVATE' for you?"

Whoops! I touched a nerve. "Oh, of course not! Private's private, Mr. Crostini."

Then, for the first time during the meal, Humphree speaks.

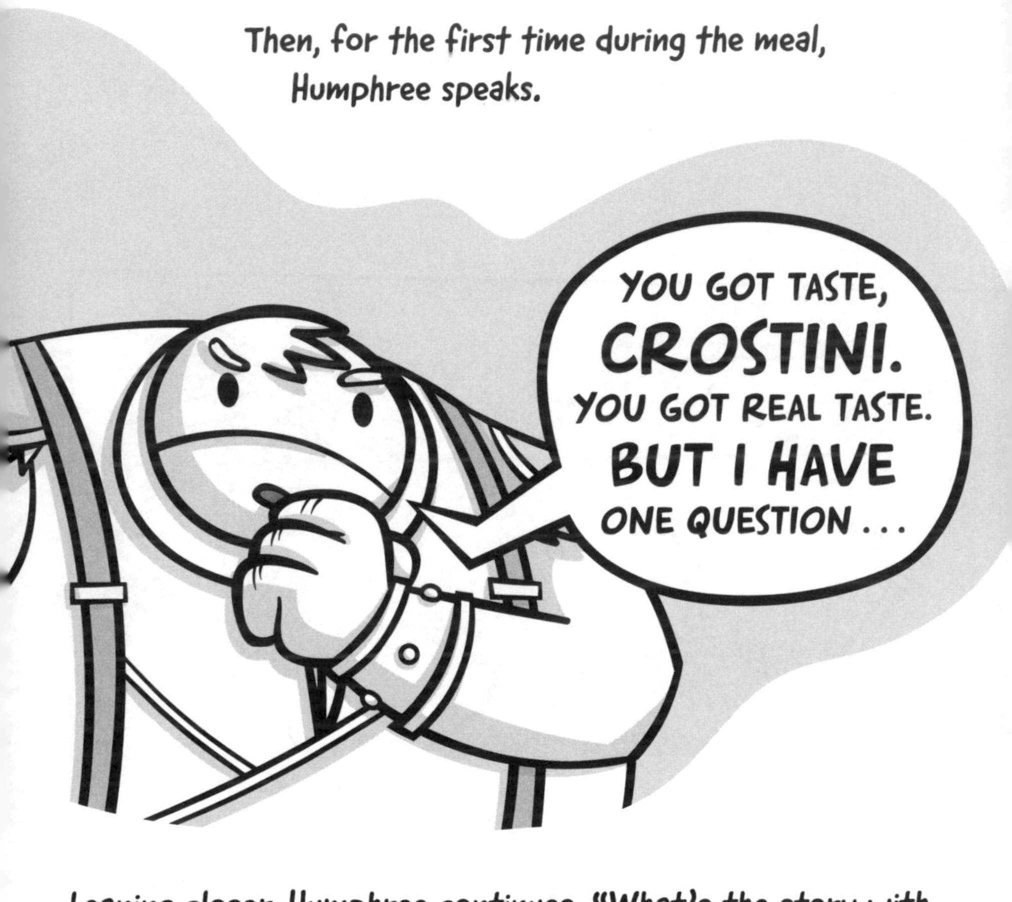
YOU GOT TASTE, CROSTINI. YOU GOT REAL TASTE. BUT I HAVE ONE QUESTION . . .

Leaning closer, Humphree continues, "What's the story with those gizmos on the animals in the creature feature?"

"Ahh, you noticed those," Crostini says with a sly smile. "Those devices monitor the creatures' health. I do everything to keep them content and comfortable."

Humphree turns to lock eyes with the wrangler. "That's funny, when you had your zappo-lasso around my neck—I don't think I'd describe myself as '**COMFORTABLE.**'"

I shoot Humps my gravest glare—he's going to offend our host!

Thankfully, one of Mr. Crostini's servants interrupts the convo. "Sir," the bot says, "we'll soon be entering an Oort cloud. This may be your last chance to contact—ahem—HER."

"Ahh, thank you," Mr. Crostini says, smoothing his shirt. "My guests, I apologize, but I must bring this evening to a premature end."

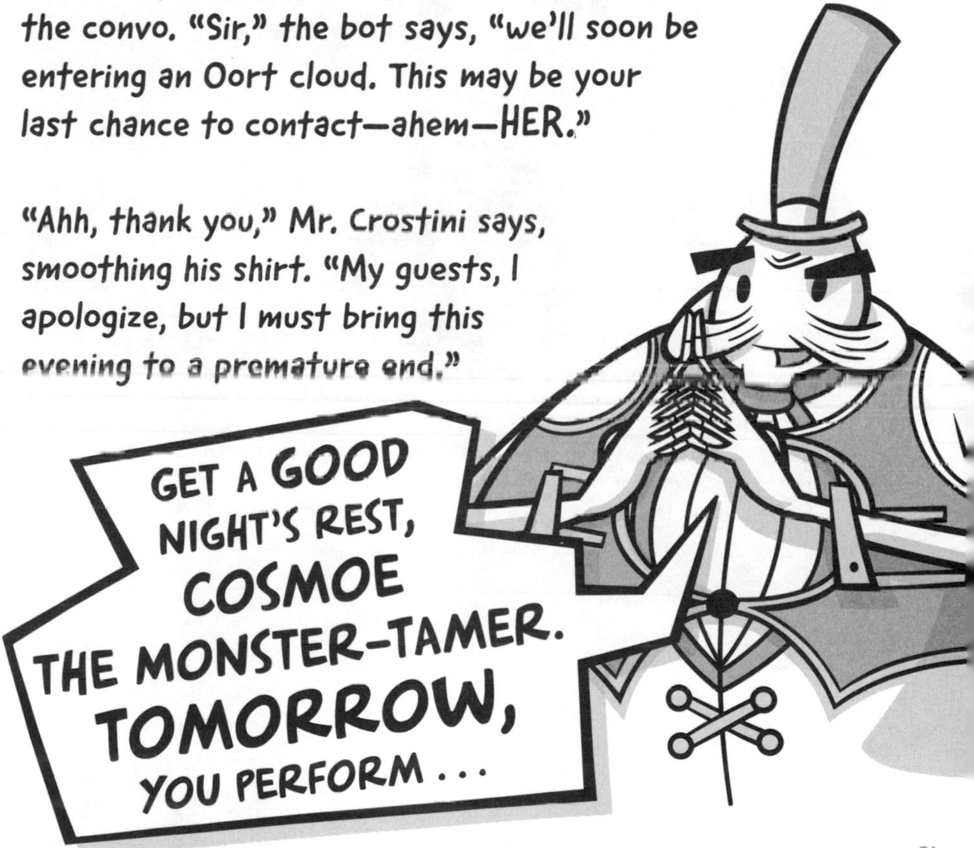
GET A GOOD NIGHT'S REST, COSMOE THE MONSTER-TAMER. TOMORROW, YOU PERFORM . . .

FEEL THE VIBE!

7

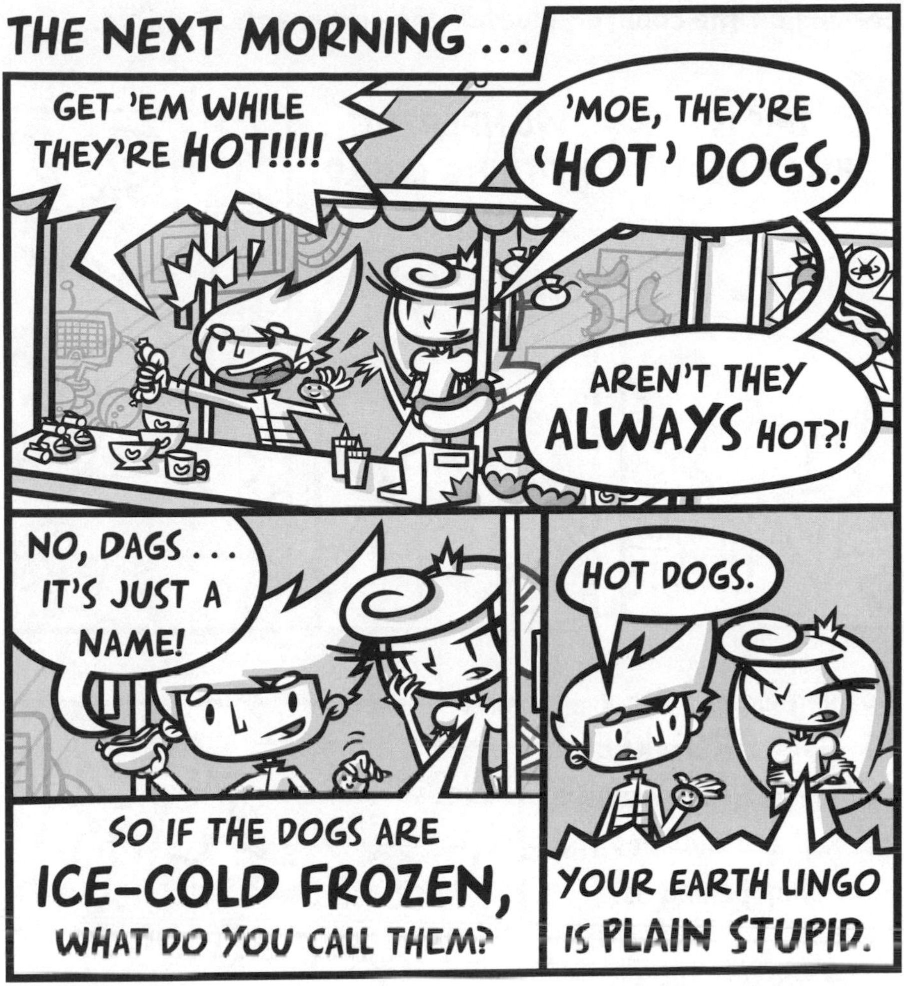
THE NEXT MORNING . . .
GET 'EM WHILE THEY'RE HOT!!!!
'MOE, THEY'RE 'HOT' DOGS.
AREN'T THEY ALWAYS HOT?!
NO, DAGS . . . IT'S JUST A NAME!
HOT DOGS.
SO IF THE DOGS ARE ICE-COLD FROZEN, WHAT DO YOU CALL THEM?
YOUR EARTH LINGO IS PLAIN STUPID.

The sun is barely up, but the carnival is already open and thick throngs of aliens are streaming through the entrance.

The energy of the whole thing hits me like an oomph cannonball straight to the chest. The carnies dashing about, the clowns tumbling, and the mammoth creatures baying and bellowing as they're led to the stadium . . . It all reminds me of the old days.

Leaning on the counter, I watch the circus action unfold.

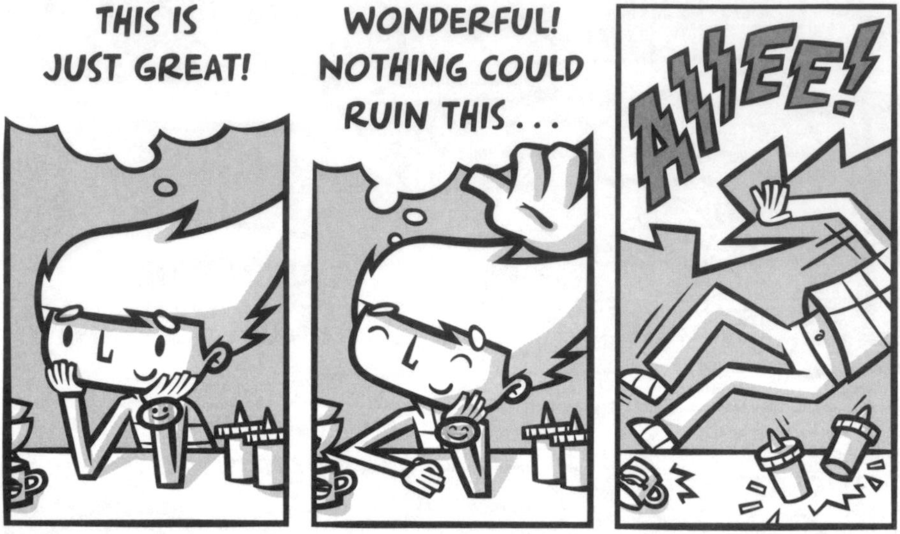
THIS IS JUST GREAT!
WONDERFUL! NOTHING COULD RUIN THIS . . .
AIIEE!

Nothing except for a **1.1 TON BRONKLE!** Humphree drags me into the hall and punches the door shut behind us.

"Hey! What's the big idea, Humps?!"

"You can't perform today, short pants. No monster-taming. I know you don't want to hear it, but we need to blow this plop-stand."

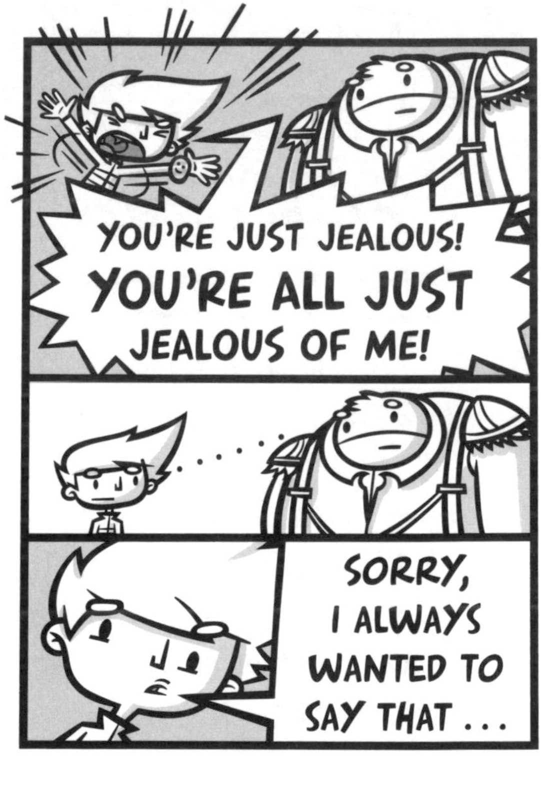
YOU'RE JUST JEALOUS! YOU'RE ALL JUST JEALOUS OF ME!
SORRY, I ALWAYS WANTED TO SAY THAT . . .

Humphree makes a crazy serious face. "I did some poking around, trying to figure out what those gizmos on the creatures' heads are. Look what F.R.E.D. found . . .

GOVERNATOR GIZMO
CAN BE USED TO CONTROL THE WEARER. IN RARE CASES, USED TO INJECT FLUIDS IN ORDER TO TRANSFORM, MUTATE, AND MANIPULATE CREATURES.

I frown. "That said 'rare cases'! Rare! You're just ticked off the wrangler put the lasso choke on you."

"Don't you feel **THE VIBE**, Cosmoe?!"

"What <u>VIBE</u>? I get no vibe. What does Dagger think? Does she get a vibe? Am I the only one not getting vibes?"

Humphree exhales. "Cosmoe, listen to me. Those gizmos are used to *mutate* creatures! That's bad—get it?!"

My hands ball up into tiny, stressed fists. At first I was hesitant. But now that we've joined—we can't just walk away. That's quitting!

"Look out there!" I finally say. "It's circus fun! Can't be bad!"

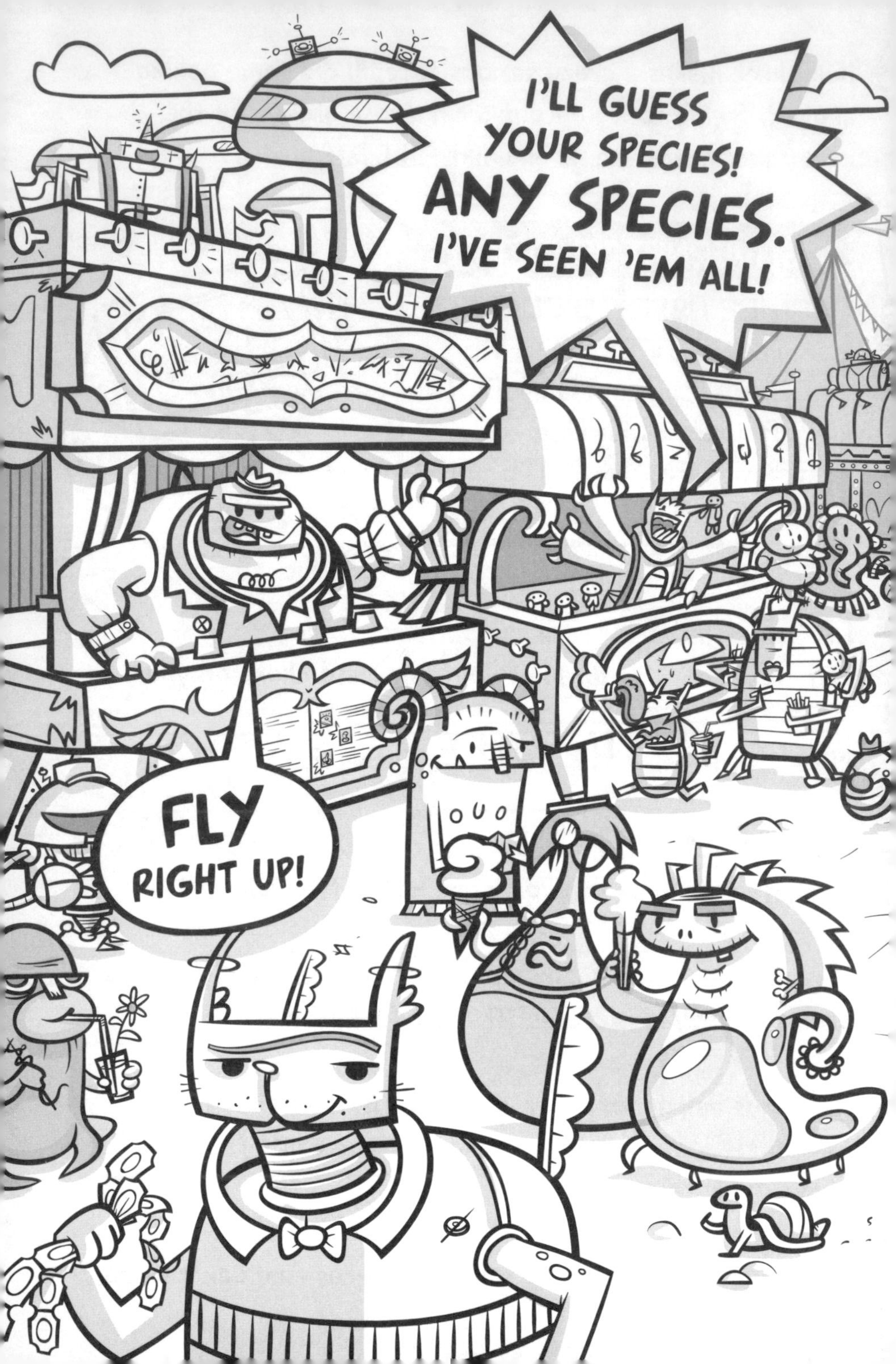
I'LL GUESS YOUR SPECIES! ANY SPECIES. I'VE SEEN 'EM ALL!
FLY RIGHT UP!

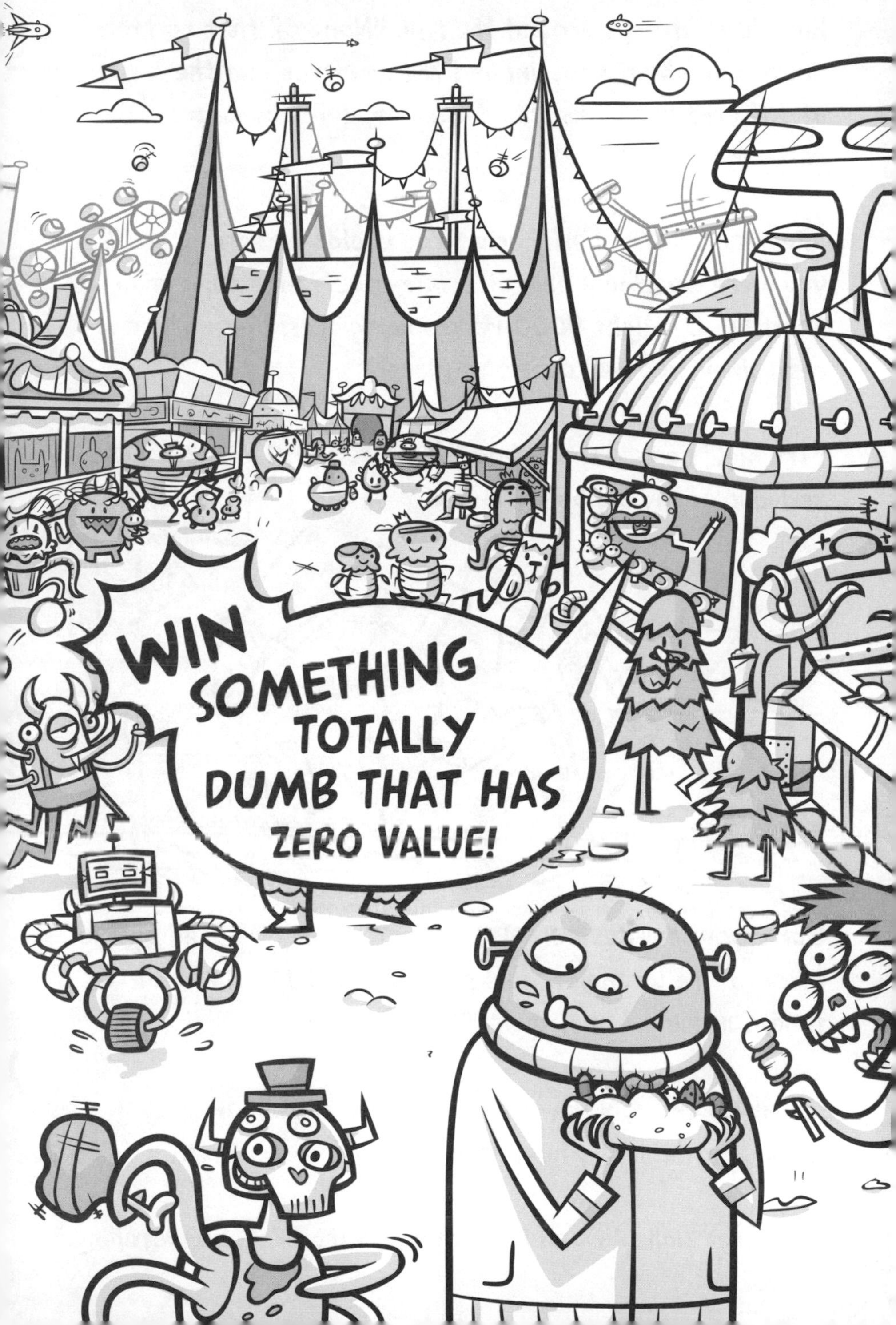
WIN SOMETHING TOTALLY DUMB THAT HAS ZERO VALUE!

Humphree stomps around the hall. "None of that matters! I'm talking about Crostini and the wrangler and the **EVIL** at the center of this thing! Cosmoe, don't make me restrain you . . ."

"Restrain **ME?**" I bark back. "You couldn't restrain me if you were wearing a pair of triple-electron, twin-turbo, Restrain-O-Might 9000 restrainer gloves! I'll be the one restraining you—all over this place!"

"Try me!" he barks, and I go **"RARRRGH!"** and leap at my big buddy and—

Our Who-Can-Restrain-Who? battle is interrupted by the voice of the wrangler. He's poking his head in the door. "It is time, Earthling," he growls. "You perform now."

I climb down from Humphree and dust myself off. "Look, this is, like, my destiny! I have to do it! Wish me luck, OK?"

Humphree sighs. "Good luck, short pants. We'll be watching."

I follow the wrangler to the arena, then down a tunnel into the stadium. Other acts rush past me: Juzzy Jugglers and Pluto Plate Spinners.

THERE YOU ARE, MY BOY! **QUICK,** SLIP INTO THIS.

I get a strange sensation in the base of my skull when I look at this spaceified monster-tamer outfit. I don't want it touching my skin. It's like I haven't EARNED it. Also, it's super-ugly—a crime against coolness.

"No, Mr. Crostini, I'll be wearing my ordinary clothes," I declare.

Mr. Crostini frowns, then grins, and then words explode from his mouth. "Brilliant! A man of the people, you are! The reubens will love it!" The odd little ringmaster then scurries through the entrance.

A second later, the wrangler is pushing me forward into the stadium, into the spotlight ...

SHOVE

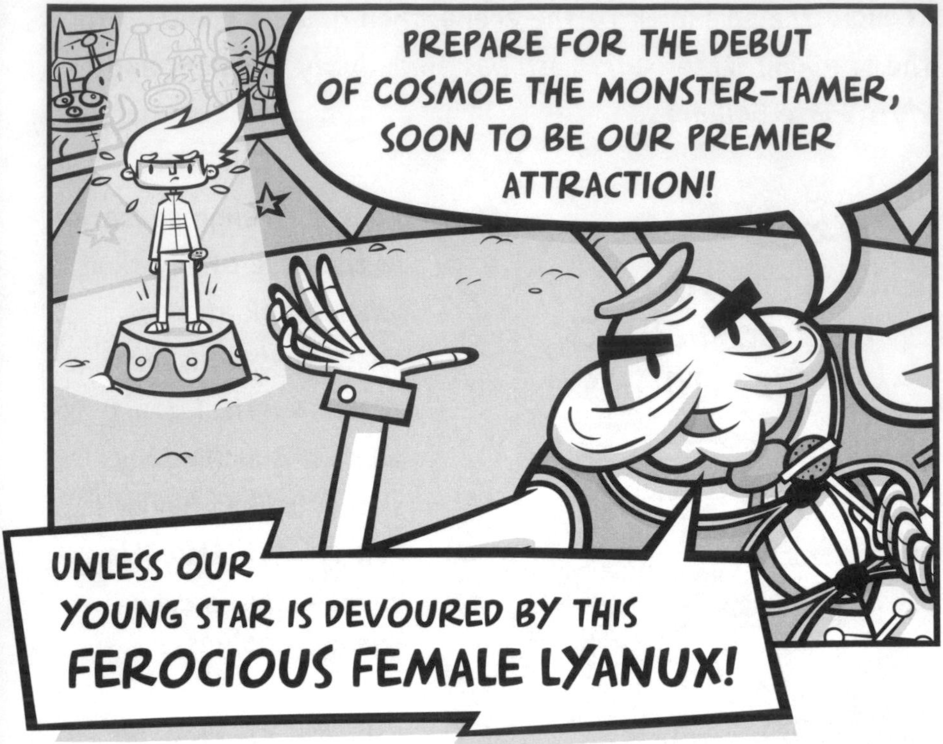
PREPARE FOR THE DEBUT OF COSMOE THE MONSTER-TAMER, SOON TO BE OUR PREMIER ATTRACTION!
UNLESS OUR YOUNG STAR IS DEVOURED BY THIS FEROCIOUS FEMALE LYANUX!

As soon as Mr. Crostini says "lyanux," the crowd cheers and stomps their feet. I try to remain calm, but I'm scared, anxious, uneasy—a whole horde of emotions are duking it out inside my skull.

The feeling of confidence? It's GONE. GONE, GONE, **GONE.** It's gone because an instant later, Crostini tips his hat to me and skitters off, leaving me alone with this thing, this wild beast, this queen of the Lunar Jungles, this lyanux.

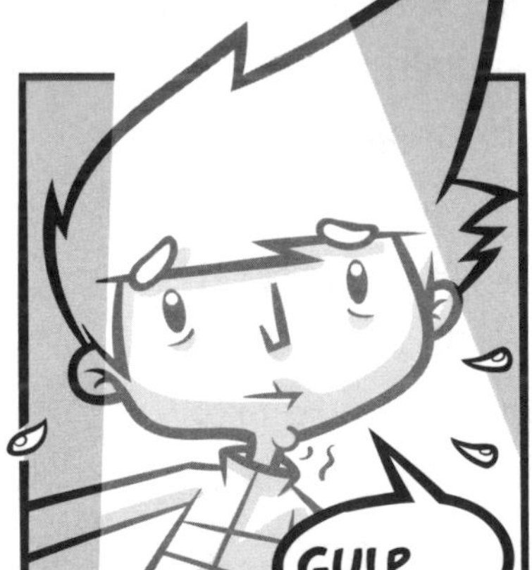
GULP . . .

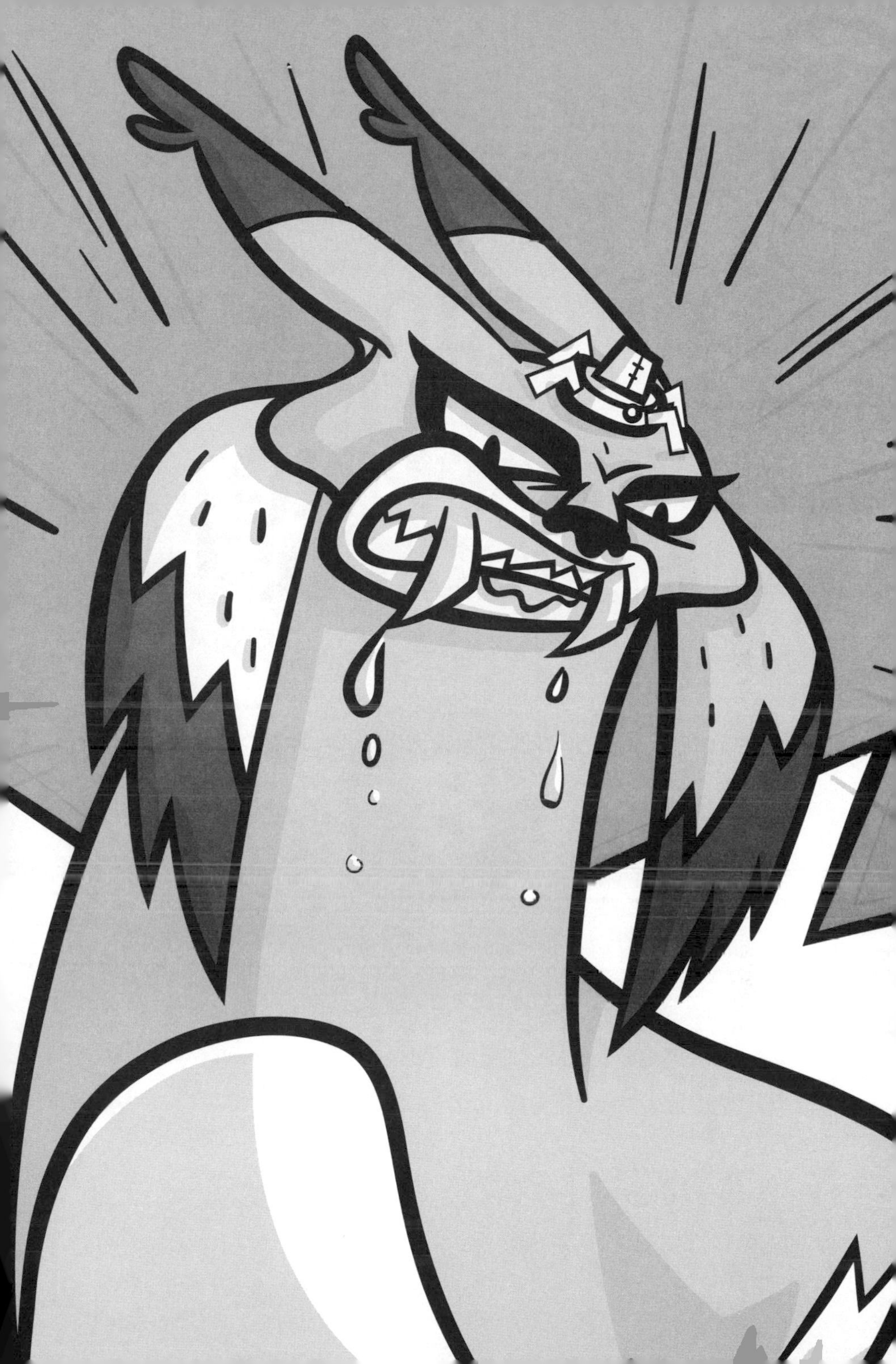

BIG AND FRAPPING FEROCIOUS!

I wish I could savor this moment. I wish I could soak it in and let my nostrils nab every last scent because, at last, I'm in the circus and in the spotlight!

But I can't. 'Cause this lyanux is **BIG.**

BIG AND FRAPPING FEROCIOUS.

But I still totally 100% no problem got this. 'Cause I'm a professional monster-tamer. And I completely, entirely know what I'm doing.

Right? Maybe right? I hope I'm right . . .

Silver stardust crackles beneath my feet as I take a step forward. "Hey, girl. Ready to put on a nice little show?"

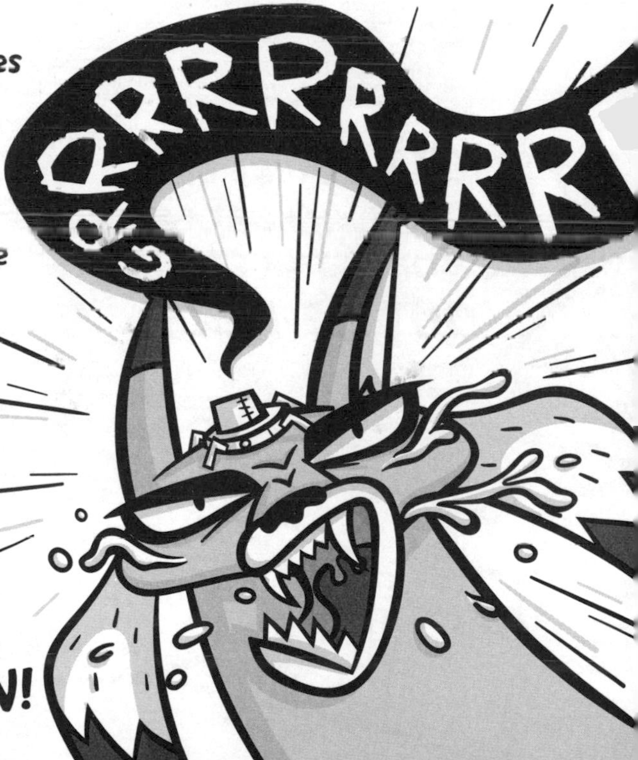
GRRRRRRRRR

NOT READY FOR A NICE LITTLE SHOW!

WHOA, WHOA, YO! I've seen lion-taming acts a thousand times, but now I can't remember the first thing about them! My mind is out to lunch. Probably downing four hot dogs with a side of koko ice-pie, if I know my mind . . .

C'mon, mind! **THINK!** Help me! Stop being lame and useless! Do something!

The lyanux looks into my eyes. It's like she sees the weakness in me—the softness of my soul, the quaking of my heart, all that poetic junk.

I spot Dagger and Humps in the front row and dash over. "Guys, I think I've decided that monster-tamer may <u>NOT</u> be the career for me . . ."

NOW YOU'RE USING YOUR SKULL, SHORT PANTS! C'MON, LET'S GET YOU **OUT OF HERE.**

OH, BUZZ OFF, HUMPS.

HE CAN DO IT! **STOP THINKING** SO MUCH, 'MOE.

JUST GO OUT THERE AND BE NATURAL, RADICAL **YOU.**

A roust-a-bot reaches over the railing and shoves me back into the center of the ring. I look up, just in time to almost wet my pants (almost, I swear, only almost).

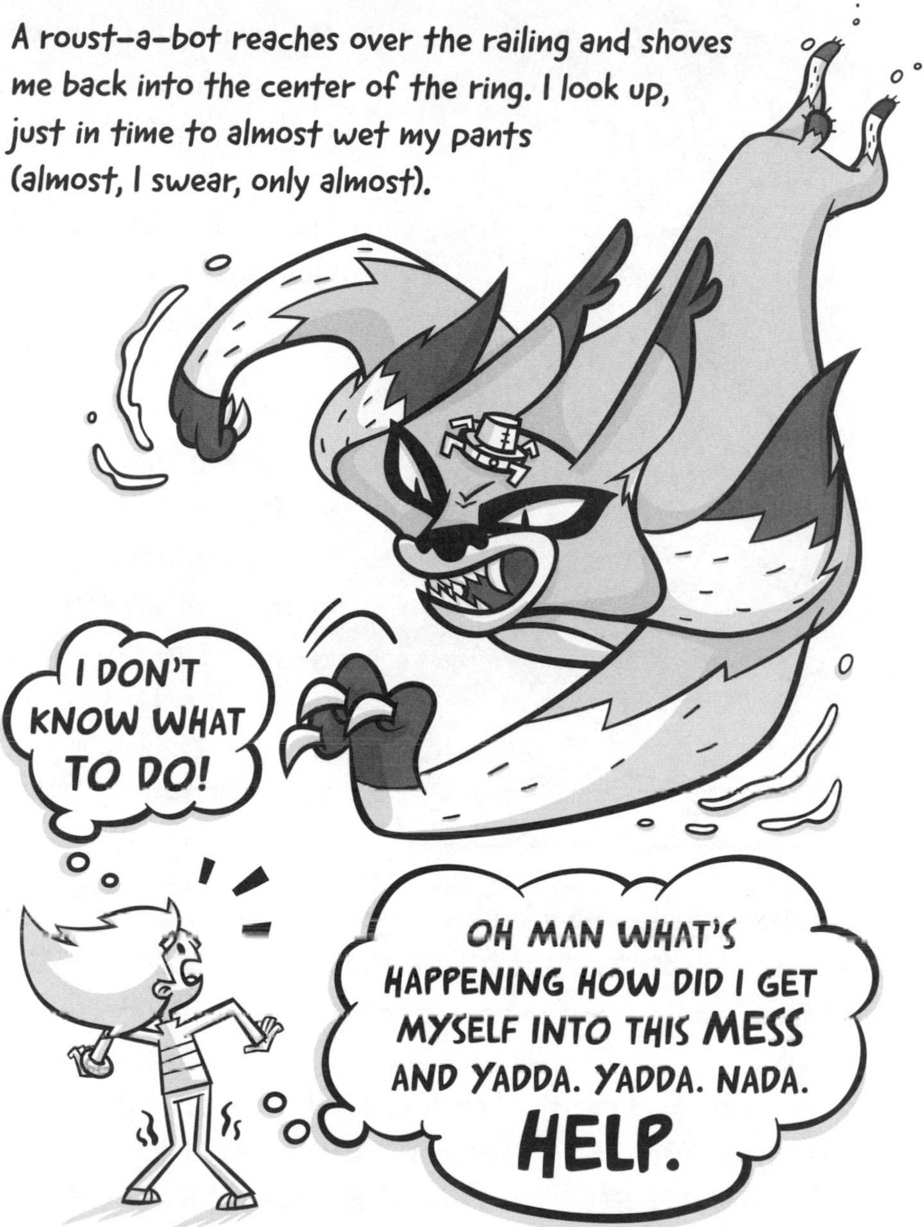
I DON'T KNOW WHAT TO DO!
OH MAN WHAT'S HAPPENING HOW DID I GET MYSELF INTO THIS MESS AND YADDA. YADDA. NADA. HELP.

Finally, my brain just goes blank like someone hit the off button, and I somehow grab hold of Dagger's advice. I STOP THINKING and I JUST <u>DO</u>, throwing one hand over my eyes and just screaming whatever comes out of my mouth . . .

FLAMING GOOBER RING OF FAKE FIRE!

The Iyanux lands beside me and the crowd explodes (not literally, that would be gross). They're big fans of the Flaming Goober Ring of Fake Fire!

The Iyanux no longer looks even the tiniest bit terrifying! Her monstrous mandibles loosen, and she flashes me a sort of beastly smile. I DID IT! I truly am Cosmoe the Monster-Tamer.

Memories come flooding back like a tidal wave on Ozak's Ocean Isle. I know **EXACTLY** what to do. I scratch behind the Iyanux's ears. "You're not so scary, are you, girl?"

The Iyanux purrs. I notice then that the Iyanux has a gizmo on her head, like the other creatures. There's a red light on top of the gizmo, like it's turned off. If the gizmos monitor the creatures' health, why would it be <u>OFF</u>?

No time for pondering. I've got a show to put on. A spectacular show!

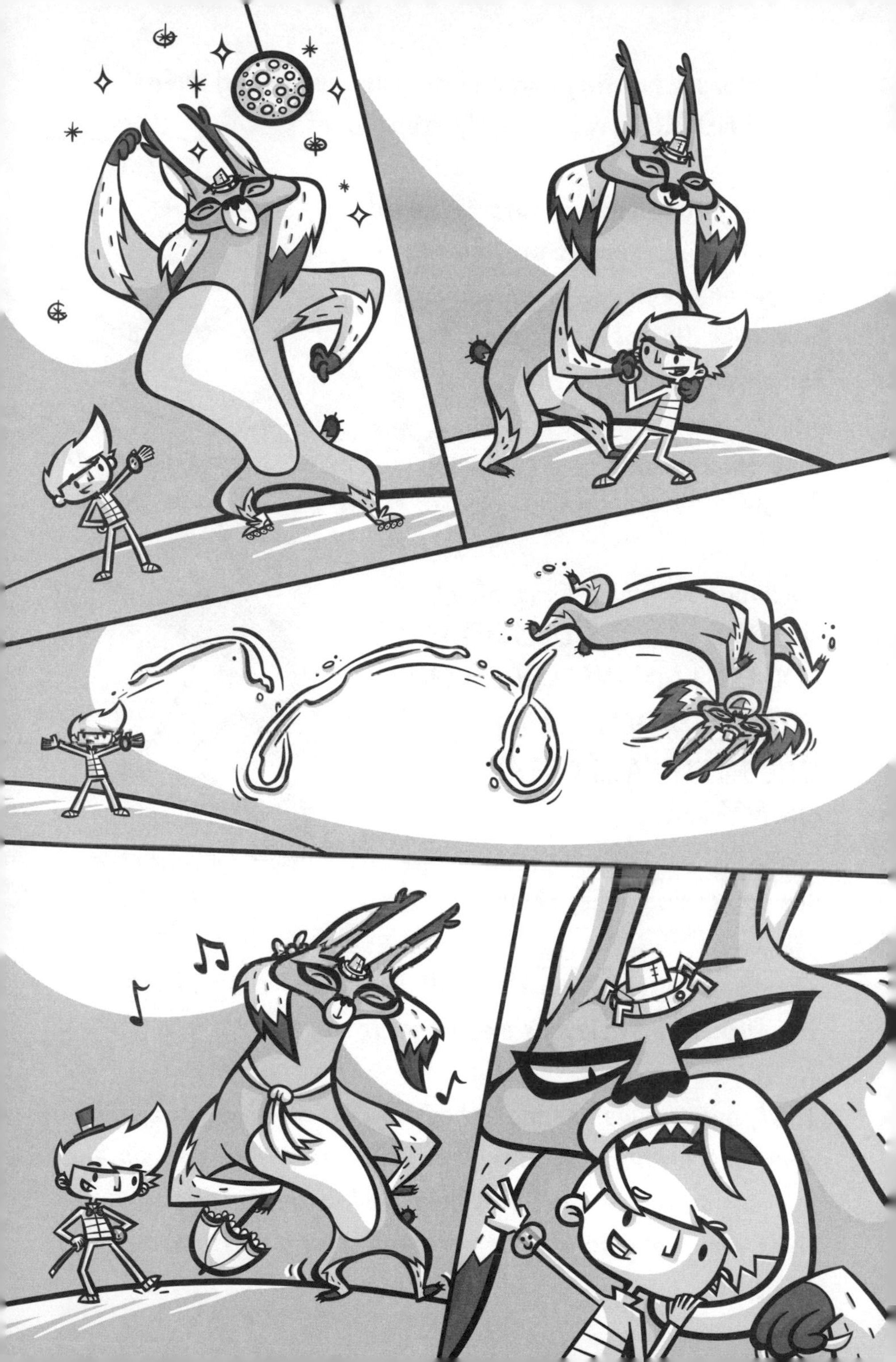

The crowd is hooting and chanting my name, and it feels **STUPENDOUS.** Well—mostly stupendous.

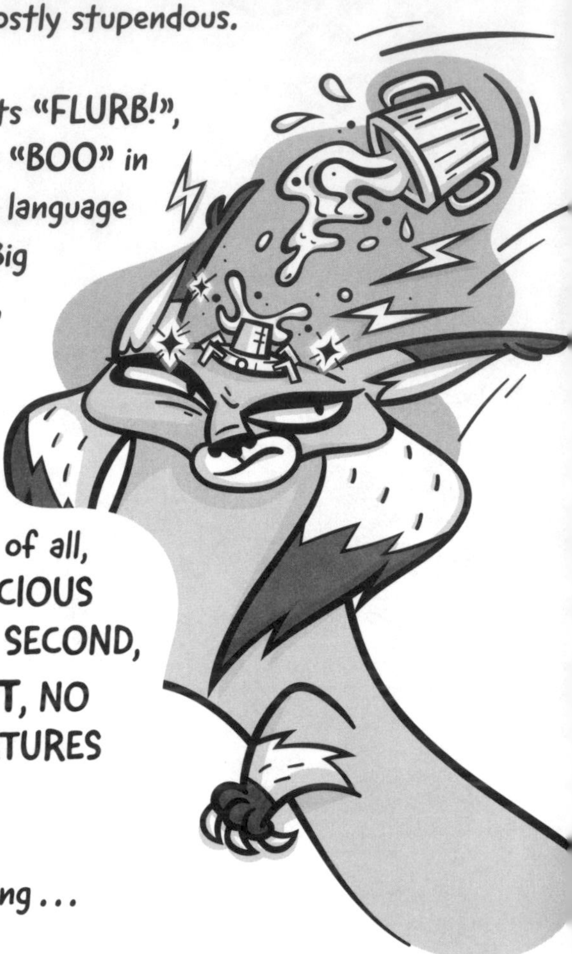

One very rude alien shouts "FLURB!", which I'm guessing means "BOO" in whatever very rude alien language he speaks. He tosses his Big Slurpo soda into the ring, and it splashes down onto the lyanux's crown.

I'm about to freak. First of all, **NO ONE WASTES DELICIOUS SODA ON MY WATCH! SECOND, MORE IMPORTANT, NO ONE MISTREATS CREATURES ON MY WATCH!**

But something is happening . . .

The gizmo on the lyanux's head sparks, and the red light on top flickers and flashes and turns to green.

The lyanux's eyes change—they turn black-black, the color of dark matter. Her hair stands on end. Her muscles throb and her legs quiver. She has this horrible look in her eyes like she's very, very sorry, but she can't stop what's about to happen . . .

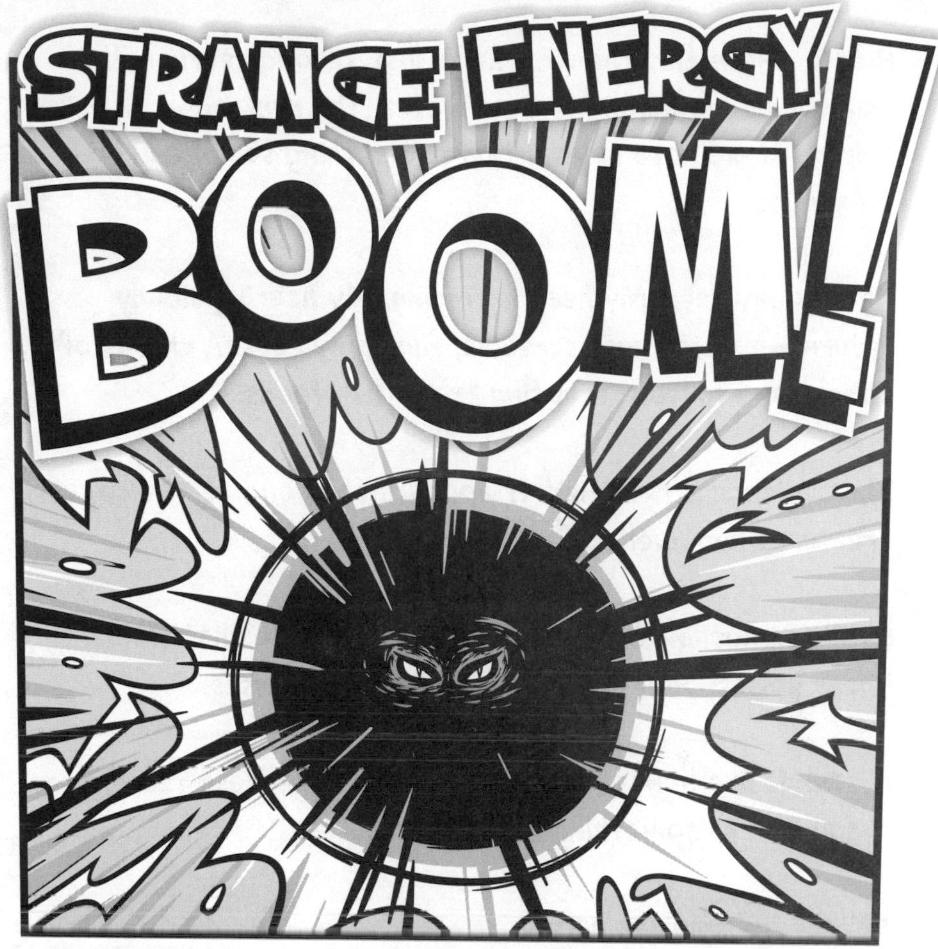
STRANGE ENERGY
BOOM!

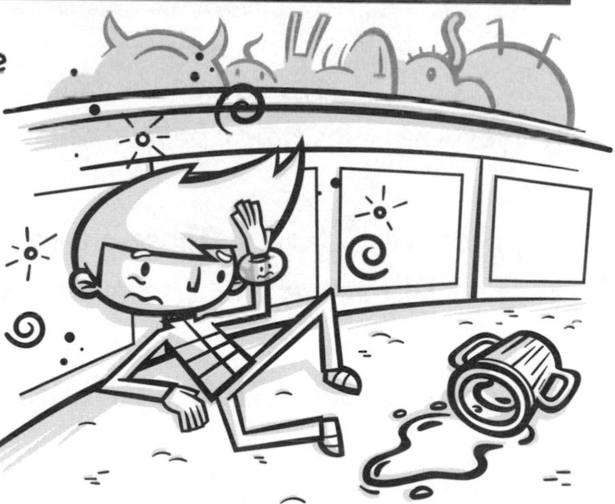

The blast hits me in the chest like a brick, and I'm hurled back, into the wall.

My mind is muddy. Confuzzled. Brain rocked, rattled, and rolled.

Purple smoke fills the air where, just seconds earlier, the Iyanux was standing. My eyes water. The rank odor of burnt hair clogs my nose holes. I taste something sooty and foul on my lips.

I get to my feet. My head is ringing. My hearing slowly returns—and it's just screams, filling my ears. A chorus of shrieks and squeals, erupting from the stands.

The audience is horrified. It appears that one of the circus creatures just, well, **EXPLODED.**

I still see nothing but smoke. But from inside that smoke, I hear noises: bone-chilling, bloodcurdling noises.

It sounds like bones breaking. It sounds like flesh tearing. It sounds like something **MUTATING.**

At last the smoke clears.

I take a deep breath and do my best not to faint. My eyes—my eyes don't believe what they're seeing.

Humphree was **RIGHT.** Those gizmos. They DO something. They just <u>DID</u> something, to the Iyanux.

She's changed. She's TRANSFORMED. She is **<u>NOW</u>** . . .

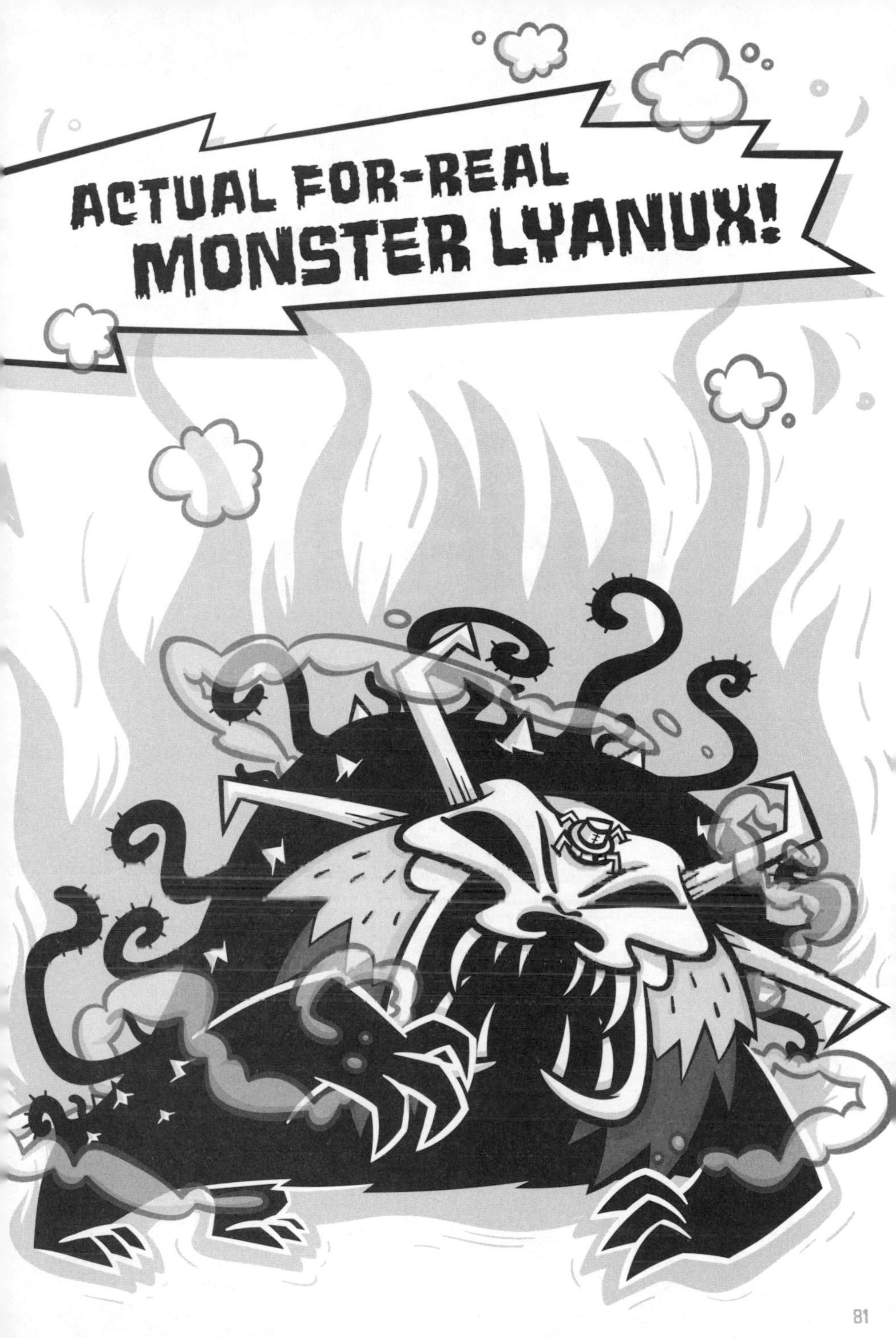
ACTUAL FOR-REAL
MONSTER LYANUX!

TOO CLOSE FOR COMFORT!

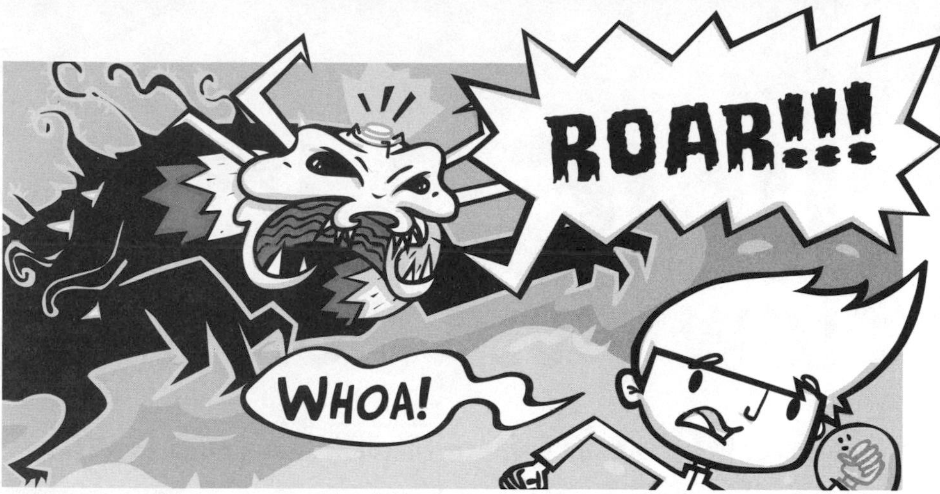
ROAR!!!
WHOA!

The mutated lyanux blasts through the exit, trampling roust-a-bots. Humphree and Dagger race up behind me. "Evilness to be stopped!" Humps says. "C'mon!"

We dash outside. The circus grounds are **A DESTRUCTIFIED-DAMAGE DISASTER**—and the lyanux-monster has only been on the loose for moments!

Dagger whips out her flash blaster, and a second later she's jetting through the crowd, hollering, "Catch up, slowpokes!"

I need a better view if I'm going to figure out how to stop this crazy mutated thing. Just then, something buzzes past me. Then another.

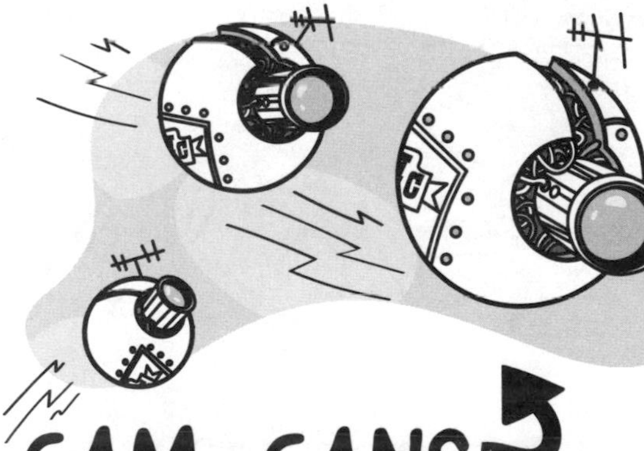
CAM-CANS

JINGO GLOW-BULB MOMENT!

"Humphree!" I shout as I watch the cam-cans race by. "Time for the ol' swimming hole launch-toss!"

Humphree hurls me, and I think, "Cosmoe, your plans are really dumb—and someday they're going to get you killed."

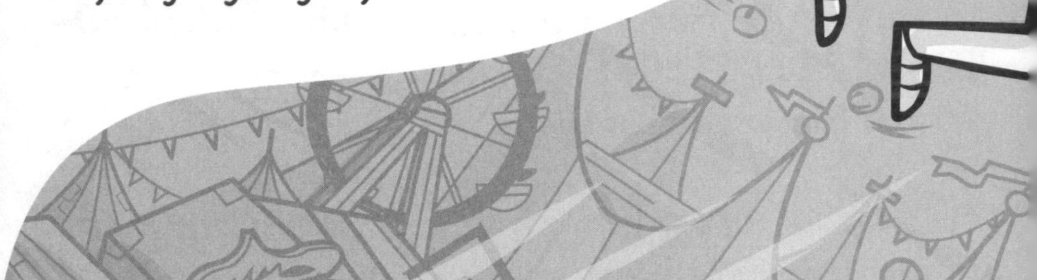

THAT'S PROBABLY TRUE . . . BUT NOT THIS DAY!

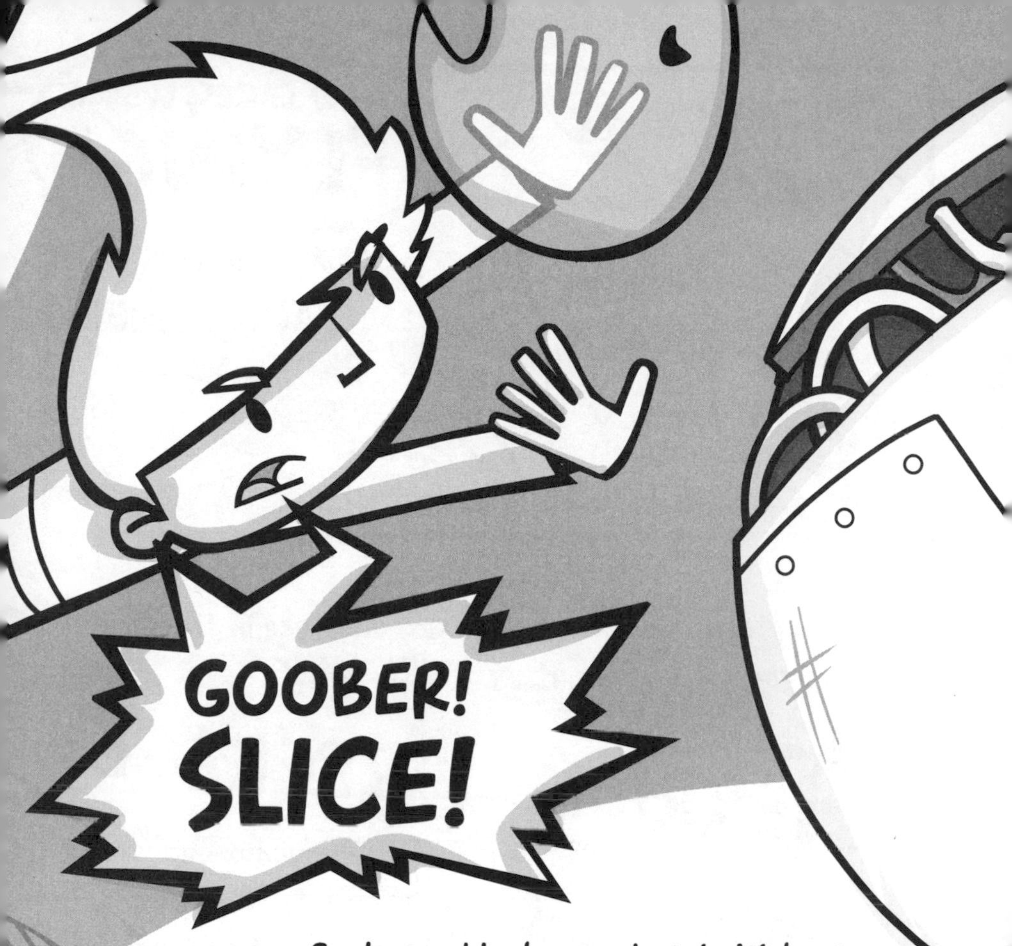
GOOBER!
SLICE!

Goober suddenly morphs into Wolverine mode—claws are coming from my hand! I slice through the cam-can's metal hull and yank on its wires. The bot emits a beeping, booping sound. Got it! It's now mine to control!

I lash out with Goober and fling another cam-can to Humps. "Hop on, big guy!"

Humphree's armored fists punch through the bot, and he tugs the wires like hoater reins.

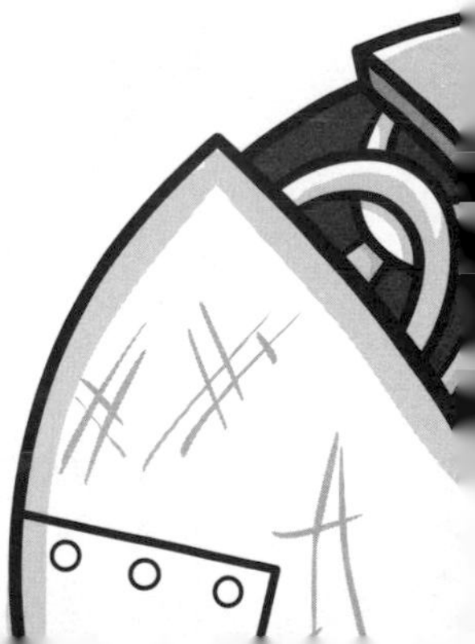

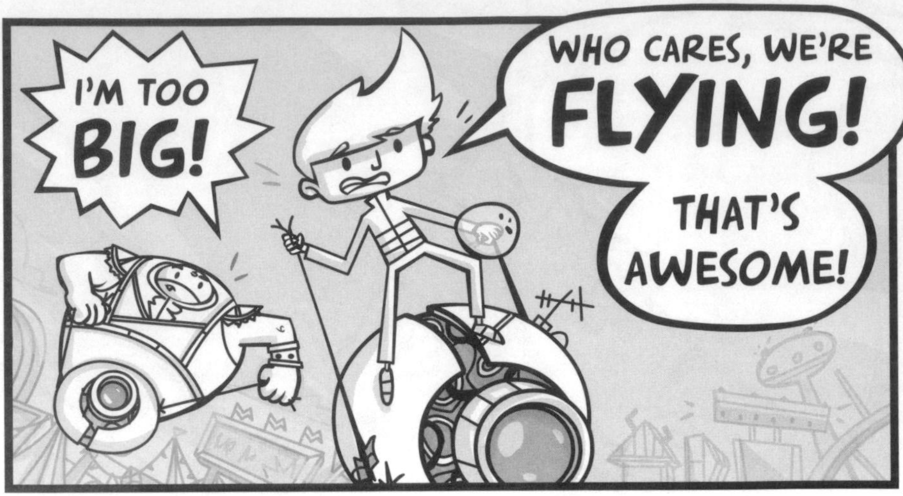
I'M TOO BIG!
WHO CARES, WE'RE FLYING!
THAT'S AWESOME!

I gasp as I steer the cam-can upward and take in the scene. As far as the eye can see, it's . . . WRECKAGE.

TERRIBLE WRECKAGE.

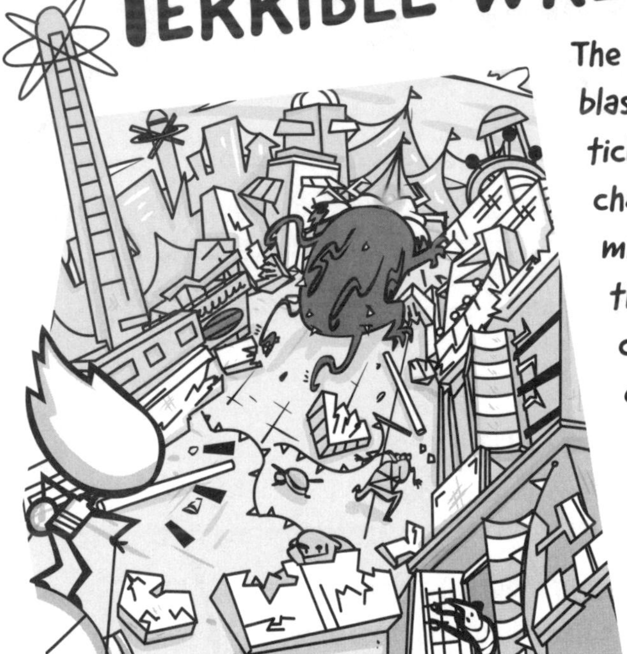

The lyanux-monster blasts through a ticket booth and charges toward the midway. I twist the wires and the cam-can dives down. Crumbling, collapsing circus contraptions nearly crush us as we blaze behind the beast . . .

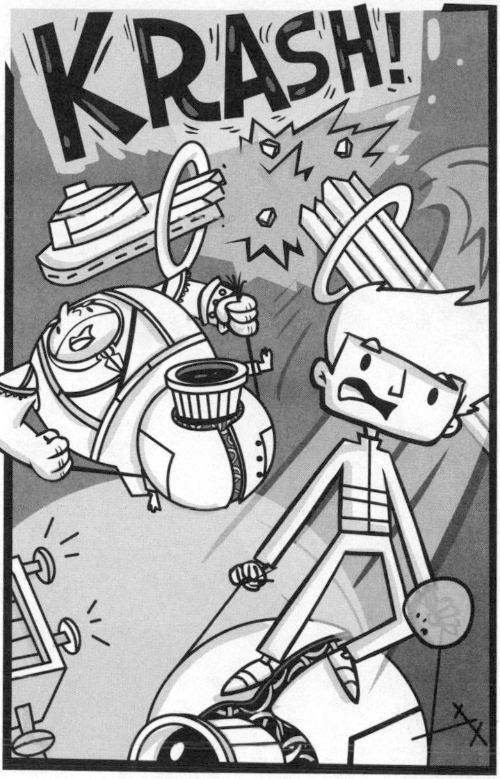
KRASH!

I swerve, tugging the cam-can's wires, barely avoiding being crushed by a falling high-strike tower, then burst out from beneath the rubble and swoop low.

"GOOBER, GO!" I shout, flinging my arm forward. Goober snakes through the air and grabs hold of the monster's tail. She tries to shake free, but Goober hangs on tight and—

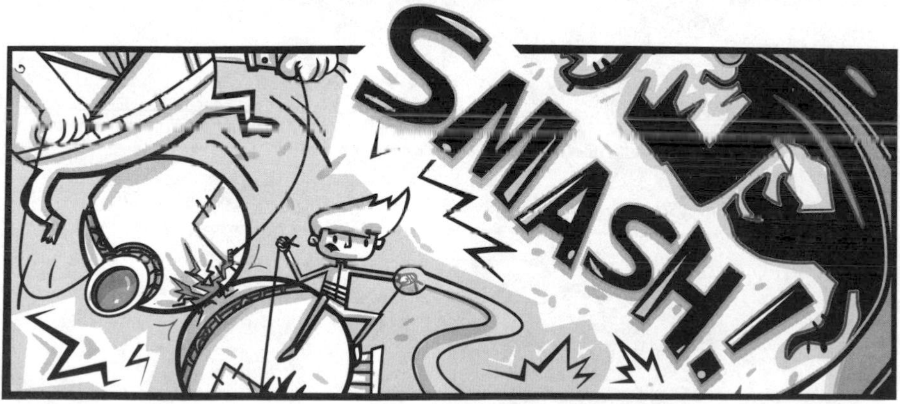
SMASH!

Humphree tumbles off his cam-can and splashes down into the debris below. But Goober still grips the lyanux-monster's tail as we whip around the corner, onto the midway . . .

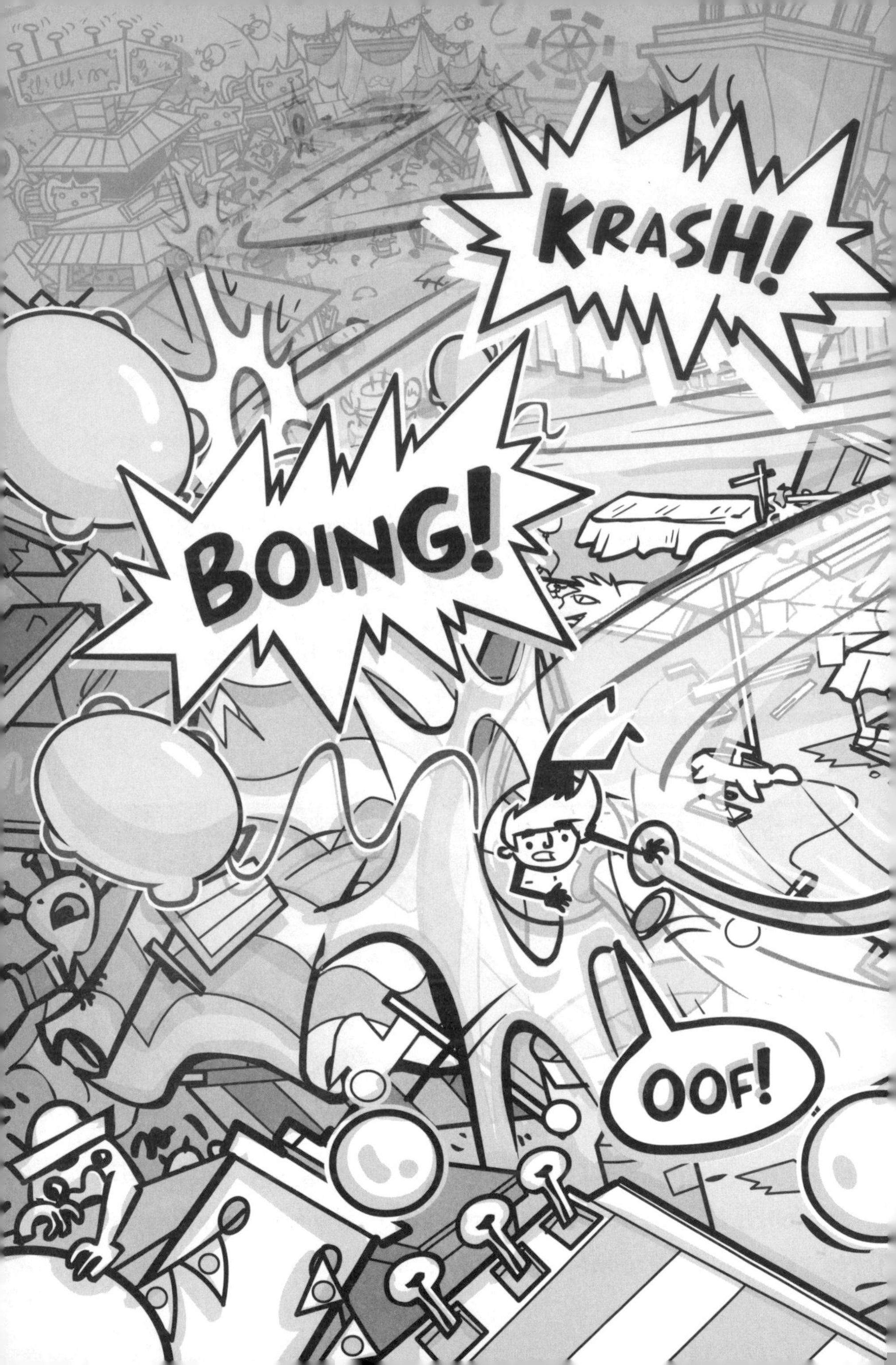
KRASH!
BOING!
OOF!

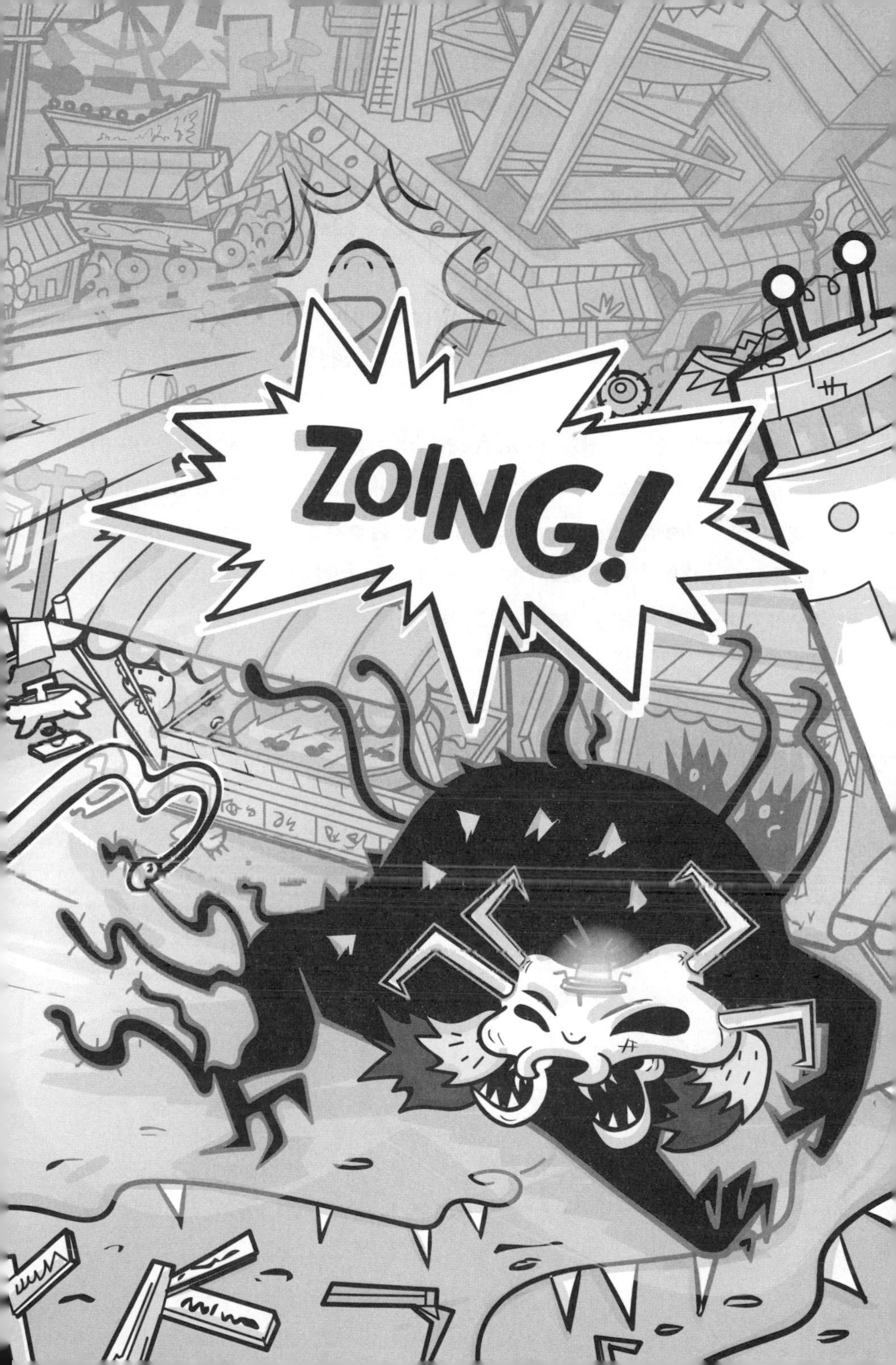
ZOING!

I burst out from the wreckage—bruised, battered, and beaten badly. I want to give up. But then I see it . . .

THE YOUNGLIES TENT!

It's full of kid aliens! If the lyanux-monster charges into there—I don't even want to contemplate the catastrophe.

I hunch over the cam-can, head low, and it rumbles beneath me as I blast past the monster. I hold my breath and—gulp—leap off! The cam-can shoots out from beneath me like a runaway bike. I'm now the only thing between the lyanux-monster and the younglies tent.

And just as I'm about to make a BIG VALIANT STAND, I hear the familiar sound of Princess Dagger's ice blaster. I look up just as she fires, and I'm . . .

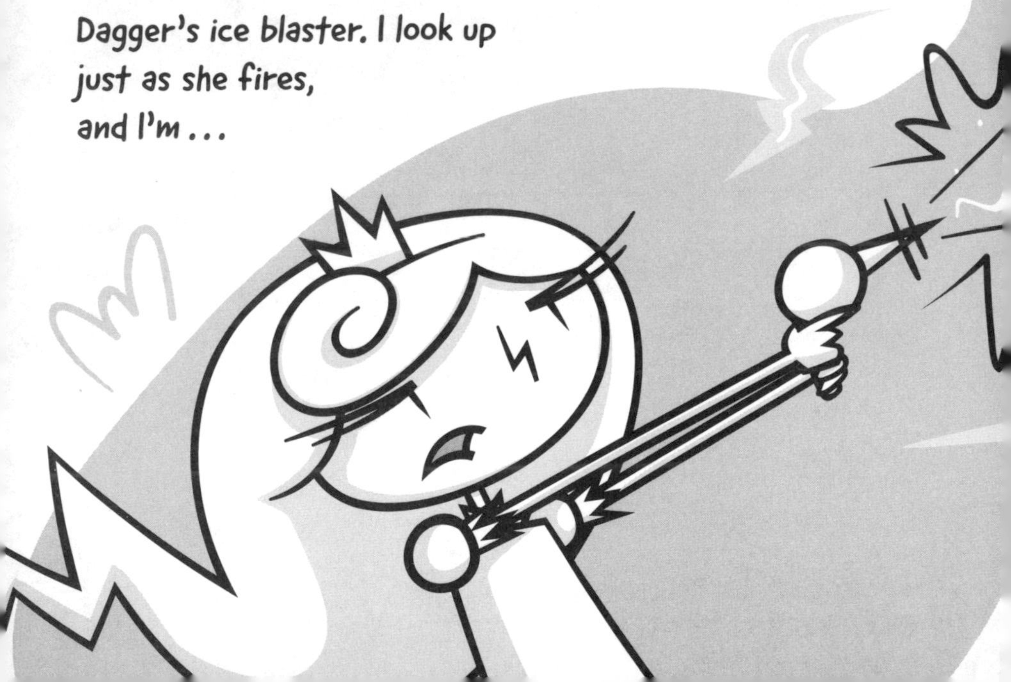

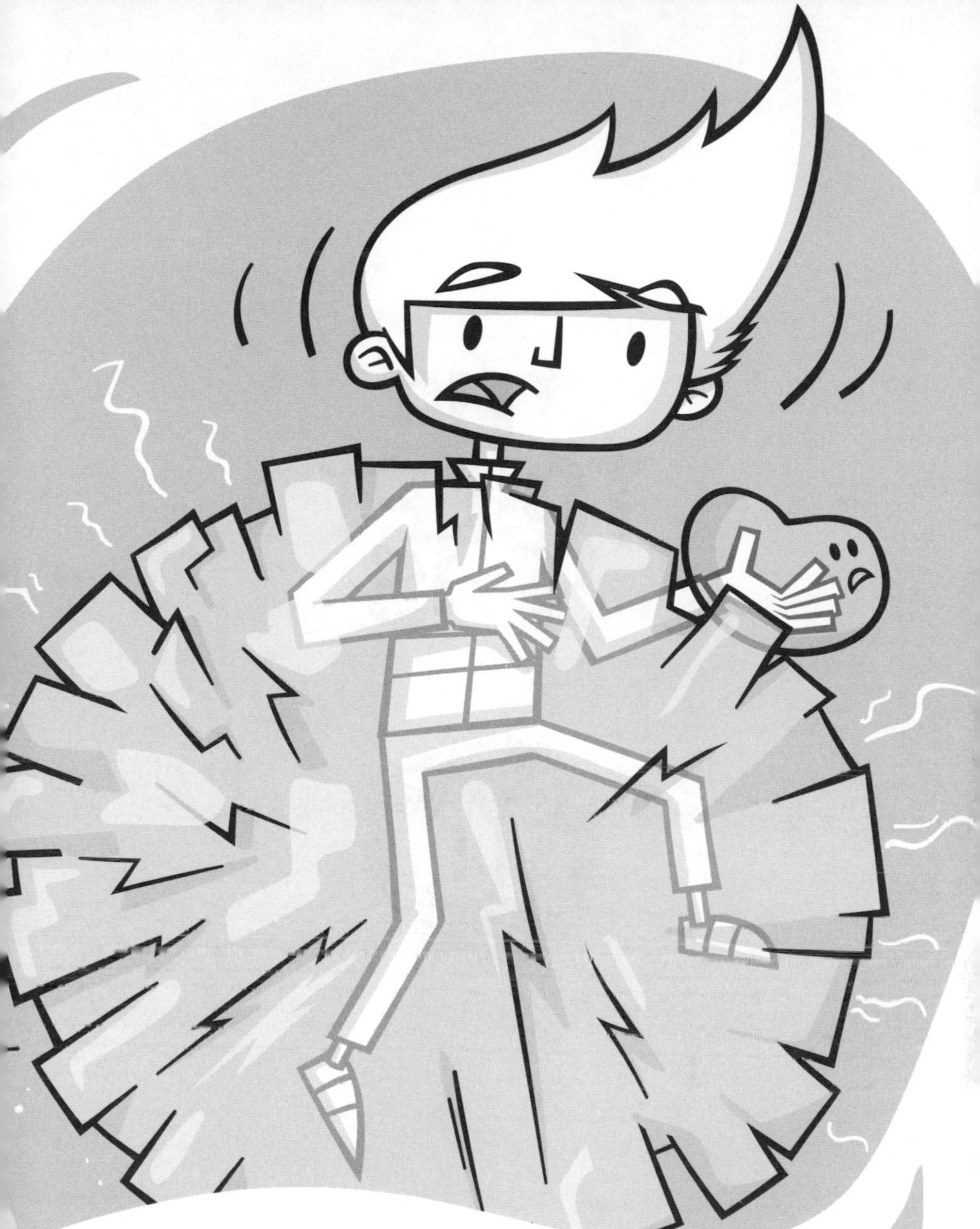

CHILLED OUT!

THE TOILET IT IS

10

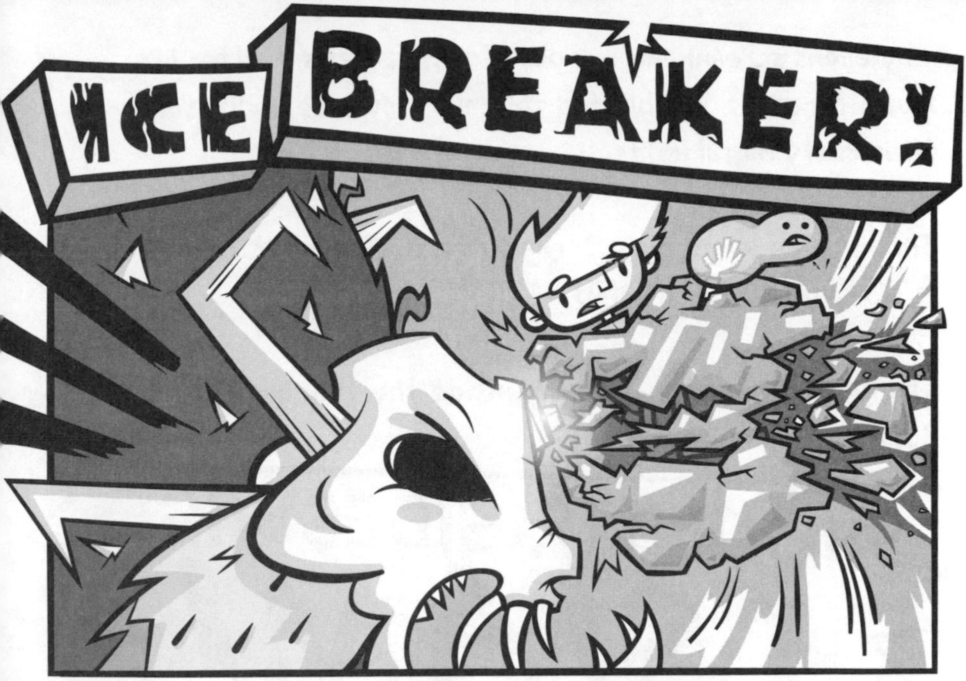
ICE BREAKER!

The ice shatters like cosmic crystal as the lyanux-monster smashes into frozen me, then barrels on.

WE NEED TO STOP HER!

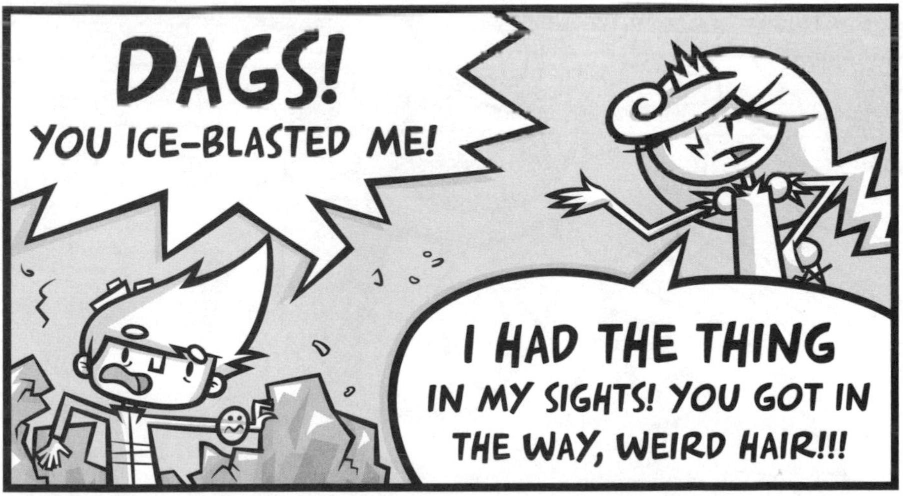
DAGS! YOU ICE-BLASTED ME!
I HAD THE THING IN MY SIGHTS! YOU GOT IN THE WAY, WEIRD HAIR!!!

Tiny aliens scream and cry out. Roust-a-bots scatter like mutant-ratzos. The blasted tin cans only care about saving their rusty metal butts.

The midway looks like a tornado tore through it. I guess it did: **A TORNADO OF LYANUX-MONSTER.**

The lyanux-monster is nearly inside the younglies tent! But then—

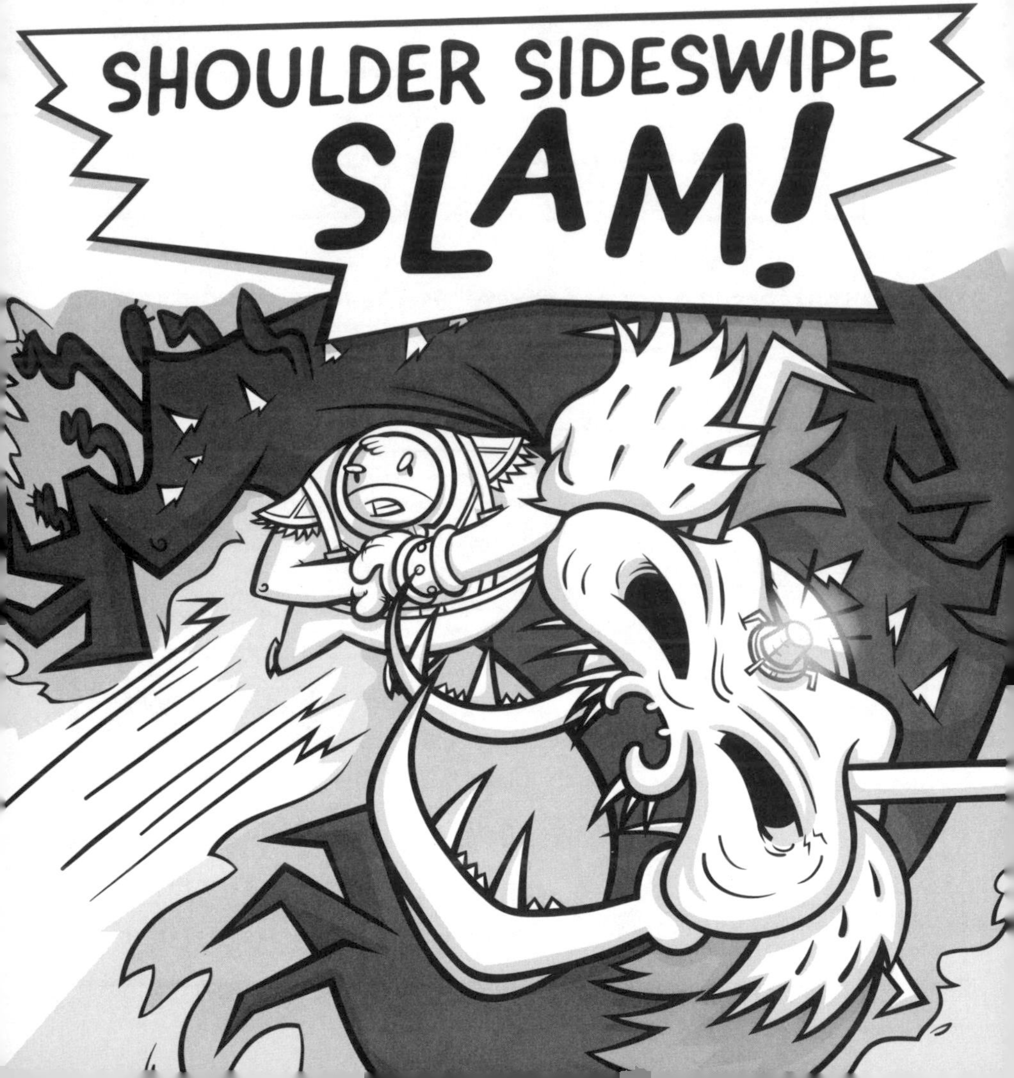
SHOULDER SIDESWIPE
SLAM!

Humphree throws his massive Bronkle shoulder into the beast's underbelly. The monster wails. Its legs buckle, and it suddenly goes into a barrel roll, flipping, end over end, missing the younglies tent by JUST barely.

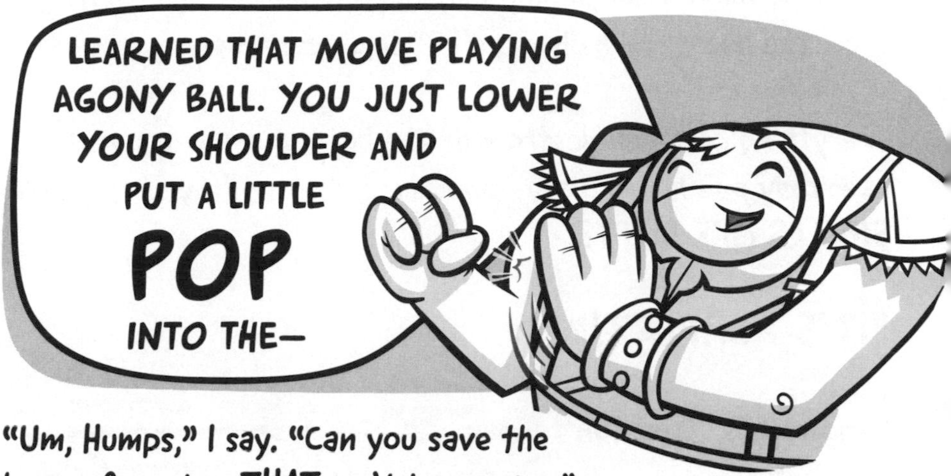
LEARNED THAT MOVE PLAYING AGONY BALL. YOU JUST LOWER YOUR SHOULDER AND PUT A LITTLE
POP
INTO THE—

"Um, Humps," I say. "Can you save the lesson for when THAT isn't happening."

That is the lyanux-monster. Her mouth opens wide, frothing with black saliva, and emits an earsplitting howl of anger.

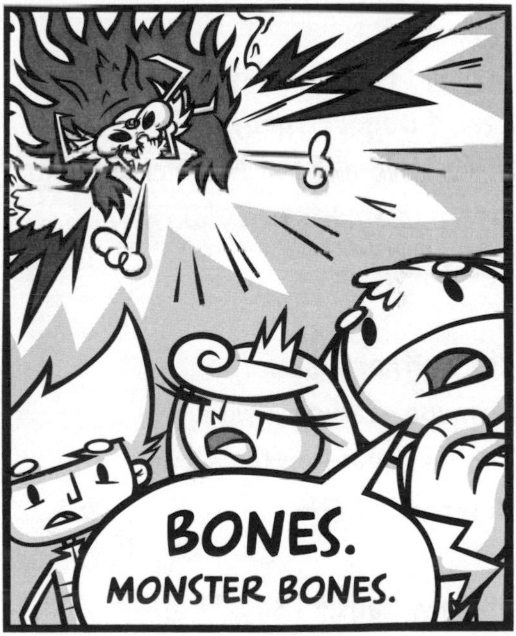
BONES.
MONSTER BONES.

She lowers her head and runs her foot across the ground like a bull, ready to charge.

GULP.

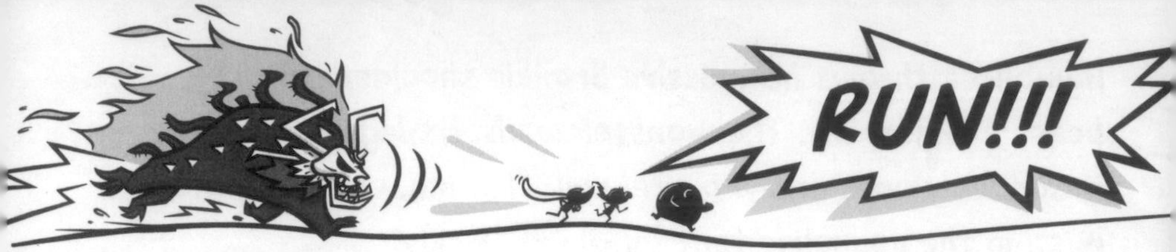
RUN!!!

We're in full-on Hollywood-blockbuster mode, booking it from the beast! "Which way?!??" Dagger shouts.

Everything has been destroyed. The big top is a ways away. I see only one hiding place—one place that's filthy, dirty, and **SMELLS LIKE BUTTS.**

"IT'S PERFECT!"

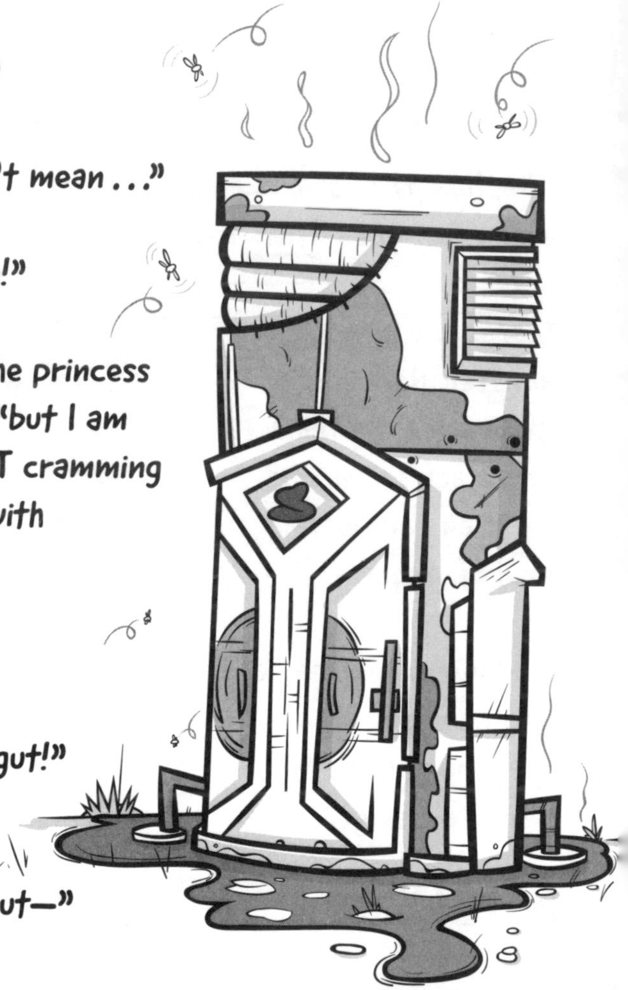

Dagger says, "You don't mean . . ."

"Yes! The transpo-can!"

"Look, I hate to play the princess card," Dagger shouts, "but I am a princess and I'm **NOT** cramming into a portable privy with you two!"

"It's either inside the transpo-can or inside the lyanux-monster's gut!" Humphree barks.

"Sorry, Dags," I say, "but—"

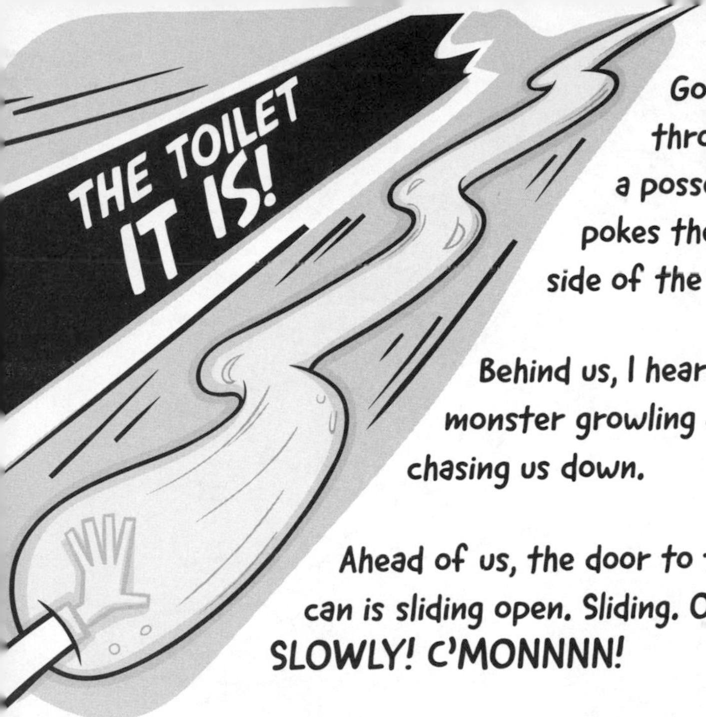
THE TOILET IT IS!

Goober slithers through the air like a possessed snake and pokes the button on the side of the transpo-can.

Behind us, I hear the lyanux-monster growling and hissing and chasing us down.

Ahead of us, the door to the transpo-can is sliding open. Sliding. Open. SO. SLOWLY! C'MONNNN!

FINALLY! IT OPENS!

We dive inside and Humphree yanks the door shut. This spot—it ain't pretty . . .

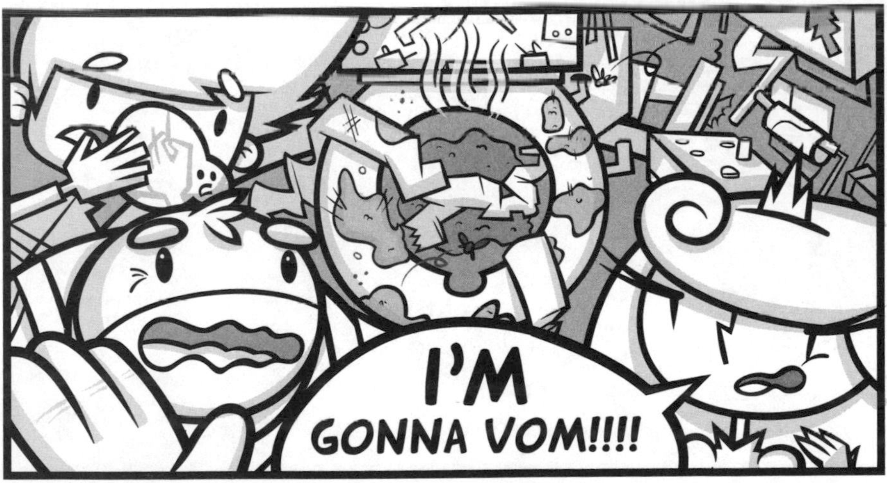
I'M GONNA VOM!!!!

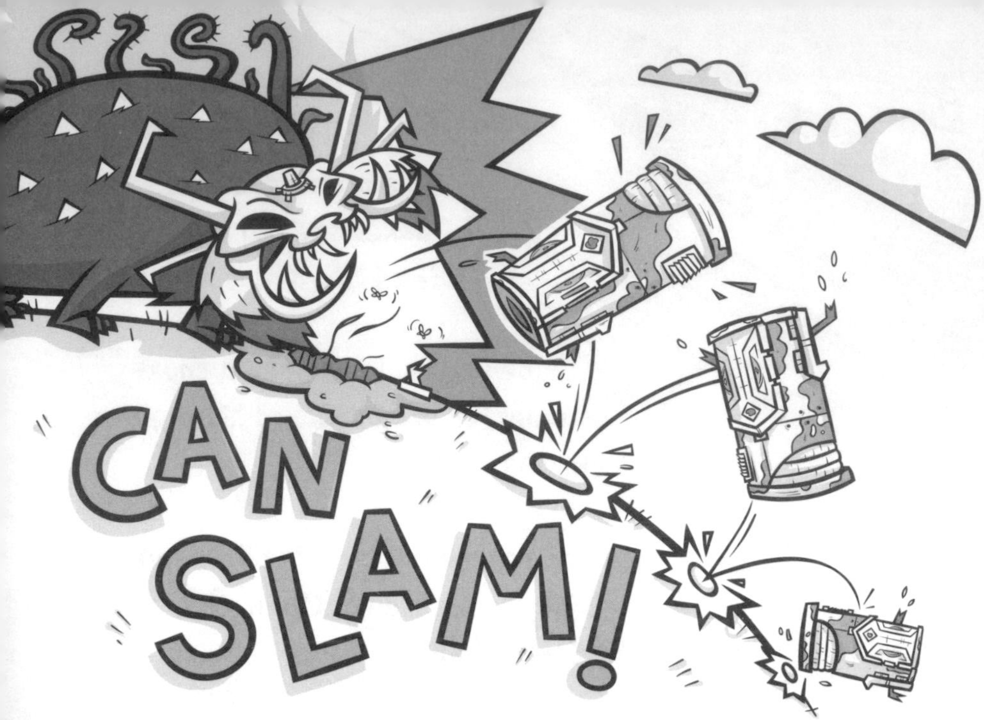
CAN SLAM!

We're tossed about! And without going into too much detail—let me just say, it's not nice and it's not clean. Finally, the tumbling toilet comes to a stop . . .

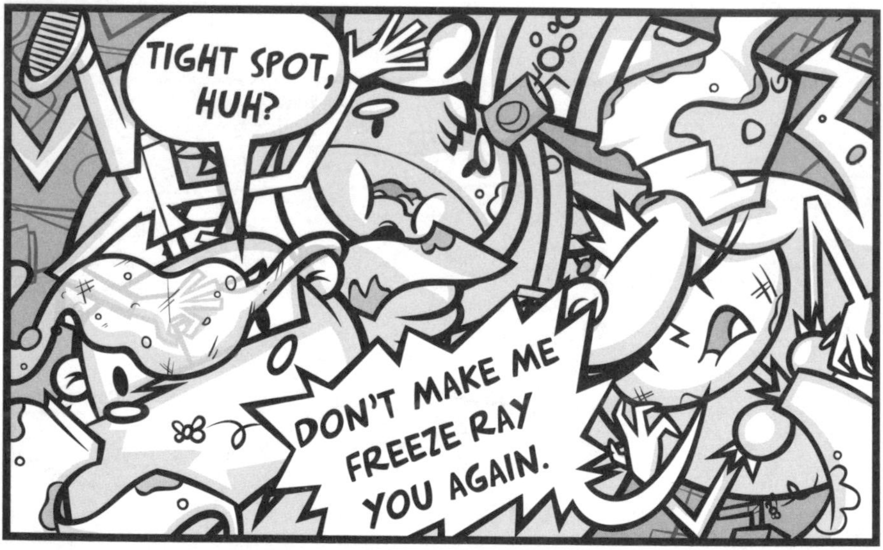
TIGHT SPOT, HUH?
DON'T MAKE ME FREEZE RAY YOU AGAIN.

I wait a moment, nudge open the door, and crawl out onto the grass. I see the *Neon Wiener* sitting just beyond the wreckage. And it gives me an idea. "I don't care how mean this monster is," I say. "No beast can resist our GRILLED WIENERS!"

I whistle, loud as I can. A second later, the Iyanux-monster is turning and rushing headlong toward me . . .

I spot F.R.E.D. hovering around the *Neon Wiener*'s serving booth. "OPEN THE <u>REAR DOORS</u>, BUDDY!" I shout.

F.R.E.D. swings around to the rear and yanks open the doors. Humphree charges past me, grabs a crate of uncooked dogs, and dumps them on the ground.

Dagger lets off a shot with her fiery flash blaster. **PFWOOM!** The doggies are instantly cooking, smelling delicious. The monster skids to a halt, opens wide, and digs in—

TAMED
BY
WIENERS!

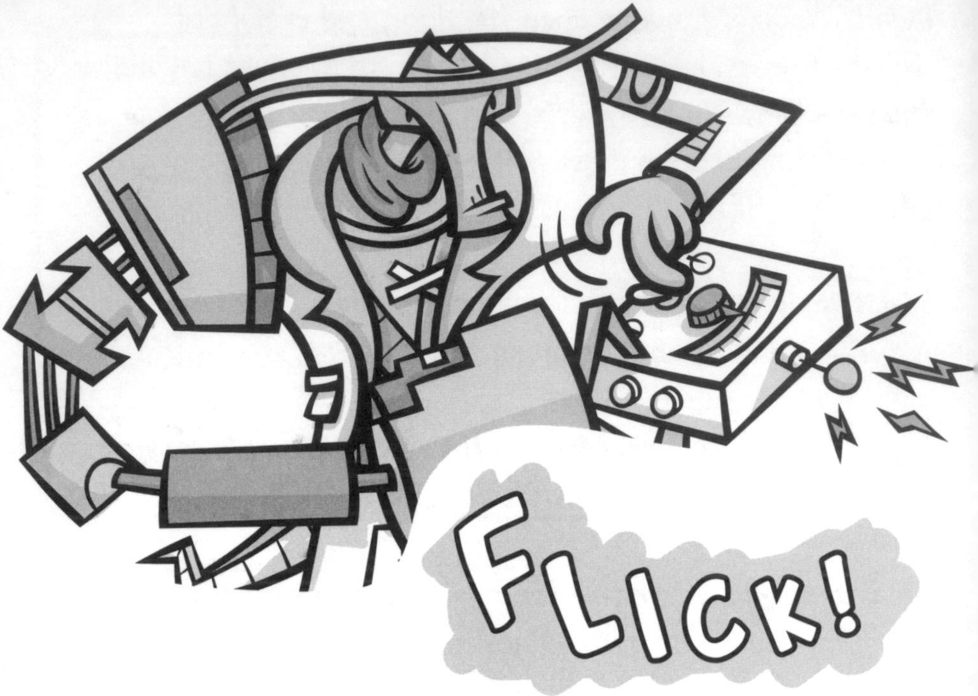
FLICK!

But the monster's meal is cut short. The wrangler is there, carrying a bizarre remote control. It looks like something from my Earth days, playing with RC cars.

Suddenly, the lyanux-monster howls. Her body is changing. Returning to what it was. Her eyes are red and cloudy. It looks like she's waking up from a dream—or a nightmare . . .

The wrangler's arm transforms, and he slings his zappo-lasso around the lyanux's neck. She yelps and kicks as the wrangler drags her away.

The lyanux watches me. Her eyes are wide and wet with fear. She's not ferocious. Not in the least. She's petrified . . .

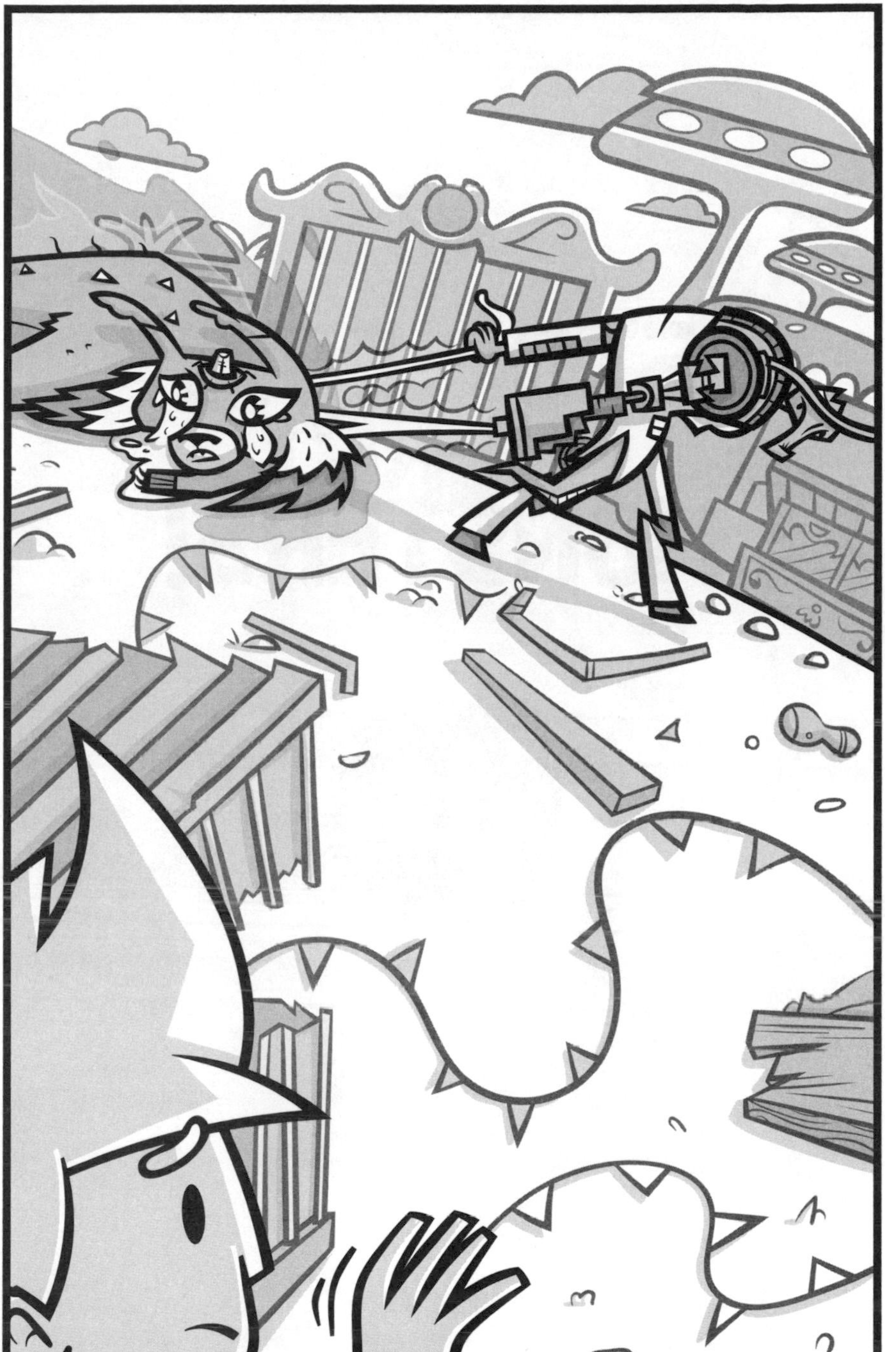

STOP EVIL ENERGY MONSTERS!

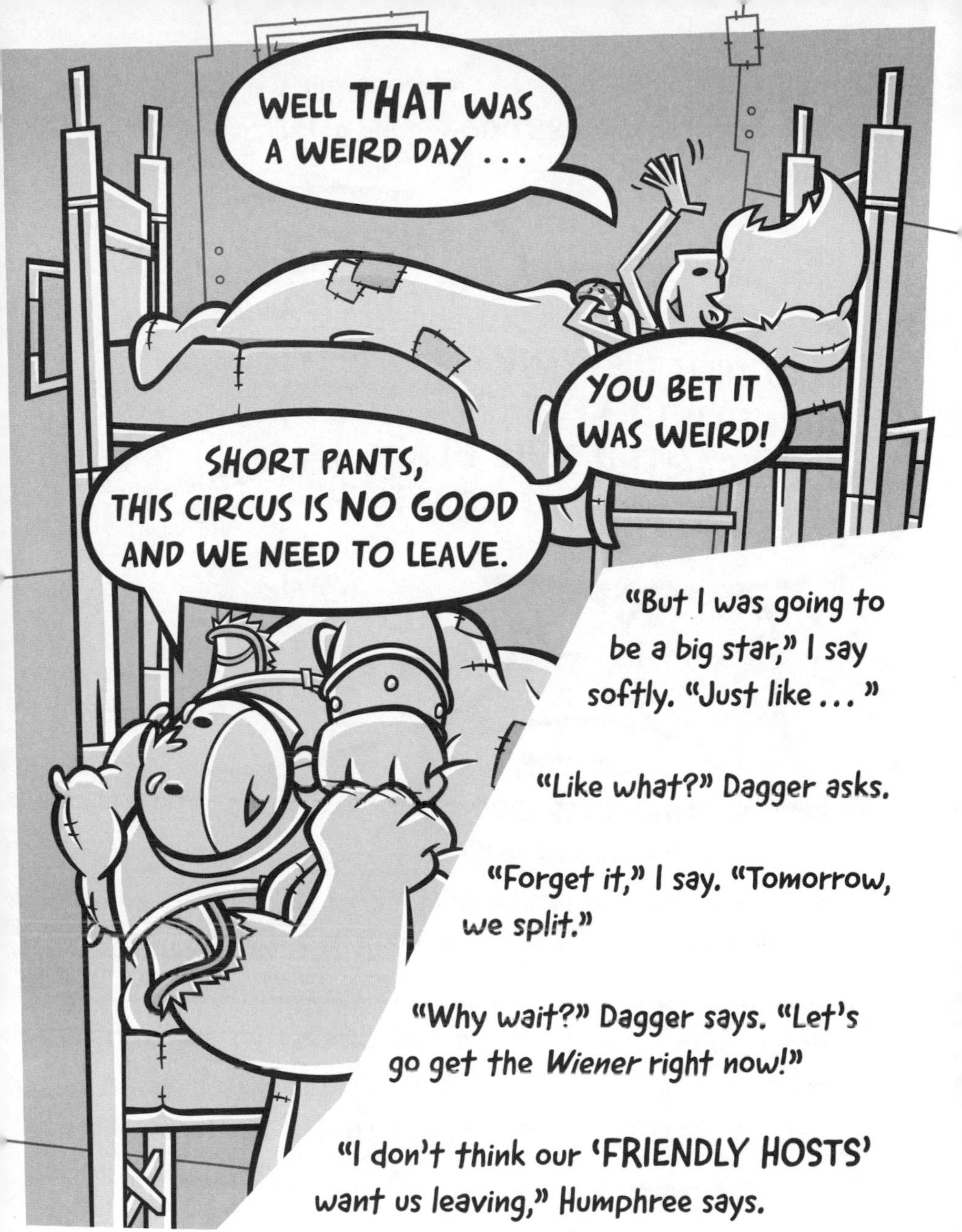
WELL THAT WAS A WEIRD DAY . . .
YOU BET IT WAS WEIRD!
SHORT PANTS, THIS CIRCUS IS NO GOOD AND WE NEED TO LEAVE.

"But I was going to be a big star," I say softly. "Just like . . . "

"Like what?" Dagger asks.

"Forget it," I say. "Tomorrow, we split."

"Why wait?" Dagger says. "Let's go get the *Wiener* right now!"

"I don't think our 'FRIENDLY HOSTS' want us leaving," Humphree says.

Three giant roust-a-bots stand guard outside, ready to box our brains if we try to split. We all realize the terrible truth: **WE'RE PRISONERS . . .**

"All right," I say. "If we agree we're leaving, we should probably talk about the 88,000-pound gorzillaphant in the room . . ."

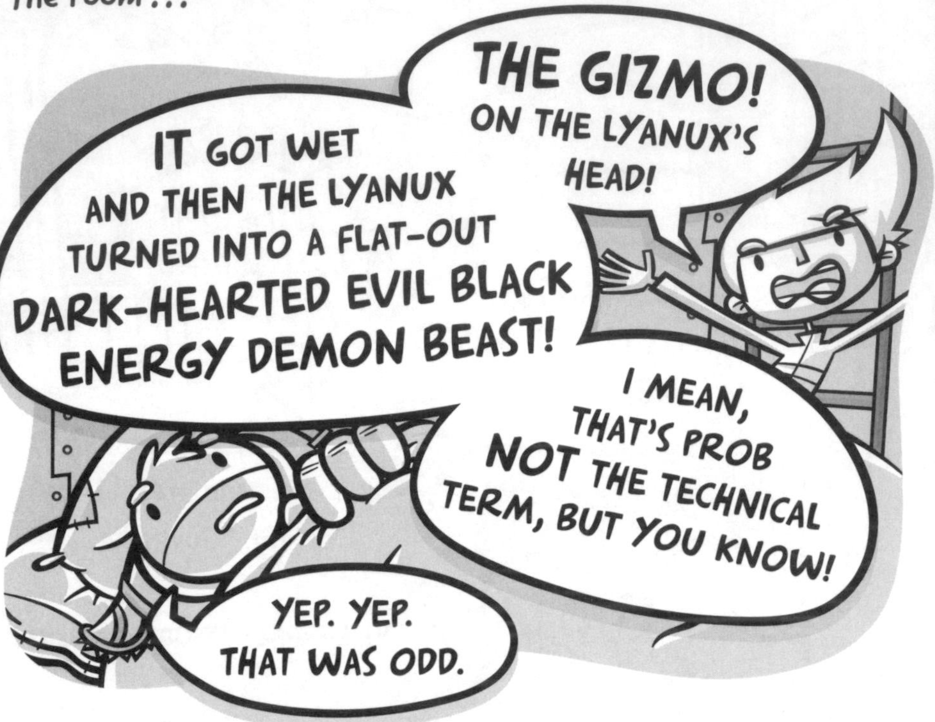
THE GIZMO! ON THE LYANUX'S HEAD!
IT GOT WET AND THEN THE LYANUX TURNED INTO A FLAT-OUT DARK-HEARTED EVIL BLACK ENERGY DEMON BEAST!
I MEAN, THAT'S PROB NOT THE TECHNICAL TERM, BUT YOU KNOW!
YEP. YEP. THAT WAS ODD.

Dagger's eyes glow, all mischievous. "Y'know what we need to do, right? Knock those nougat-heads in their noggins!"

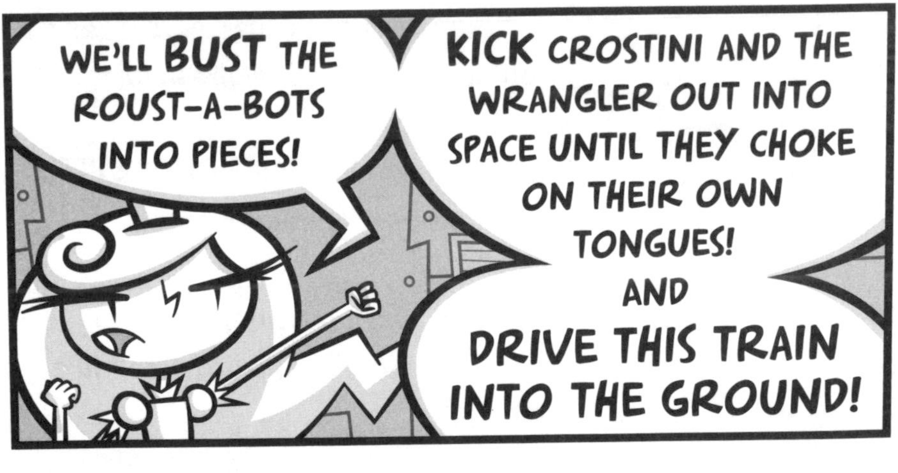
WE'LL BUST THE ROUST-A-BOTS INTO PIECES!
KICK CROSTINI AND THE WRANGLER OUT INTO SPACE UNTIL THEY CHOKE ON THEIR OWN TONGUES!
AND DRIVE THIS TRAIN INTO THE GROUND!

"Um, let's just take a step back here," I say. "What if, instead of all the tongue choking and noggin knocking, we—wait for it—organize a boycott **OLD SCHOOL!**"

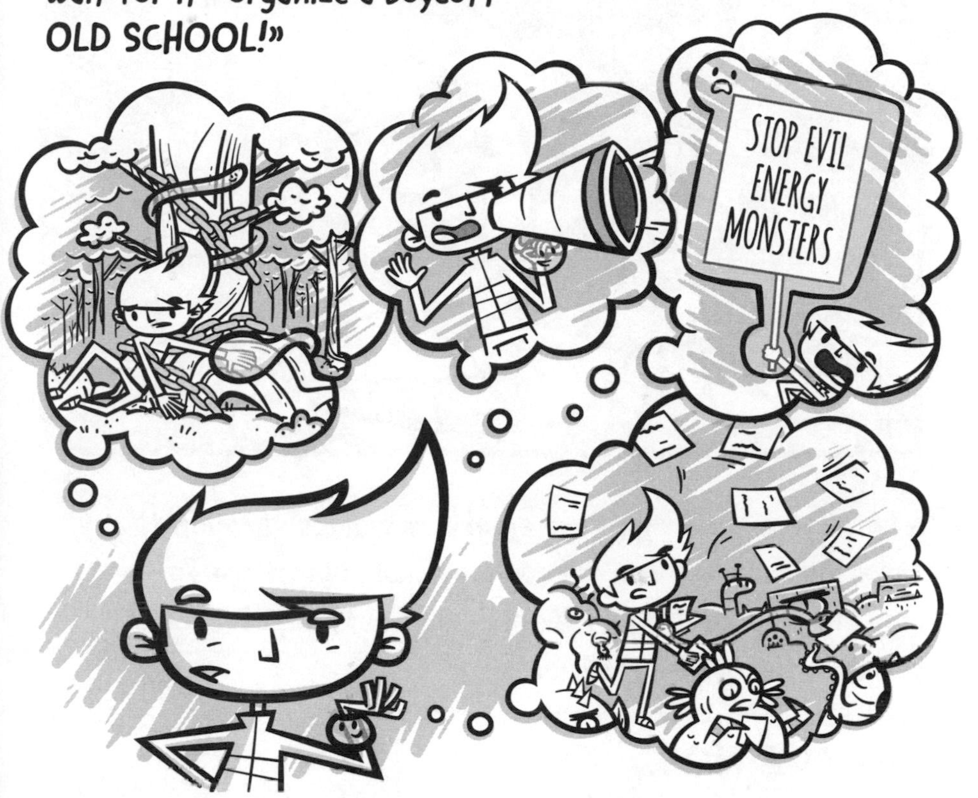
STOP EVIL ENERGY MONSTERS

Humphree and Dagger look at me like I'm a nut. "Fine, fine," I groan. "You're right. We need to give it to them good. We'll figure out something rad."

Dagger smiles happily, then flicks the light knobber. "You two get some rest. I'll keep an eye on those robo-thugs."

I lay my head down on the big, comfy pillow. I thought I was fulfilling my destiny, here. But as I fall asleep, all I can think is: **IT'S OVER.**

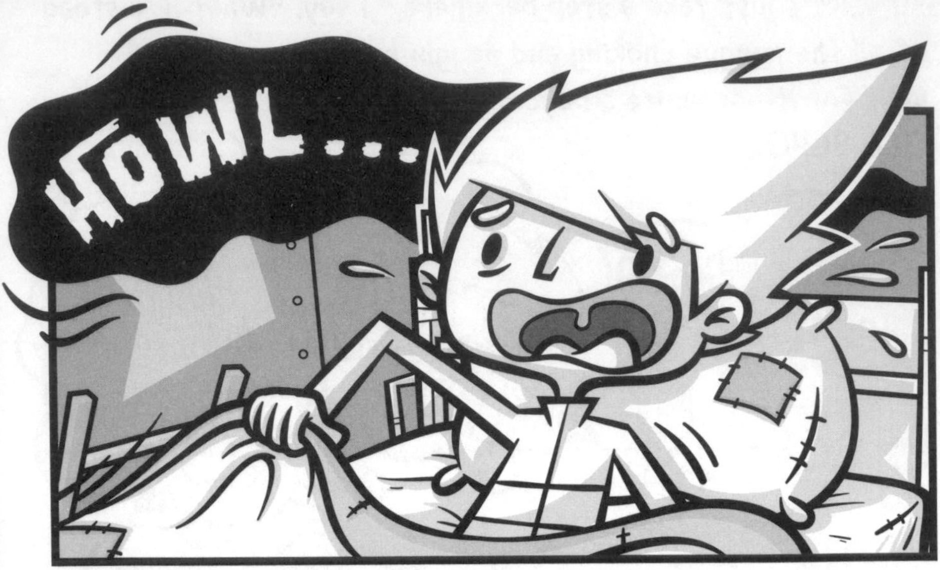
HOWL...

A horrifying howl snaps me awake. It echoes through the train, through our car, through my skull. I lie there for a moment, hoping it's just an arc-wing rattling or a loose screw in the grav-stabilizer.

BUT IT'S NOT.

"'Moe, get up," the princess whispers, shaking me. "You hear that? Sounds like something's being, um, tortured ... Let's go check it out! Do some exploring. Maybe we'll get to kick something!"

"If we're exploring, we need heavy-duty backup," I say.

Unfortunately, getting our "HEAVY-DUTY BACKUP" to stop snoozing is no easy task ...

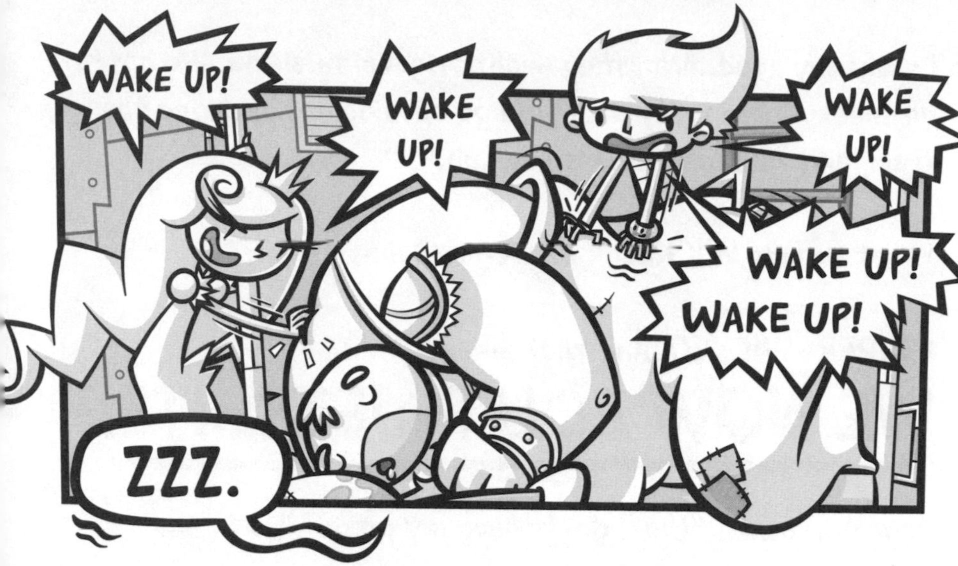
WAKE UP!
WAKE UP!
WAKE UP!
WAKE UP!
WAKE UP!
ZZZ.

Another howl slices through the air. I gulp. We need to move—with or without the big guy. "C'mon, Dags, we'll have to do this one just the two of us."

I peer through the door. The roust-a-bots are still out there. Their thick fists hang, ready to crack our craniums. "I can take those metal-heads out!" Dagger brags.

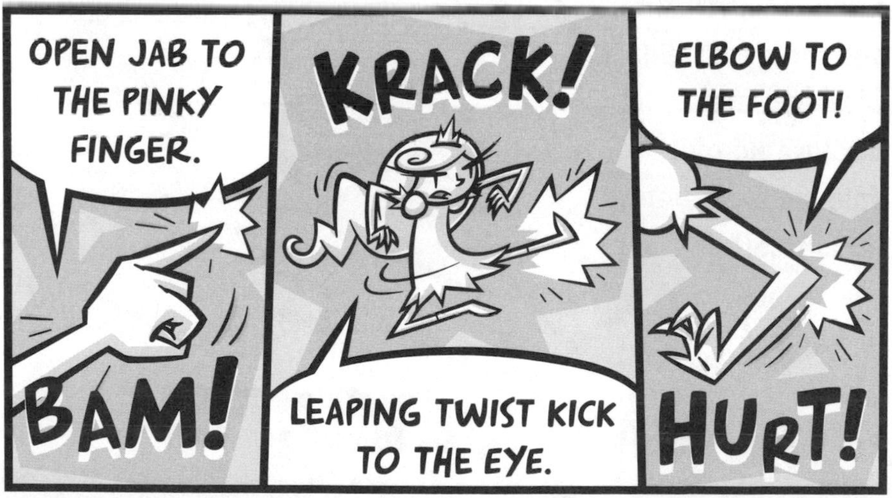
OPEN JAB TO THE PINKY FINGER.
BAM!
KRACK!
LEAPING TWIST KICK TO THE EYE.
ELBOW TO THE FOOT!
HURT!

I shake my head. "No, they might trigger an alarm. We gotta be sneaky-pants. My plan? We go outside, creep along the train, and find whatever's howling."

"That sounds **WICKED!**" Dagger exclaims.

"SUPER-WICKED. And that means . . .

WE NOW EQUIP JETSUITS!"

Dagger frowns. "Um, I don't have my jetsuit."

"WHAT? Whaddya mean? Where's your jetsuit?"

Dagger shrugs. "In the *Wiener*."

"Why's it in the *Wiener*?!"

"You didn't tell me to bring my jetsuit!" she shouts. "I didn't plan for jetsuiting, because no one told me we'd be jetsuiting!"

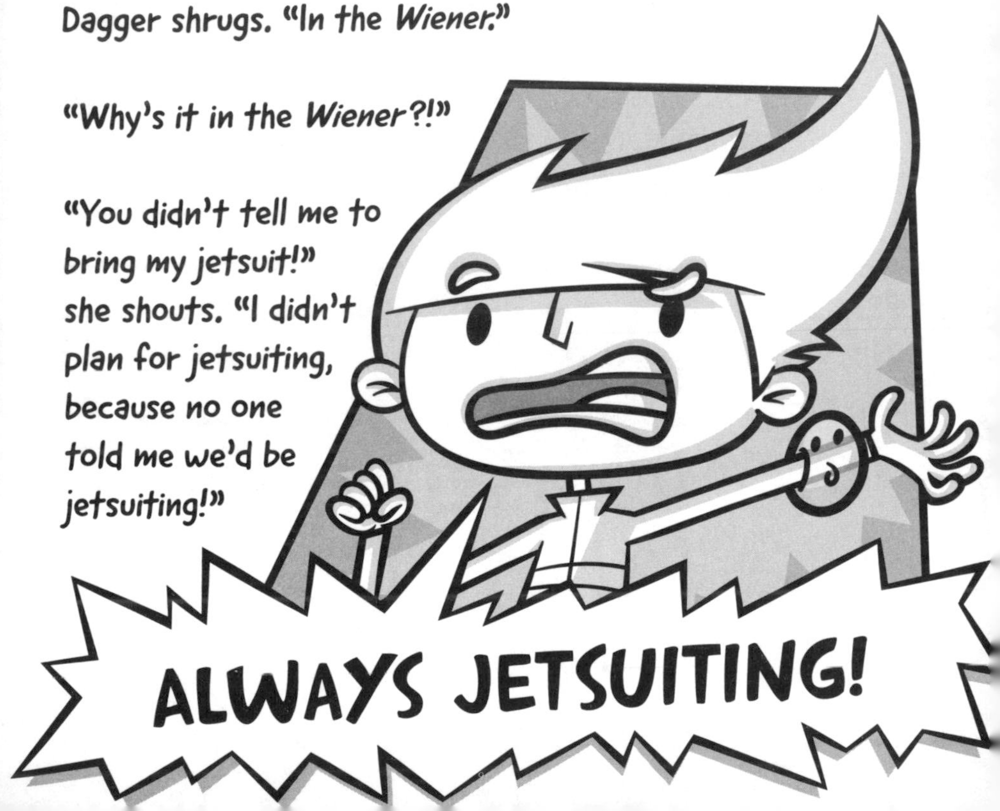
ALWAYS JETSUITING!

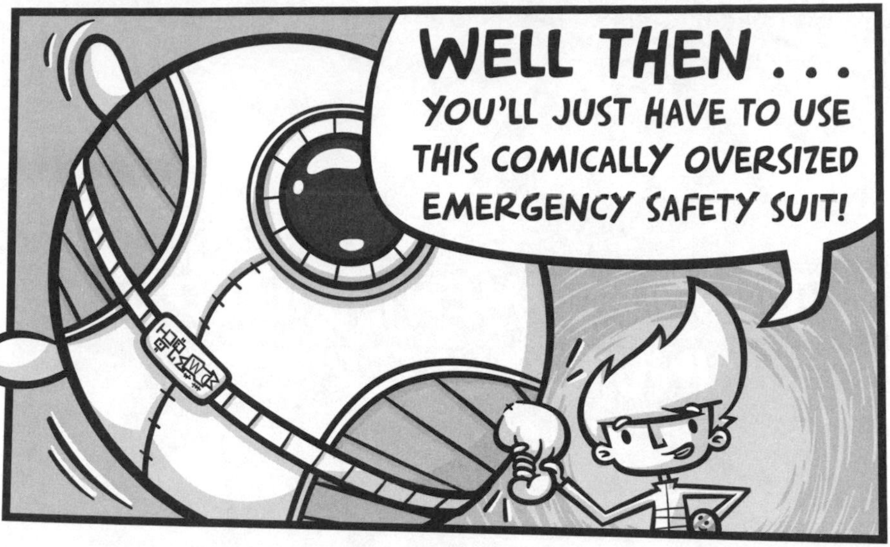
WELL THEN . . .
YOU'LL JUST HAVE TO USE THIS COMICALLY OVERSIZED EMERGENCY SAFETY SUIT!

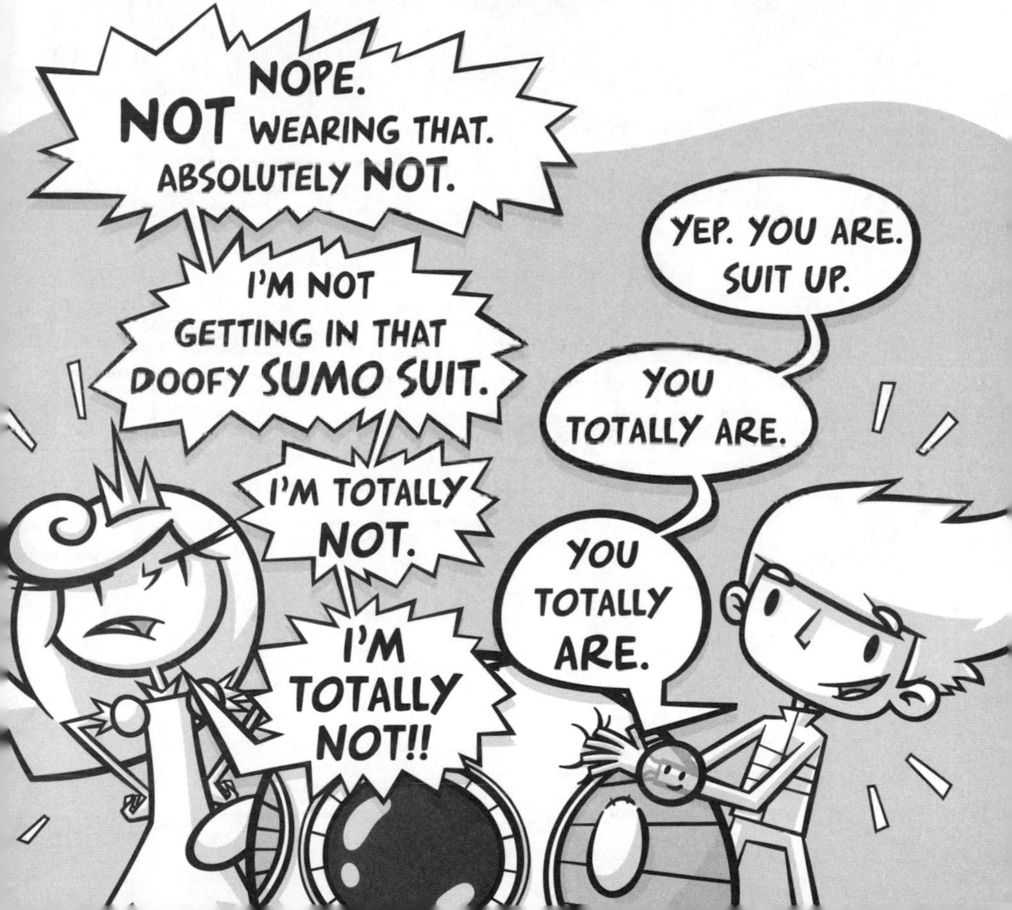
NOPE. NOT WEARING THAT. ABSOLUTELY NOT.
YEP. YOU ARE. SUIT UP.
I'M NOT GETTING IN THAT DOOFY SUMO SUIT.
YOU TOTALLY ARE.
I'M TOTALLY NOT.
YOU TOTALLY ARE.
I'M TOTALLY NOT!!

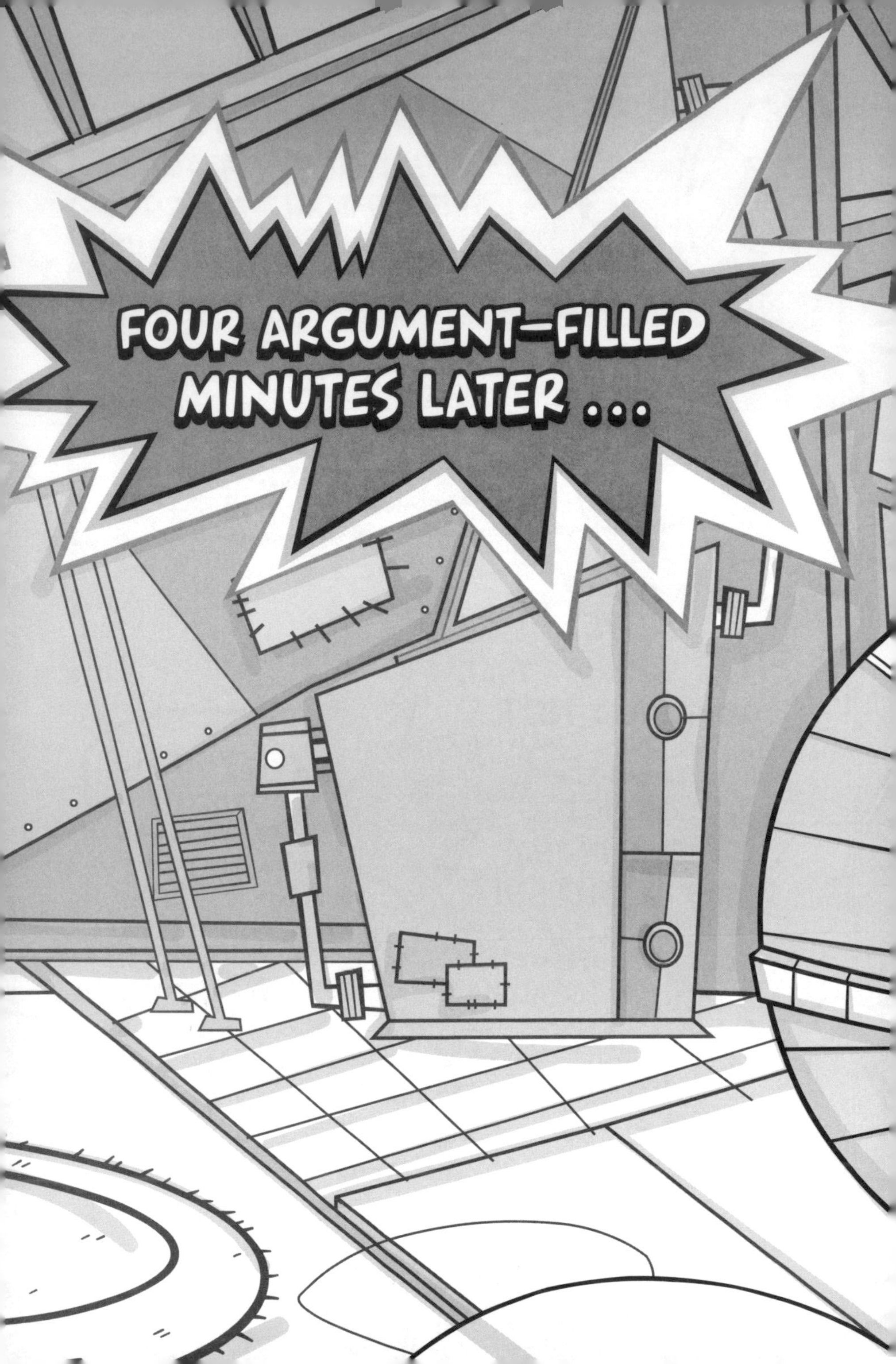
FOUR ARGUMENT-FILLED MINUTES LATER . . .

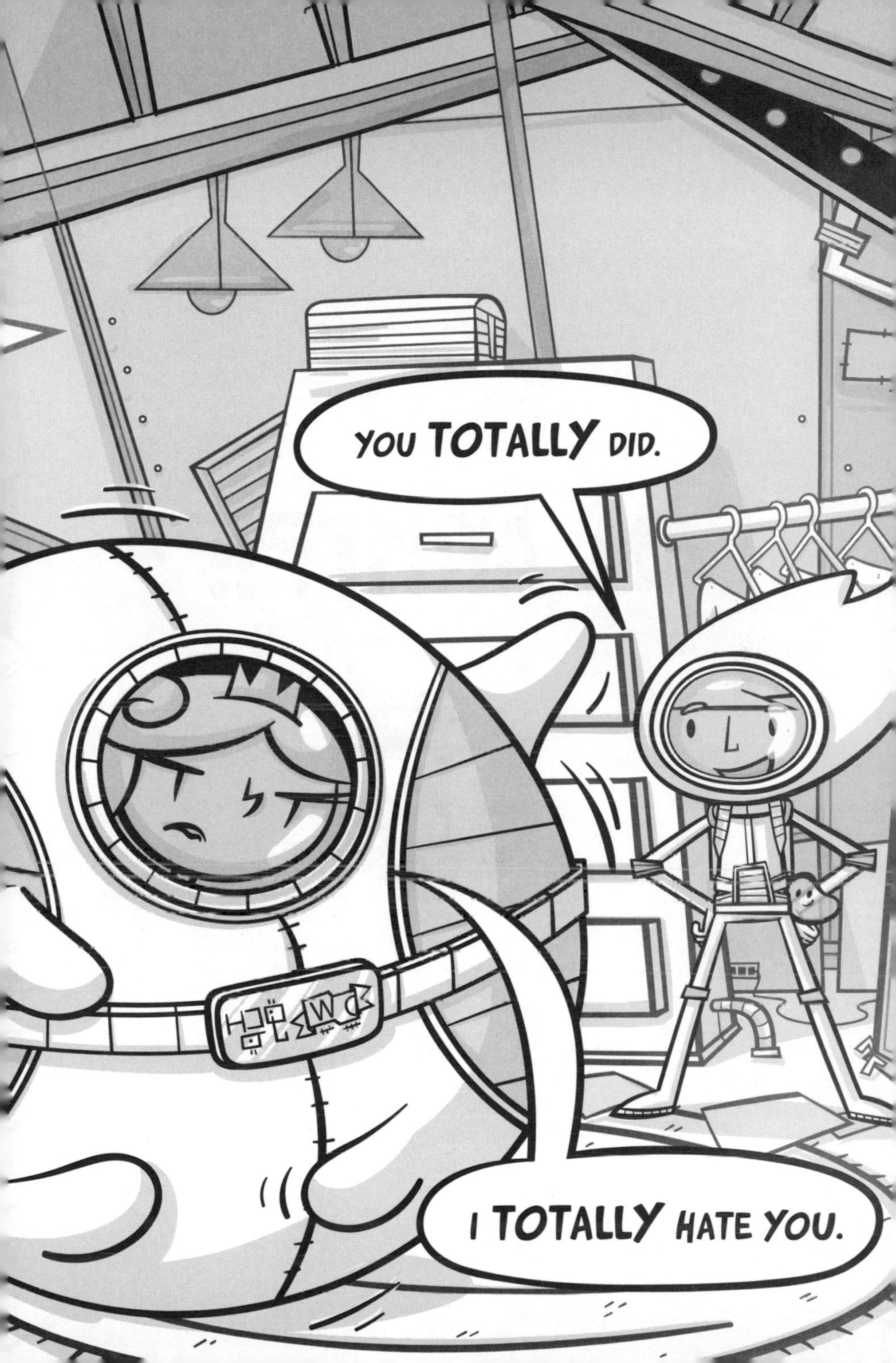
YOU TOTALLY DID.
I TOTALLY HATE YOU.

AN ARMY?!?!

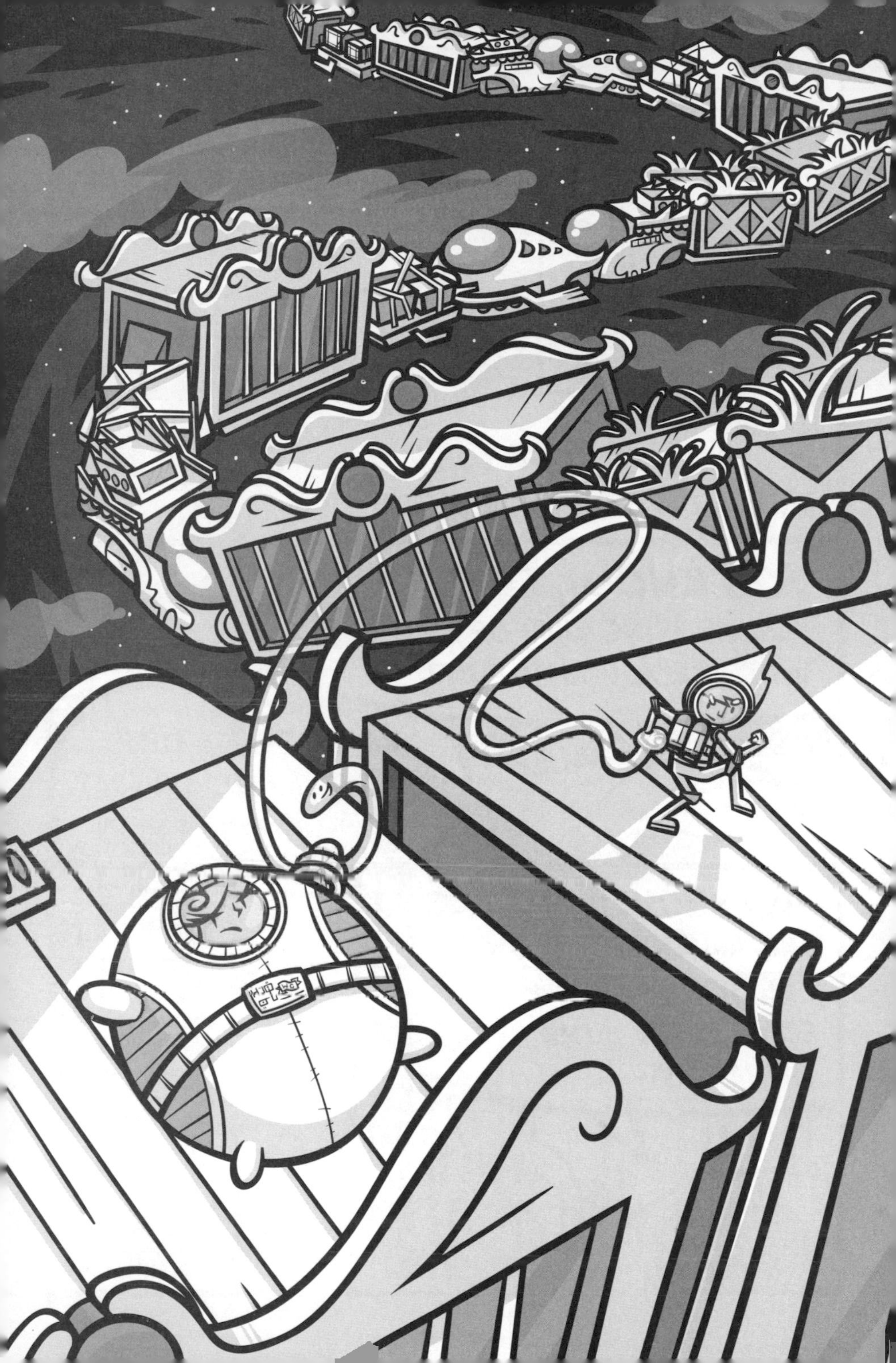

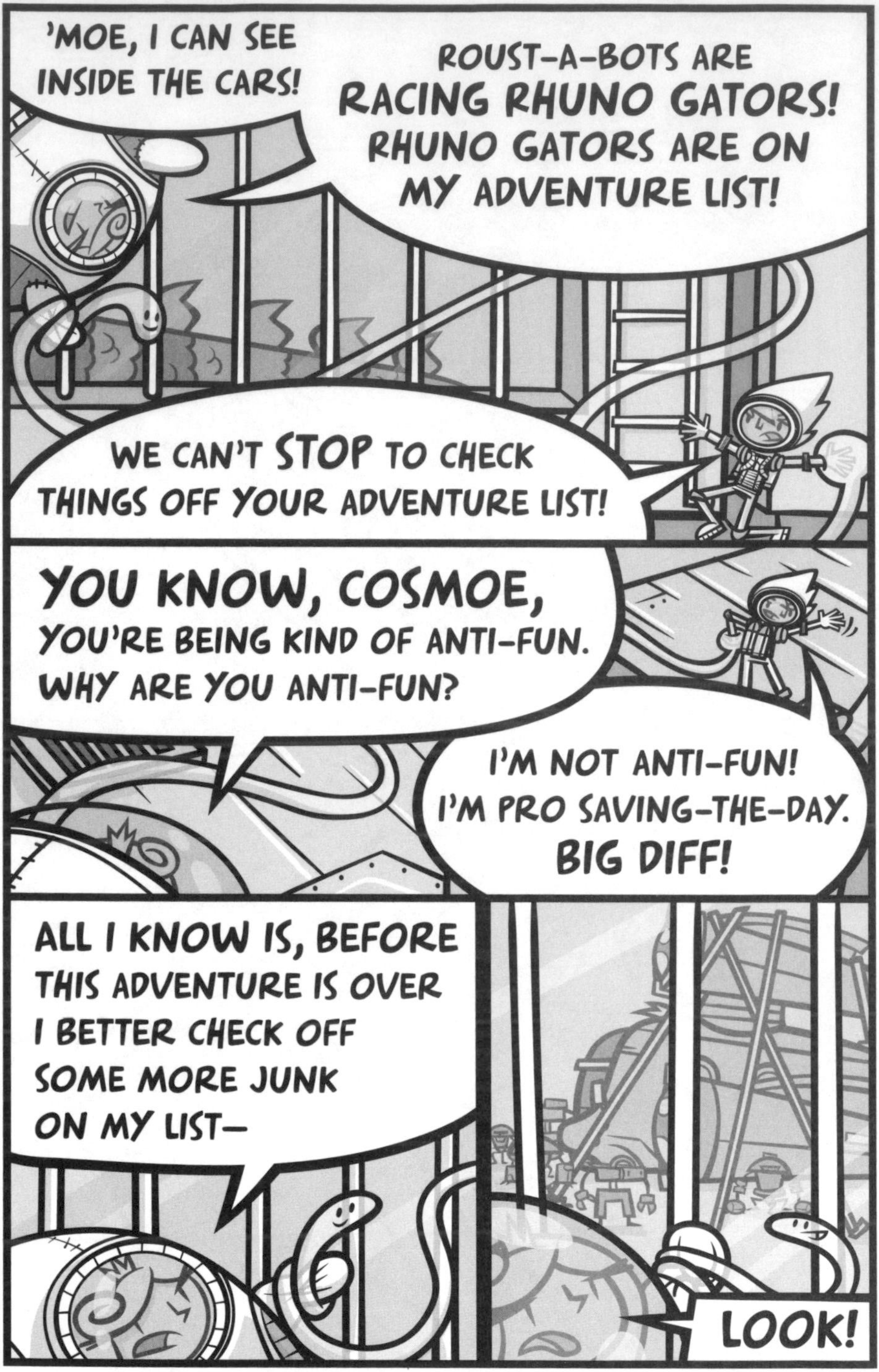
'MOE, I CAN SEE INSIDE THE CARS!
ROUST-A-BOTS ARE RACING RHUNO GATORS! RHUNO GATORS ARE ON MY ADVENTURE LIST!
WE CAN'T STOP TO CHECK THINGS OFF YOUR ADVENTURE LIST!
YOU KNOW, COSMOE, YOU'RE BEING KIND OF ANTI-FUN. WHY ARE YOU ANTI-FUN?
I'M NOT ANTI-FUN! I'M PRO SAVING-THE-DAY. BIG DIFF!
ALL I KNOW IS, BEFORE THIS ADVENTURE IS OVER I BETTER CHECK OFF SOME MORE JUNK ON MY LIST—
LOOK!

THE *WIENER* IS SURROUNDED BY ROUST-A-BOTS! THEY DEFINITELY DON'T WANT US LEAVING . . .

"I see it," I say. "We'll escape tomorrow."

We continue past clown cars and creature cars until we finally reach the rear of the train. Through the porthole window, I see the room where we had dinner. I see the huge metal door to the "private" car that Crostini wouldn't let us enter. And I realize . . .

The howl is coming from inside Crostini's private car! The car is covered in metal panels, concealing what's inside.

It's time to play space-spy. Goober snakes underneath a panel and SNAP! The panel flips off and drifts away. We press our faces against the glass.

IT'S LIKE . . .

LIKE SOME SORT OF MAD SCIENTIST LABORATORY!

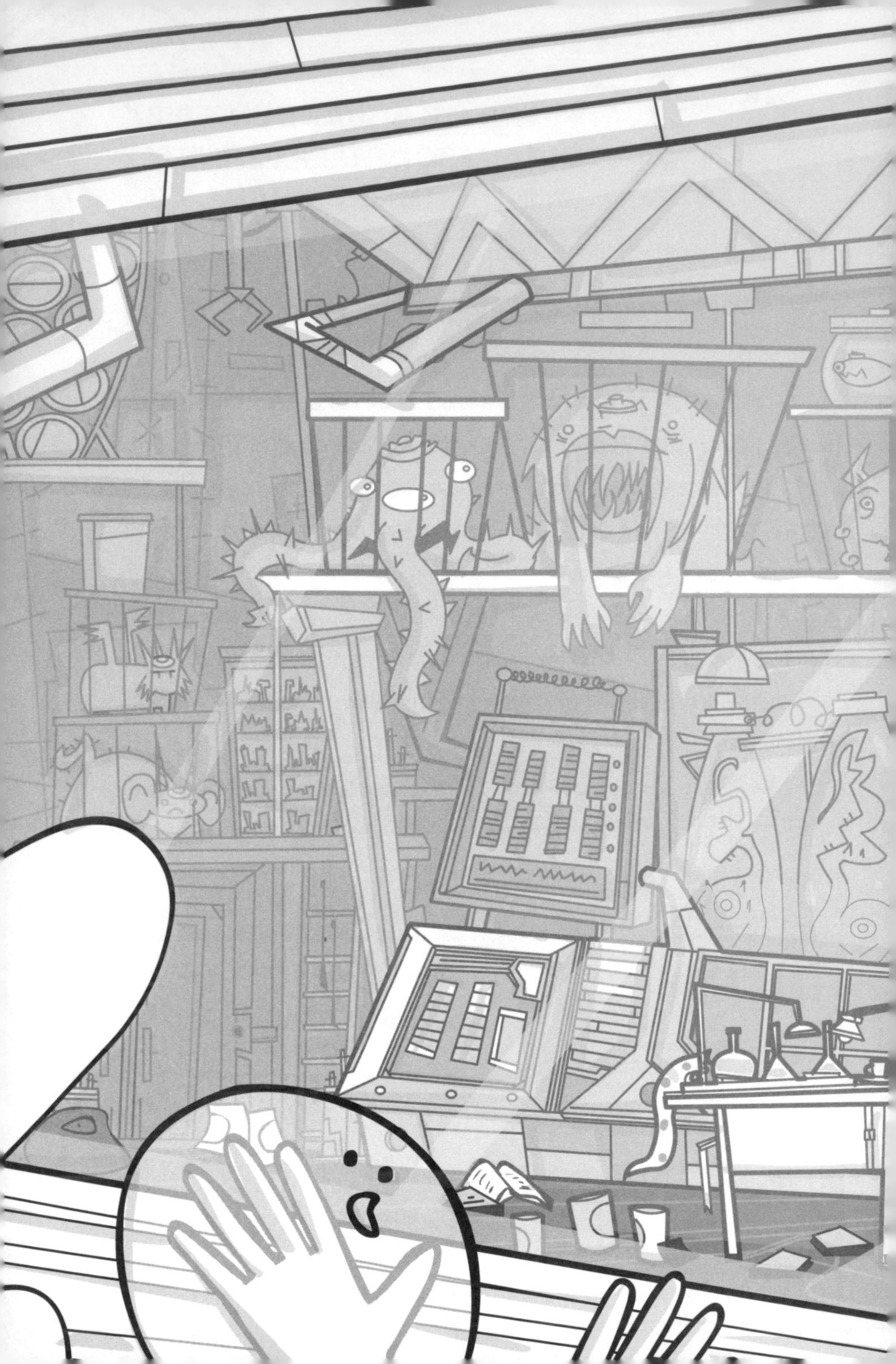

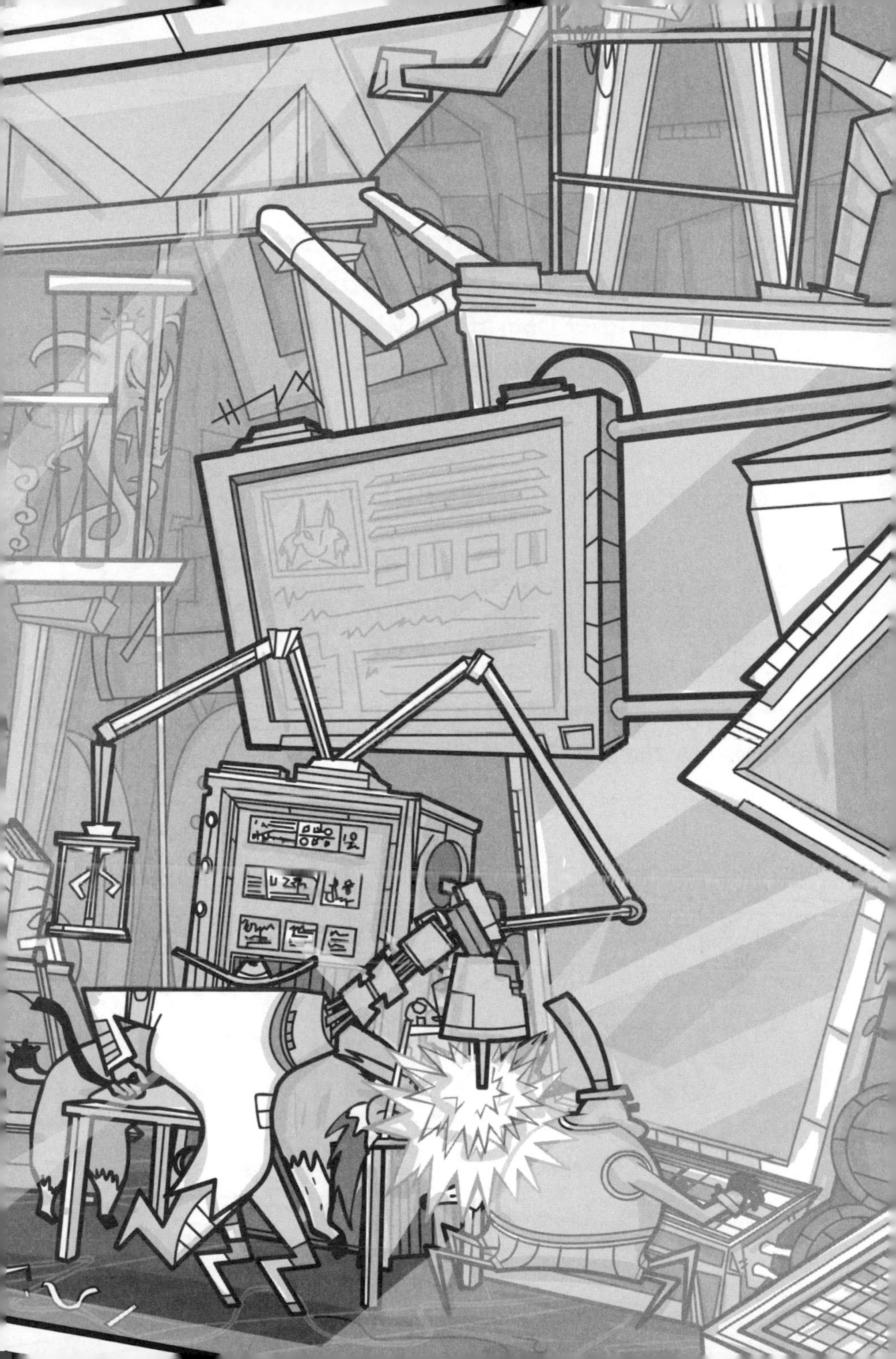

"OK, let's not get carried away . . ." I say. "It MIGHT not be a mad scientist laboratory."

"Cosmoe, my mom has a whole *team* of mad scientists. I know a mad scientist laboratory when I see a mad scientist laboratory, and **THAT, BUDDY**, is your classic mad scientist laboratory. Weird tools. Buzzing equipment. Creatures in cages."

I groan. The lady is right. It does appear to be your classic mad scientist laboratory.

I place my face to the glass, trying to get a better view. I spy the wrangler, towering over a table. A moment later, he steps to the side, revealing . . .

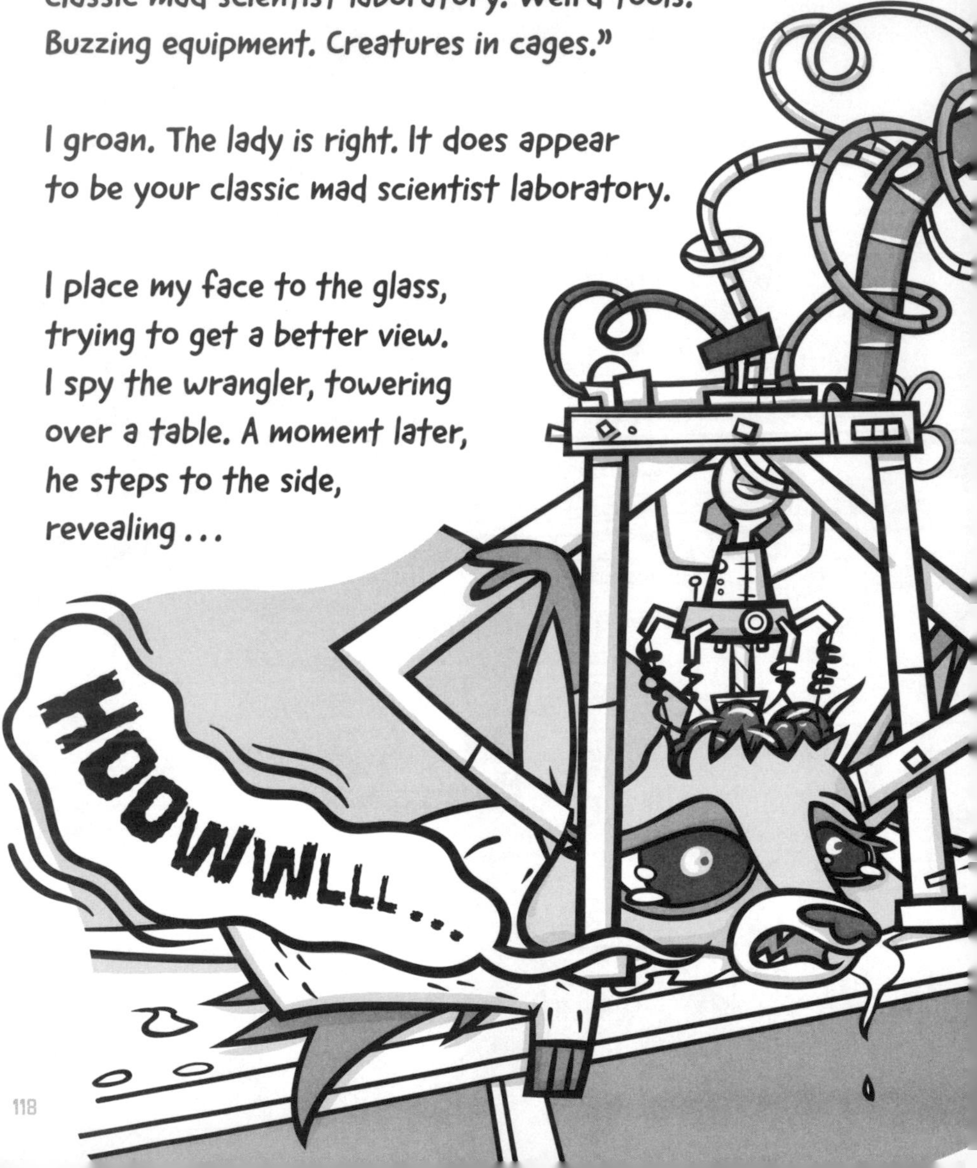
HOOOWWLLL . . .

"The lyanux!" I exclaim. "**SHE** was howling. Those jerks are hurting her! We need to hear what they're doing, Dags. WAIT! My ear-bugs!"

COSMOE FUN FACT:

Ear-bugs are fantastically gross. The twin faces of the ear-bug crawl inside your ears, then you place the ear-bug's mushy butt center on a window and you can hear **EVERTHING INSIDE.**

I smush the ear-bug against the train car, then one face crawls into my suit and inside my ear. I slap the other face on Dagger's visor, and it osmosisizes through the glass and slithers up into her nose (since the princess has no ears).

And we hear bad, bad stuff.

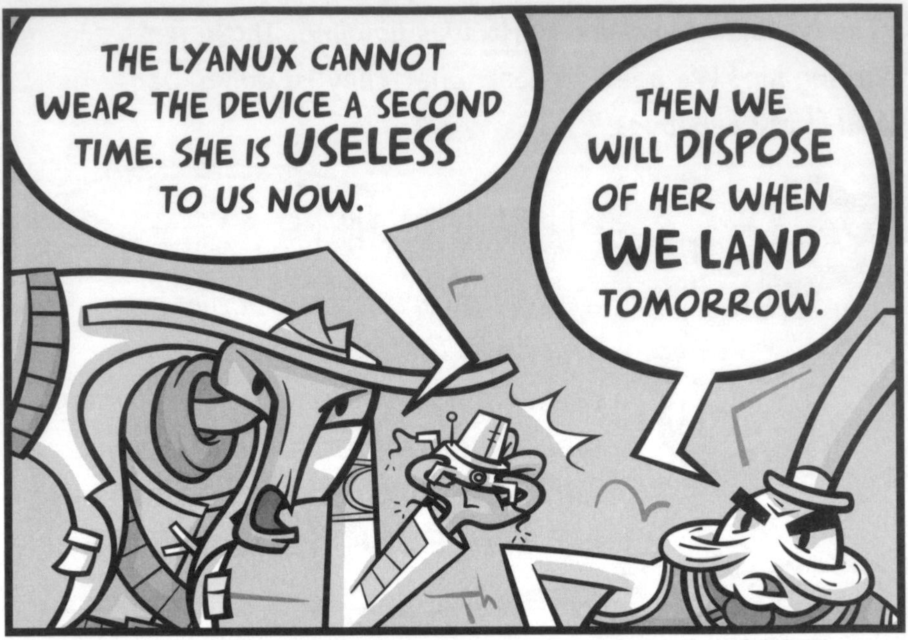
THE LYANUX CANNOT WEAR THE DEVICE A SECOND TIME. SHE IS USELESS TO US NOW.
THEN WE WILL DISPOSE OF HER WHEN WE LAND TOMORROW.

"Did you hear that?" I exclaim, turning to Dagger. "Dispose of! Crostini said DISPOSE OF! They're going to just dump the lyanux on some planet! To—to—to DIE!"

Dagger doesn't say anything. Her eyes are wide, and blue freckles begin to dot her face. Nervous freckles! Something has her spooked.

I turn back to the window. What I see freezes me. It's like my heart is spring-loaded—and that spring-loaded heart just leaped up into my throat. Sweat pours off my forehead, fogging up my visor.

Someone from our past has appeared on the screen. Someone from our past is involved in this wicked plot . . .

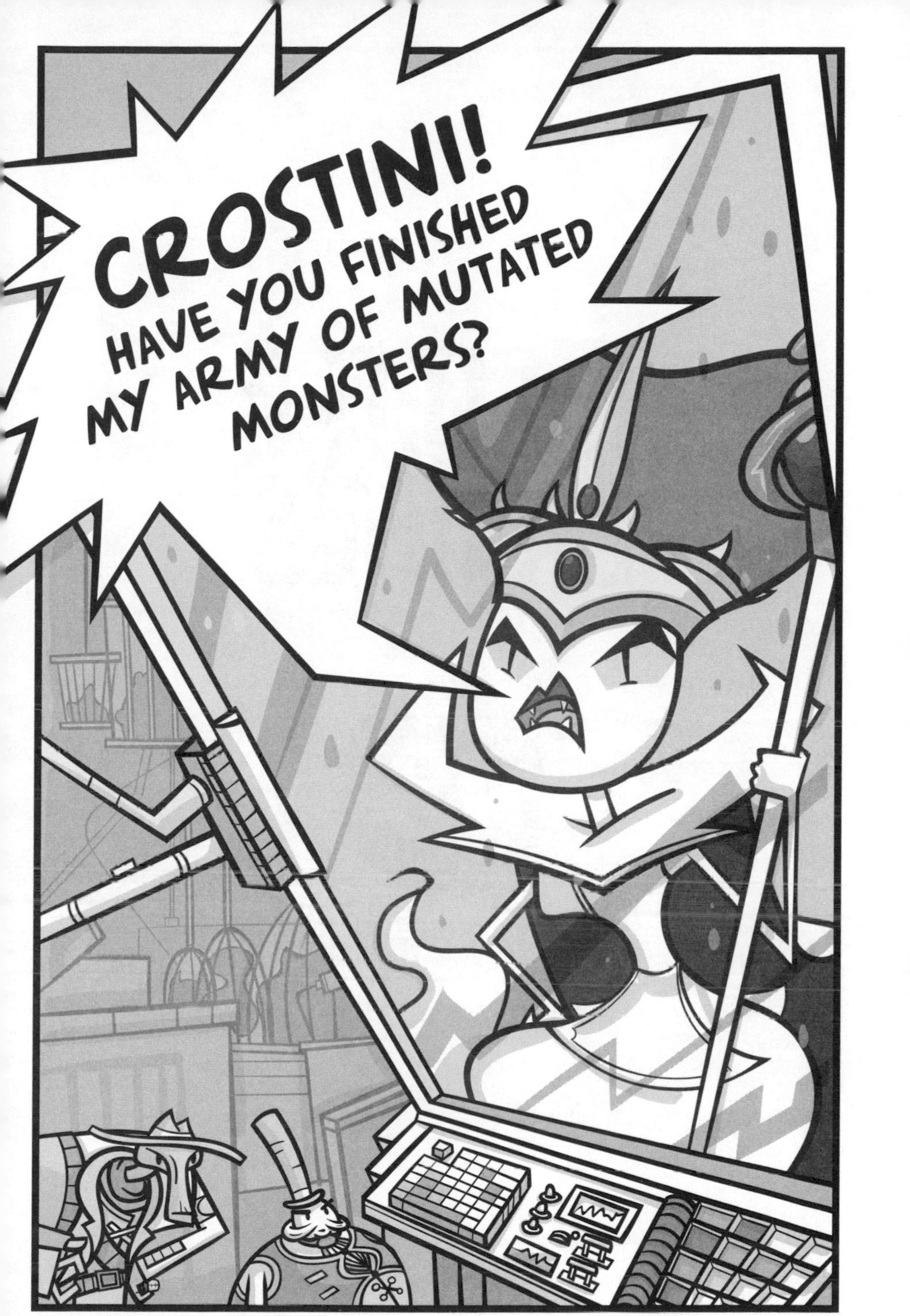
CROSTINI! HAVE YOU FINISHED MY ARMY OF MUTATED MONSTERS?

A LITTLE BIT SPACE BRAINED

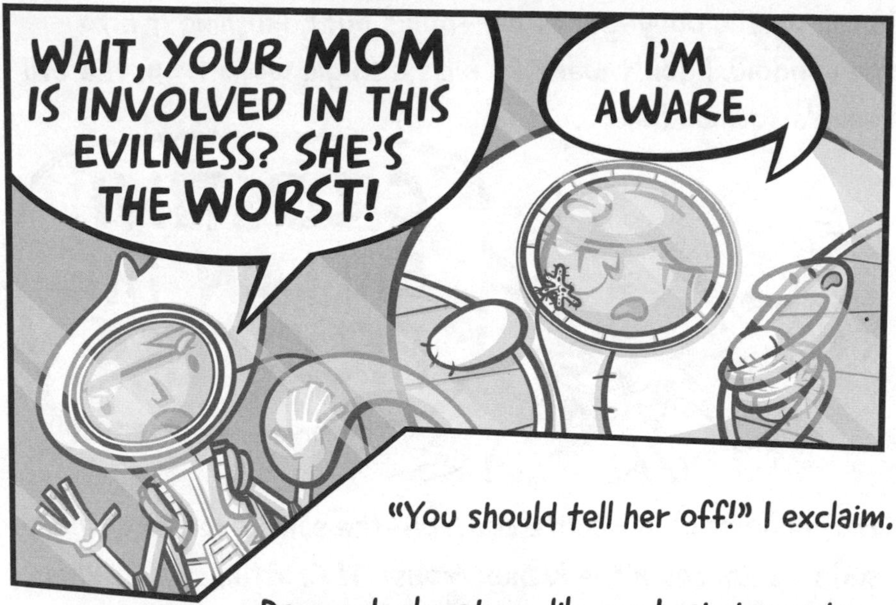
WAIT, YOUR MOM IS INVOLVED IN THIS EVILNESS? SHE'S THE WORST!
I'M AWARE.

"You should tell her off!" I exclaim.

Dagger looks at me like my brain is moving in super slo-mo. "Uh, I did . . . Remember? It was a whole dramatic thing? With battling and space chasing?"

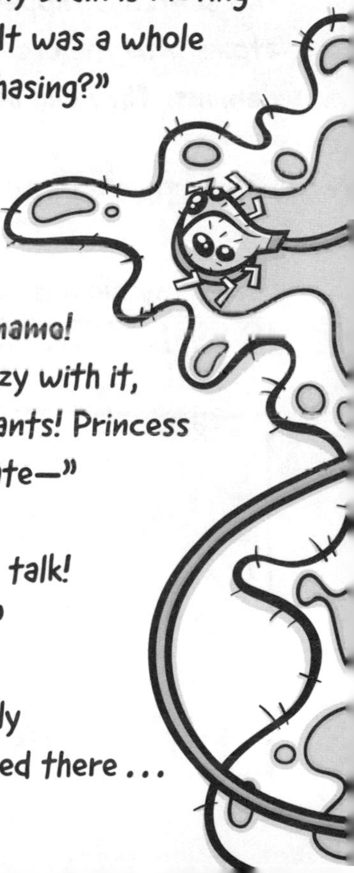

Ohhhh yeah. Duh. Sometimes my brain *does* move in super-slo-mo.

"Well," I say, "you could change your last name! So you're not associated with her. Get crazy with it, something totally fresh! Princess Power Pants! Princess Explosion Fists! Princess Annoying Roommate—"

"Cosmoe!" she barks. "Knock off the goof talk! The bad guys are explaining their big plan!"

Oh. Right! Villain speeches. I should probably pay attention. Got a little bit space-brained there . . .

I push on the ooey-gooey ear-bug's butt, mushing it into the window. I don't want to miss a single word from the evil queen's squawk box . . .

CROSTINI, EXPLAIN THE PROCESS.

Crostini holds up a remote control—the same one the wrangler used to shut down the Iyanux monster! Crostini says, "When this switch is flipped, the governator gizmo pumps evil energy atoms into the creatures' brains, turning them into energy demons. They will be the weapons in your army!"

I gasp. That's <u>EXACTLY</u> what happened to the Iyanux!

"Wait, my mom is taking the circus creatures and turning them into **WEAPONS?!**" Dagger says.

SHE REALLY IS THE WORST.

TOTES THE WORST.

AND WHAT ABOUT THE **GARGANTUID?** WHERE IS IT? I WANT IT! **GIVE IT TO ME!**

I glance at Dagger. Gargantuid? We both shrug. Never heard of it. Of course, it's a big galaxy and there are at least, like, fifty-nine different species of creatures out there. Or more. Yeah, probably more. I'm not so good with numbers.

From the way his little crab legs are click-clacking, I can tell Crostini is terrified of the queen. I mean, who isn't?? The lady's an expert in execution! She's got a doctorate in destruction! A masters in mayhem!

"The gargantuid is too dangerous, your evilness," Crostini cries. "To capture it would be death!"

It looks like Queen Dagger's crown is about to poke through the monitor. "NO!" she roars. "I want the gargantuid. I **NEED** it! I will ride atop it as I lead my monstrous new army!"

The wrangler takes a single, slow step forward. He bows slightly. "My queen, I will capture the creature for you. You have my word."

Queen Dagger squeals with delight, then immediately goes back to being evil and scary. "Don't you two bungle this! If you fail me, the penalty is . . . hmm . . . well, I'll think of something. And it won't be fun! And it'll probably involve power drills. And stabby needles. Evil Queen <u>OUT!</u>"

The big monitor blinks off. My mind is galloping. Army? We're supposed to stop an ARMY?!

"Maybe you could just call your mom?" I say. "Ask her to knock it off? Hatch a different evil plan?"

"Well, Cosmoe—I *could* have done what I wanted to do earlier. Remember . . . Kick Crostini and the wrangler out into space until they choke on their own tongues!"

"But you ruined it," Dagger says, "<u>WITH THE SUMO SUIT.</u>"

"We need to tell Humps," I say. "He was in big battles galore when he was a pirate. He'll know what to do."

"He's all the way back at the other end of the train!" Dagger says. "We just spent FOREVER getting here. And now you want to go back?!"

Argh. I don't know what to do! If we just burst in there now we'll get all beat up! And then we won't save the creatures. We *have* to save them. Especially the lyanux . . . it's my duty!

Dagger snaps her fingers in my face. "COSMOE! Now! Goober hammer, crack this glass, and let's handle business!"

Our chat is cut short. A long shadow falls over us. And when a long shadow falls over you, it's never good. It's never like, "A long shadow fell over us—and I turned to see it was some guy bringing me a million bucks and a Choco Taco!"

No. Never.

It's always something BAD.

And this time, it's MORE
BAD THAN EVER . . .

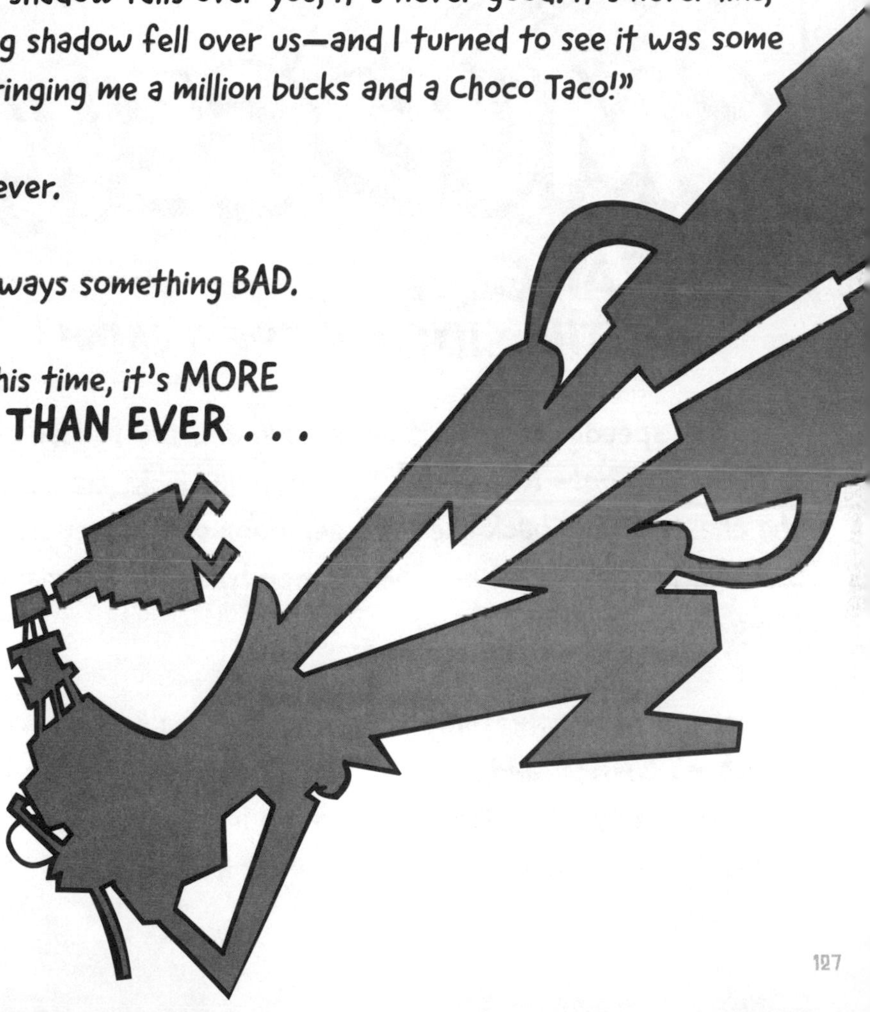

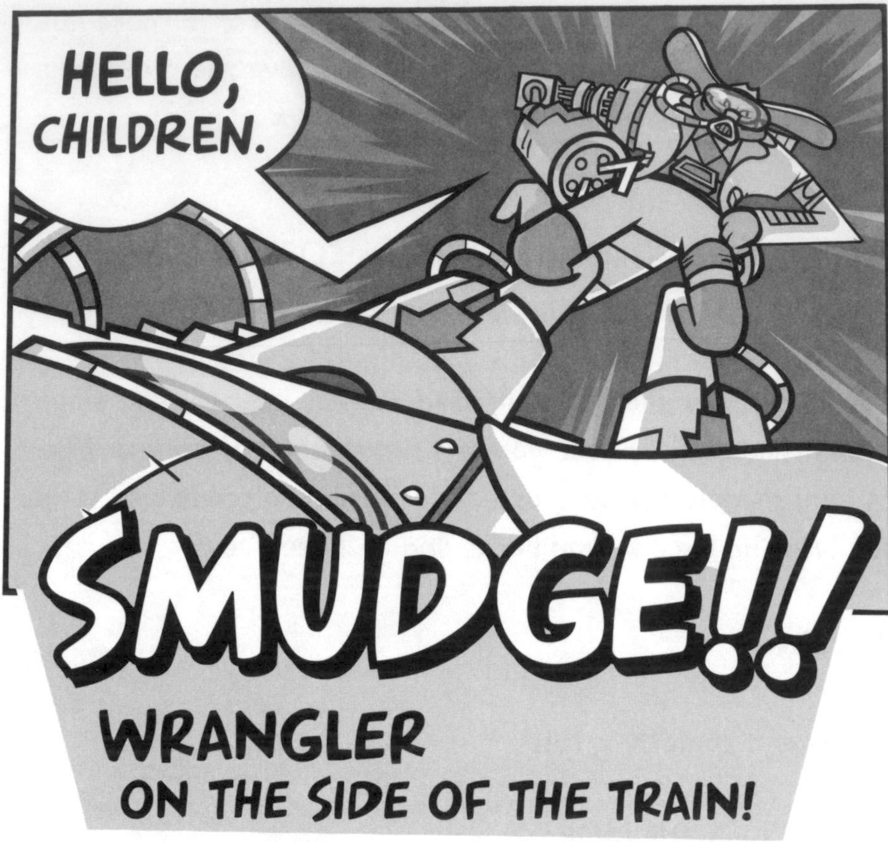
HELLO, CHILDREN.
SMUDGE!!
WRANGLER
ON THE SIDE OF THE TRAIN!

I grip the speeding train with one hand and try to lash out with Goober, but—KRUNCH! The wrangler kicks me square in the chest. I swing back like a screen door on a windy day and SLAM into the train. I'm nearly seized by the jet stream and flung into open space.

Dagger yells out something that sounds like a Bruce Lee "HEE-YEAH!" and leaps at the wrangler. But she's not super-maneuverable right now, so she just sort of punches and kicks the air while ever so slowly drifting toward him. Her every move is . . .

HAMPERED BY THE SUMO SUIT!

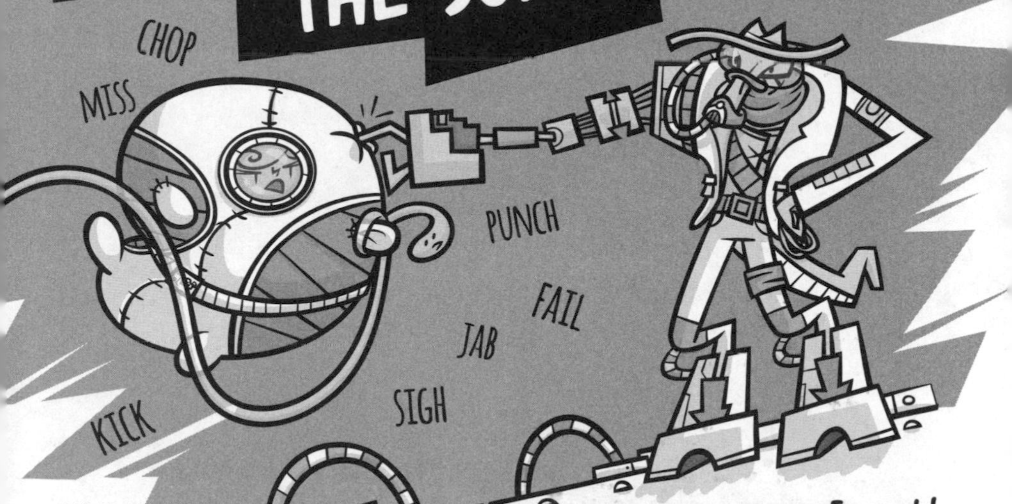
CHOP
MISS
PUNCH
FAIL
JAB
SIGH
KICK
NOPE

Enough! There's **NO WAY** we're winning this fight. We need to peace out! I hit the jets on my suit, hoping we can zoom to a getaway.

But there's a sudden mechanical grinding sound and the wrangler's hand transforms into a jagged sword! I see a silvery flash and the glint of metal as the blade slices through the air, and then . . .

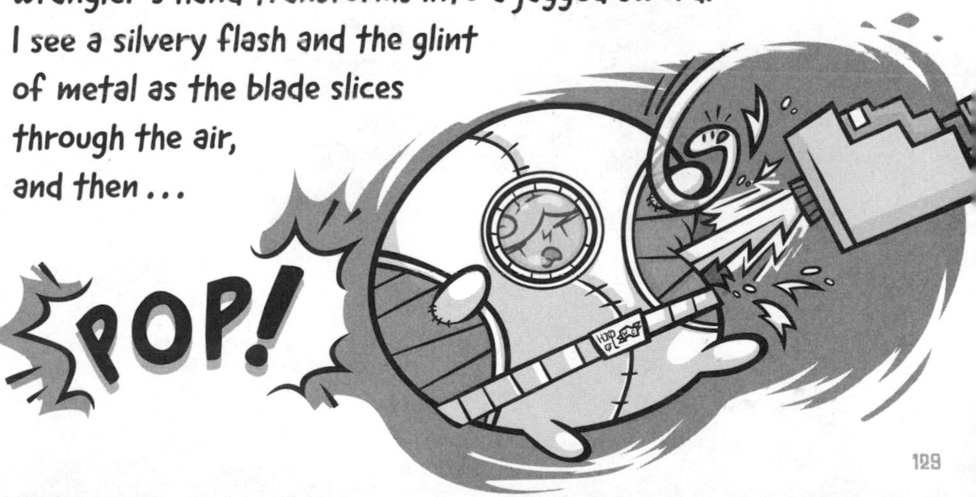
POP!

The wrangler snatches hold of Dagger, lifting her into the air. "UNHAND ME!" she hollers. "UNHAND ME THIS INSTANT!"

The wrangler's masked head cocks to the side. His eyes flash—a burst of cruel darkness. "If you insist, Princess . . ."

And then—staring at me,
beady eyes boring holes
into my brain—
he lets go.

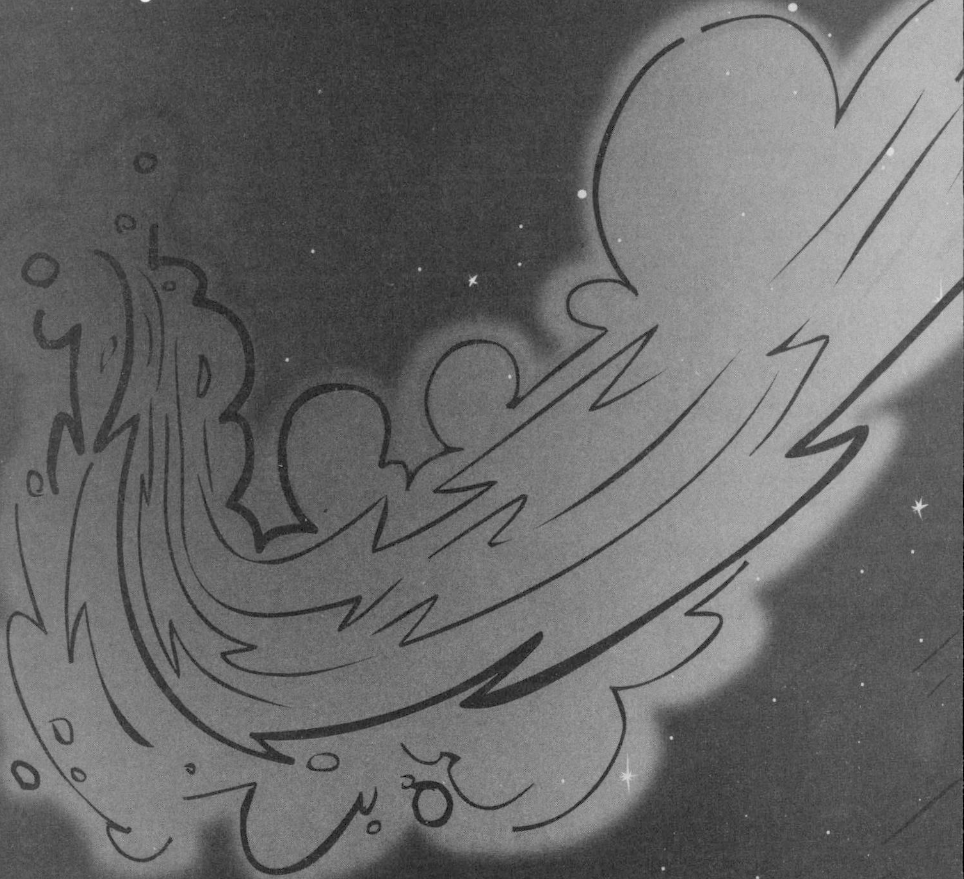

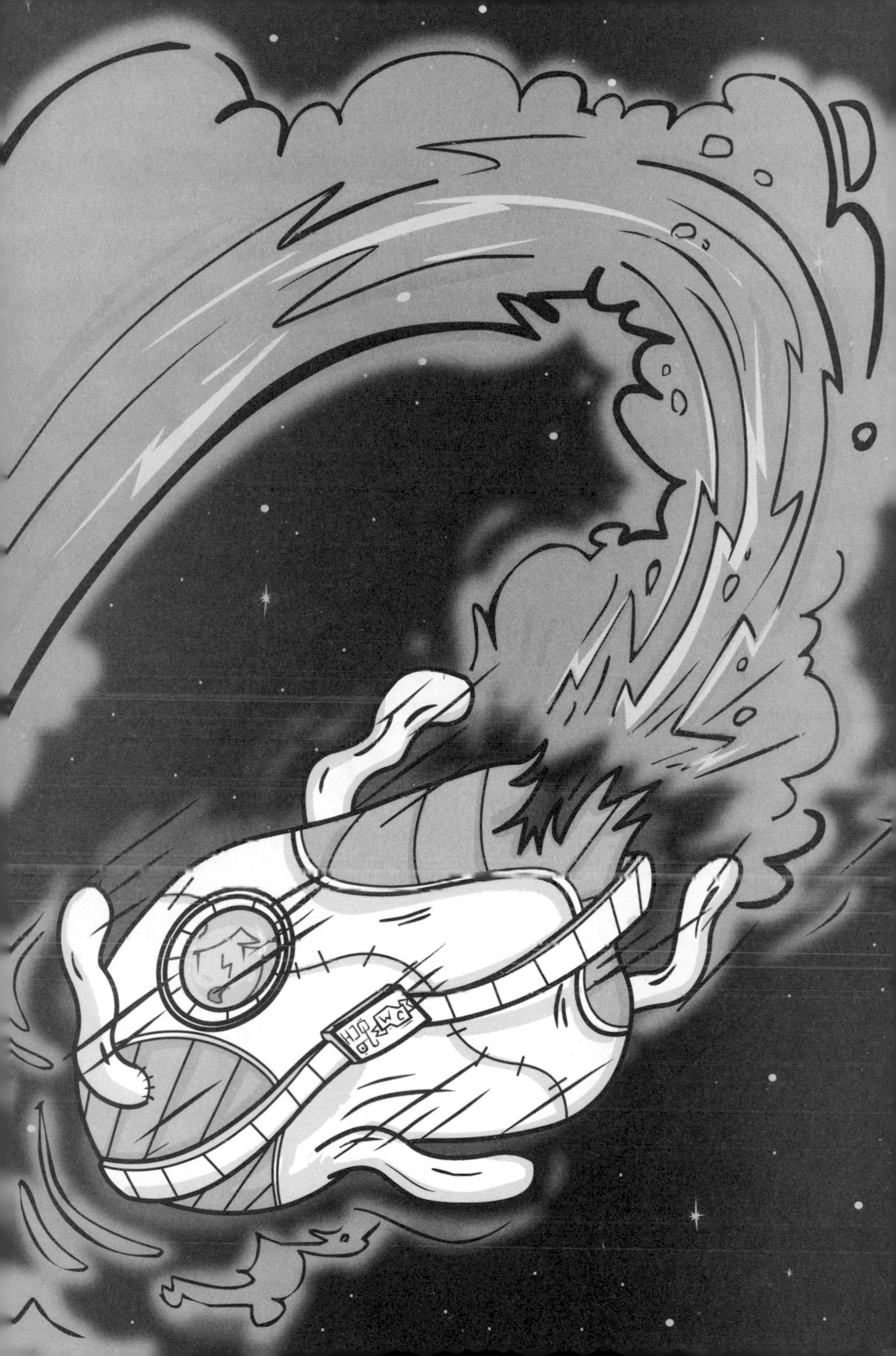
WC

ANGRY REVENGE MOLDY PIZZA

14

I'm stunned to the point of paralysis. I grip the speeding train, Goober whips about, but I'm completely frozen.

DAGS . . .

She had no control. She had no jetpack. She was just like a big balloon, bobbing along with my help. And then the wrangler POPPED that balloon. She's in **SUPREME PERIL!**

I've never felt such fury. My brain is like a frantic tornado of frappin' furious thoughts. And **TWO THOUGHTS** are bigger than the rest:

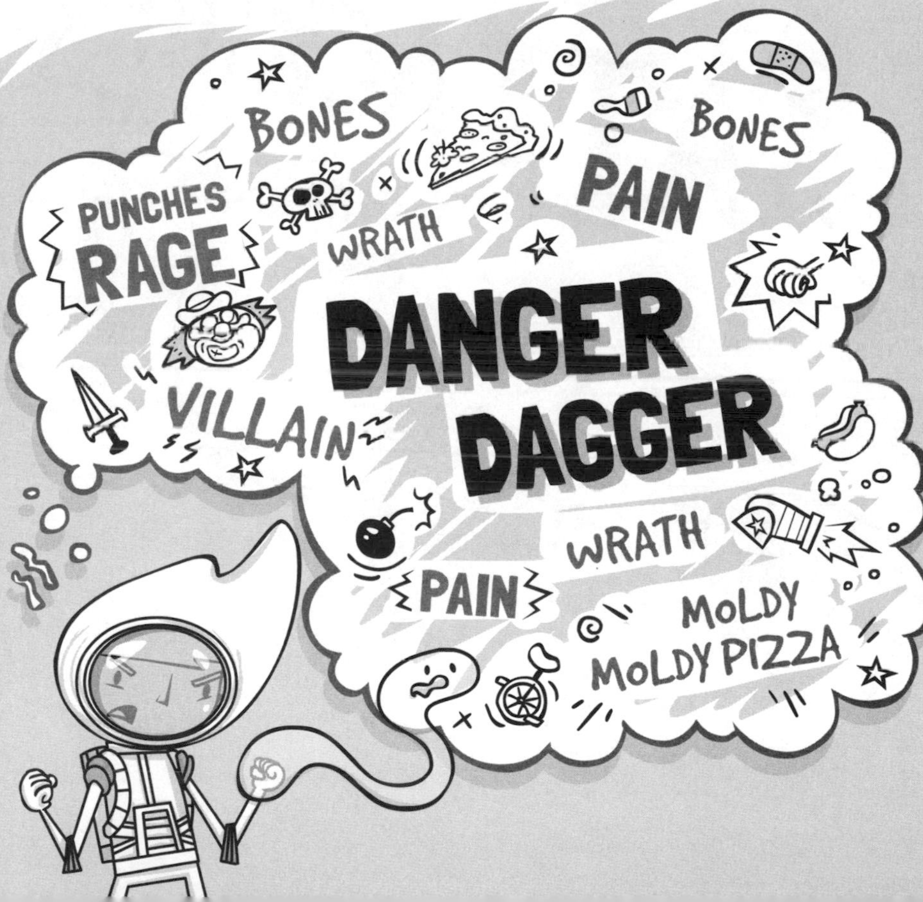

BONES
BONES
PUNCHES
RAGE
PAIN
WRATH
DANGER
DAGGER
VILLAIN
WRATH
PAIN
MOLDY
MOLDY PIZZA

I need to act with quickness. I can't get past the wrangler—the hulking villain blocks the way. There's only one way I can catch up to Dagger and save her: I need to knock this big baddie right off his feet.

I grit my teeth, ball my fists, summon up all my fury, and unleash a devastating . . .

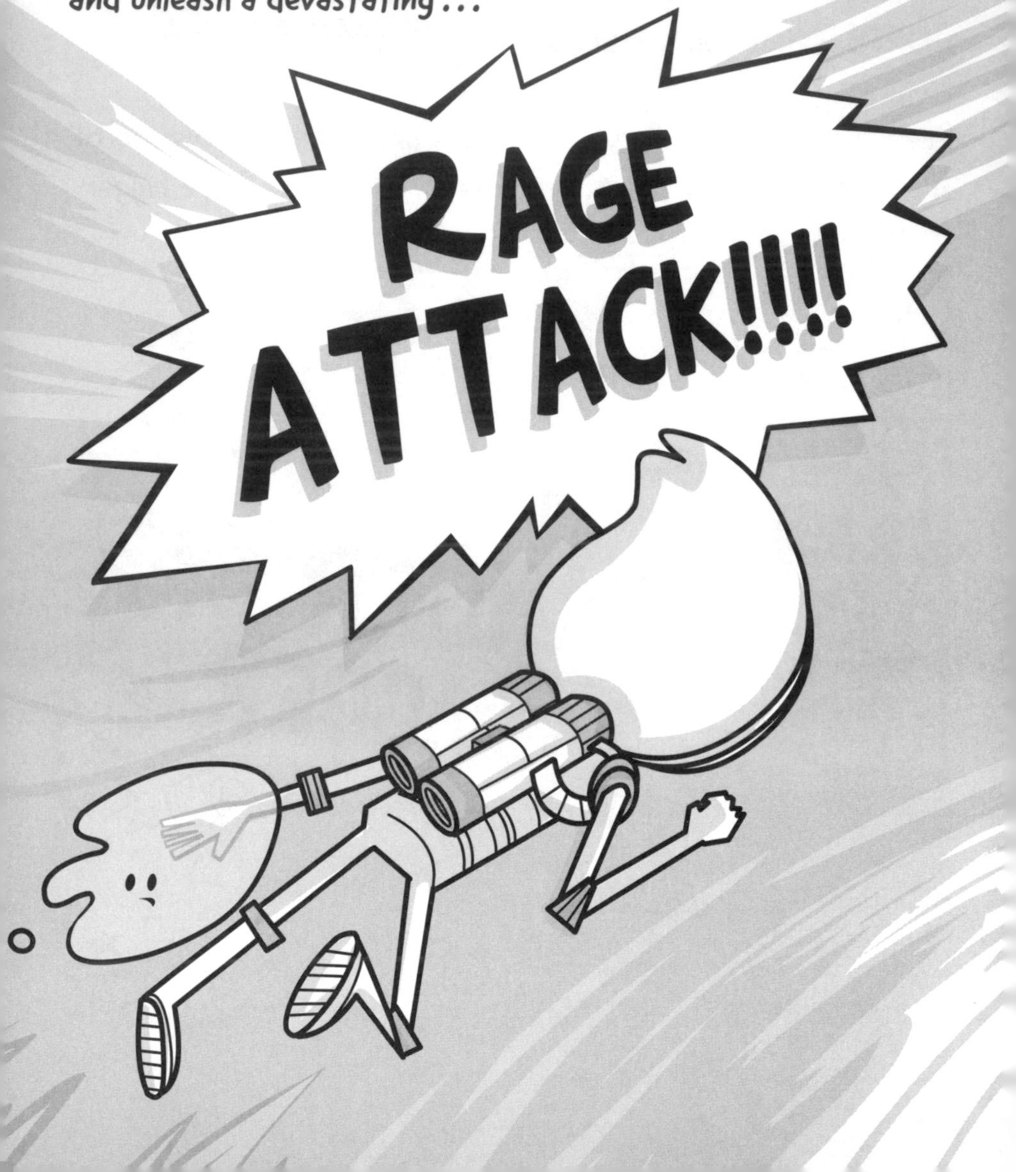
RAGE ATTACK!!!!!

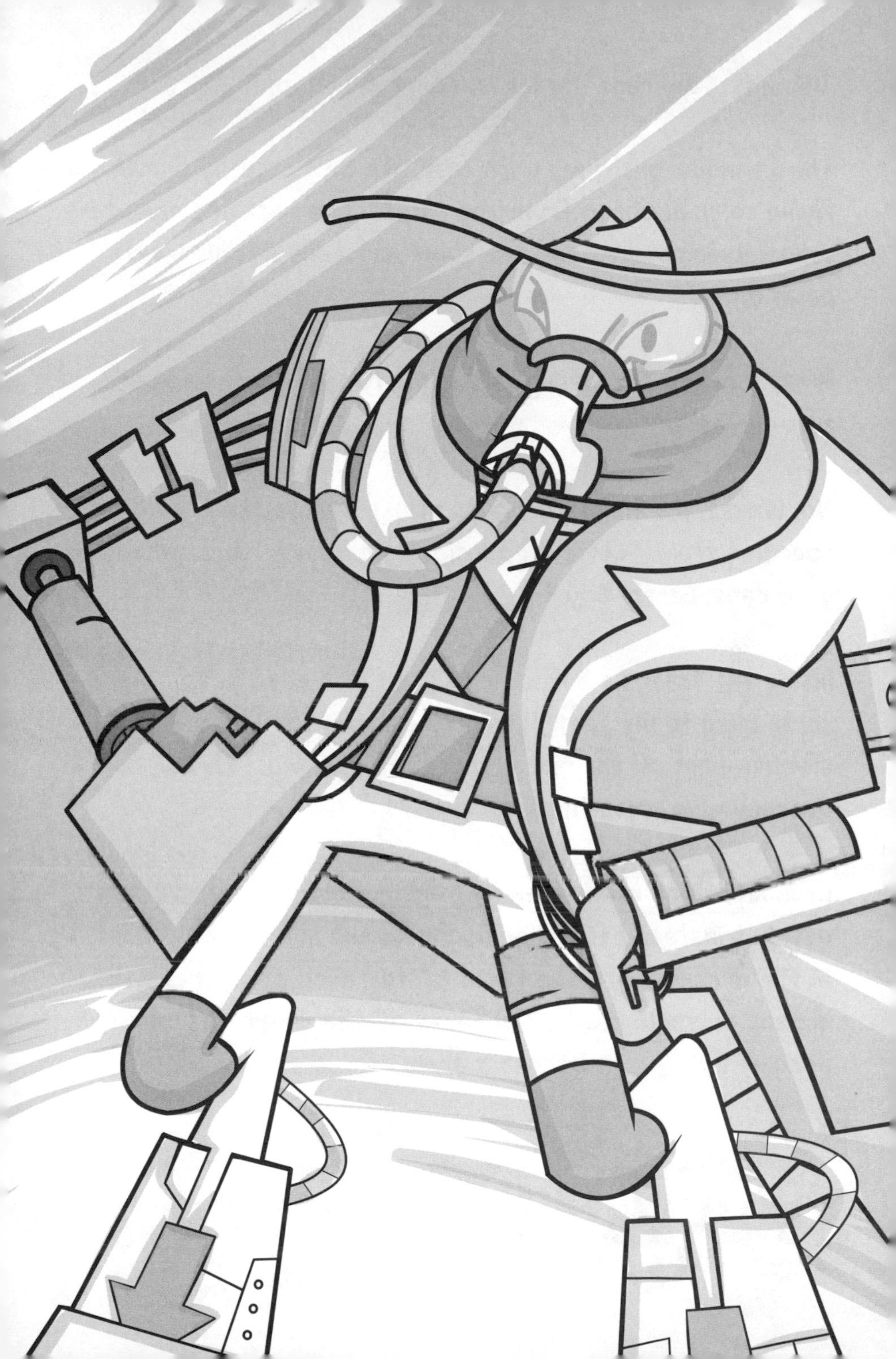

Annnnd . . . my rage attack is a big **FAT** flop.

The wrangler grabs me with ease, like he's casually plucking a flying solar discaroo from the air. It's like back in elementary school, being picked on—like some jerk bully has his meaty paws on me.

What's next? The wrangler's going to stuff me inside a zero-G locker?

No. Worse. His magnetic boots stomp across the roof of the speeding train. "Let's step inside," he hisses. "And get you in your cage, Earth-Boy."

Inside the train, he hurls me to the floor. But I'm up, scrambling to my feet, trying to escape. The lights from the electro-bars on the blaze-cages are blinding. I throw an arm over my eyes, squinting.

I run left, then right, then left again. I'm looking for a way out, but instead I find a midnight-movie horror show! Glowing in the darkness are the faces of terrified creatures with gizmos on their heads. The faces of the creatures who will become Evil Queen Dagger's army of . . .

MUTATED MONSTERS!

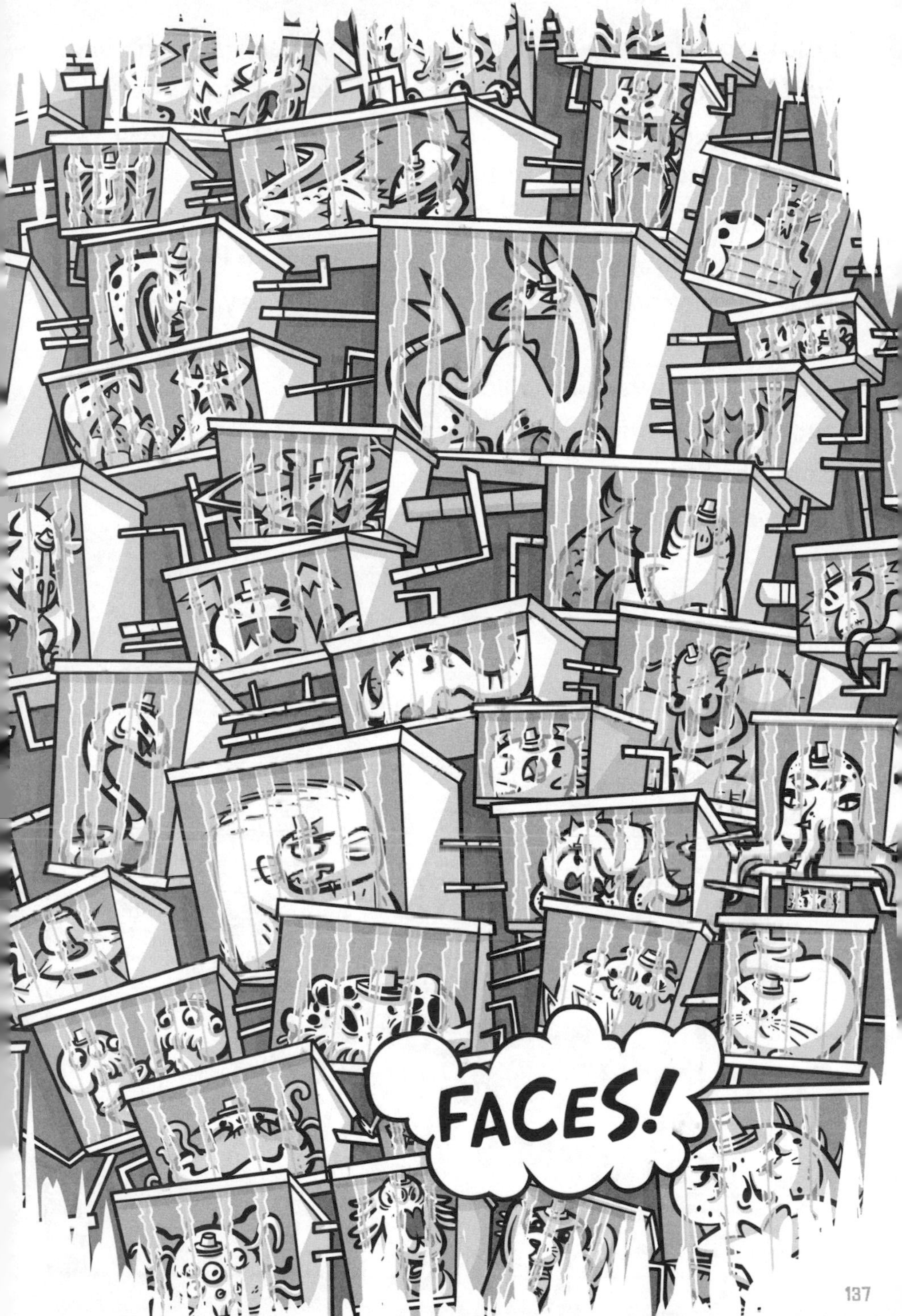
FACES!

I race around a cage holding a winged gozarian, then trip and tumble right into the arms of Crostini. He chuckles cruelly. "Cosmoe, why did you have to be so inquisitive? We could have made so much money together . . ."

I flick the visor on my space suit. It retracts so I'm face-to-face with the villain. "Keep your money," I growl.

Suddenly, the wrangler whips me around and stuffs me into an open blaze-cage. The bars slam shut, then hum with laser static.

"Now," Crostini says, with an especially sinister smile, "it's time to go find your oversized friend."

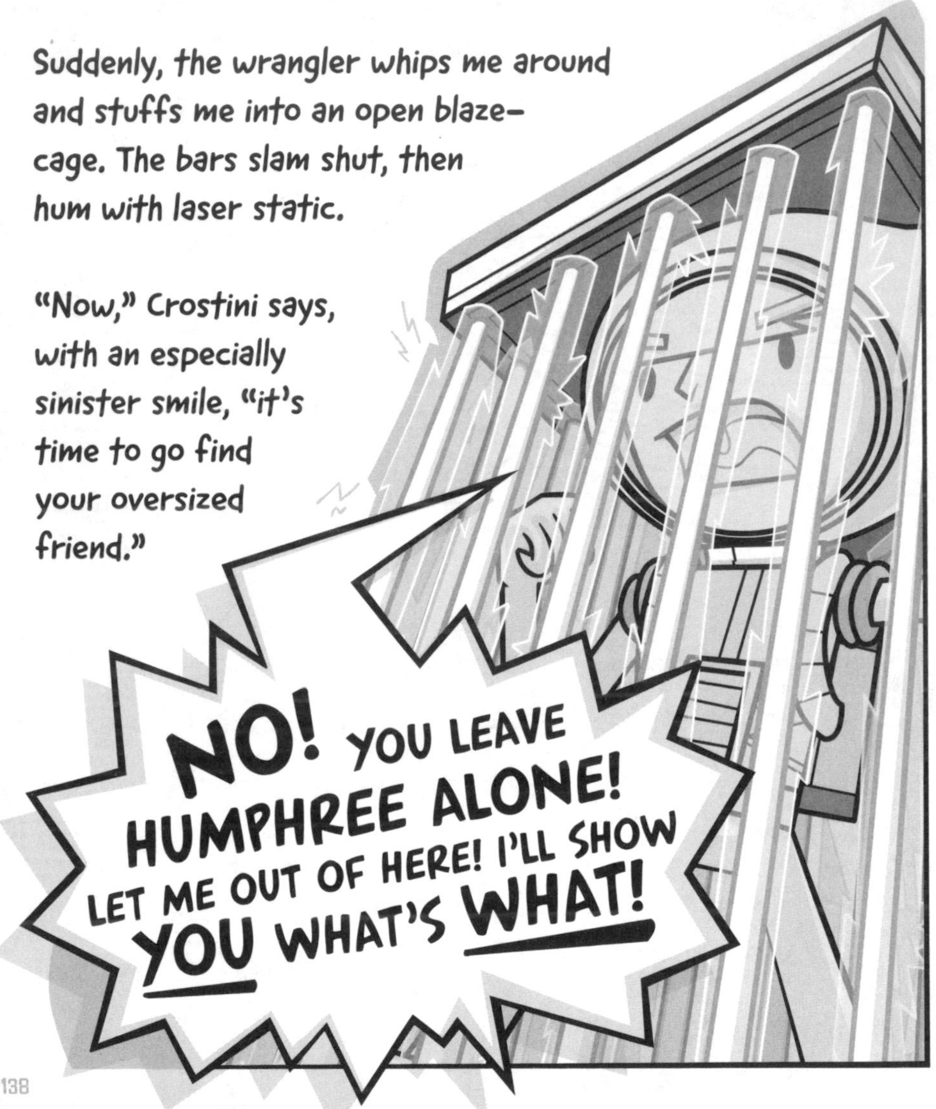
NO! YOU LEAVE HUMPHREE ALONE!
LET ME OUT OF HERE! I'LL SHOW YOU WHAT'S WHAT!

So things are, like, really bad right now, huh? I ignored Humphree when he said there was something hinky about Crostini and the wrangler. I ignored my own gut, which told me the circus was straight-up terrible. I ignored Dagger when—well, I kind of always ignore Dagger, but whatever . . .

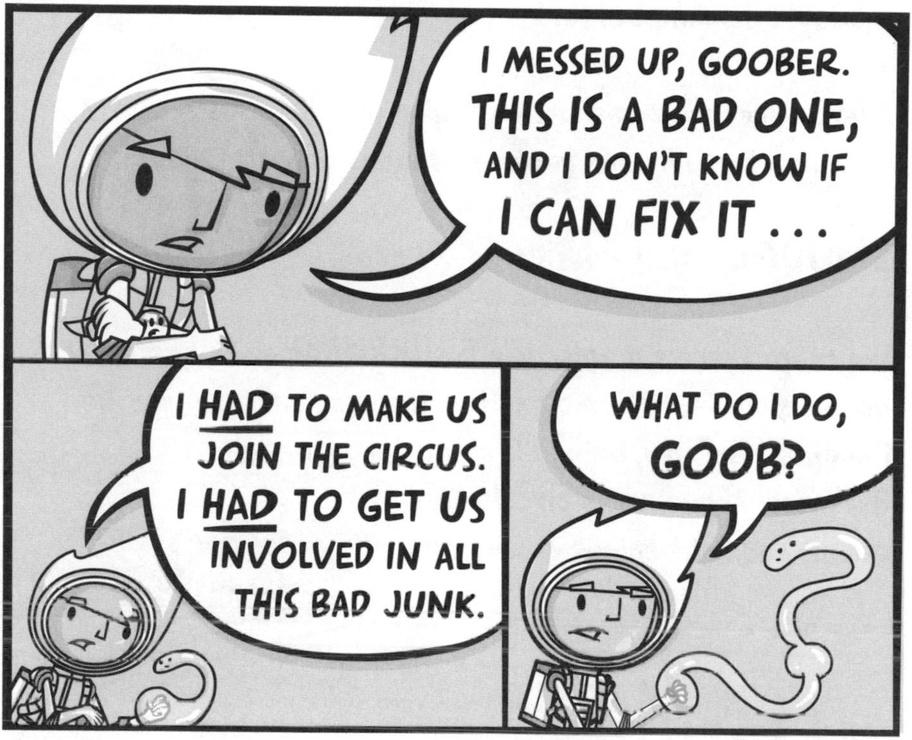
I MESSED UP, GOOBER.
THIS IS A BAD ONE, AND I DON'T KNOW IF I CAN FIX IT . . .
I HAD TO MAKE US JOIN THE CIRCUS. I HAD TO GET US INVOLVED IN ALL THIS BAD JUNK.
WHAT DO I DO, GOOB?

"A question mark . . ." I sigh. "Great. A lot of help you are."

I'm sick with fear and choked by worry. All I can do is shut my eyes. The strange snoozing snores of a thousand astounding creatures surround me.

And soon, I'm snoozing right along with them.

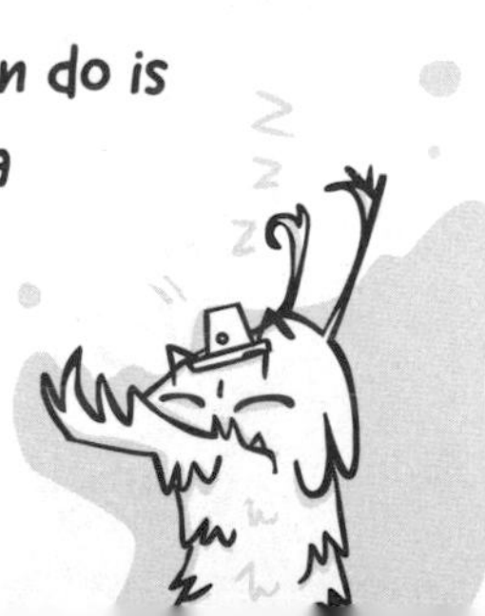
Z
Z
Z

I'm jostled awake. The blaze-cage is on the move. Someone's dragging it. It's pitch-black—can't see anything. I hear distant voices. A vast crowd somewhere. The smell is different now: damp. We've landed.

"Hey, I'm a **MONSTER-TAMER!**" I bark. "This treatment is shoddy! I demand better!"

A voice I recognize as the wrangler says, "This is the last treatment you'll ever receive—shoddy or not. Enjoy it."

SMUDGE. That doesn't sound good.

We stop. There's a noise like **BRRRRUMP**, and my stomach does a slow flip. I'm moving up. The cage falls around me. I'm on a platform, being lifted up through the darkness. Above me, a circular hole opens, and light shines down.

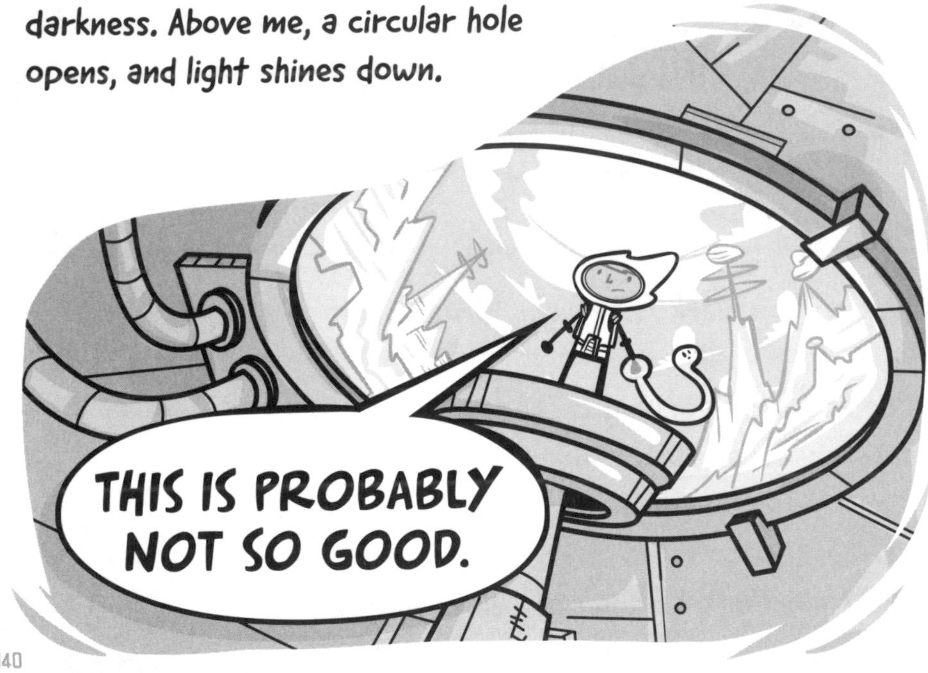
THIS IS PROBABLY NOT SO GOOD.

I rise up through the ground. It takes a second for my eyes to adjust—coming out of that darkness, it's blindingly bright, like I'm staring at a double sun.

I blink away the sunspots and take in my surroundings. I'm in some sort of rocky arena. It's a small canyon, surrounded by tall jagged rocks, like stone walls. Perched on the rocks are hundreds of roust-a-bots and clown-bots. High-pitched hisses and battery-operated boos fill my ears.

This is bad. Real bad. What are they going to do? Feed me to some beastly behemoth? A six-footed ooze demon? I've never seen one, but Humphree once fought one and said they are **FOUL.**

I **COULD** just fly out of here. I mean, I am still wearing my jetsuit. But Crostini knows that. He could have taken it from me, but he didn't. Why?

Suddenly, Crostini's voice booms. He's on the highest rock, forty feet up, looking down like some sort of Roman emperor watching a gladiator duel. The wrangler stands beside him—the classic savage sidekick. I want nothing more than to wipe the ground with these weasels.

Crostini spreads his arms and bellows, "Welcome to planet Rocc, Cosmoe the Monster-Tamer! We've seen you battle the deadly **SKORLAX!** We've seen you tame the wild **LYANUX!** But how will you fare against a . . ."

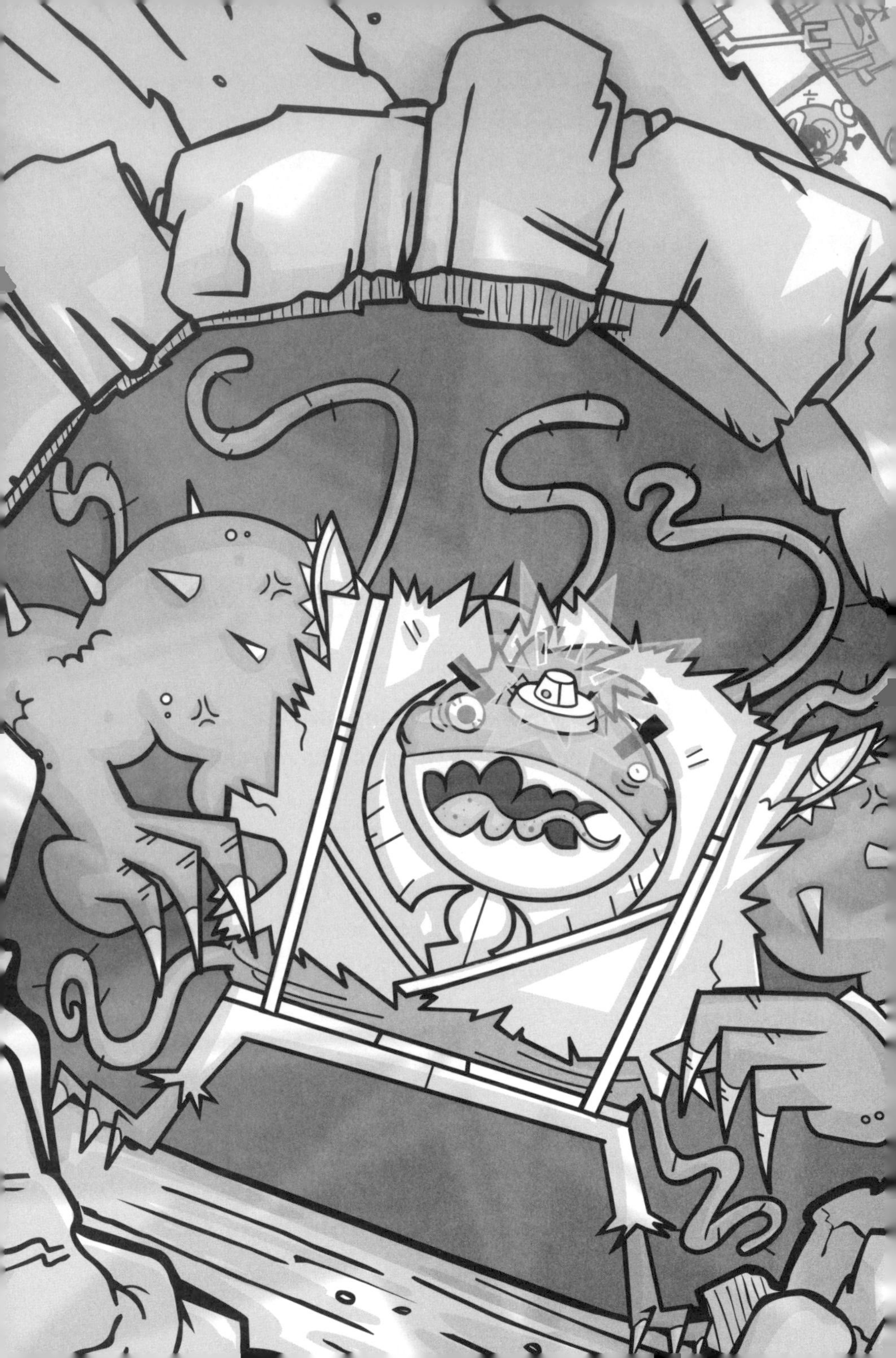

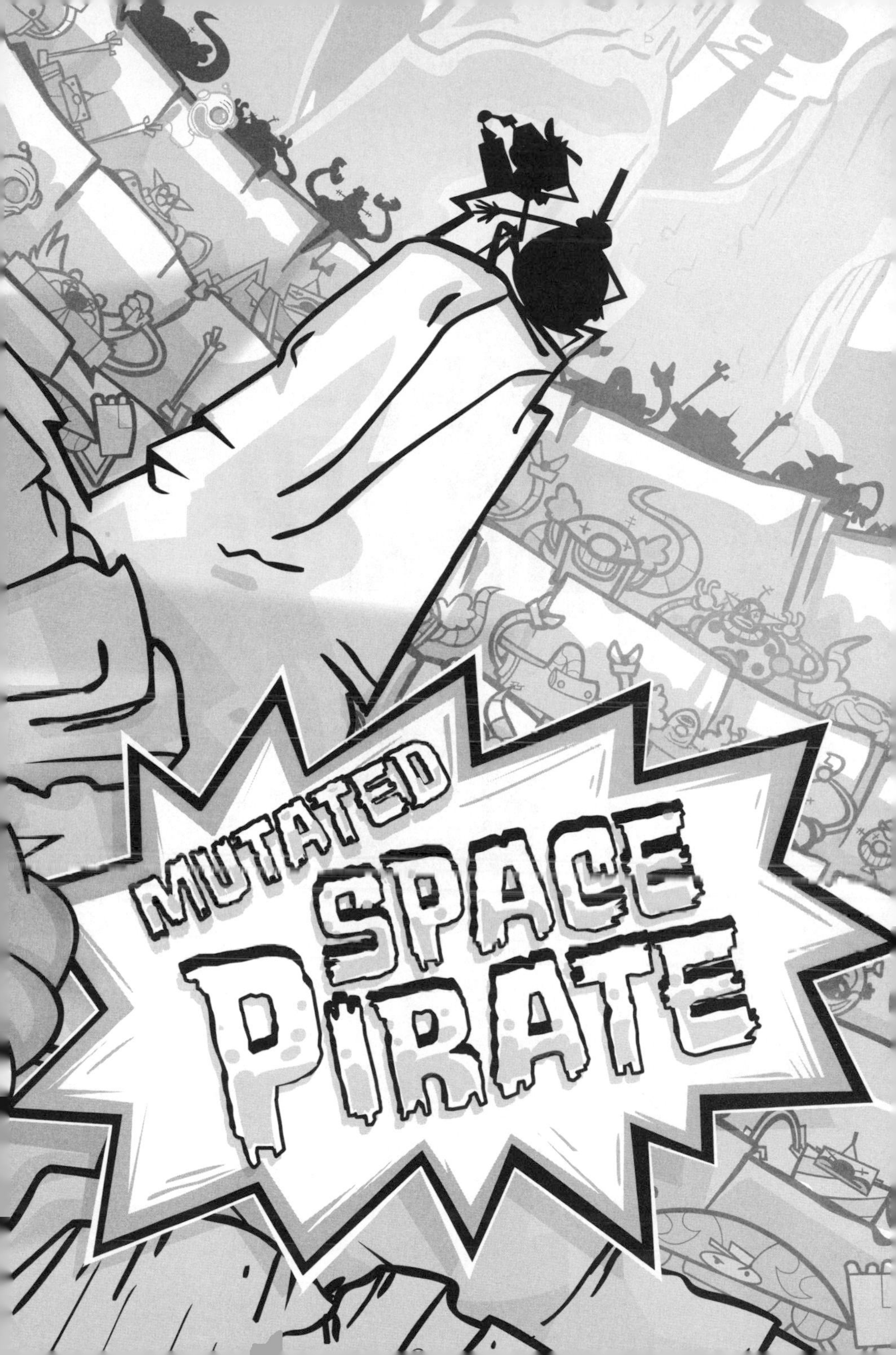
MUTATED
SPACE
PIRATE

DARK-HEARTED HUMPHREE

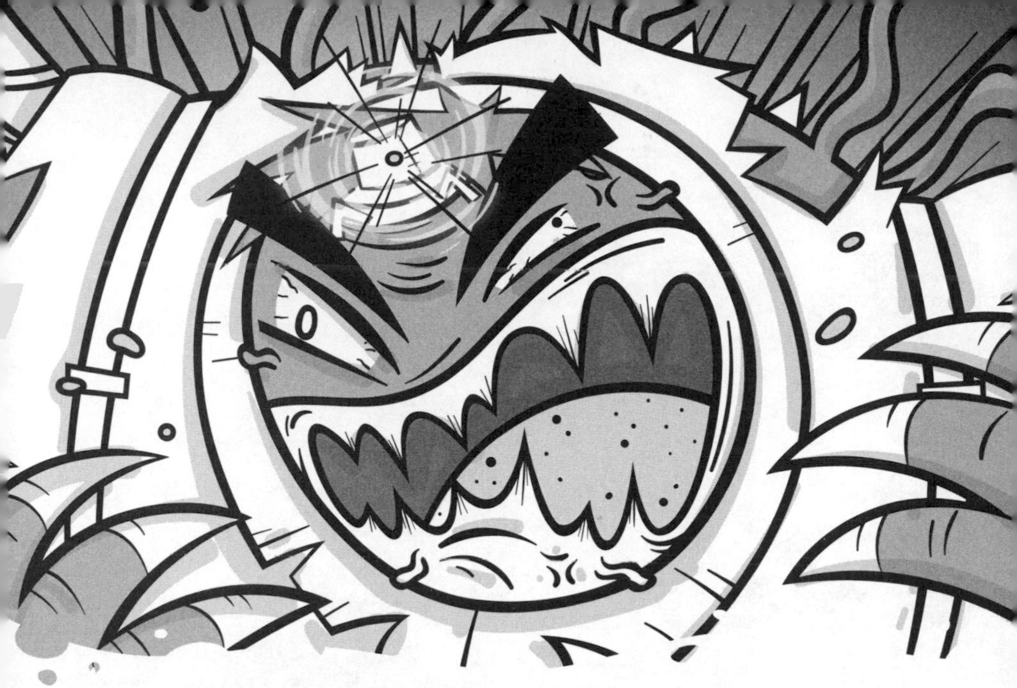

My stomach flips. Crostini slapped one of those gizmos onto my best friend's head! I have no words . . .

I'm hoping that, y'know, FRIENDSHIP WILL OVERCOME!

Because that's what happens, right? Friendship solves everything! Humphree will look inside his heart of hearts and see that he's **NOT** an evil energy monster. He's my best bud.

I stare into his eyes. He twitches. His huge shoulder jerks to the side. And then he's barreling toward me like a force of frapping nature!

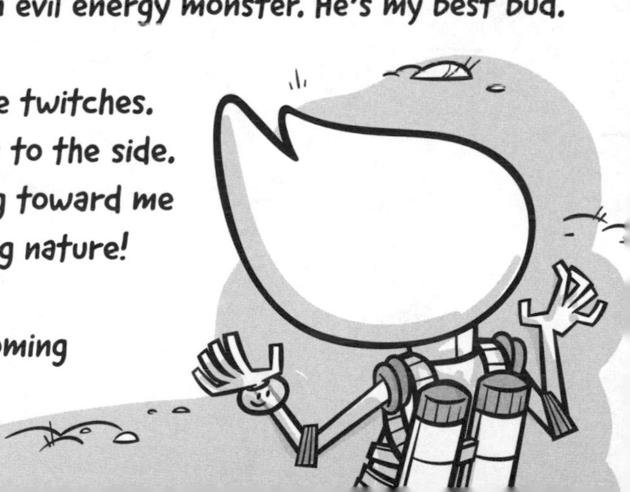

Friendship isn't overcoming squat right now . . .

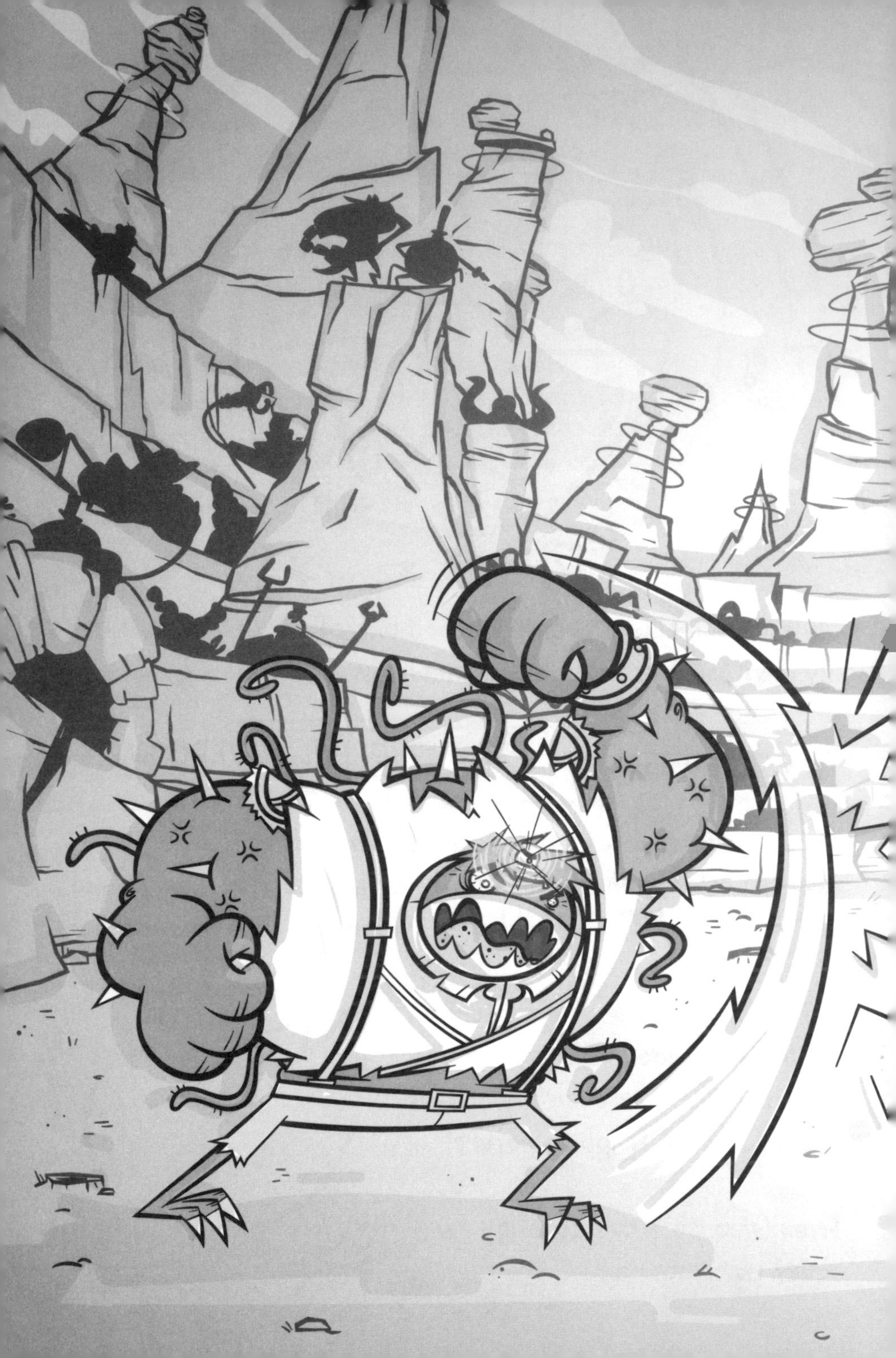

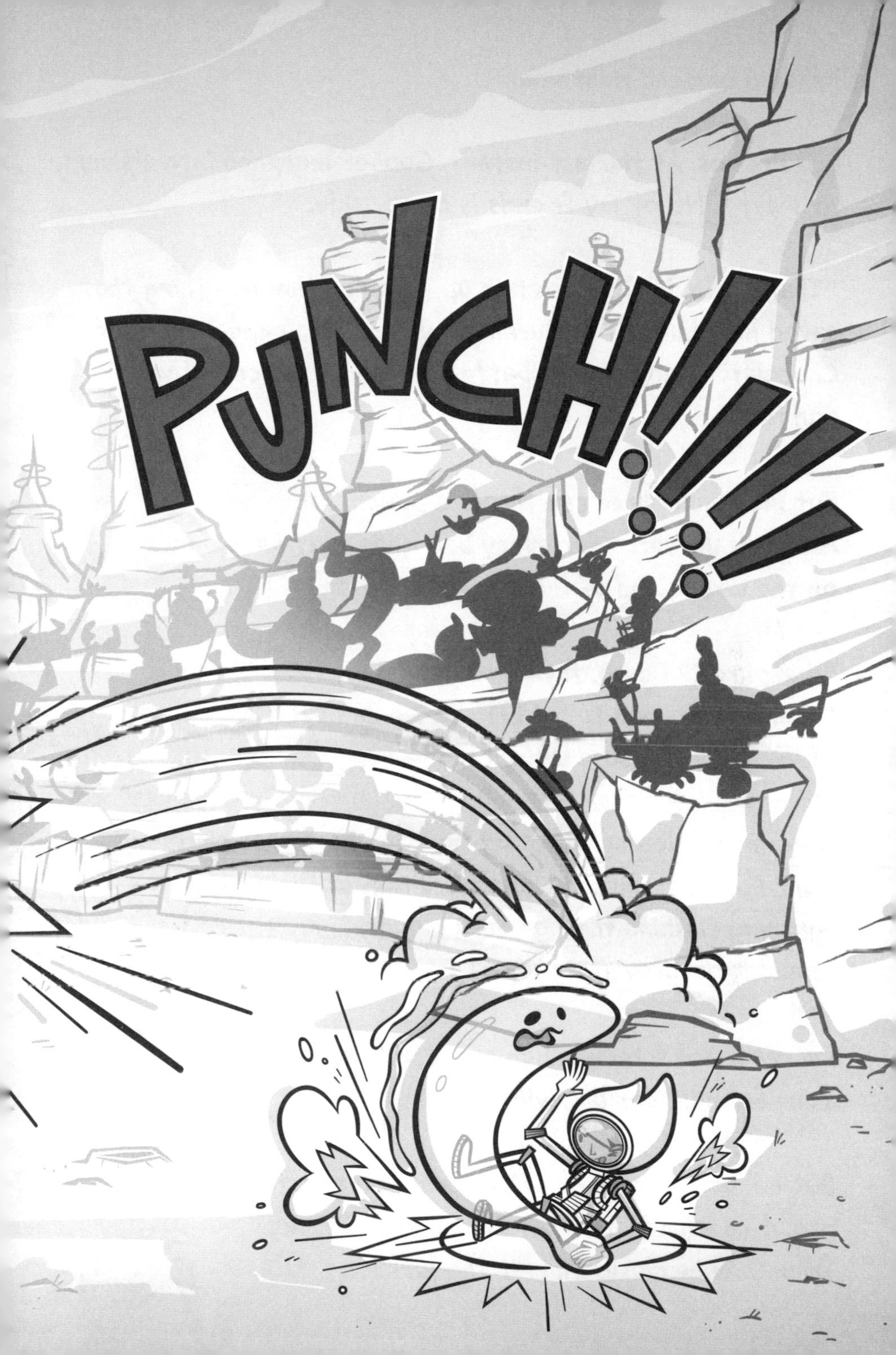
PUNCH!!!!

I should be dead right now.

But I'm not. At the last instant, Goober morphed into a shield. At least ONE of my friends is on my side.

"Thanks, Goob," I say, sitting up. "You're the only thing that saved Humphree from turning my face into pancake batter. Chocolate-chip pancake batter, if I had a choice in the matter . . ."

But man, Humphree can throw a punch. I suddenly feel really, really sorry for every bad dude that wound up on the wrong end of Hump's furious fist.

"Humphree," I gasp, trying to get to my feet. "It's me. Cosmoe. You need to **STOP** so we can **WORK TOGETHER** because **DAGGER IS—**"

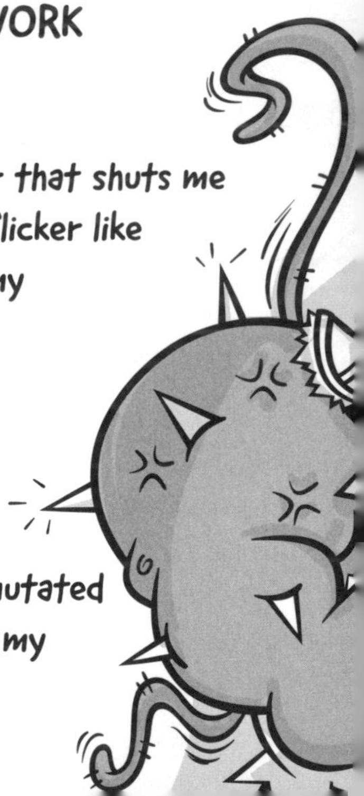

Humphree unleashes a planet-quaking roar that shuts me right up. He stomps toward me. His eyes flicker like lightning flashing through dark clouds. Is my friend lost forever in there?!

I scream and scream. "Humphree, it's me! Your friend! Your buddy!"

But he just charges forward, emitting a mutated growl—a sound that I barely recognize as my friend. As he closes in, I hit the jets . . .

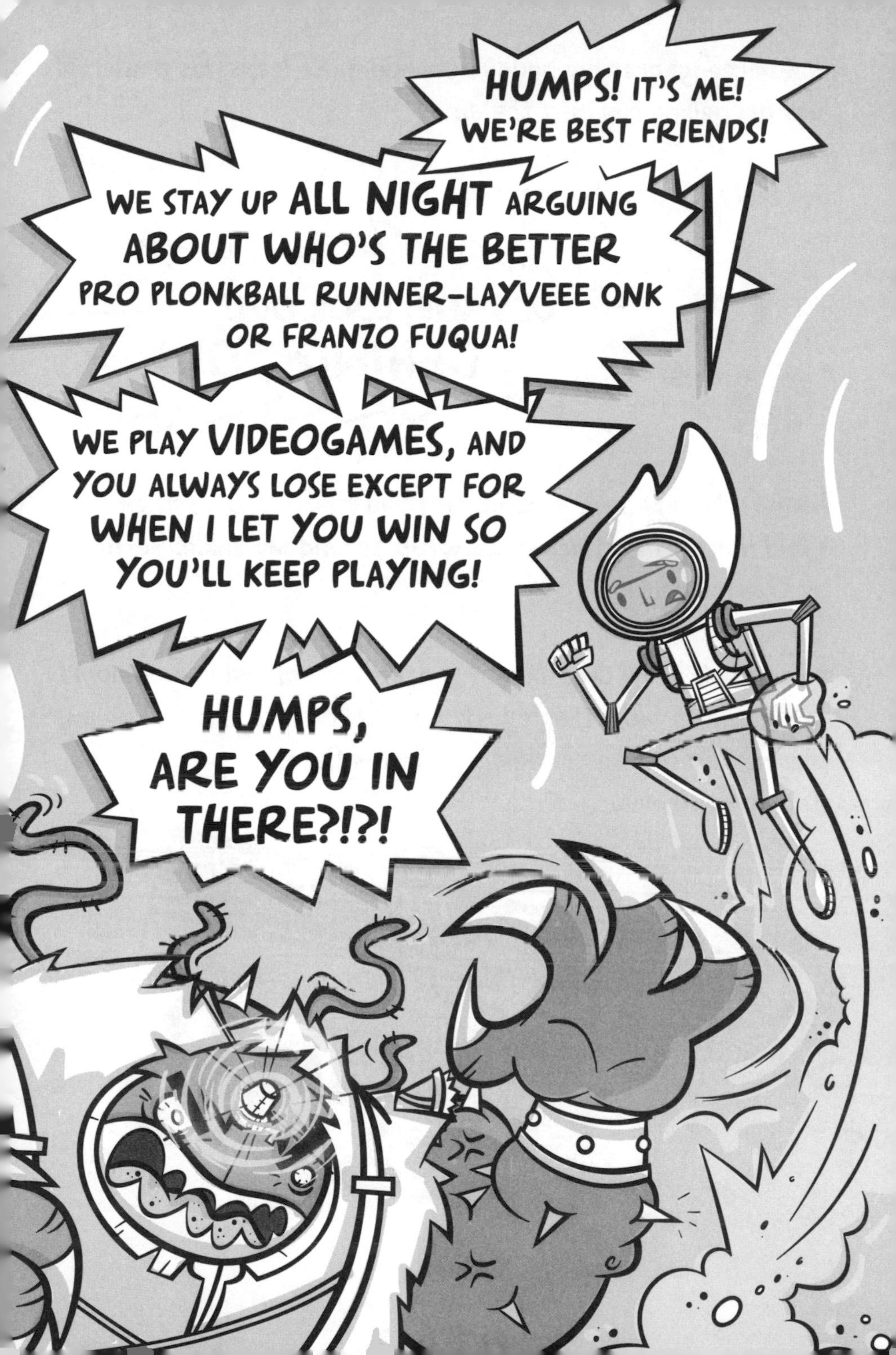
HUMPS! IT'S ME! WE'RE BEST FRIENDS!
WE STAY UP ALL NIGHT ARGUING ABOUT WHO'S THE BETTER PRO PLONKBALL RUNNER–LAYVEEE ONK OR FRANZO FUQUA!
WE PLAY VIDEOGAMES, AND YOU ALWAYS LOSE EXCEPT FOR WHEN I LET YOU WIN SO YOU'LL KEEP PLAYING!
HUMPS, ARE YOU IN THERE?!?!

Humphree ignores my buddy reminders. He leaps, his powerful legs propelling him into the air.

Suddenly, Crostini hollers,

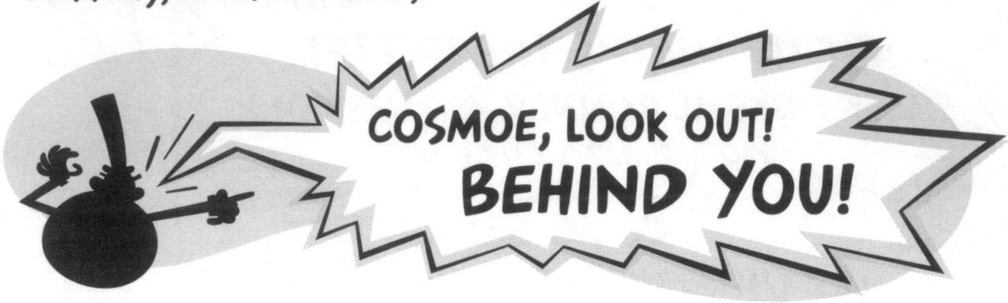
COSMOE, LOOK OUT!
BEHIND YOU!

Huh? I whip my head around. Nothing there . . . Just then I feel Humphree's thick paws wrap around my ankle. He tugs as Crostini cackles.

I can't believe it! Crostini got me with the ol' made-you-look! trick. That's BAD. That's just plain EMBARRASSING. I mean, please, just revoke my Galactic Action Hero ID card right now.

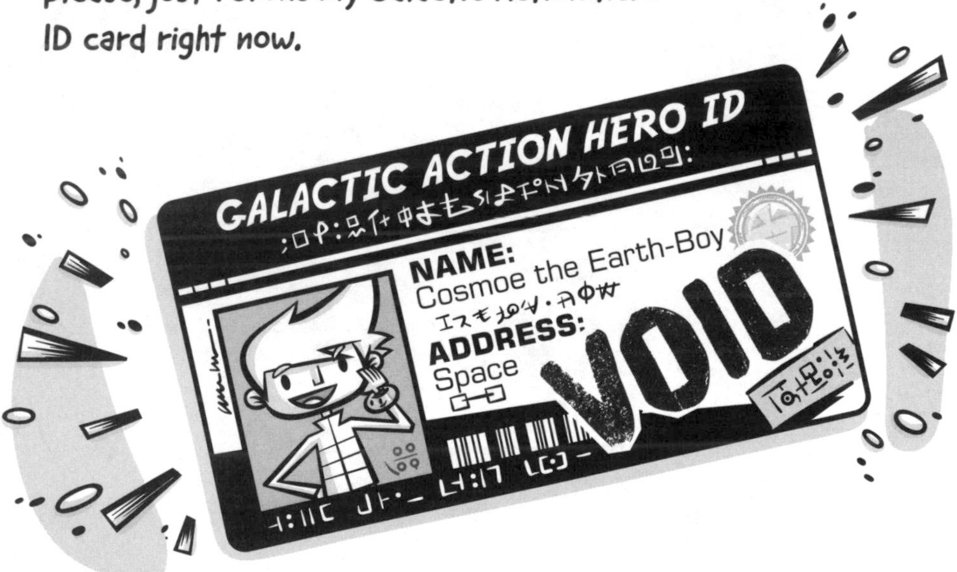
GALACTIC ACTION HERO ID
NAME:
Cosmoe the Earth-Boy
ADDRESS:
Space
VOID

Humphree yanks my leg, jerking me closer. My jetpack howls, kicking up dirt and sand.

"Please, Humphree," I say, practically begging. "It's me, short pants? You call me that—short pants. I don't know why. I guess because my pants are shorter than yours? Which is weird . . . But really you call me that because it's a nickname and best friends give their best friends nicknames! And I'm your best friend!"

Humphree grunts.

"Humps. Just, please, don't . . ."

He does.

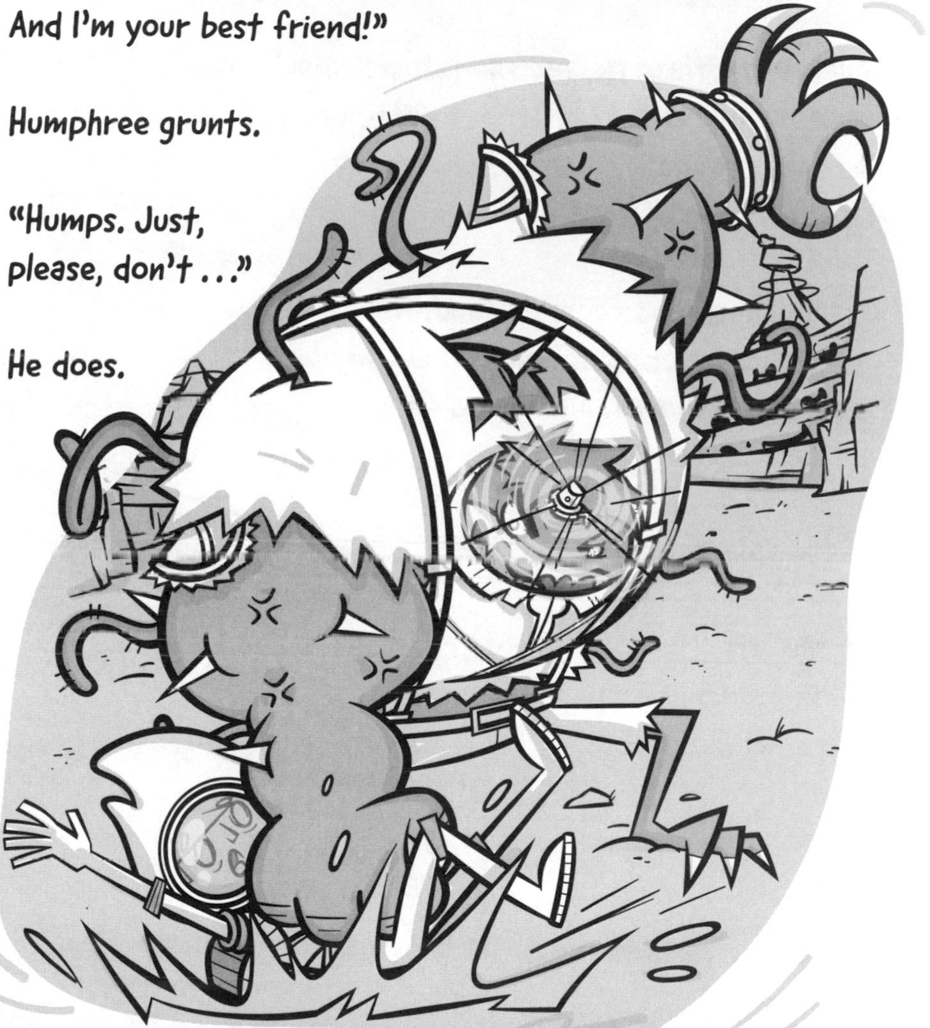

My mouth emits a strange, foreign gurgling sound. Humphree may have broken my insides. My jetsuit is slightly armored and gives me a tiny bit of protection, but really, trust me, **IT AIN'T MUCH.**

And the fun's not over.

Humphree raises one colossal foot, ready to squash me.

I squeeze the throttle and the jetpack sparks and spits fire just as Humphree **STOMPS.** I skitter and bounce across the rocky ground. The crowd cheers my near-death experience.

I arch my head and zoom upward, finally gaining control and hovering in the air. I eye my big buddy. Sorry, Humps, but I need to fight back. An army is being constructed—and I can't stop it if I'm splattered.

I hit the jets, the rockets roar, and I'm suddenly torpedoing toward my monstrous friend . . .

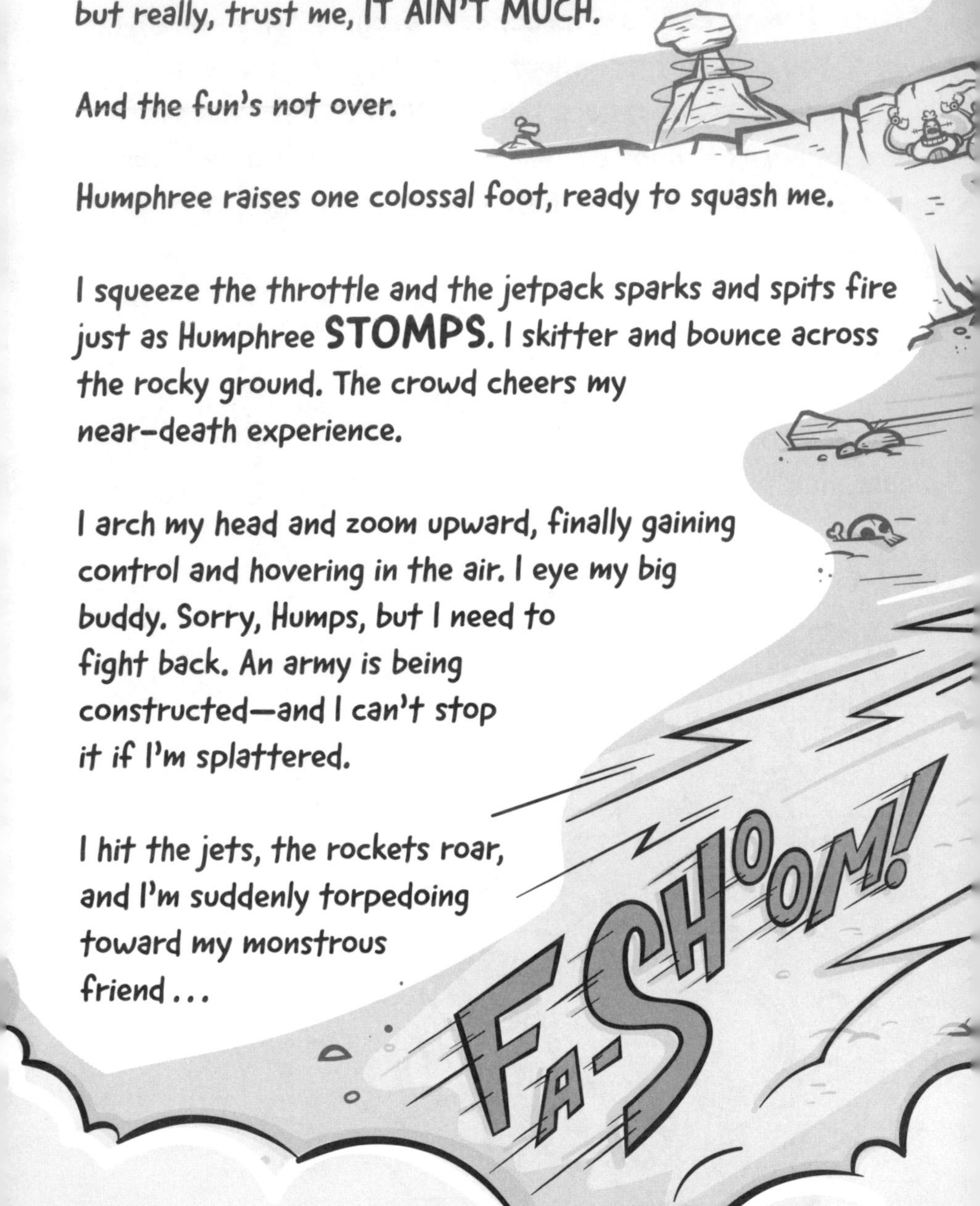
FA-SHOOM!

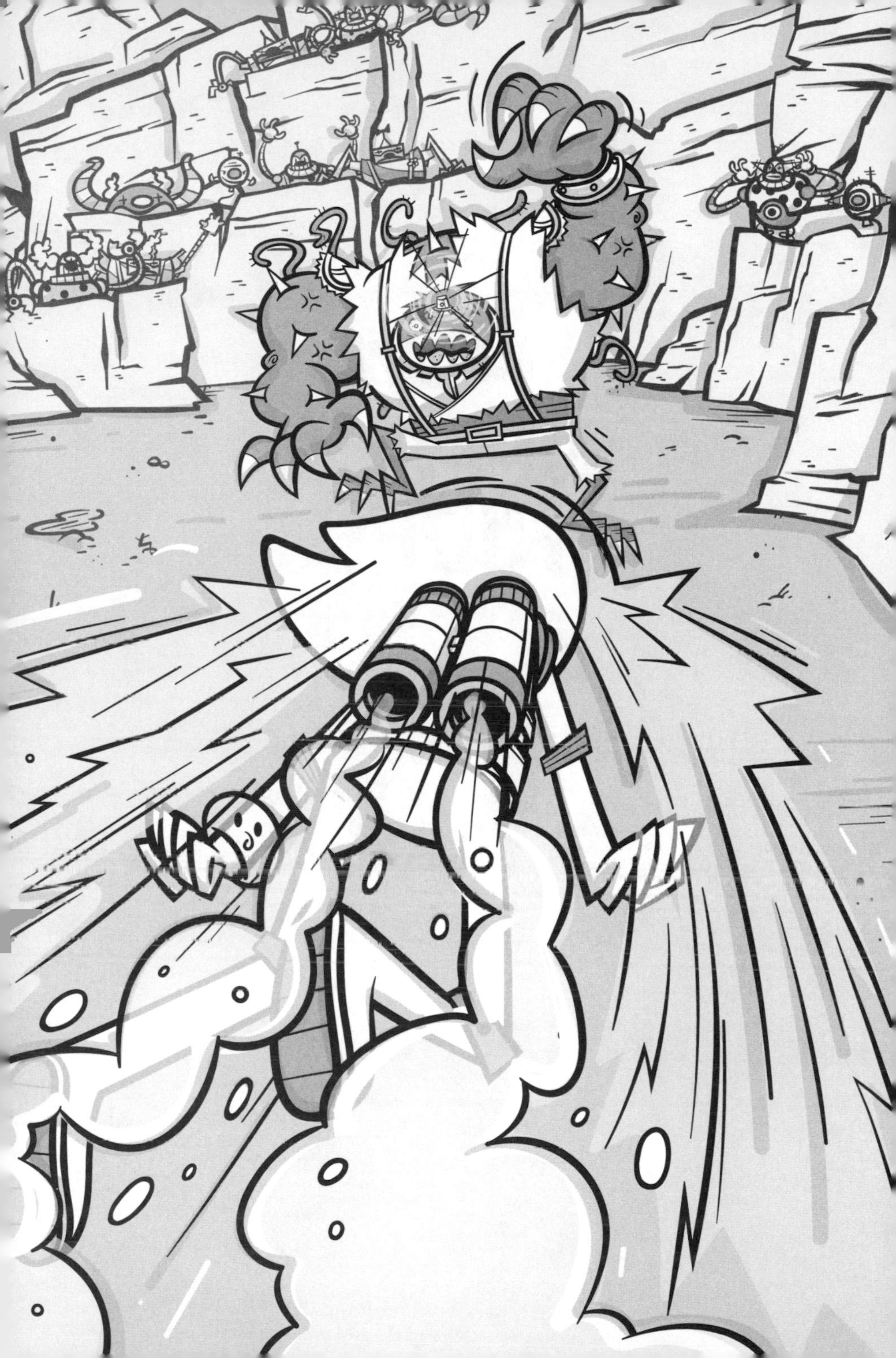

HEY!
NEED A
RIDE?

16

As I rocket forward, Humphree widens his stance. His massive, mutated arms extend and his huge hands open. He's going to squash me like a bug.

But at the last possible instant, I lower my head and . . .

I DIVE!

The jetpack's fire burns hot as I whizz beneath Humphree's legs, twist in the air, and zip up behind him.

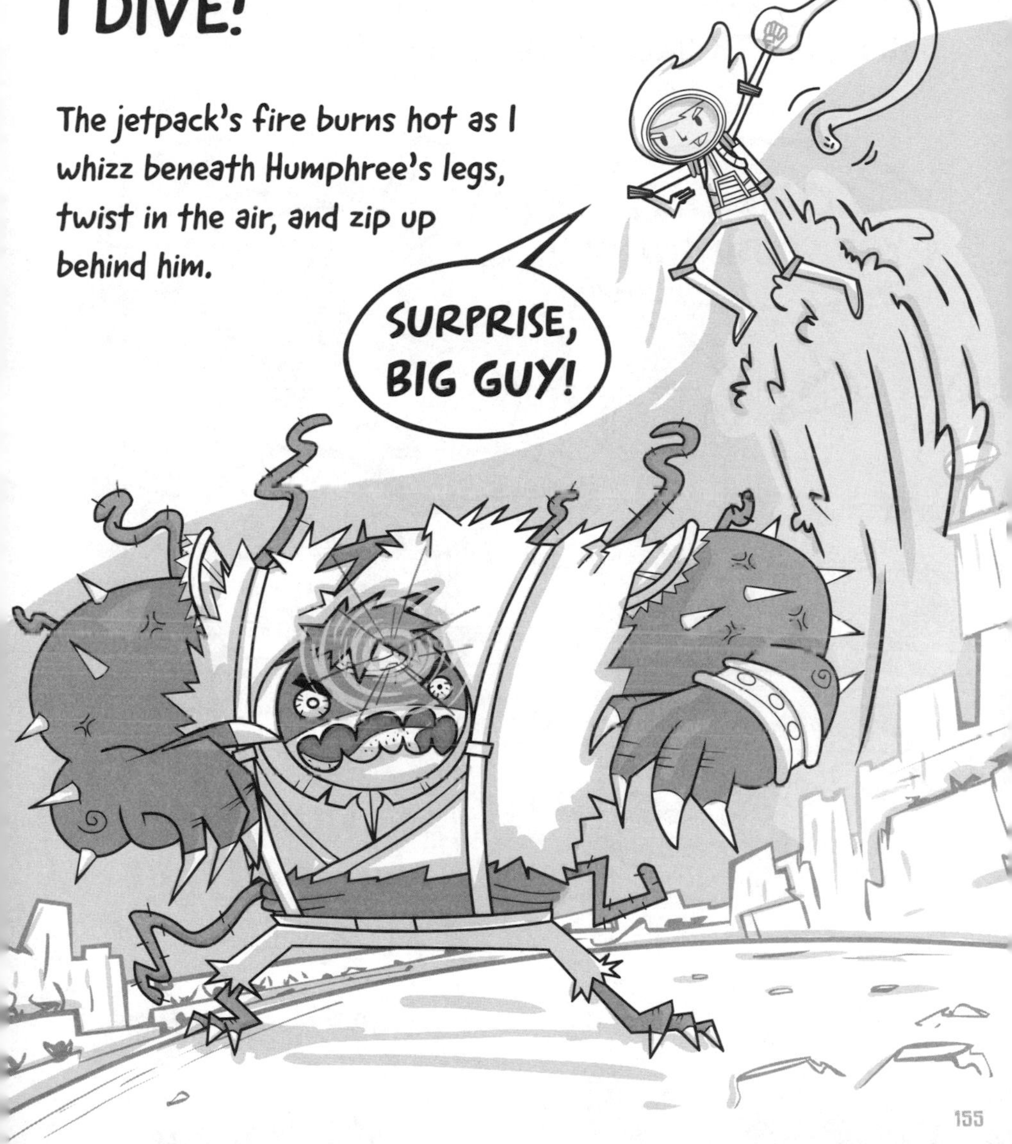
SURPRISE, BIG GUY!

I pound away at the gizmo with a heavy Goober mallet! Soon, the gizmo cracks and sparks. With my other hand, I yank the thing. If I can just get the gizmo off, maybe I can fix my friend . . .

Humphree roars and thrashes. He lands a devastating blow to my chin. My eyes spin. "STOP PUNCHING, YA BIG DUMB BRUTE. I'M TRYING TO **SAVE YOU!**"

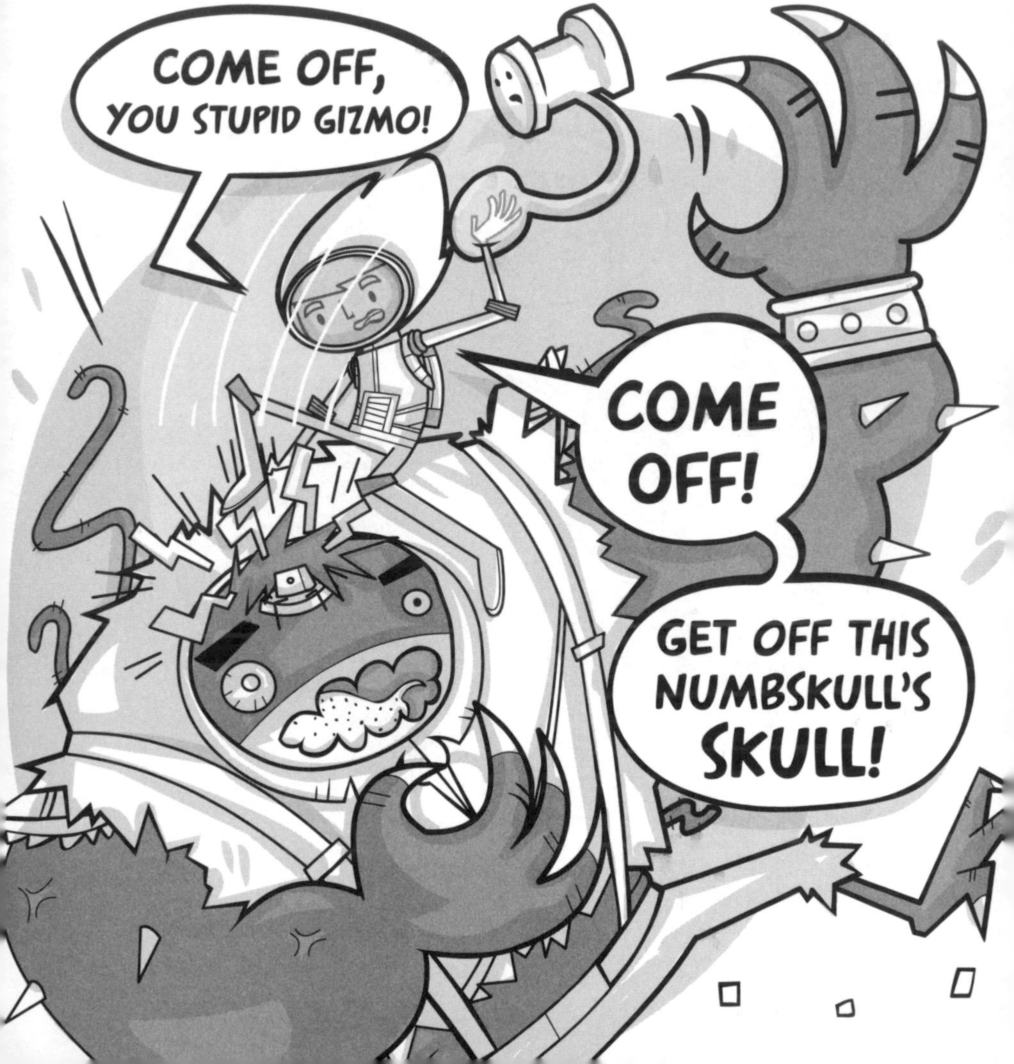
COME OFF, YOU STUPID GIZMO!
COME OFF!
GET OFF THIS NUMBSKULL'S SKULL!

A heavy slap from Humphree's powerful hand causes the jetpack to buzz and spark. His gigantic fingers rip my collar.

GULP.

My fingers graze the gizmo. I grasp for it. But it's too late—Humphree flings me through the air.

KRASH! I careen across the soil like a tiny human tumbleweed. Humphree roars and pounds his chest like King Kong on steroid-Z3.

Crostini calls down, laughing, "You cannot stop him, Earth-Boy!"

I raise my fist. "Hey, Crostini . . ."

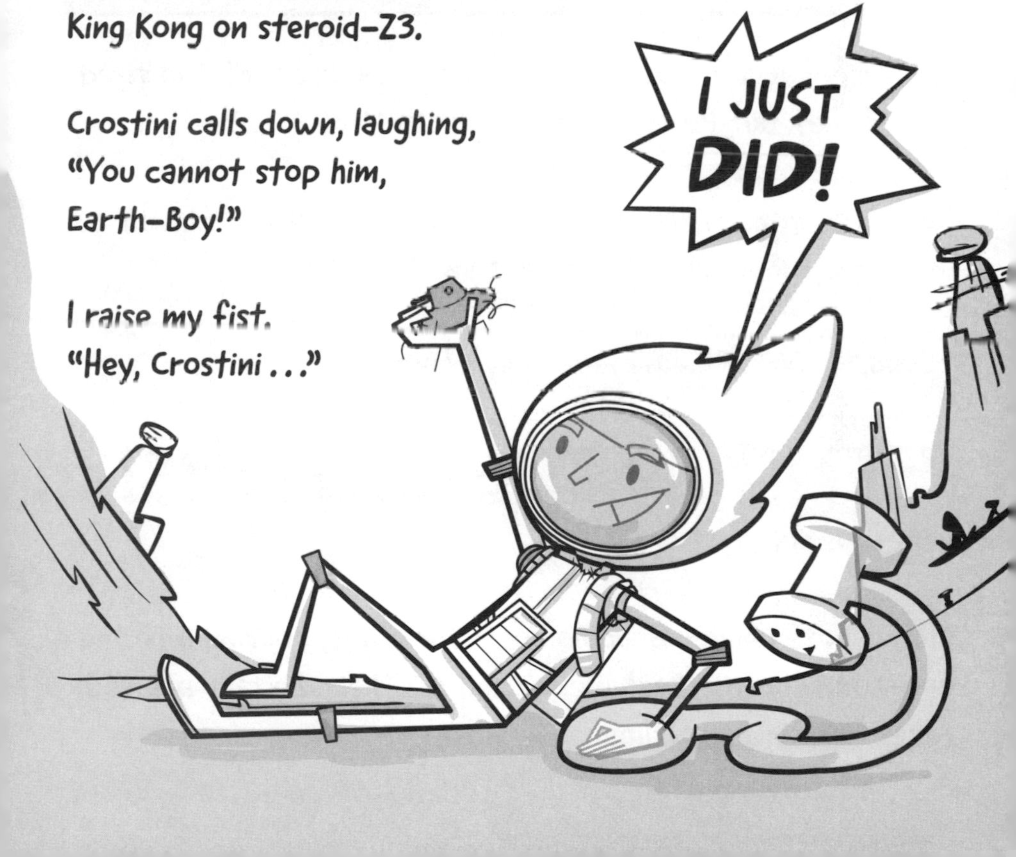
I JUST DID!

Humphree howls! He's on his knees, transforming, returning to his true form—his BEST FRIEND FORM! It's the same as the lyanux—shrinking, changing. I toss the busted gizmo to the ground and sprint over.

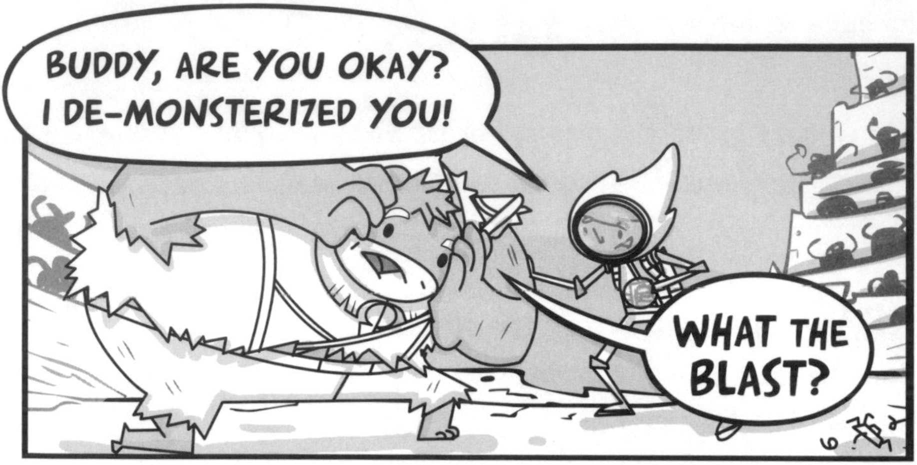
BUDDY, ARE YOU OKAY? I DE-MONSTERIZED YOU!
WHAT THE BLAST?

"Humps, I know you're confused and weak and hurt and tired and all that, but I'm afraid this fight isn't over . . ."

Humphree grunts. "Never too confused and weak and hurt and tired and all that to battle some bots."

"Good," I think. "'Cause here they come . . ."

"SEND IN THE CLOWNS!"

yells Crostini.

Clown-bots come cascading down the cliffs, pouring into the arena. In seconds they've encircled us. Their digitally painted faces flash in the sunlight.

I can do some serious Goober damage. And Humphree's got fists of fury. But there are HUNDREDS of these jester jerks. I could suffocate from the smell of greasepaint alone.

Humphree seems to read my mind. "Let's go down swinging, huh, short pants?"

But just then I feel a tremendous blast of heat. And then the deafening roar of engines. Over the crazed cackling of the approaching clown-bots, I hear a familiar hum and a friendly voice.

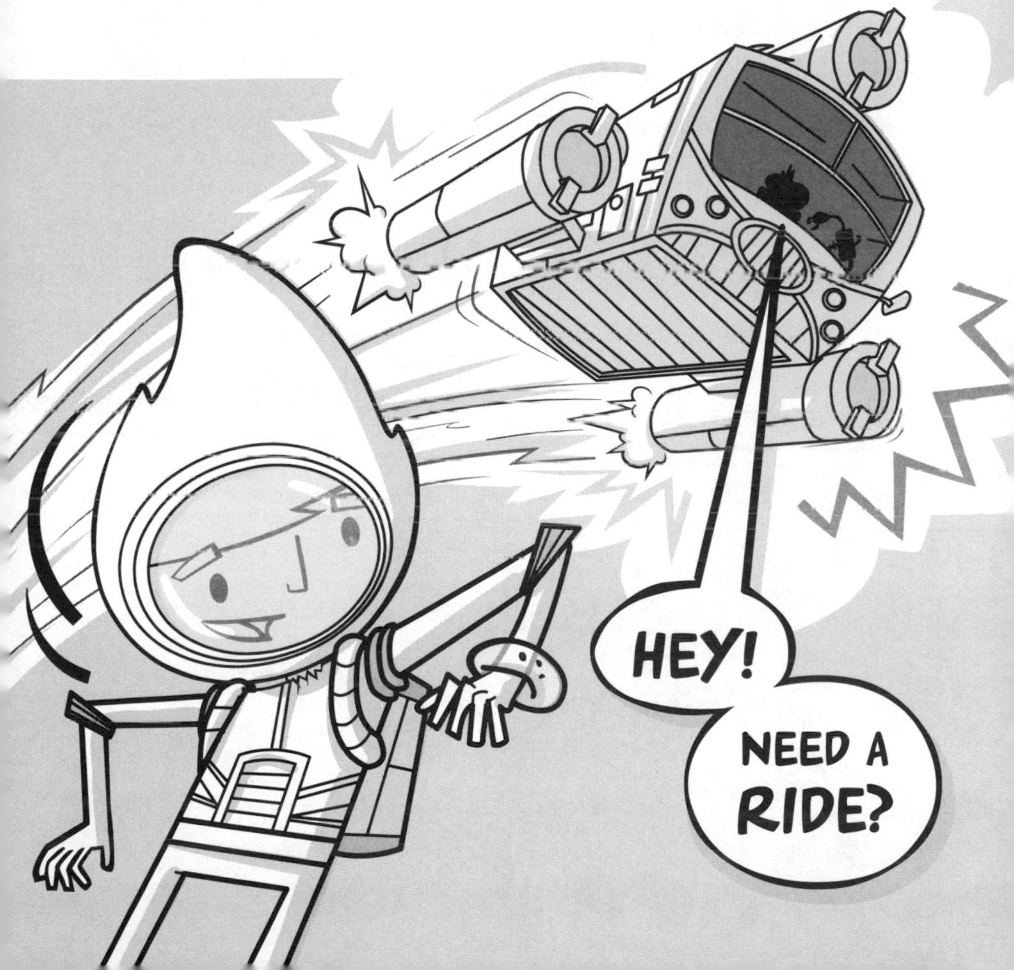
HEY!
NEED A RIDE?

It's Dagger, here for a last-minute rescue! And of course she's okay! What was I even worrying about?! It's Dags!

"Cosmoe!" Humphree shouts. "Time to pound ourselves a climbing pile!"

Clown-bots pounce from every direction. I swing a massive Goober mallet. Humphree's punching and pummeling and powering his way through the clown-bot horde.

The busted robo-bodies are piling up, forming a perfect tower for us to make our escape.

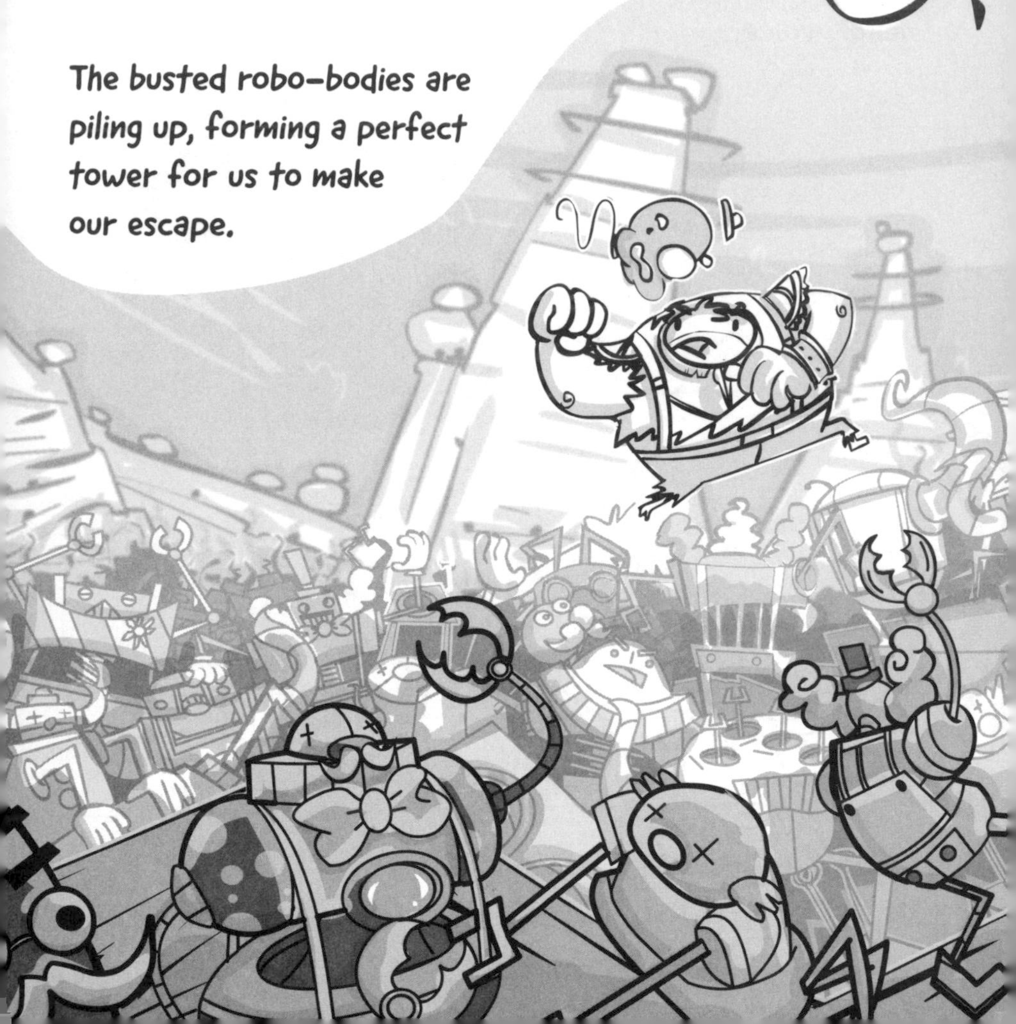

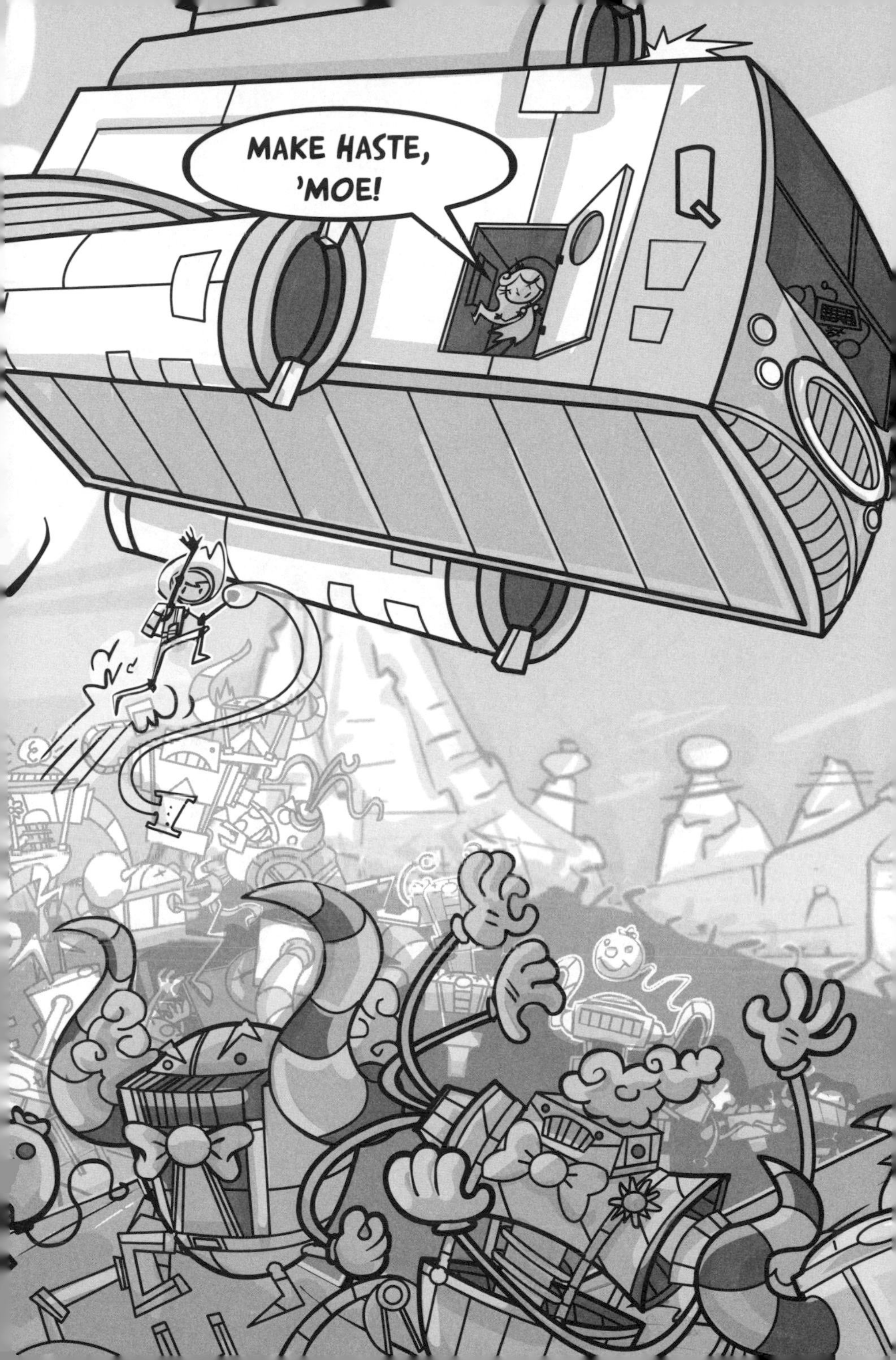
MAKE HASTE,
'MOE!

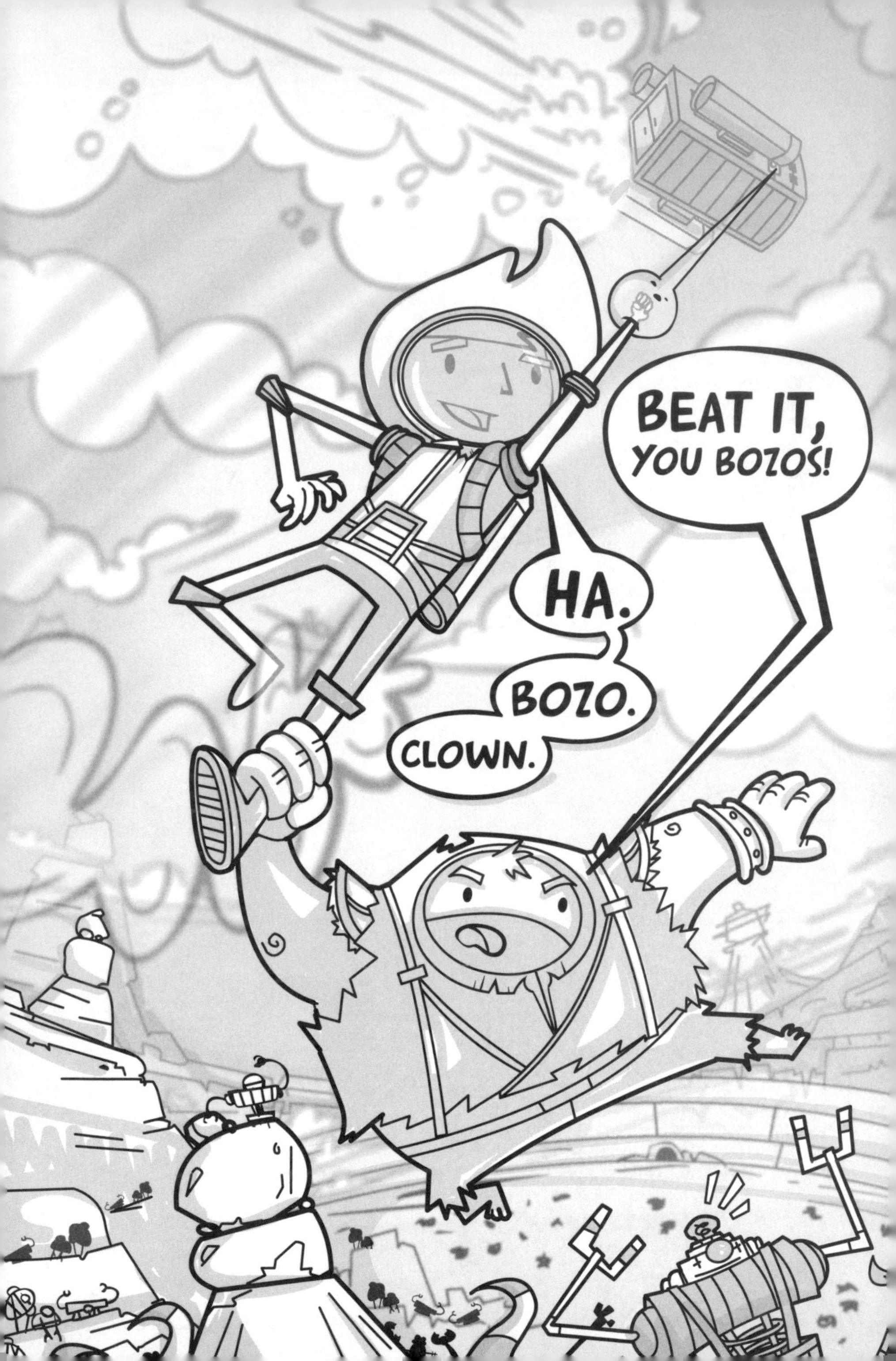
BEAT IT, YOU BOZOS!
HA.
BOZO.
CLOWN.

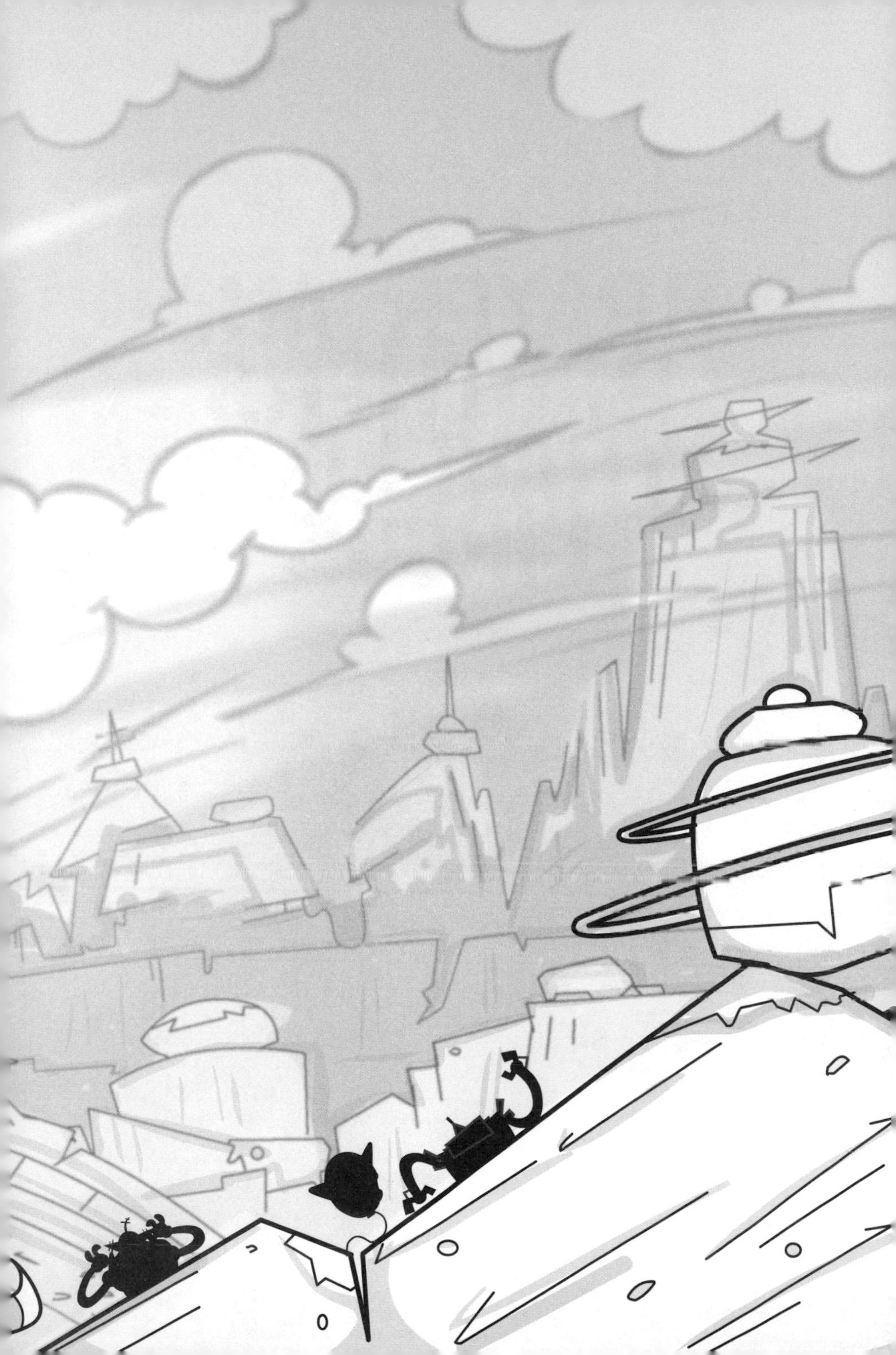

BRAYER AND BROTHERS TRAVELING CIRCUS

A FEW SPACE HOURS LATER . . .

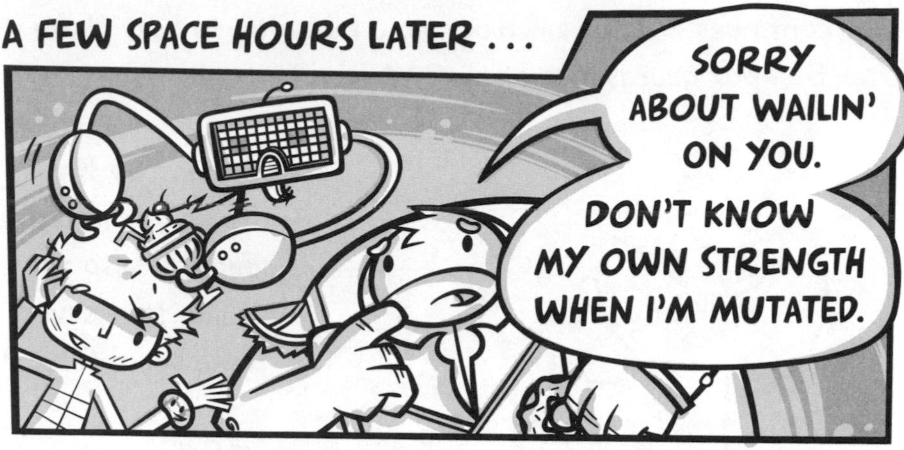
SORRY ABOUT WAILIN' ON YOU.
DON'T KNOW MY OWN STRENGTH WHEN I'M MUTATED.

My head is pounding from those Humphree punches—but I've got F.R.E.D. holding a milk shake to my noggin', numbing the pain. "All good, bud," I say. "You weren't yourself! Like me in the morning before my Super-String Cola."

Humphree chomps on a Drizzle Donut as I fill him in on all the crazy stuff that went down: the mad scientist room, the lyanux, and Evil Queen Dagger's involvement in the wicked plot.

Humphree's silent for a moment, then he exclaims, "Sizzling sunspots! I told you guys the circus was no good!"

"And what about you, Dags?" I ask. "I thought you were gone! For good! I was so worried, you have no idea . . ."

Dagger grins. "Can't keep a good princess down. You'll be pleased to know, Cosmoe—your stupid sumo suit snagged on to a busted old antenna . . .

She continues, "Then remember how I wanted to bust those roust-a-bot guards into pieces? Well ..."

I grin. "So the thing you hated most is also the thing that saved you. Beautiful ..."

"Yeah, yeah. So now what? Hit me with the STATUS!"

"Okay," I say. "So ... Crostini is going to deliver an army of monsters to your mom to do some really evil junk with—take over planets, whatever. Bottom line, evil-time."

Humphree and Dagger nod. "But ..." I continue, "he can't deliver the army until he finds THE GARGANTUID! Whatever that probably totally terrifying thing is ..."

F.R.E.D. beeps twice, "THE GARGANTUID IS ONLY FOUND ON ONE PLANET IN THE KNOWN GALAXY. PLANET ALZION."

"Jingo!" I say. "So that's where they're going next! And that's where we'll foil their plan with ...
A HOLLYWOOD-STYLE TRAIN HIJACKING!"

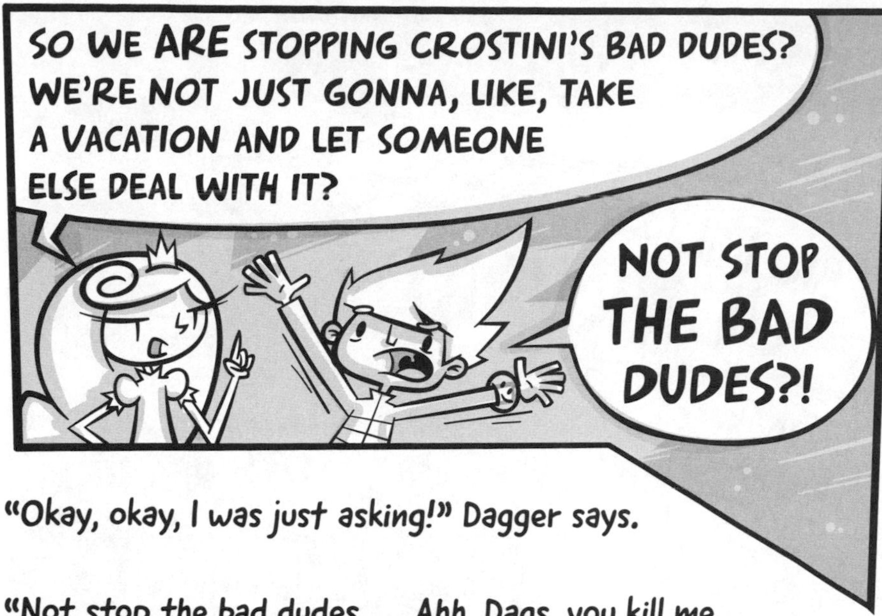
SO WE ARE STOPPING CROSTINI'S BAD DUDES? WE'RE NOT JUST GONNA, LIKE, TAKE A VACATION AND LET SOMEONE ELSE DEAL WITH IT?
NOT STOP THE BAD DUDES?!

"Okay, okay, I was just asking!" Dagger says.

"Not stop the bad dudes . . . Ahh, Dags, you kill me. NOT stop the bad dudes???! Hilarious! I missed you."

Humphree's back to focusing on the plan. "As soon as we set foot on that train, it's going to be fight night."

Sigh. I was *hoping* no one would bring that up. I was *hoping* we could just try out my plan and wish for the best. Because I *do* know another way—but I don't like it . . .

I ask myself, can I do this? Is it time? I think maybe it is. All right then . . . I exhale deeply and say, "F.R.E.D., set coordinates for Sand City, Utah."

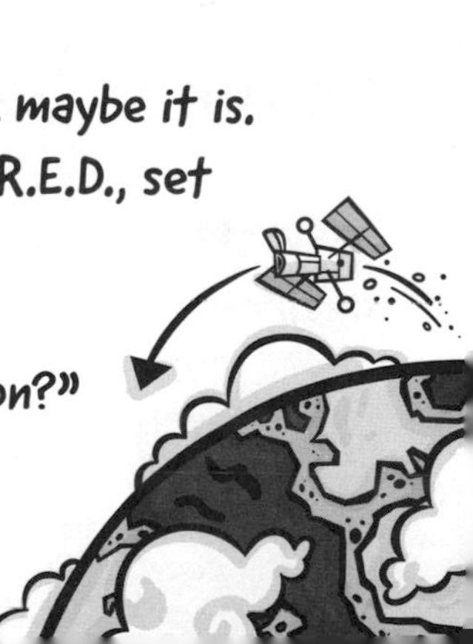

Dagger frowns. "Huh? What planet is that on?"

"Earth," I say. "It's on Planet Earth."

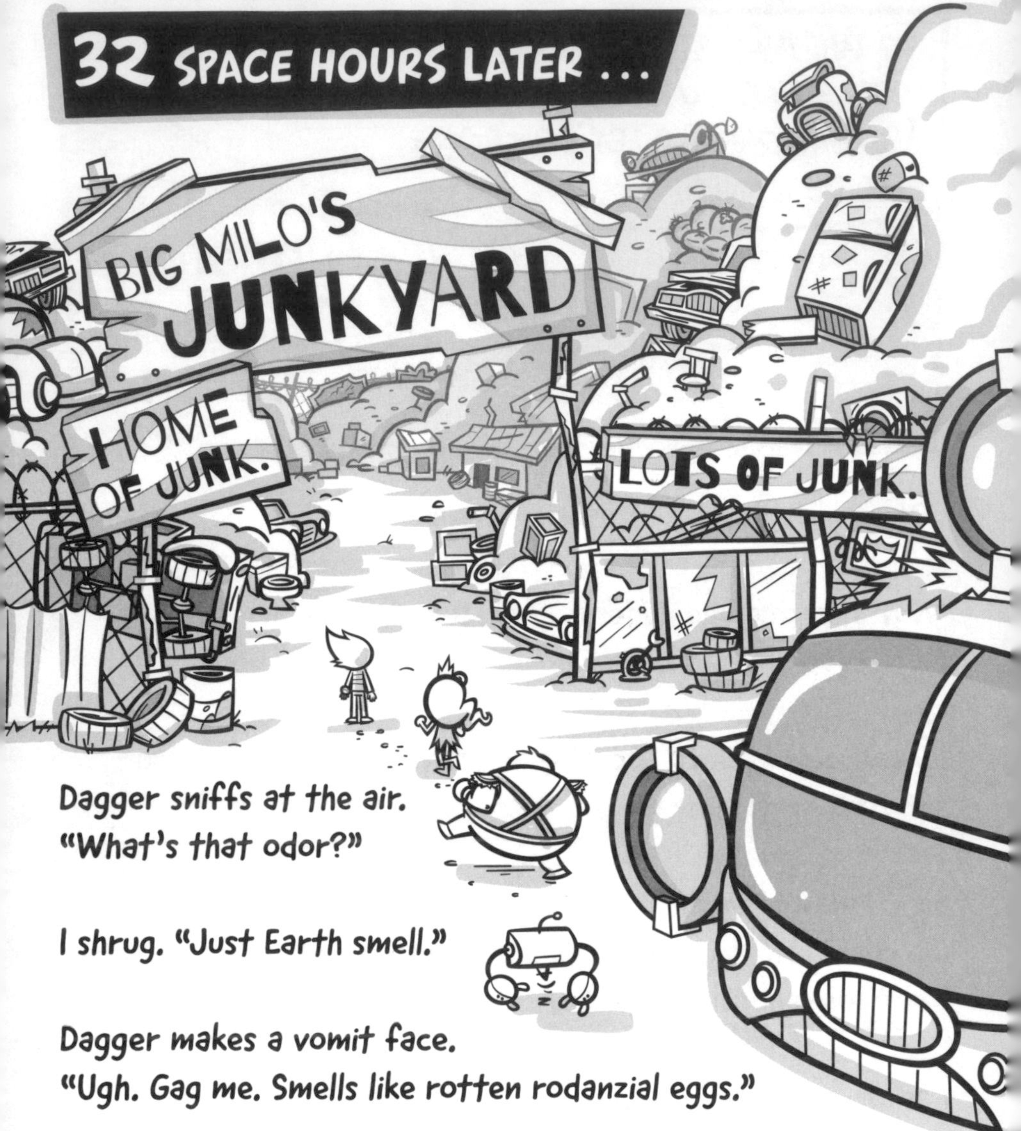
32 SPACE HOURS LATER ...
BIG MILO'S
JUNKYARD
HOME OF JUNK.
LOTS OF JUNK.

Dagger sniffs at the air. "What's that odor?"

I shrug. "Just Earth smell."

Dagger makes a vomit face. "Ugh. Gag me. Smells like rotten rodanzial eggs."

"Hey!" I bark. "It smells delicious! It's Earth smell, and it's the smell of where I come from, and it's yummy for the nose!"

"Geez, okay, relax 'Moe. No need to get all weirdly emotional on us."

The rusty gate to Big Milo's Junkyard swings open, screeching as we step inside the junkyard.

OK, so... **WARNING:** Dagger is correct. I probably <u>AM</u> about to get weirdly emotional. I'm not an emotional dude. But sometimes you just can't help it. For me, this is gonna be one of those times. I feel it coming. Sentimental city.

The junkyard is jam-packed with rusted, rotting Earth garbage. Piles and piles of broken-down cars and school buses and mounds of metal. Dagger is a bit confused by it all...

WHAT A STRANGE CREATURE... HELLO? YOU ALIVE?

Excitedly, Humphree says, "Short pants, this place is loaded with metallic material! We haul some of this to Port Beemore and sell it to Bruzzles the junk-bot and we'll make a killing!"

"That's not what we're here for, Humps," I say.

Stepping around a towering pile of busted old toilets, I see it. It's strewn across the ground, stretching the length of a football field.

"That," I say. "We're here for that."

"This is Brayer and Brothers Traveling Circus," I tell them. "It was a traveling circus and carnival train. Like Crostini's. But, you know, not evil. Just regular and nice and fun."

Dagger and Humphree look at me like "Yeah, and . . . ?"

"And this is where I used to live."

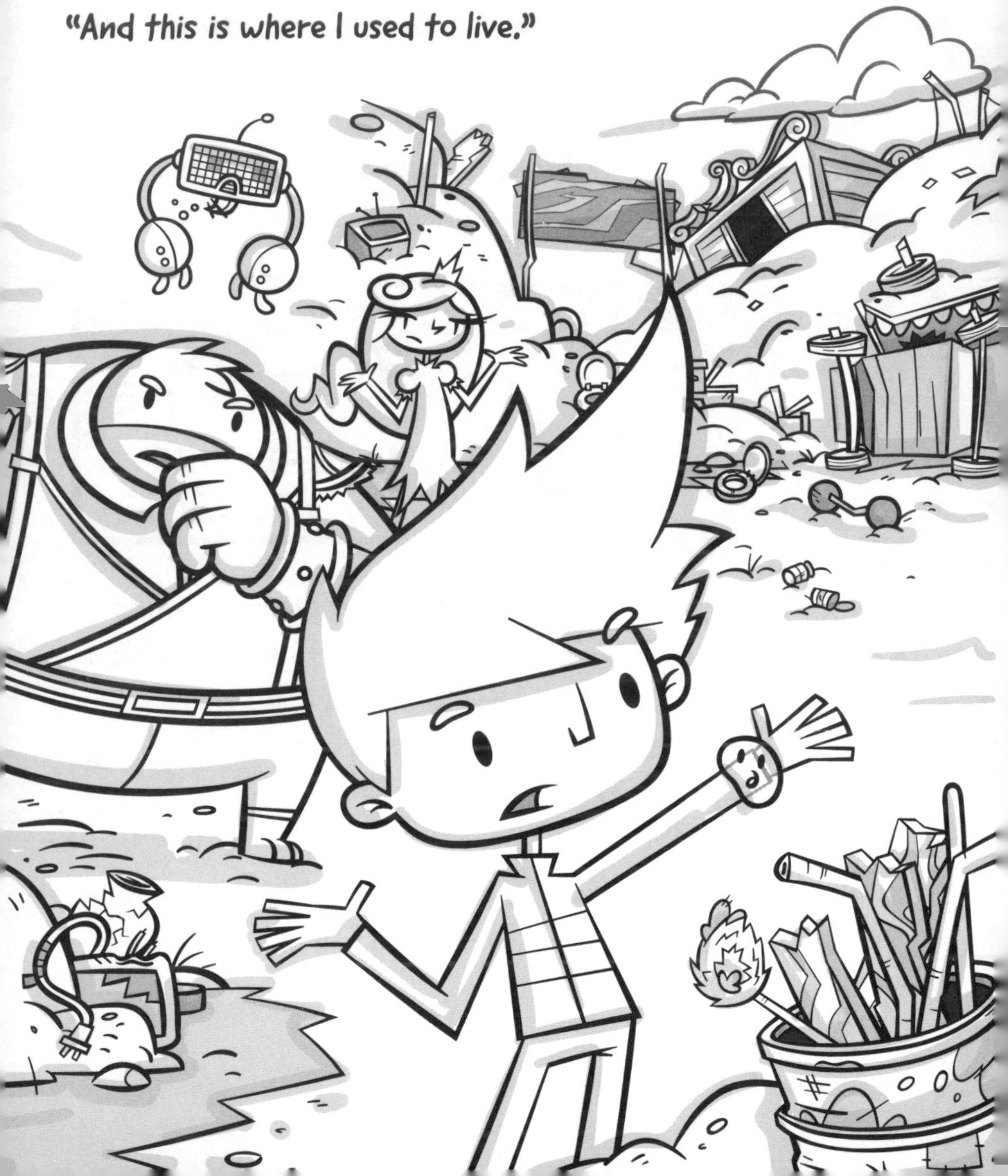

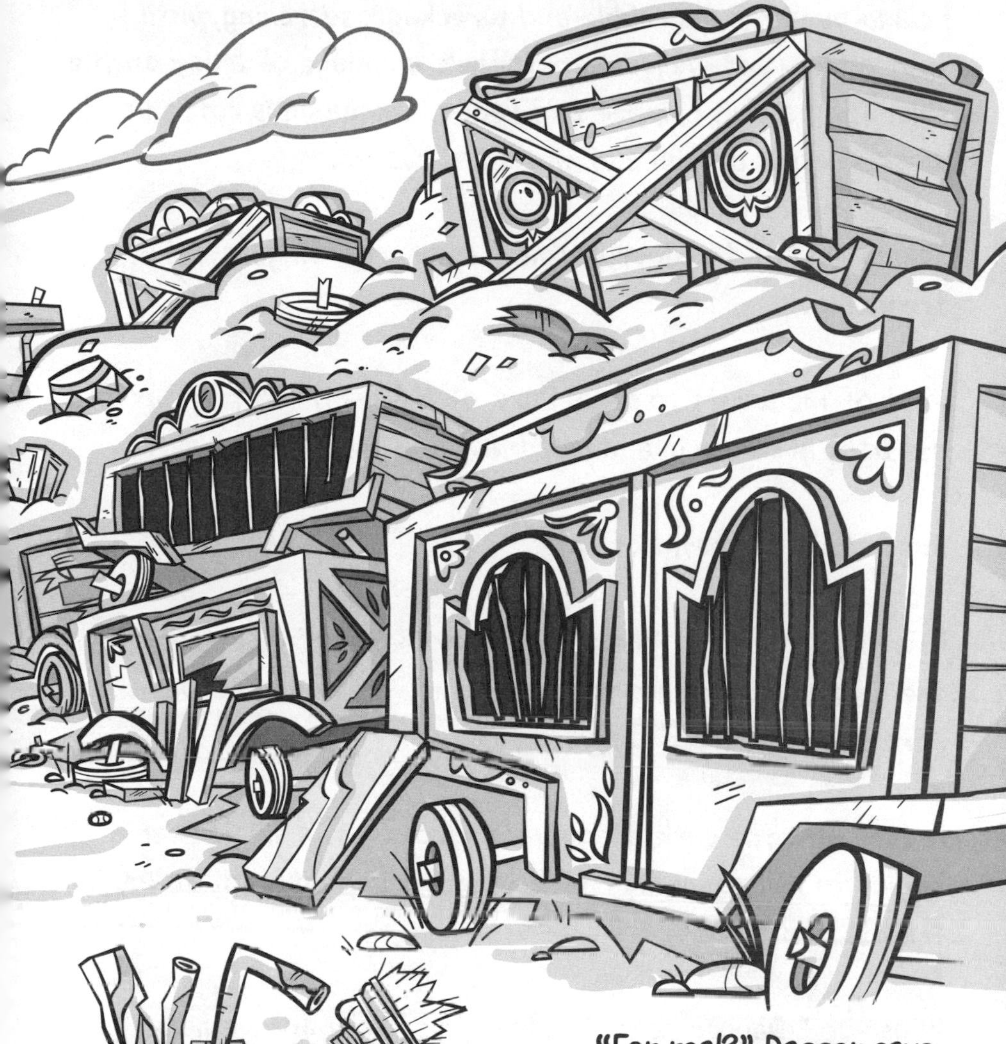

"For real?" Dagger says. She cocks her head, unimpressed. "Looks like it's seen better days."

I frown. Dagger's right, for sure. This train used to be the most grand and glorious thing you ever saw—the last of the great traveling circus trains. And then it all came to an end . . .

I climb over the old rubble and wreckage, searching, until I spot a blue-and-yellow car. There's an image of a lion on the side. The paint is chipped and faded. The wood is rotten and weak. Glass is broken and metal has rusted.

Taking hold of the door handle, I realize my fingers are trembling.

Part of me wants to stop. Part of me wants to turn around, get back in our ship, and just blast off.

But I can't do that. Not now.

I swallow, then pull. The entire door immediately comes off the hinges and crashes to the ground. The sound echoes across the deserted junkyard.

I stare into the dark, shadow-lit circus car. A single tear begins to roll down my cheek. I quickly wipe it away so my friends don't see.

"Cosmoe," Dagger says, "what is this? Why are we here?"

It takes me a moment to answer. When I do, I speak slowly—trying to keep my voice from cracking.

"This was our car," I say. "Me and my parents. This car is where I lived until I was eight years old."

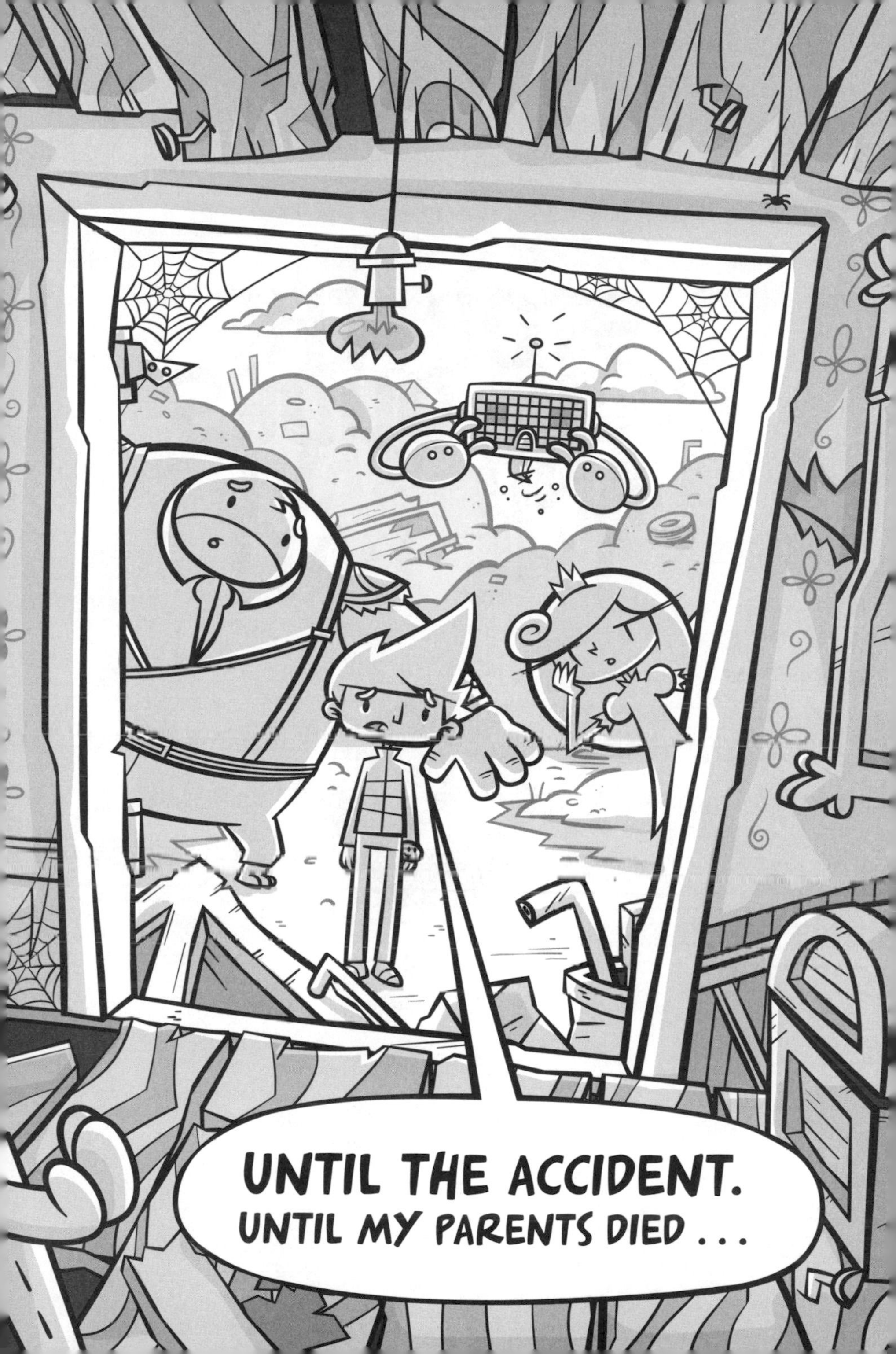
UNTIL THE ACCIDENT.
UNTIL MY PARENTS DIED . . .

STOP THE EVIL DUDES AND SAVE THE DAY!

18

WAIT.
COSMOE,
YOUR PARENTS
DIED?
HERE?

Dagger sighs.
"Oh, Cosmoe. I'm sorry."

I feel Humphree's and Dagger's eyes on me.
They want to know the details. But they don't want to ask.

Dagger and I are sitting on the foldout bed I'd slept on every
night until I was eight, with the 1970s *Jetsons* bedsheets.
They used to be my dad's. I wrap my fingers around the
sheets and squeeze them tight.

"It's not a long story," I start. "There was an accident. The
ringmaster was greedy—he only cared about money. Not
safety. And one day, the big top collapsed. My parents didn't
survive. I did. The circus closed down after that . . ."

"What happened then?" Dagger asks softly. "Where did you
go and live?"

I laugh quietly and get to my feet. "That, Princess, is a story
for ANOTHER TIME . . ."

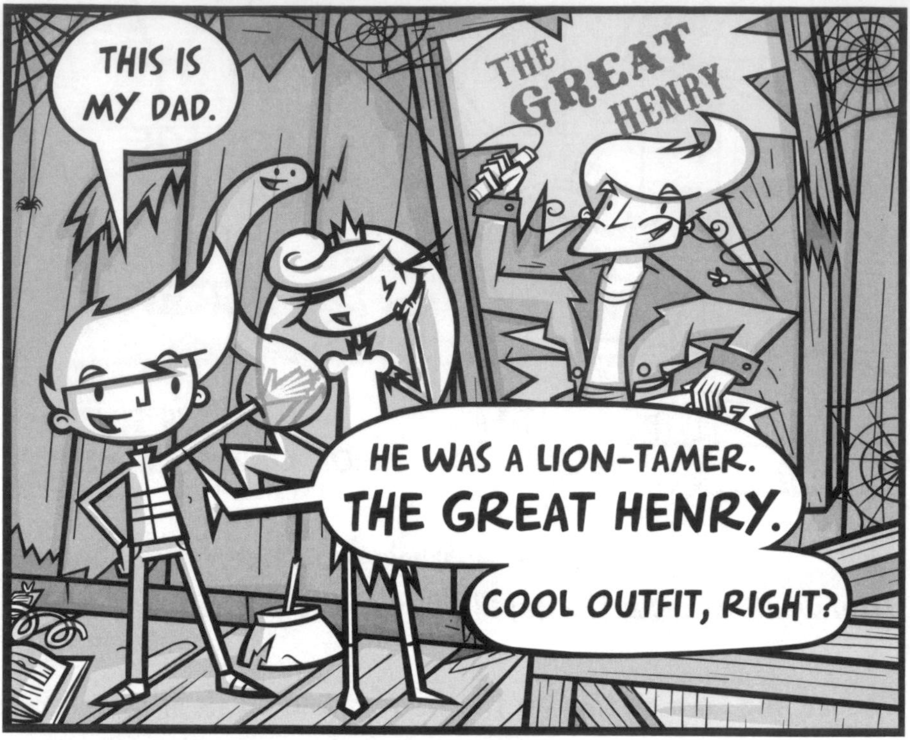
THE GREAT HENRY
THIS IS MY DAD.
HE WAS A LION-TAMER. THE GREAT HENRY.
COOL OUTFIT, RIGHT?

"So that's how you knew to do all that monster-taming stuff?" Humphree asks. "You watched your old man?"

"More than watched!" I say. "While the train was traveling from city to city—long, nighttime rides—he would stay up for hours, teaching me everything he knew."

Dagger leans against me. "He was handsome," she says. "I mean, for a human."

I stare at the poster. My father. The wonderful man who raised me and the wonderful man I haven't seen in five years—and will never see again. "Yeah, I guess he was, huh?"

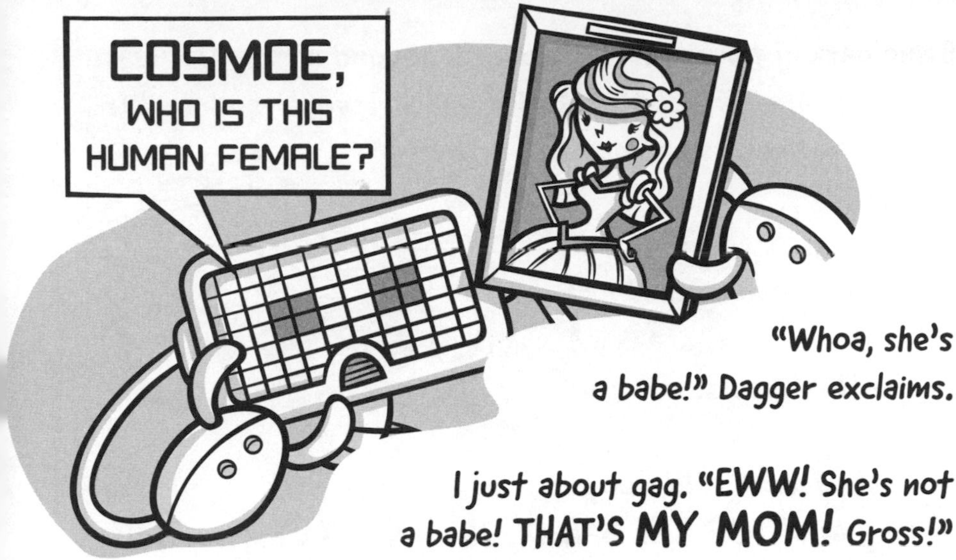
COSMOE,
WHO IS THIS
HUMAN FEMALE?

"Whoa, she's a babe!" Dagger exclaims.

I just about gag. "EWW! She's not a babe! THAT'S **MY MOM!** Gross!"

"She's total hot sauce!" Dagger says. Then she scrunches up her nose and looks me up and down and grins. "Y'know, I'm surprised you didn't do better in the looks department."

I laugh and shake my head. "My mom was a clown. Like, literally. Her clown name was Blossom, but her real name was Judy."

"Wow," Dagger says softly.

Humphree leans against the wall. The wood creaks and just about breaks under the weight of his big Bronkle frame. "Cosmoe, buddy," he says, "I never knew any of this."

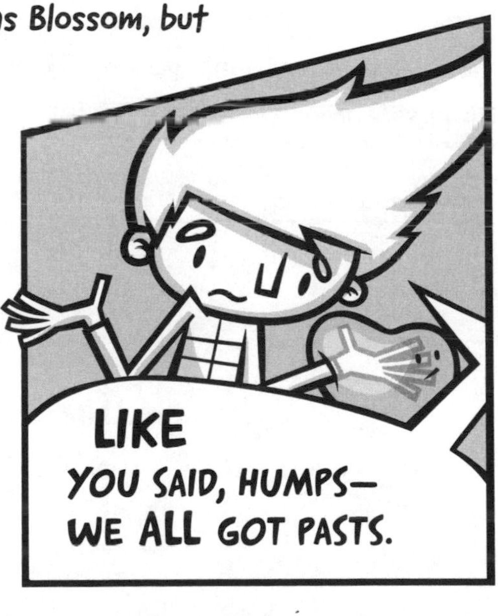
LIKE
YOU SAID, HUMPS—
WE ALL GOT PASTS.

Being back in this train car is weird. Beyond weird. This was my home. The last time I was here, well, I won't go into the details, but it was not good.

I wonder if my parents would be proud of me?

I hope they would.

I bet they would. No, you know what? I KNOW they would—as long as I **STOP THE BAD DUDES AND SAVE THE DAY!**

Which reminds me! Our adventure! Our action! It's time to knock off all this reminiscing and melancholy remembering. Life gets sad sometimes—it happens to everyone. And that's what best buds are for: When the sadness comes, you look at them and they look at you, and you laugh and you smile together and you remember it isn't ALL sadness, ALL the time. And sometimes, you're OK to just have them be sad alongside you.

So, with that said ...

IT'S TIME TO STOP CROSTINI **AND THE WRANGLER** AND SHUT DOWN THE WHOLE **EVIL CIRCUS!**

"F.R.E.D.," I say, "do me a favor and bring up the blueprints of Crostini's circus train."

WE ENTER **HERE**, AT THIS CLOWN-FACED STORAGE CAR.

THAT'S THE WEAK POINT.

I continue. "Then we sneak, sneak, sneak into that secret room of Crostini's, do some fighting, take control of the train. Humps, you're the wheelman—you hook the *Neon Wiener* up to the train. Once we handle Crostini and the wrangler, you steer us all to a Galactic Roamer Outpost, we turn in the bad dudes and—**BOOM**—we've saved the day!"

Humphree shakes his head. "And how do we 'sneak, sneak, sneak' through the train without getting caught?"

"DISGUISES!" I say. I kick open a chest at my feet like I'm playing Zelda. Dust flies out and a daddy longlegs shoots across the floor. I pull a clown costume from the chest. "Dagger, this was my mom's. Want to wear it?

She smiles. "I'd be honored."

11 EARTH MINUTES LATER . . .

Humphree suddenly stops. "Wait a parsec, Cosmoe . . .
If I'm just the wheelman, how come I got all dressed up?"

"I just wanted to see you looking doofy!" I say with a grin.

Dagger dashes ahead, practically skipping. She leaps over
a rusted old red pickup truck, then does a flip.

"Earth is fun!" she shouts. "Once you get over the smell . . ."

"THERE'S NO SMELL!" I shout, laughing and sprinting
after her.

Our little game of junkyard tag is interrupted by . . .

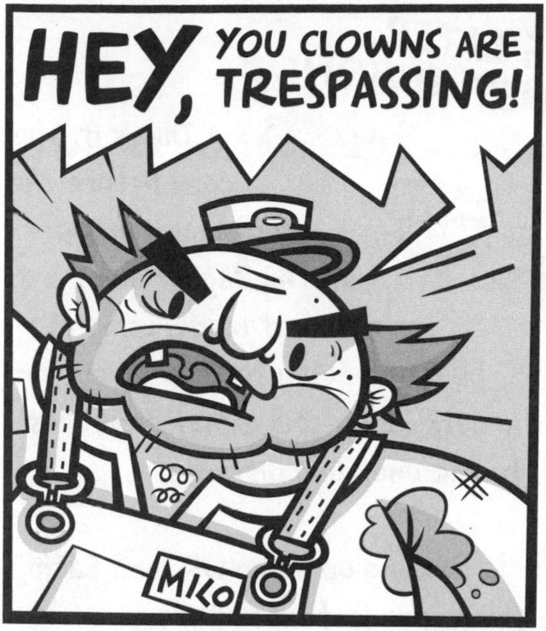
HEY, YOU CLOWNS ARE TRESPASSING!
MILO

Dagger immediately reaches for her flash blaster, ready to put this guy on ice. "No, Dags!" I bark. "This isn't space! You can't just turn people into ice cubes!"

Suddenly, the old man's face goes white. His lip starts quivering. I turn to see . . .

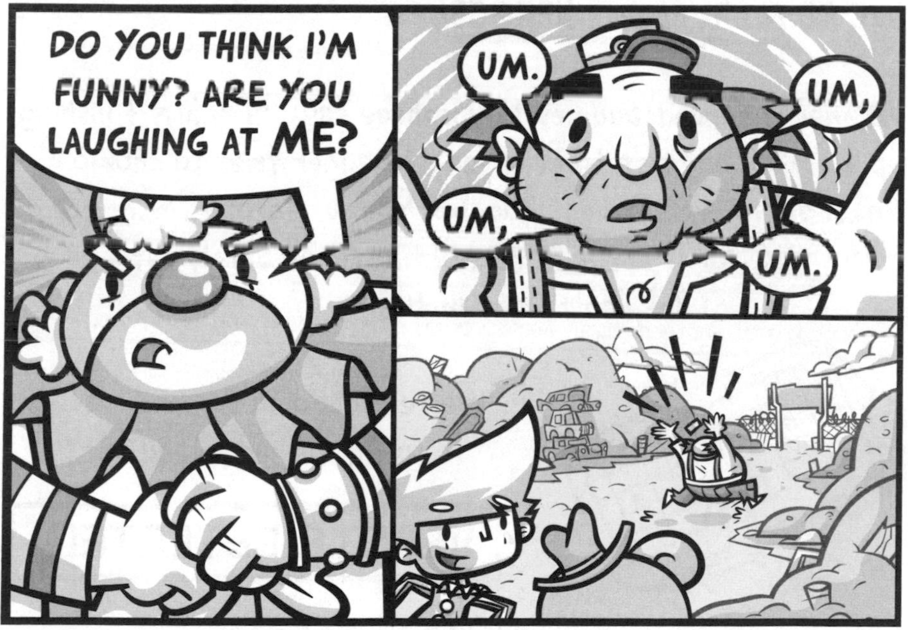
DO YOU THINK I'M FUNNY? ARE YOU LAUGHING AT ME?
UM.
UM,
UM,
UM.

Dagger laughs. "That human? He was NOT so handsome."

37 SPACE HOURS LATER, HIGH ABOVE PLANET ALZION ...

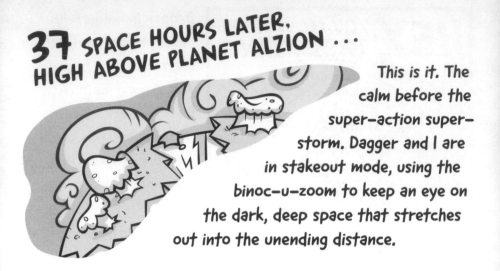

This is it. The calm before the super-action super-storm. Dagger and I are in stakeout mode, using the binoc-u-zoom to keep an eye on the dark, deep space that stretches out into the unending distance.

Humphree's on the grill. He's cooking up some wieners. Each of our favs—just in case this is our last meal. But ...
SPOILER ALERT! IT PROBABLY WON'T BE 'CAUSE WE'RE <u>MARVELOUS HEROES!</u>

"Dinner is served, buddies," Humphree says. "I'm just finishing up work on one last, 'special' dog." Dagger tries to chomp down on a Purple Delight dog, but she just groans. "Cosmoe, this clown suit is all restricting. I can barely eat. I def can't fight in this!"

"We're not going to need to fight. Just in and out."

VEHICLE DETECTED.

I squint. Out there, in the darkness, I see two tremendous headlights. **THE CIRCUS HAS ARRIVED ...**

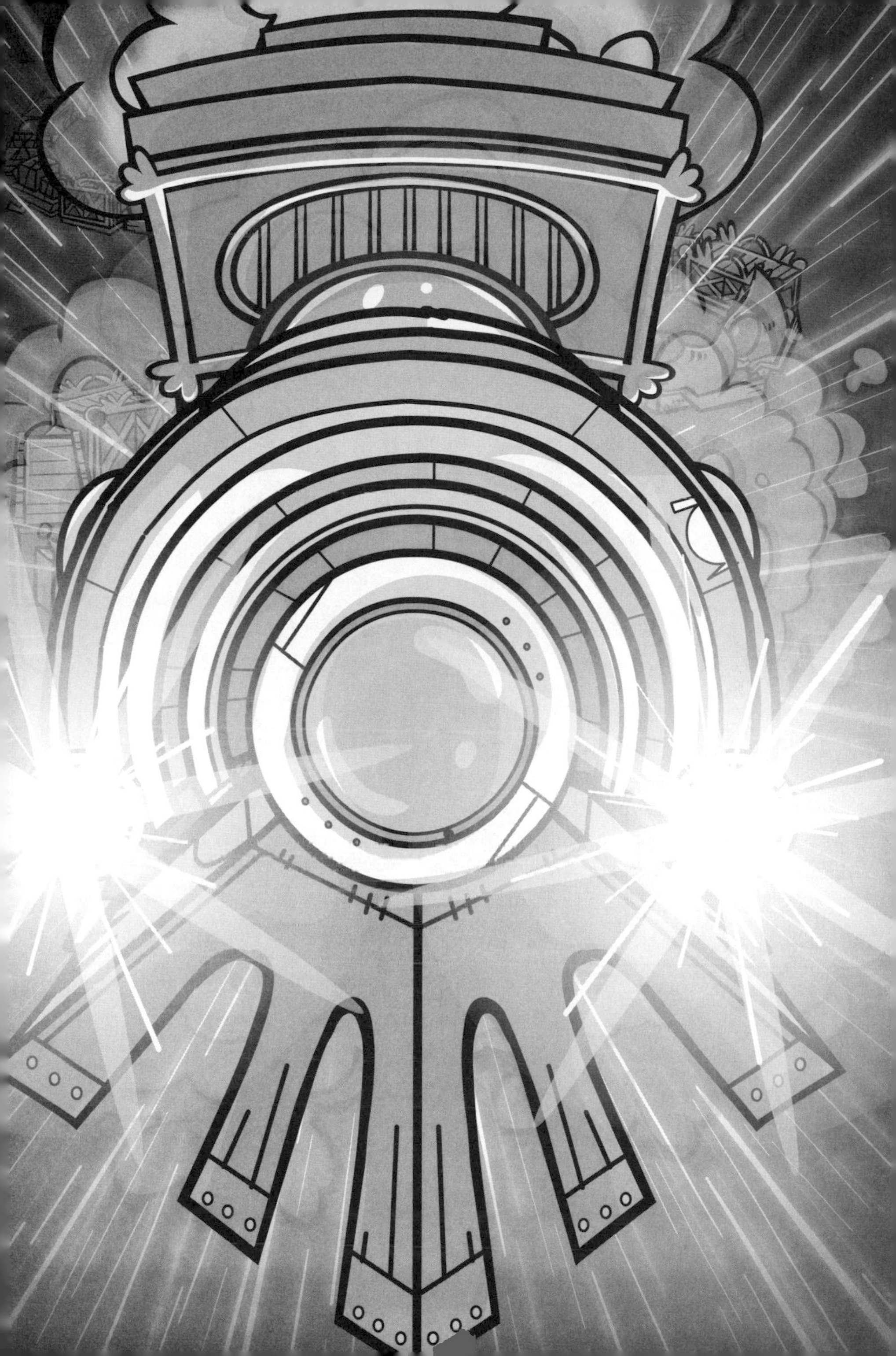

THIS DOG'S DA BOMB!

ALL RIGHT, **CLOWNS.** TIME TO GO HIJACK US A TRAIN.

Dagger looks at me all confuzzled.
"Why are you holding up a sneeze-sheet?"

"It's a handkerchief!" I exclaim. "'Cause I'm doing a Wild West train-robber thing! I'm all like: *I just want to get the job done. Nobody hurt. Get away clean. That's my code.*"

Dagger groans. "Wait. More disguises? I have no idea what a **'WILD WEST TRAIN ROBBER'** is, but you can't add another disguise! That's two disguises! You don't layer disguises. **TOO MANY** disguises, Cosmoe!"

"But I feel so cool when I'm a Wild West train-robber type!"

Dagger glares. She doesn't give a what about my coolness feelings right now.

"Fine ..." I toss my Wild West getup to the side. "Let's frapping hijack us a space circus, buds!"

Humphree flips a toggle and the *Neon Wiener* goes into midnight mode. Totally dark: no headlights, no double-bright headlights, no dials radiating red. The only light comes from F.R.E.D.'s screen, and even that dims to romantic candlelit-dinner mode.

Crostini's Cosmic Carnival and Wonder Circus rumbles toward us, exploding out of the darkness of space like some gigantic hulking piece of evil engineering. Humphree nudges the throttle and the *Neon Wiener* silently glides low. We speed ahead and then loop back around, so we're cruising alongside the train. Planet Alzion glows beneath us.

"THAT'S where we air-dock," I say, pointing.

The turbulence knocks the *Neon Wiener* back and forth, but Humphree manages to keep her steady as we fly alongside the speeding train. Steady enough for F.R.E.D. to begin the air-docking . . .

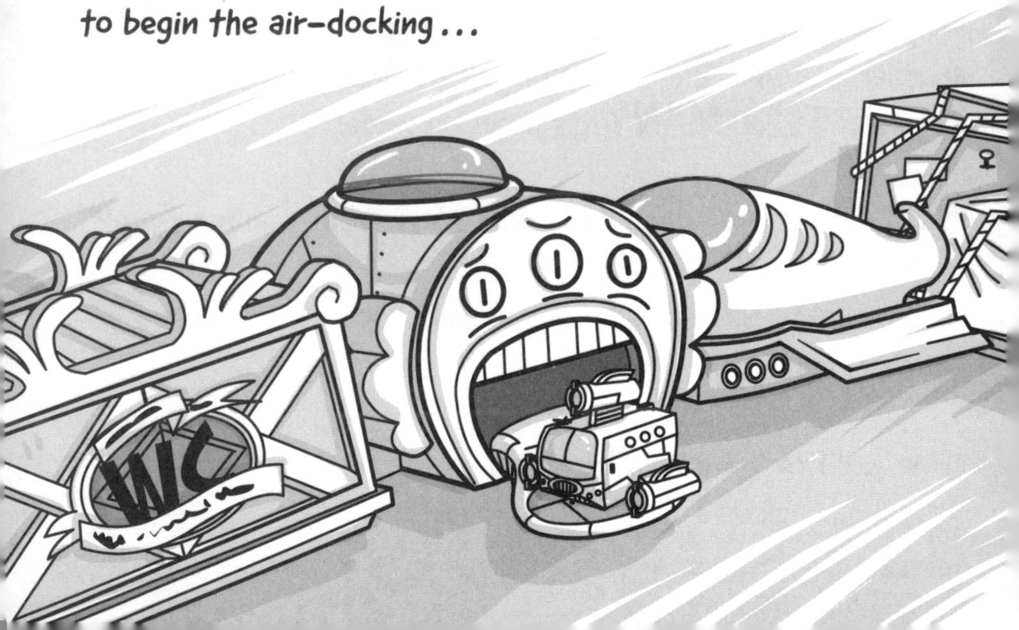
WC

Suddenly, there's a ding from the kitchen. "My special hot dog is done!" Humphree says. "Cosmoe, take the wheel!"

"We're in the middle of air-docking to a mile-long circus train, and you're making me take the wheel?!" I exclaim.

"Trust me, bud!" Humphree hollers as he dashes into the kitchen. A second later, he returns.

TAKE **THIS.** AND **MAY** THE **WIENER** BE WITH YOU.

"Why are you handing me a random hot dog right before we storm the bad guy base?"

Humphree grins and slips the wiener into my pocket. "Trust me. When you get to that heavy door of Crostini's, you'll be happy you've got that wiener."

F.R.E.D. completes the air-docking, and Dagger and I step out. The sound is thunderous. Goober twists the gigantic lock on the train's door, there's an earsplitting hiss, and the door slides open.

Time to hijack a train like some **SUPER-SPACE BANDITS!**

Dagger and I step into a storage car full of crates and dunk tanks and midway games. Through the porthole window, I see Humphree flash us a thumbs-up. The air-dock retracts and the *Neon Wiener* banks away, silently jetting through space—just a blip in the darkness.

We're alone now on the train. Behind enemy lines! Just me, Dags, about two thousand robo-villains, and a seriously cruel ringmaster and wrangler . . . Don't freak out, Cosmoe.

DON'T FREAK OUT!

"Okay, Dags," I say, doing my best to be a brave dude. "We need to walk through like fifty train cars without anyone noticing that we don't belong here—that we're not clown-bots. That means . . . ROBO-WALK!"

"Robo-walk?" Dags asks, looking at me like I've gone lunatic.

"You know, like, ah, this . . ." I say as I demonstrate.

"You look like a total clown," Dagger groans.

"Exactly!" I say. With that, I hit the open-door button, and we robo-walk our way into one seriously bustling clown car.

"I feel all their beady robo-eyes watching us!" Dags whispers. "Like any moment, they're all going to pounce!"

"Just keep robo-walking," I say. But Dags is right. The suspense is serious. It's all like: Suspense. Suspense. Heartbeats. Pounding. Suspensafying.

We pass clown-bots hooked up to charging stations and clown-bots practicing their clown gags. Soon, we're in a rhythm: moving through roust-a-bot cars and clown-bot cars and storage cars. No one suspects a thing. We're going to make it! Or not ...

Suddenly, I feel a blast of cold liquid on my face! I blink twice. Seltzer water drips over my lips. I taste wax on my tongue. I look at Dags. Yellow-and-pink makeup is running all down her shirt!

A clown-bot grips a seltzer bottle. Its electro-eyes buzz, and it barks out, **"YOU'RE NO CLOWNS!"**

OH SMUDGE.

I push Dags behind me and step forward. "We are totally clowns! This is just, um, cutting edge robotic-skin stuff," I say, tugging on my cheek. "It's crazy hi-tech."

The clown's eyes flash red. A dozen clown-bots rise up, forming a circle around us. "Prove you're clowns!" one barks.

I gulp. Okay. I spot three juggle-globes on a hover-table and scoop them up. I begin juggling, like my mom taught me. "See, I'm a clown-bot. The clowniest clown-bot ya ever heard of!"

Metal joints squeak and scrape as clowns surround us. I don't think they're buying it. I need to make a move here, or we're French toast. "And now," I announce, "for my final trick..."

I toss the juggle-globes high in the air. The clowns focus on the globes, not understanding. And then...

COSMOE CLOWN KICK!

"DAGS!" I shout. **"RUN!"**

We erupt through the clown-bots and sprint through a seemingly endless line of creature cars. Beasts roar as the clown-bots tear after us. At last I spot Crostini's dining car. The same car where we ate the fancy-pants meal, back when I thought this circus was awesome.

We dash inside, and I throw the door shut. There's a loud **THUD, BANG, BONK** as clown-bots slam into the door. But I'm not worried about the bots behind us. I'm worried about the super-steel door ahead of us ...

"How are we ever going to get through there?" Dagger asks.

"The wiener!" I say. I quickly slip out the single hot dog that Humphree gave me earlier. "He said we'd need it when he came to the super-steel door, and here we are."

Dags peeks over my shoulder and eyes the doggie. "I don't get it. It just looks like a regular ol' standard Galactic Hot Dog. A totally plain, boring, normal dog, too. How's it supposed to help us?"

"Well," I say with a shrug, "let's see just how plain, boring, normal it is . . ."

With that, I take a mighty CHOMP. "Hmm, tastes ordinary," I say. "Properly seasoned. Expertly grilled. A little heavy on the salt, maybe."

But that's when I see the words inside the wrapper. It's a message, from Humphree. And I get it . . .

The hot dog begins to jiggle and just about jumps out of my hand! It's sizzling and shaking and thick green smoke pours from one end.

Quickly, I place the wiener at the foot of the door. "Dags," I say, "I think we should step back. I have a feeling things are about to get hot . . ."

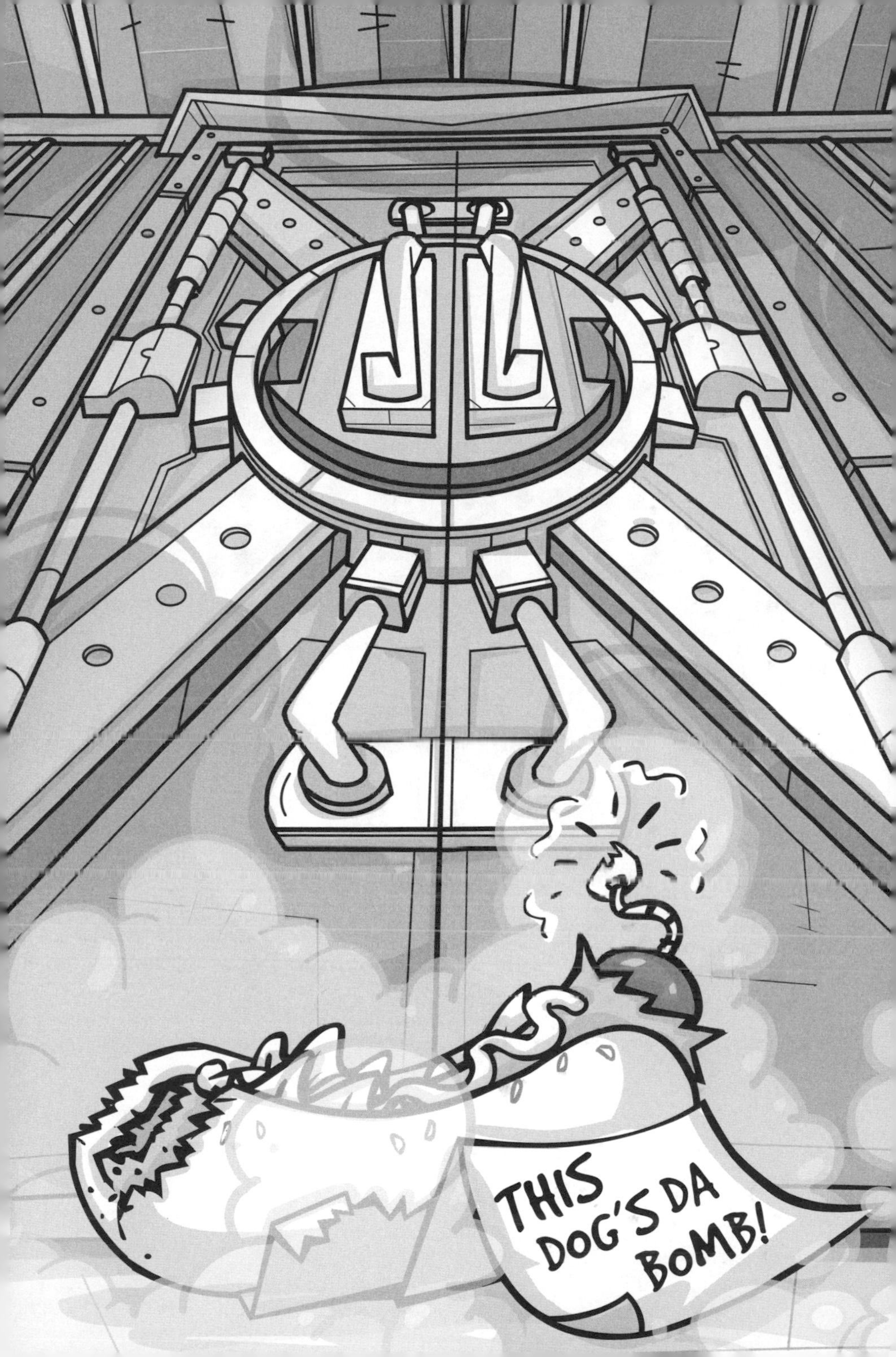
THIS DOG'S DA BOMB!

HURTLING, FLAMING, PLUMMETING

20

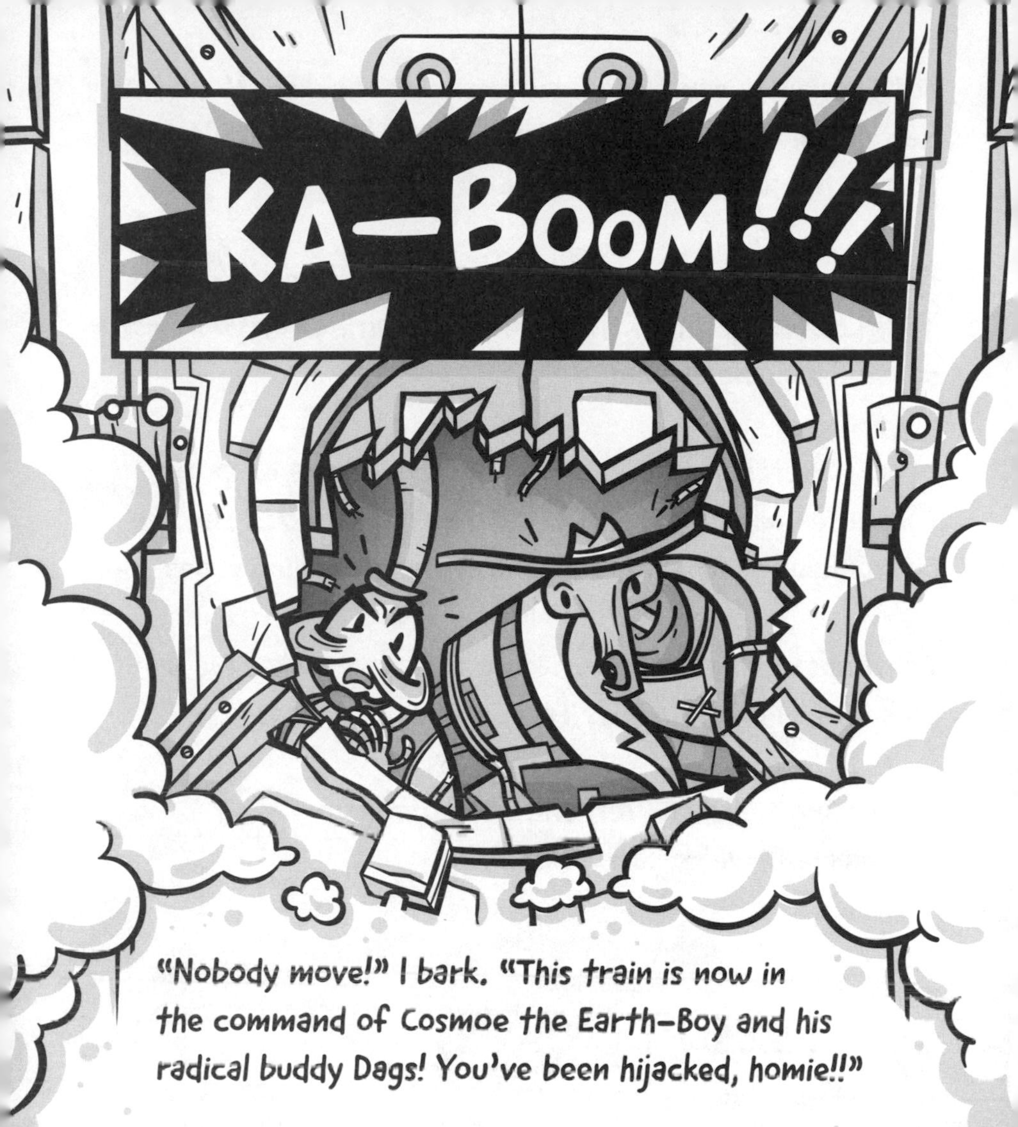
KA-BOOM!!!

"Nobody move!" I bark. "This train is now in the command of Cosmoe the Earth-Boy and his radical buddy Dags! You've been hijacked, homie!!"

With a sharp snap of my wrist, Goober wraps around Crostini's thick waist and sends him spinning.

Dags has her flash blaster trained square on the wrangler. "Move one inch," she snarls, "and you're toast, wrangle-head. *Burnt* toast."

But Crostini doesn't seem surprised or shocked. Not at all. He's giving me a look that makes me go, man, I didn't think this all the way through . . .

"I suspected you might reappear," Crostini says. "So I **TRIPLED** my security. They've been waiting for you. Just sort of hanging around . . ."

I feel something splash against my shoulder: a drop of foul green oil. I look up. **ROUST-A-BOTS!** I see the bottoms of their feet, dangling from the ceiling tubes.

Crostini grins a really infuriating grin that makes me want to sock him in his wrinkly face.

The ceiling tubes clatter, and the bots drop. In a moment we're surrounded . . .

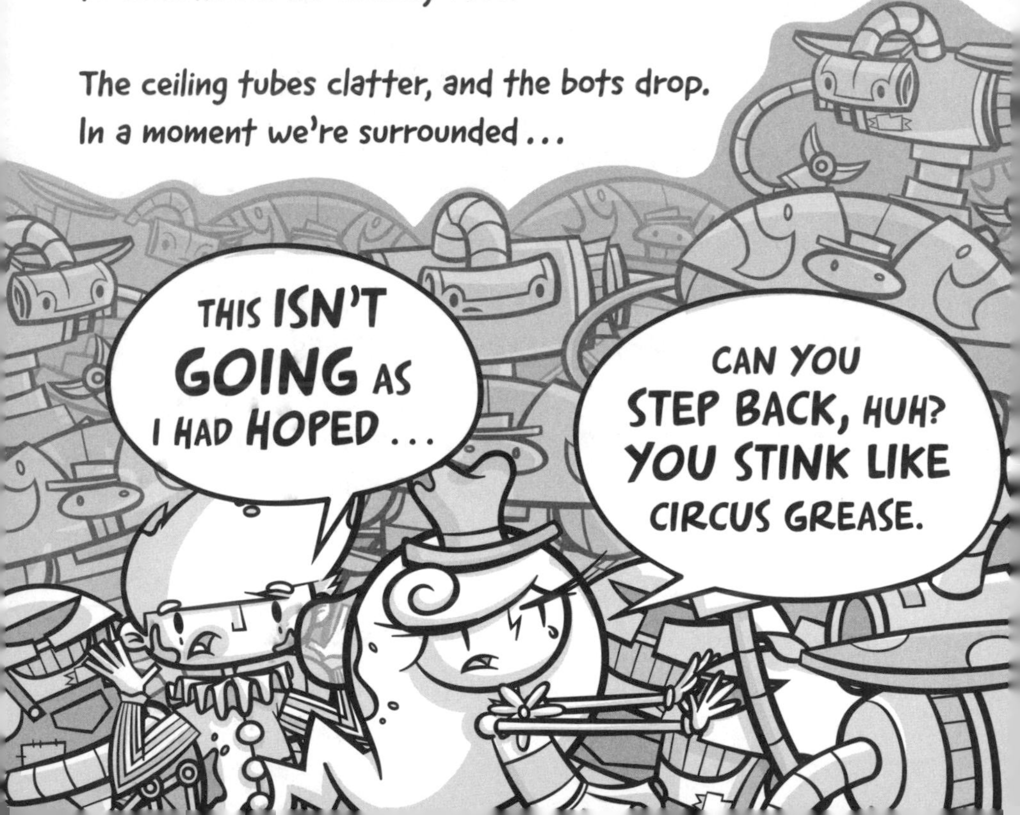
THIS ISN'T GOING AS I HAD HOPED . . .
CAN YOU STEP BACK, HUH? YOU STINK LIKE CIRCUS GREASE.

Crostini skitters toward a control panel. "And now," he says, "to find the large one. HUMPHREE." Crostini taps the panel. Suddenly we're looking at space from cameras positioned along the train's exterior.

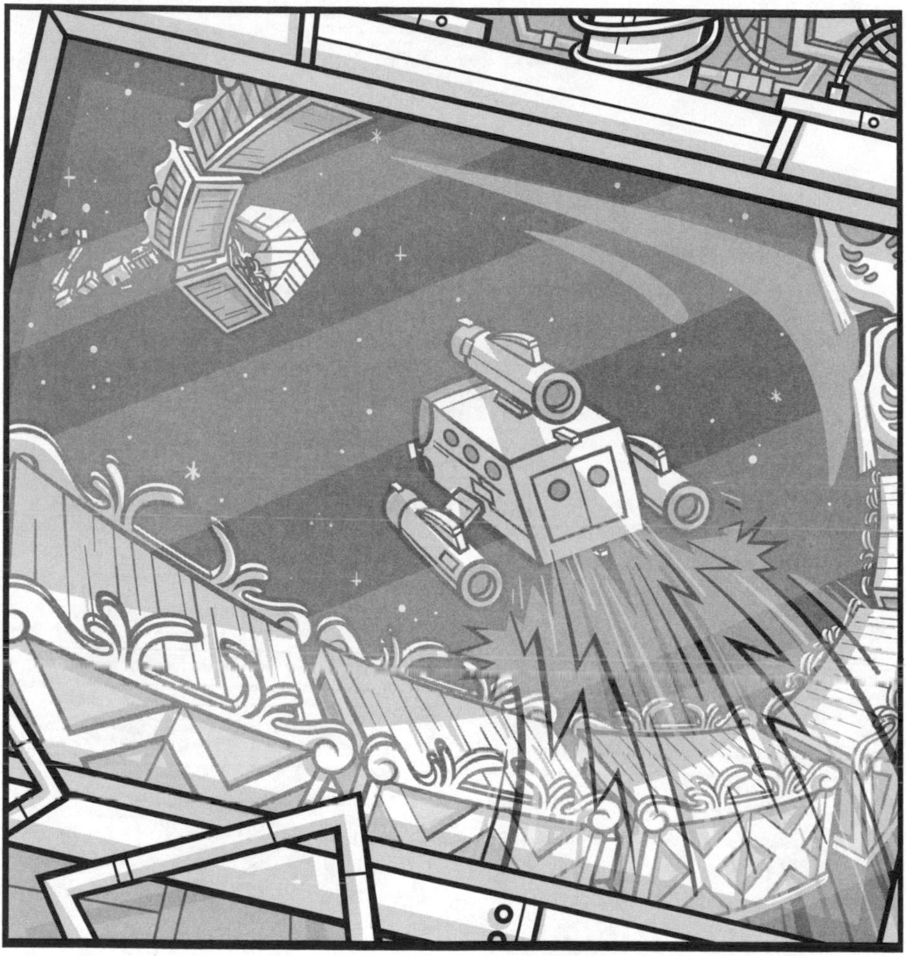

The wrangler growls. "There's the ship. I'm going to the roof." As he stomps out, his arm begins transforming, growing, until it forms one crazy colossal cannon . . .

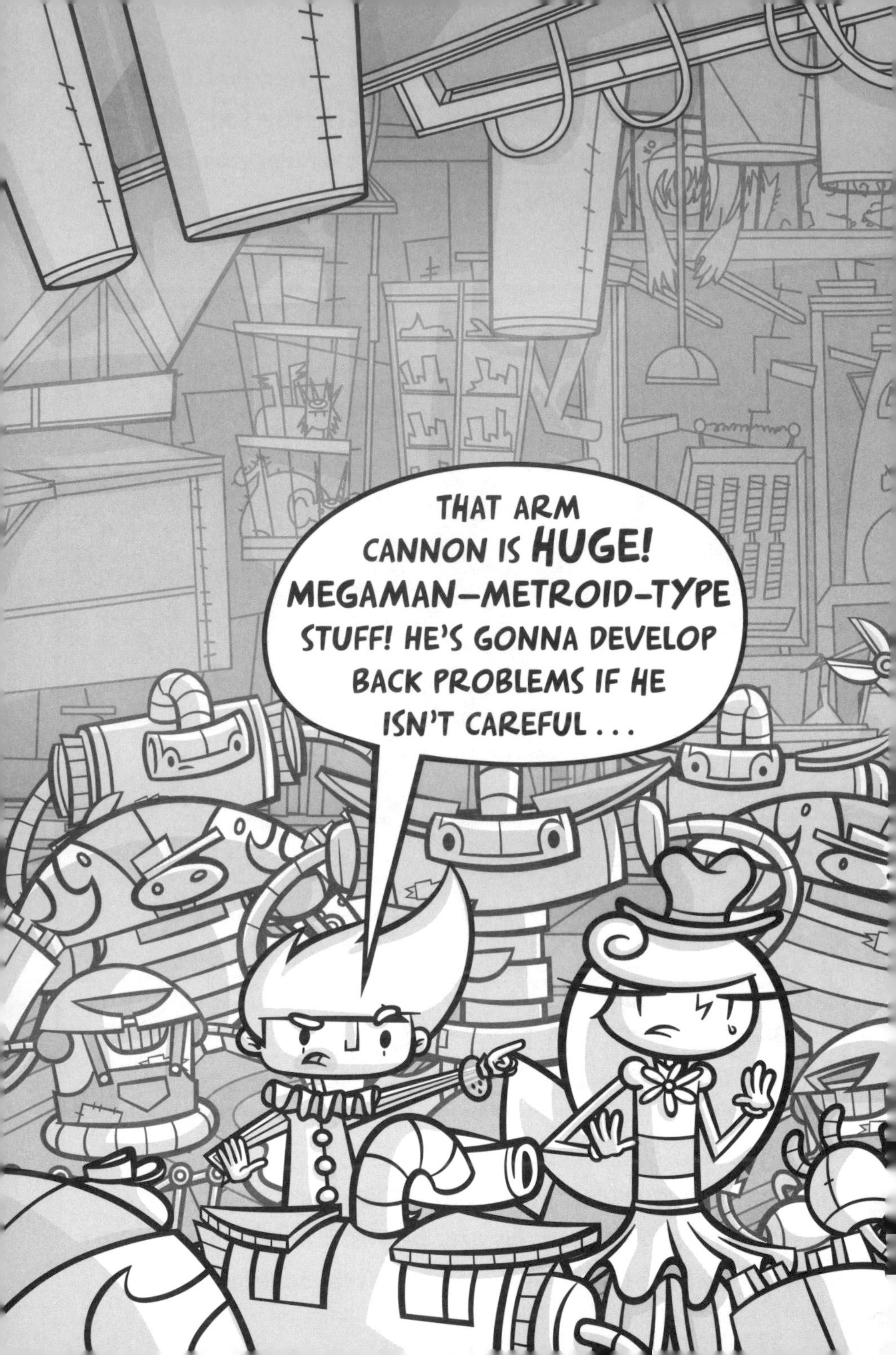
THAT ARM CANNON IS HUGE! MEGAMAN–METROID–TYPE STUFF! HE'S GONNA DEVELOP BACK PROBLEMS IF HE ISN'T CAREFUL . . .

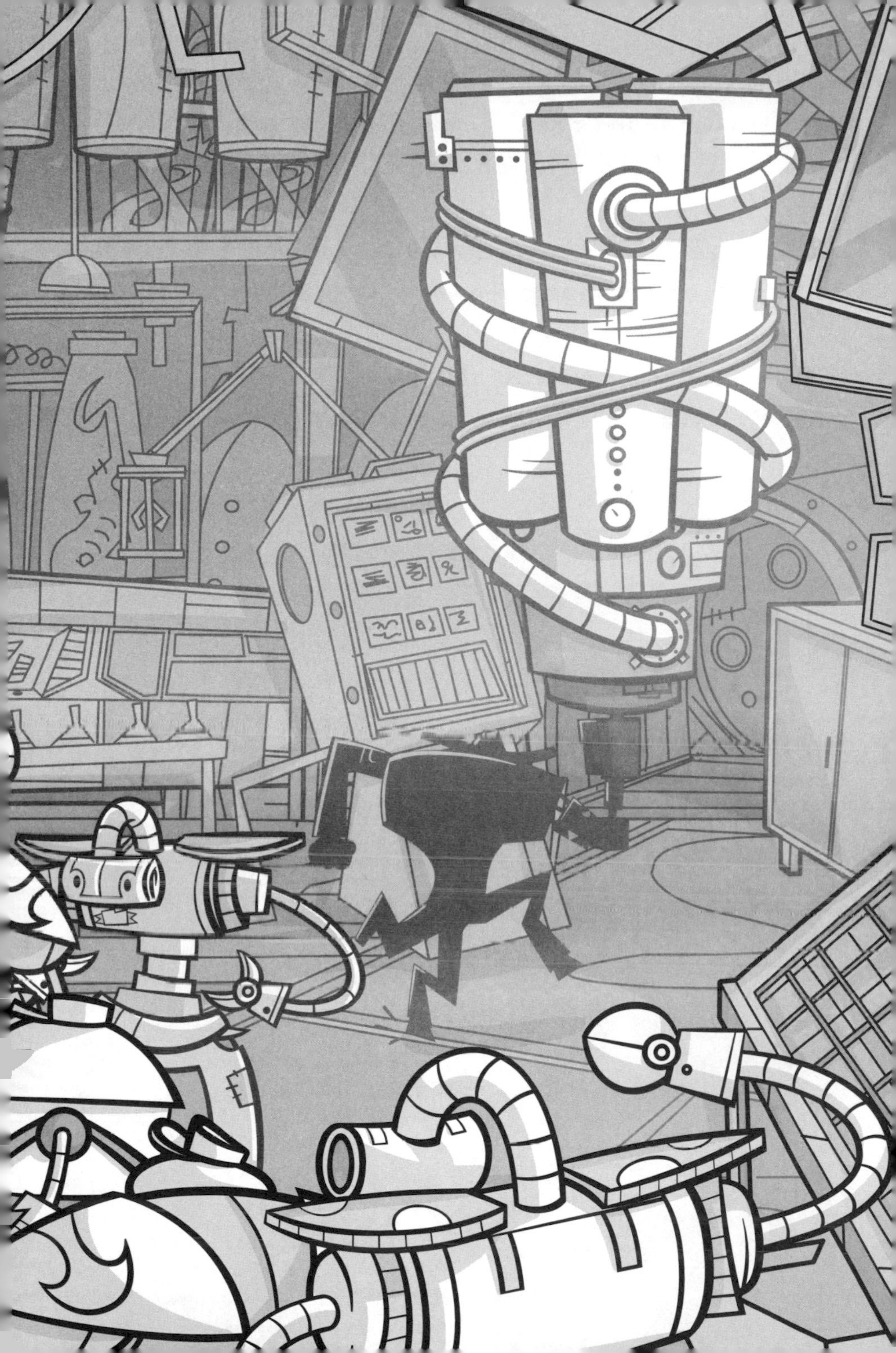

Crostini's lips curl into a vile smile. "Cosmoe, you will now witness your friend's demise. And the utter annihilation of your SILLY LITTLE *WIENER* CRAFT."

The wrangler's arm cannon is a furious weapon. Energy blasts erupt with so much force the whole train seems to shake.

A fiery blast whizzes across the *Neon Wiener's* bow. The ship curves, banks, and swings around.

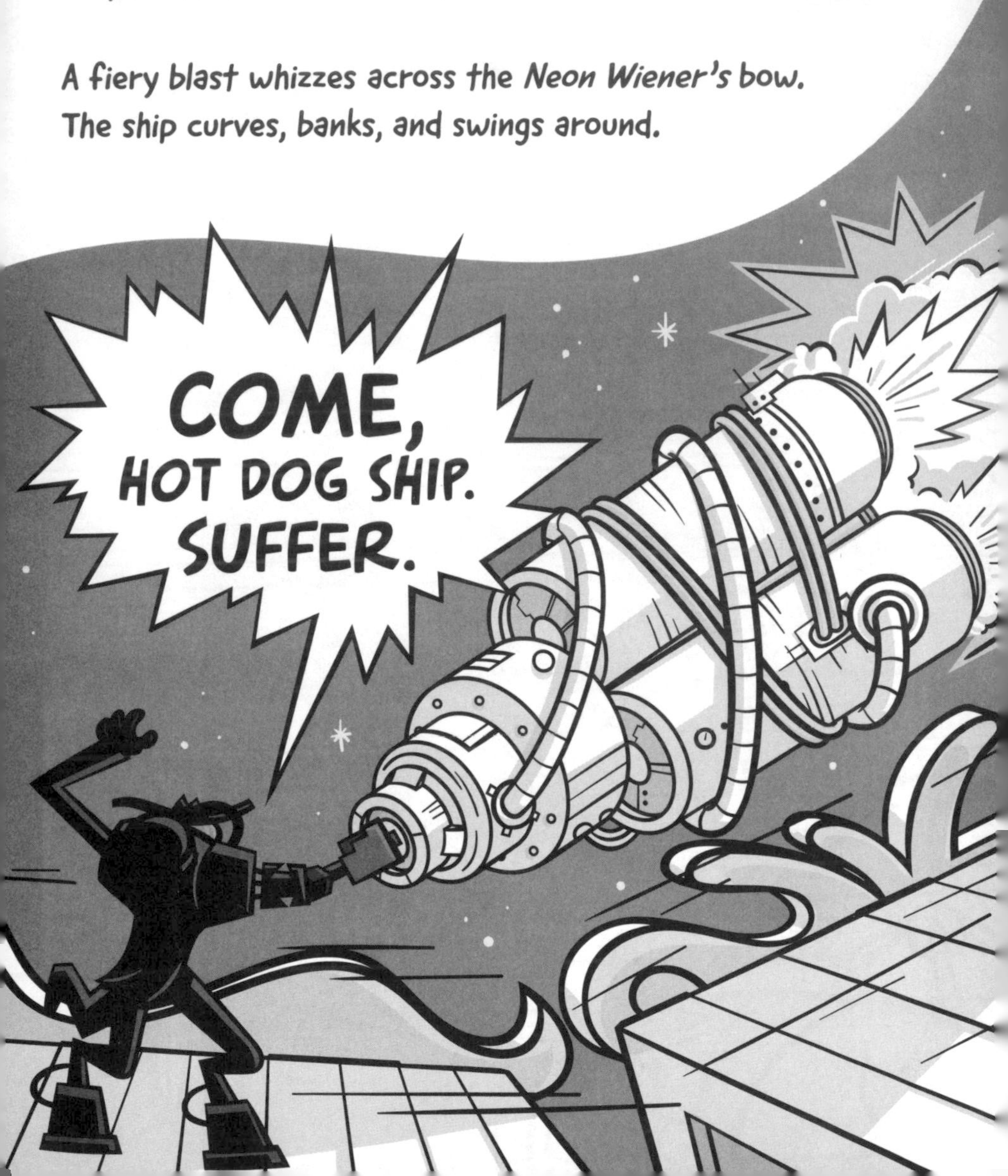
COME, HOT DOG SHIP. SUFFER.

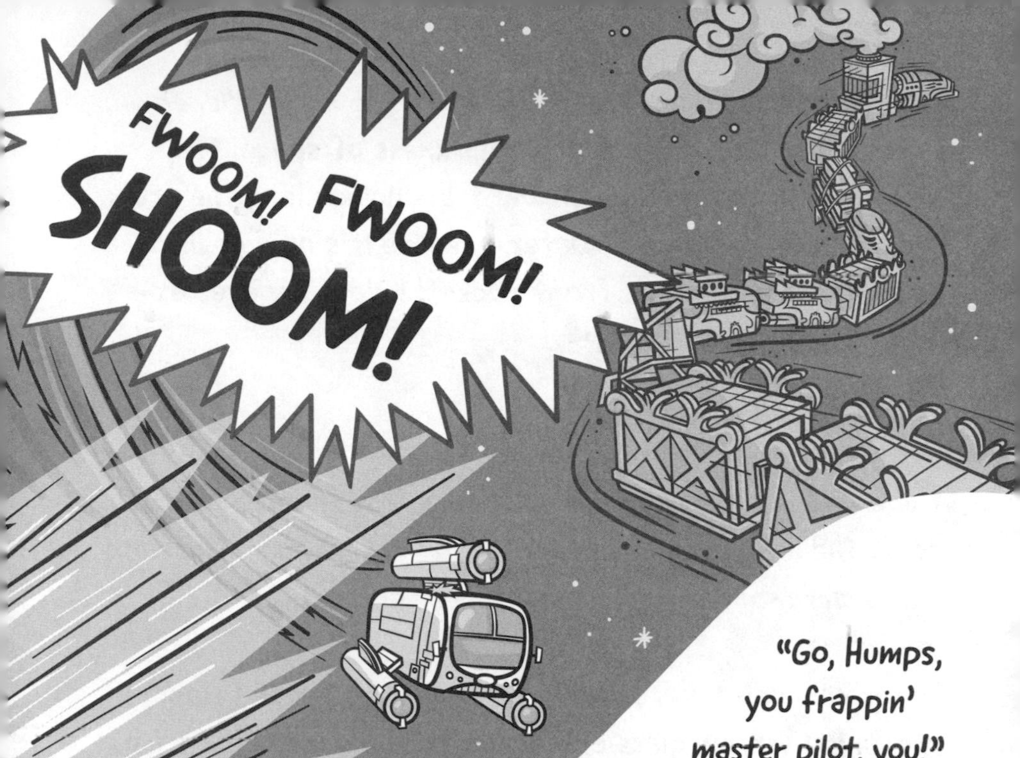

FWOOM! FWOOM!
SHOOM!

"Go, Humps, you frappin' master pilot, you!"

Crostini roars in frustration. He grabs a radio and barks, "Pilot! Steer us hard right, into the *Wiener* craft!"

The pilot comes over the radio, sounding uneasy. "But, Mr. Crostini, sir, the whole train could be . . ."

"I don't care!" Crostini roars. "We will destroy the hot dog vessel! Hit it! Hit it now, I say!"

SLAM! My eyes shoot to the monitor as the train plows into the *Wiener*. Smoke erupts and the *Neon Wiener* spirals through the air like a comet.

The train thrusts upward—KRUNCH—the *Neon Wiener* flips. Sparks shower, filling the darkness of space. The *Neon Wiener* is tumbling forward, bouncing along the train like a pebble skipping on water. I realize it's on a collision course with the train's front rocket! I close my eyes as—

KA-SLAM!

The entire train shakes and goes dark. The front rocket is gone. The main engine is nearly destroyed. My stomach flips like an acro-bot as the train pitches forward.

Everything spins. I'm tumbling through the room. I slam into the jumbo screen, glass cracks, and my clown costume rips. I hear Dags shriek as she crashes into a roust-a-bot.

"Dags!" I yell. **"GRAB ON TO ME!"**

"Huh?" she shouts. "Eww. No. Gross."

"Dags, just do it! No time for saying things are gross!"

"Fine!" she barks. Somersaulting through the room, Dags manages to latch on to my hand.

"Goober!" I shout. **"KEEP US SAFE!"** With that, Goober begins bubbling up, and soon he's surrounding us in a giant rubbery ball. And just in time . . .

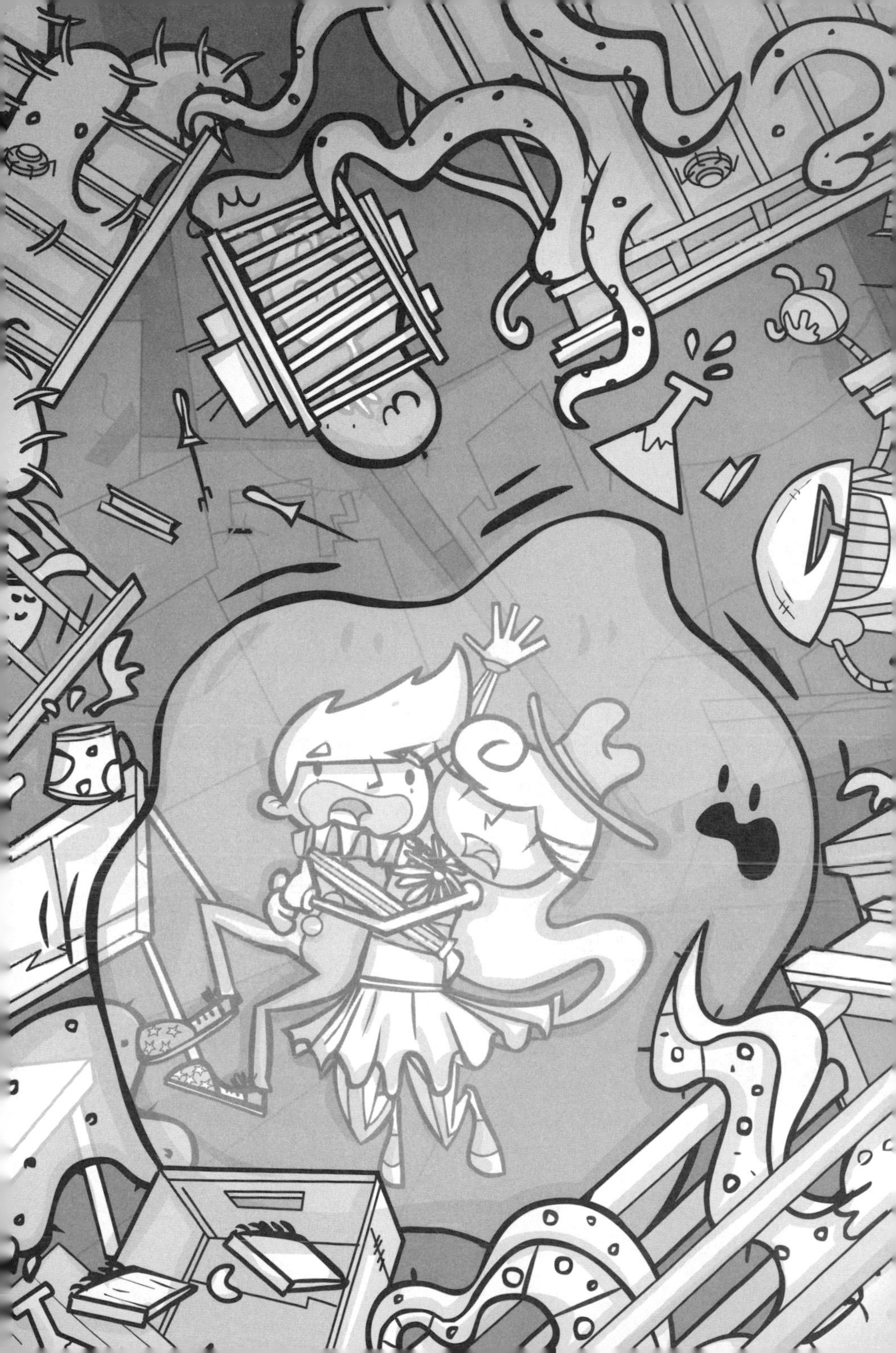

Crostini's Cosmic Carnival and Wonder Circus train is 100% out of control—HURTLING, FLAMING,

PLUMMETING

like a comet toward planet Alzion far, far below . . .

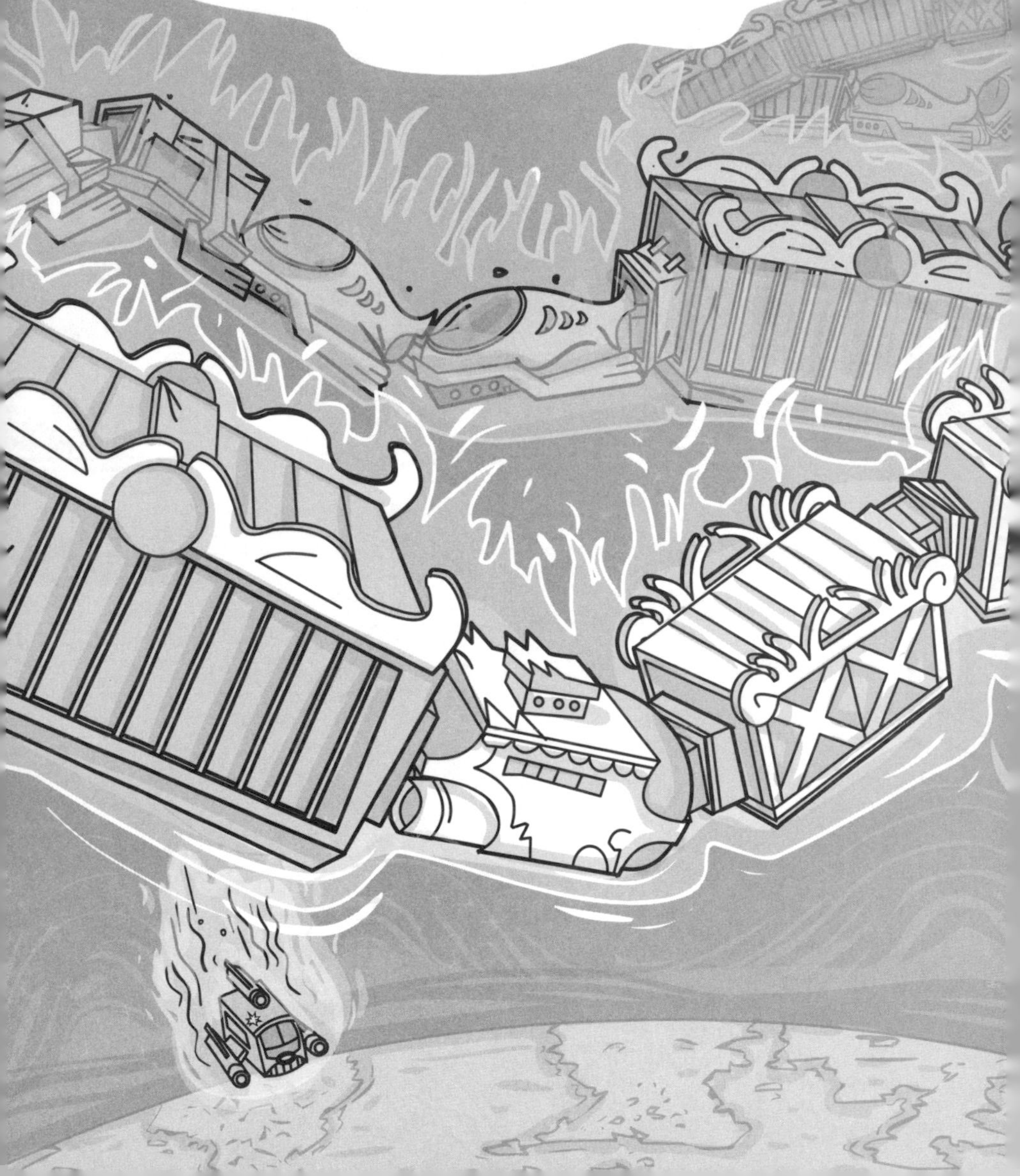

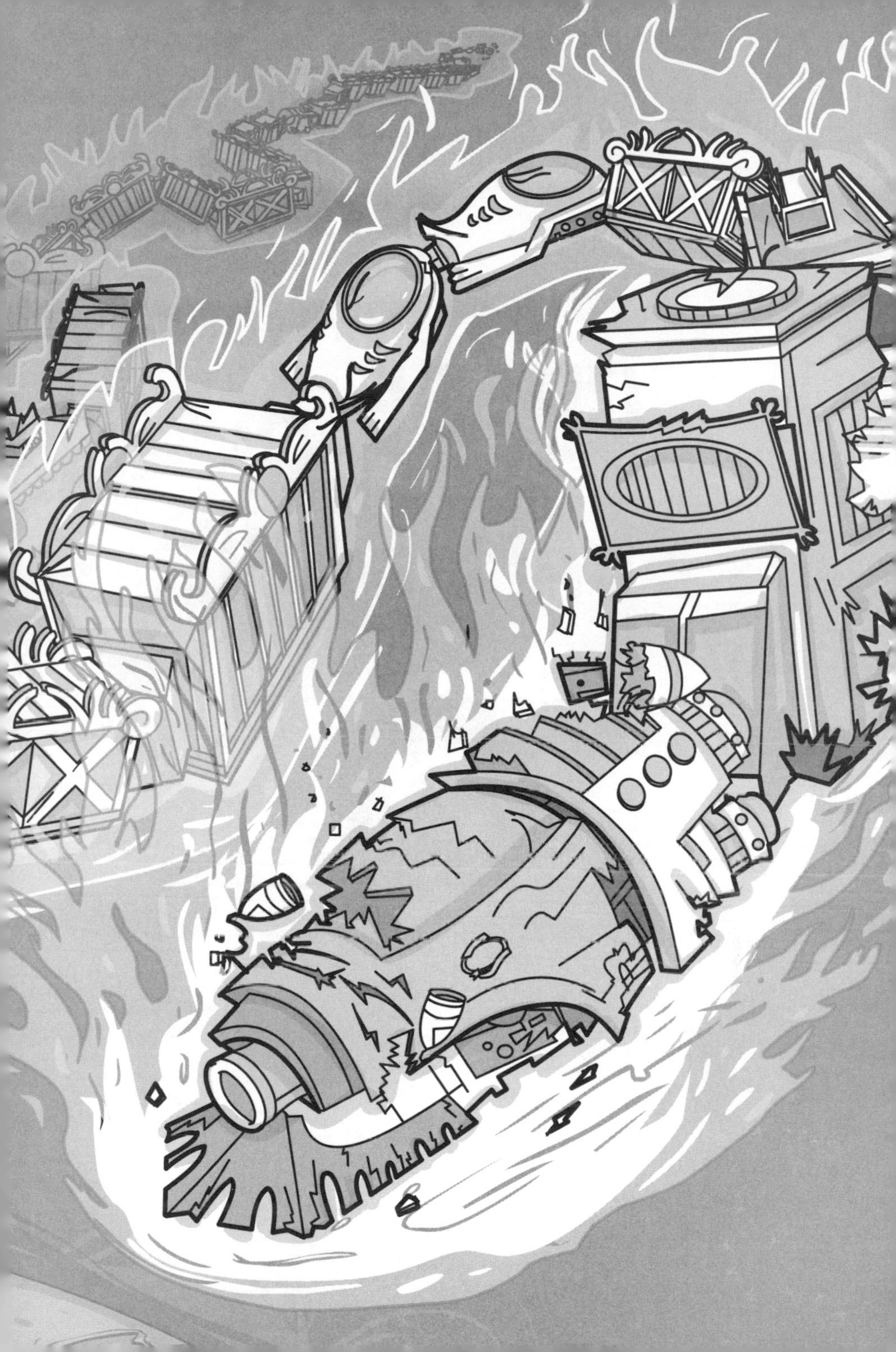

GRADE A, TOP TEN, SLAM-BANG

21

THERE'S A CRASH.

I think. There MUST be a crash, right? But I don't feel it. All I know is my ears are ringing like the school fire alarm, and there's so much smoke in my nostrils, I'll probably never grow nose hairs. Not complaining. Nose hairs are nasty.

Dagger is still gripping my arm. Goober's still enveloping us in a rubbery cocoon. I flex my wrist, and Goober returns to my side. "Dags, you alive?" I whisper.

"I think so," she says. "I *feel* alive. Also, a little hungry. Just putting that out there."

And then it hits me like an Astro Derby bat to the belly. Humps. The *Neon Wiener.* It's such a small ship. And it fell **SO FAR.** From **SO HIGH.**

I almost lost Dagger.
And now Humphree?

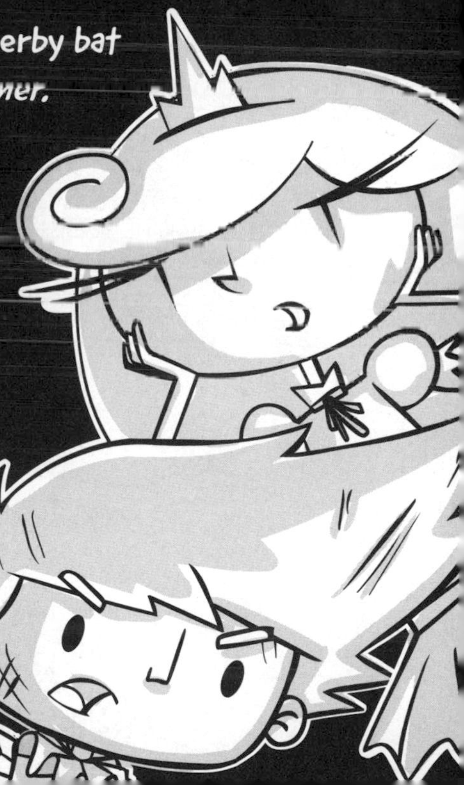

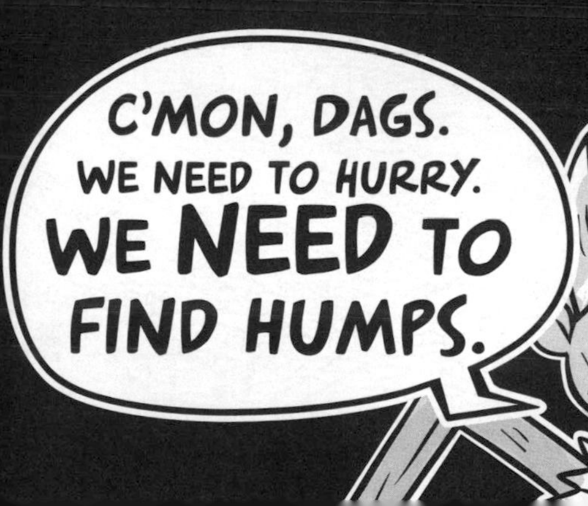
C'MON, DAGS.
WE NEED TO HURRY.
WE NEED TO
FIND HUMPS.

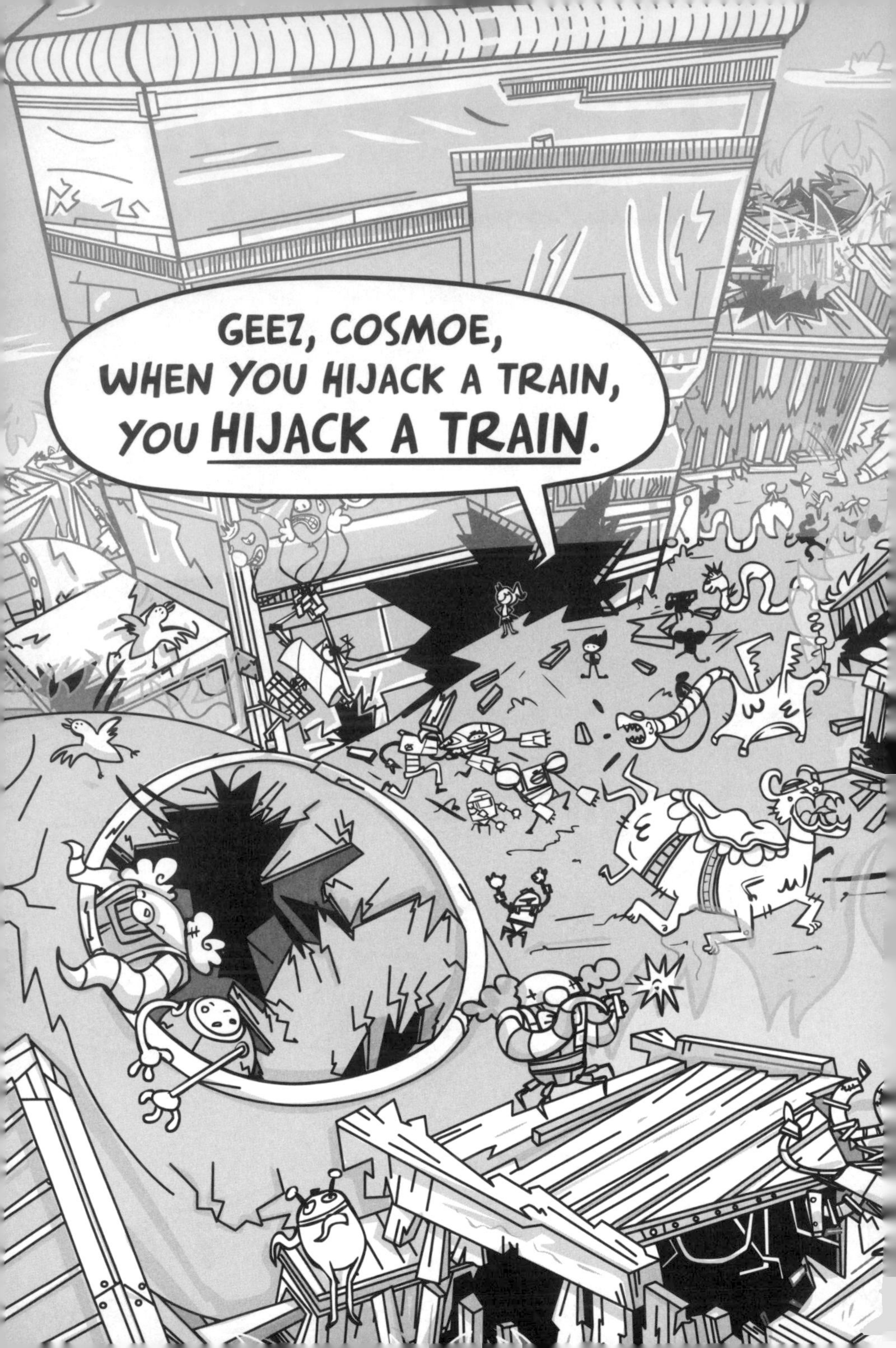
GEEZ, COSMOE, WHEN YOU HIJACK A TRAIN, YOU HIJACK A TRAIN.

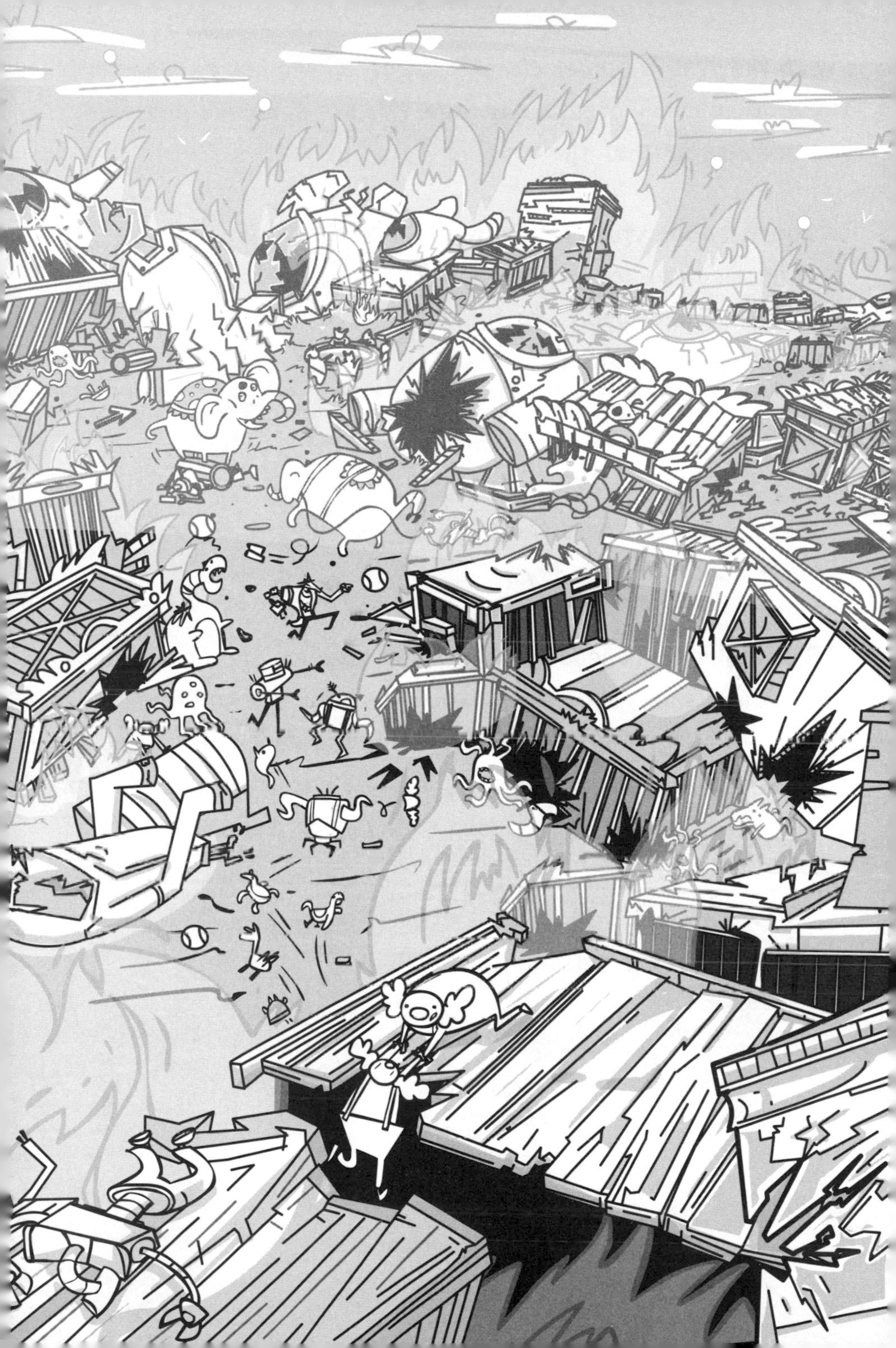

With the train's power circuits kaput, all the blaze-cages are now open. Every creature is free! It's like someone just flung open every gate at the zoo.

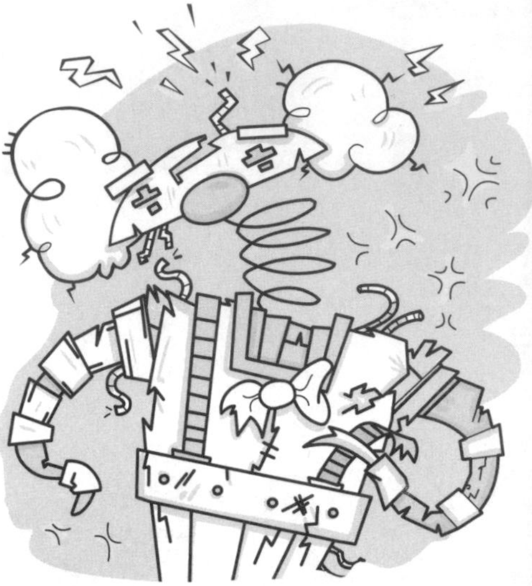

A roust-a-bot stumbles past me, his electro-noggin sparks twice, and he crumples to the rocky ground. Clown-bots pour out of the train—confusion all over their digital face-screens.

"These bad dudes have seen better days . . ." Dags says.

Stretching out ahead of us is the jagged, colorful surface of the planet Alzion. Huge mountains dot the horizon. Cliffs and rocky bluffs far ahead. A thin tendril of smoke rises up from a gorge in the distance. Could that be the *Neon Wiener* . . . ?

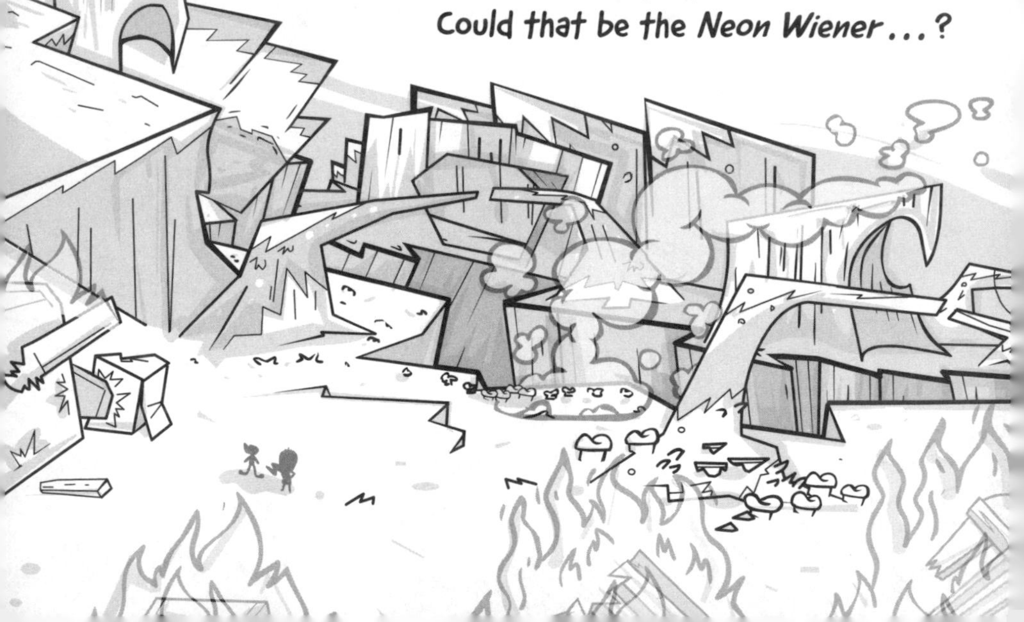

"C'mon, this way!" I say, taking hold of Dagger's hand. We push through the mob of bots and creatures.

"You think the *Neon Wiener* crash-landed down there?" Dagger asks. "It could have just blown up. EXPLODED. Ball of flame. All, like, fwoom red-hot!"

"**DAGS!!!**" I shout. "Don't say that! You can't say that stuff! What's the matter with you?"

"What? It's true. It could have."

I scowl at my part-evil friend. I don't have time to explain normal-person emotions to her.

We skid to a stop at the brink of the cliff. I'm so terrified of what I might find that I'm shaking. If Humps is gone, I don't know what I'll do. I'll be lost. I'll never forgive myself. My heart hammers as I peer over the edge . . .

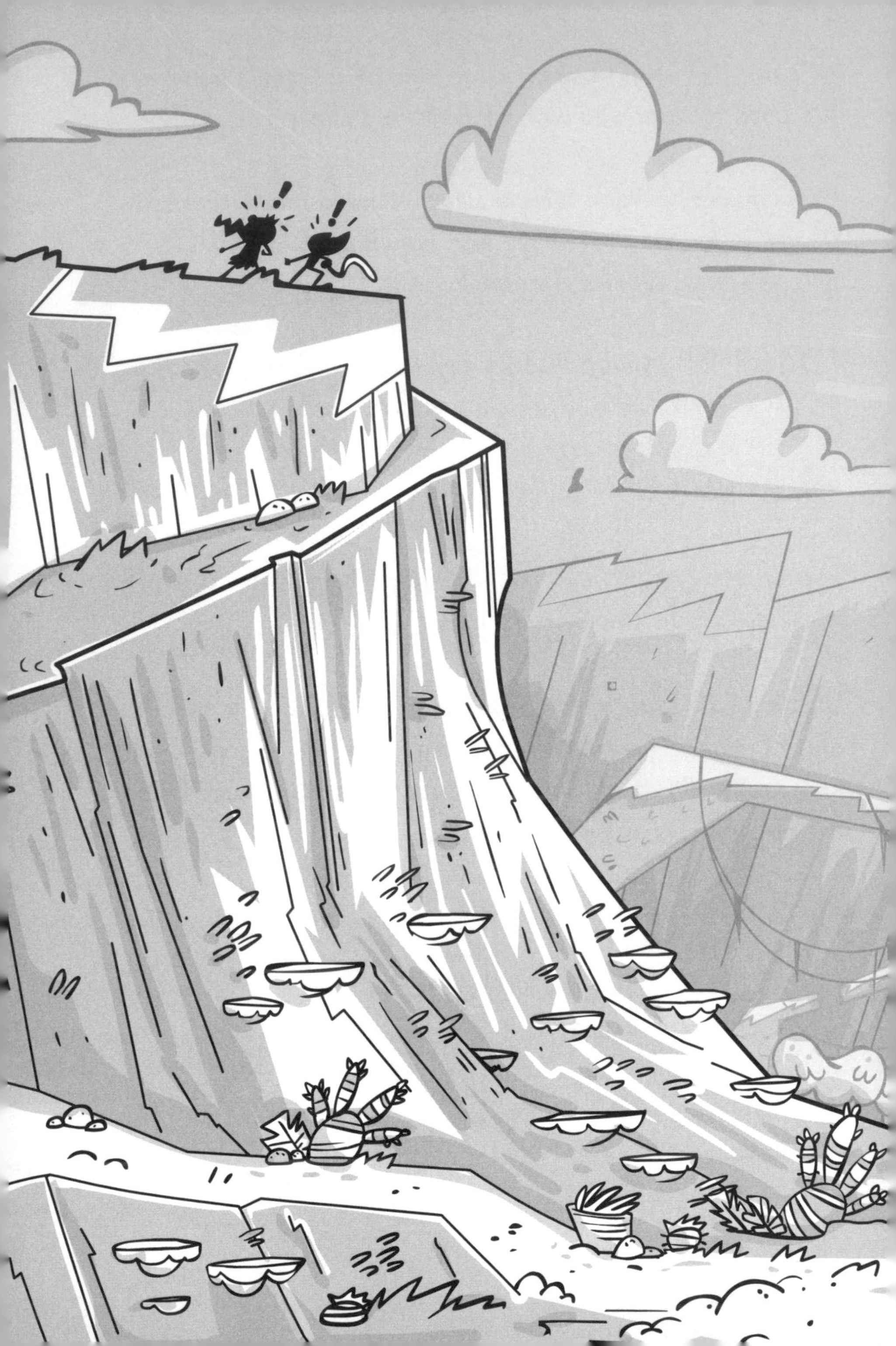

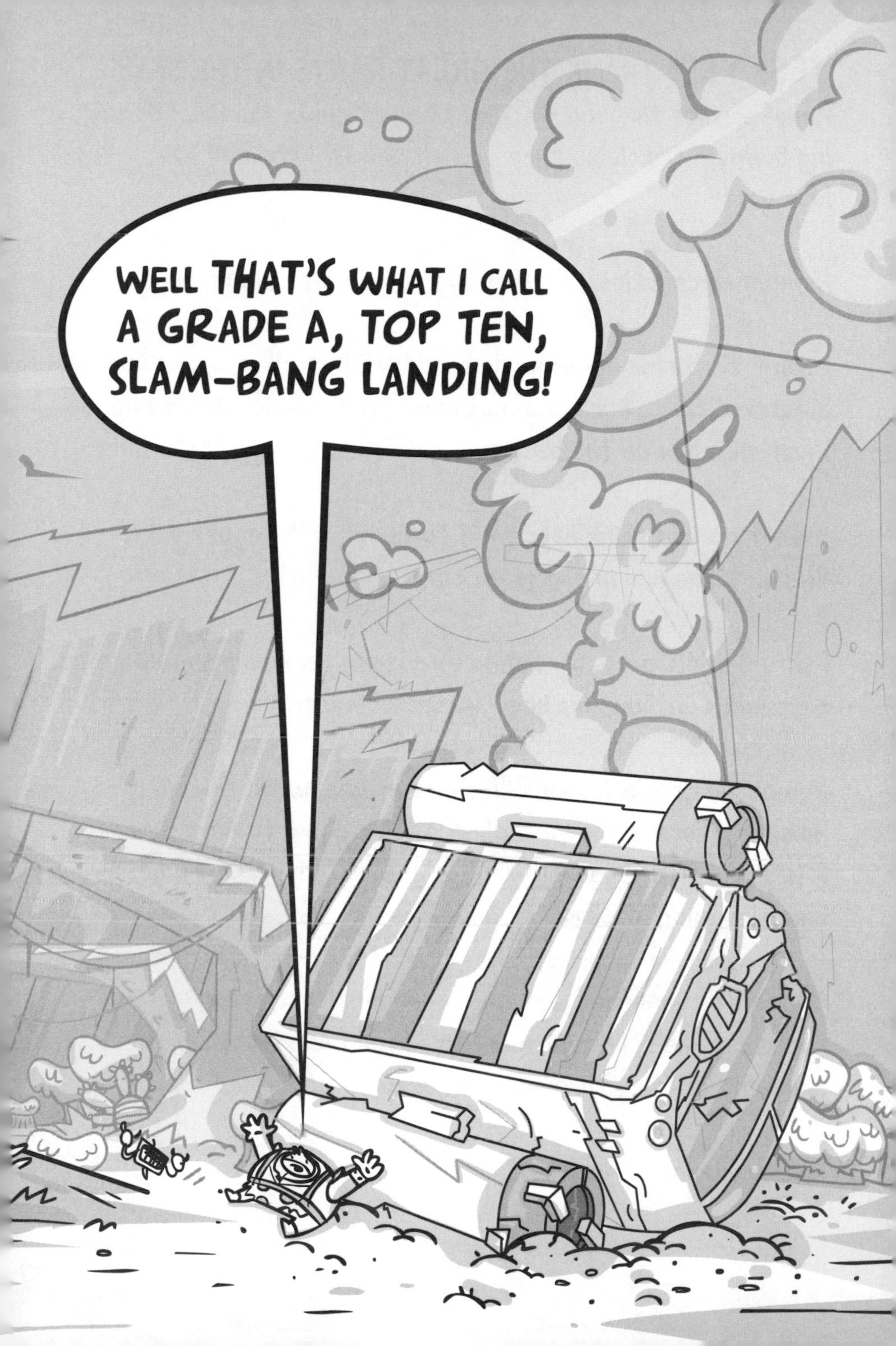
WELL THAT'S WHAT I CALL A GRADE A, TOP TEN, SLAM-BANG LANDING!

YES. YES! THANK THE GREAT PANTS IN THE SKY!

Relief rushes through me, and I bound down the hill. "Buddy, big buddy!" I exclaim. "Are you all good?! I thought we lost you!"

Humphree chuckles. "I'm too big to get lost, short pants."

I want to throw my arms around him. But y'know, I'm an awesome space hero and awesome space dudes don't hug. So I just slap him on the back and grin so wide my cheeks hurt.

"What do you think happened to Crostini?" Dagger asks. "I didn't see him in the train car."

I shrug. "He's probably hiding and crying somewhere. He's no big shakes without his heavy—the wrangler."

Humphree cracks his knuckles and makes his ol' rumbling noise. "Where is the wrangler? We're going to have words, **HIM** and **ME**. Shootin' our ship out of the sky—I'll get my knuckles good and bruised over that."

"Dude, the wrangler was on the roof of the train," I say. "So unless he's, like, Terminator-type indestructible, he's probably drifting through the cosmos right now."

And suddenly, I grin. That means . . .

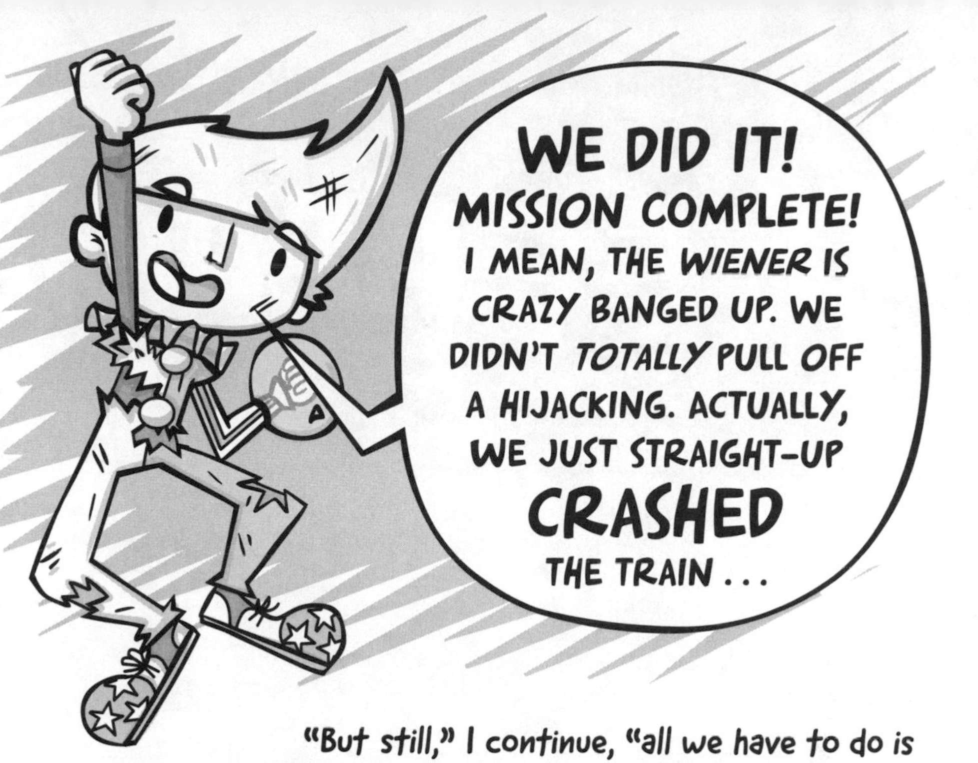
WE DID IT!
MISSION COMPLETE!
I MEAN, THE *WIENER* IS CRAZY BANGED UP. WE DIDN'T *TOTALLY* PULL OFF A HIJACKING. ACTUALLY, WE JUST STRAIGHT-UP
CRASHED
THE TRAIN . . .

"But still," I continue, "all we have to do is go back and put Crostini on lockdown, and we're done . . ."

Humphree nods. "Blow me up, short pants. You're right. And once Crostini's done, I bet all the bots fall right in line."

Dagger does a double backflip. "ROCK ON! We fix up the train, hook the *Wiener* to the front, and we're done! Game over! Creatures saved!

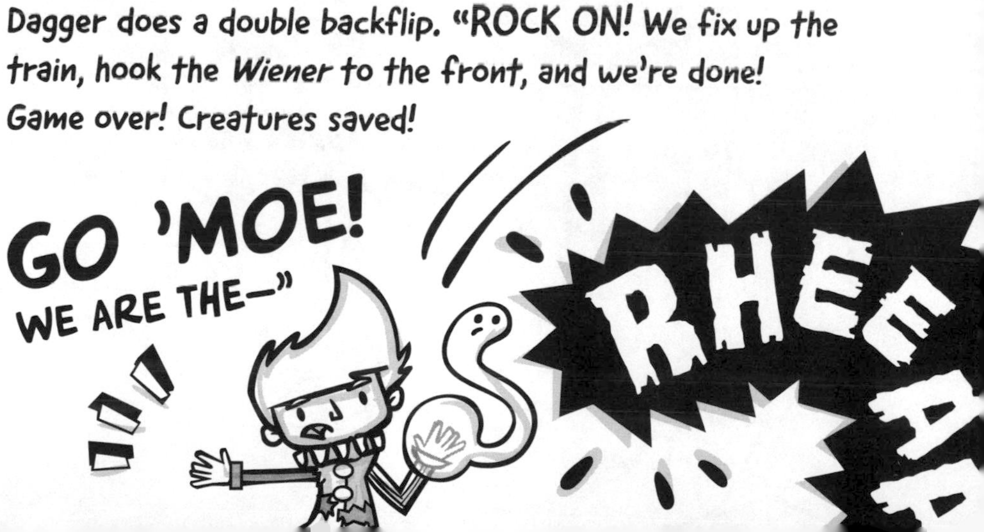
GO 'MOE!
WE ARE THE—"
RHEEA

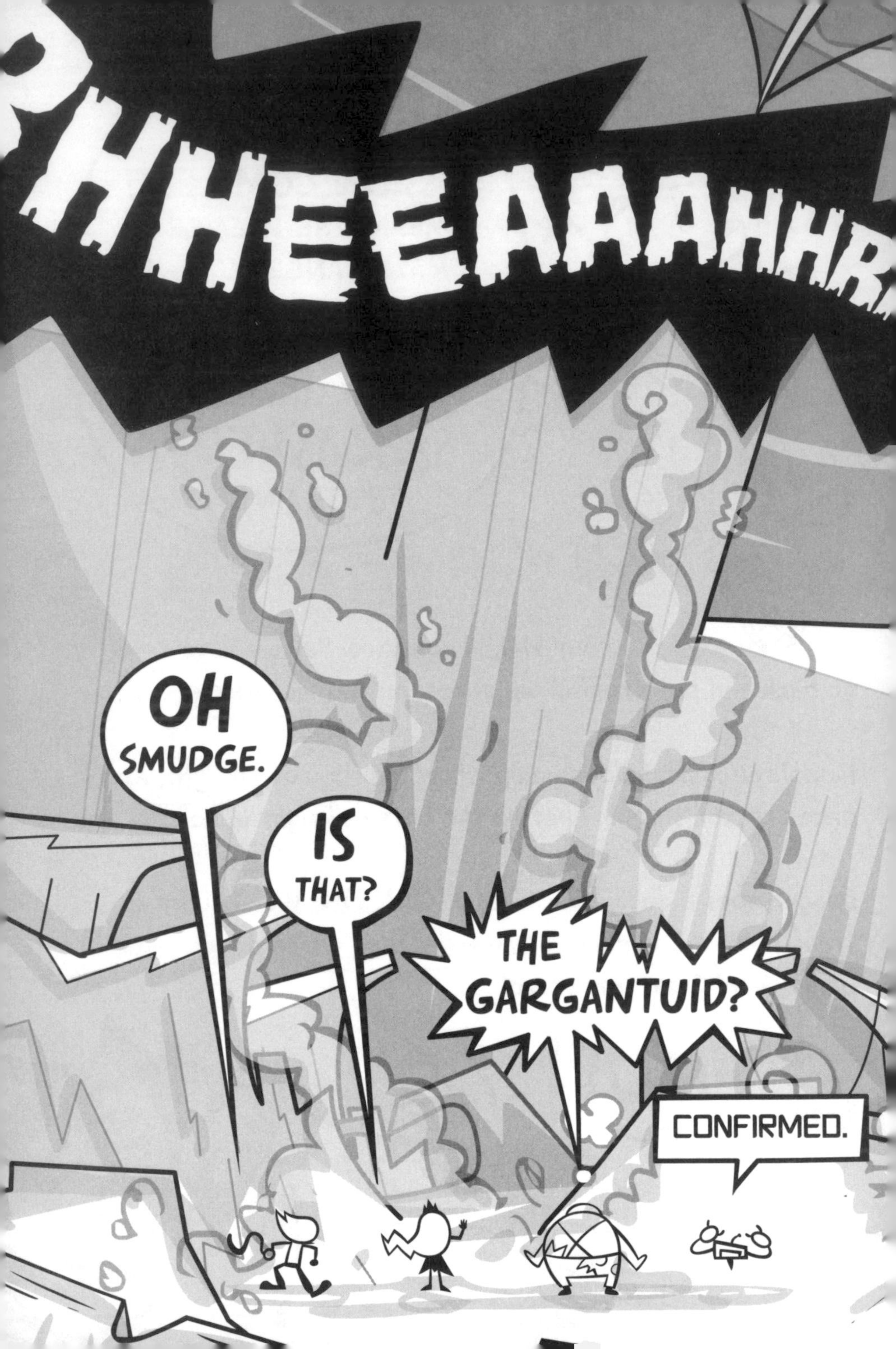

RHHEEAAAAHHR
OH SMUDGE.
IS THAT?
THE GARGANTUID?
CONFIRMED.

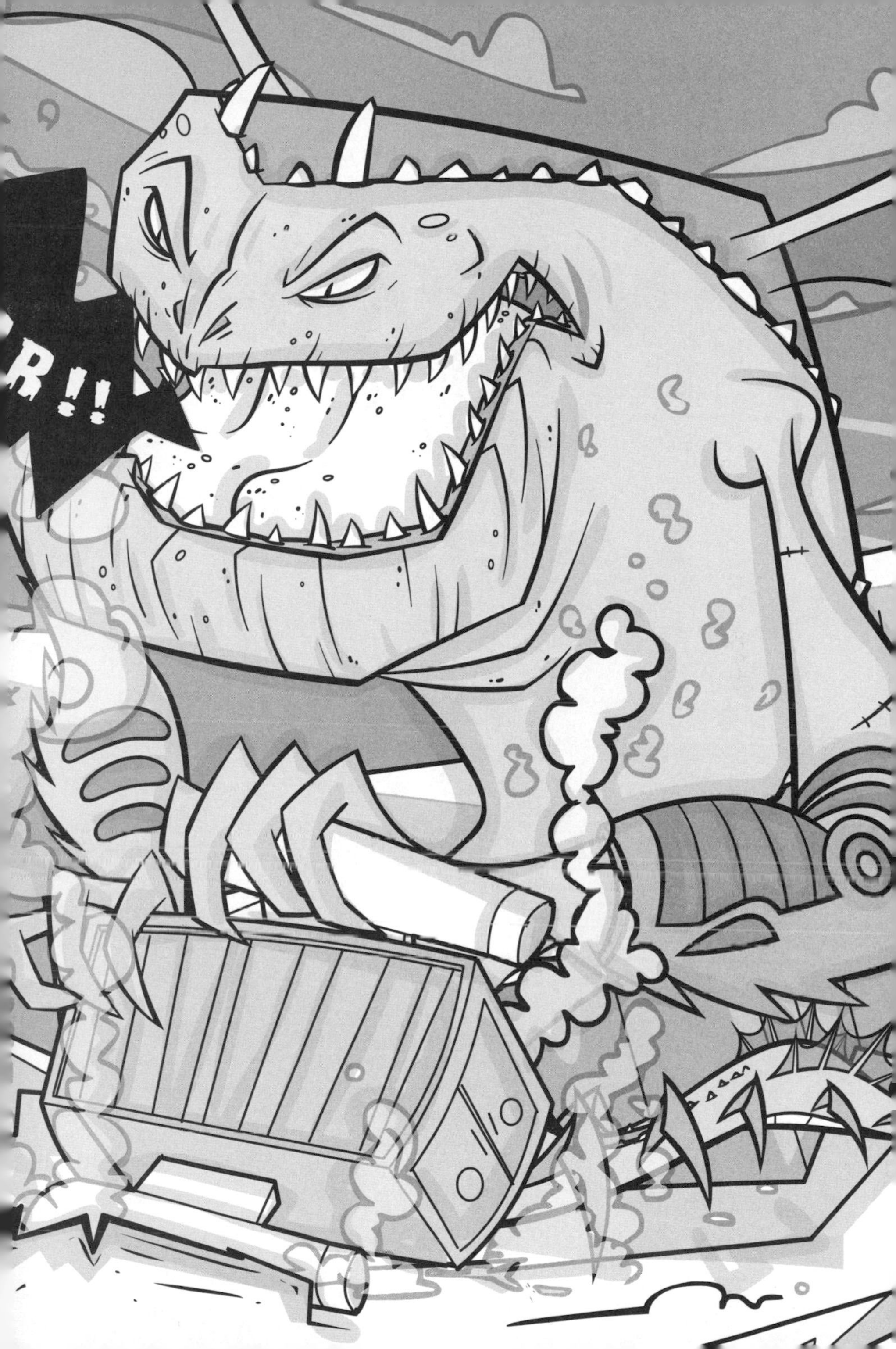
R!!

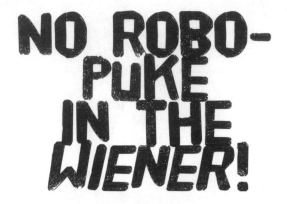

NO ROBO-PUKE IN THE WIENER!

22

There's an **EAR-EXPLODING RUMBLING**, like Humphree's stomach when he hasn't eaten in a few hours. I realize . . . It IS a stomach!

THE GARGANTUID'S STOMACH!

The gargantuid's gut thunders again, and its huge neck cranes to the side. It's eying the circus creatures.

"It's going to eat them!" I exclaim, suddenly realizing. "It's going to eat all the circus creatures! We need to lead the gargantuid away from the train, somehow. If only the *Neon Wiener* wasn't upside down—"

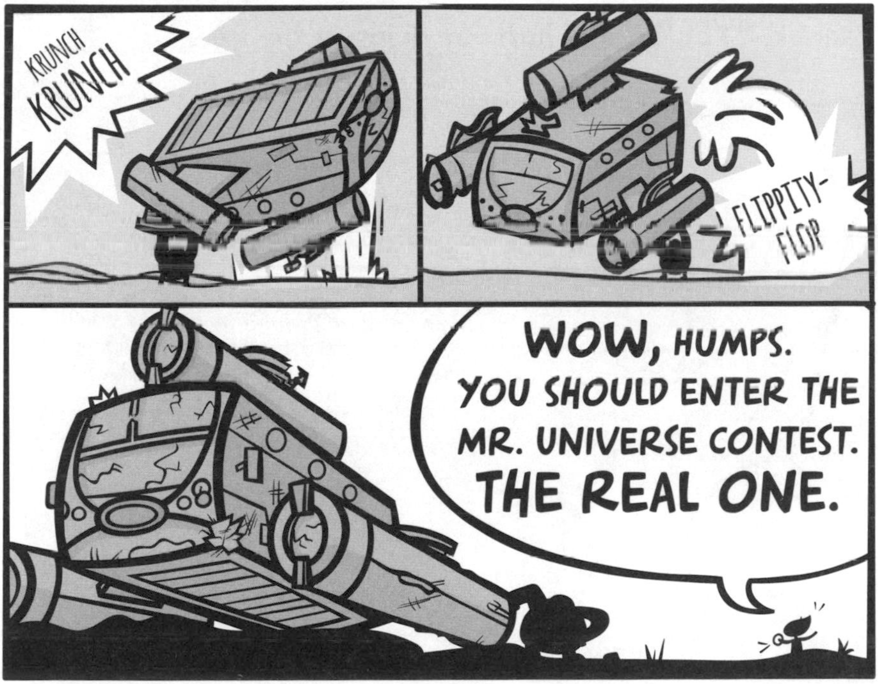
KRUNCH
KRUNCH
FLIPPITY-FLOP
WOW, HUMPS. YOU SHOULD ENTER THE MR. UNIVERSE CONTEST. THE REAL ONE.

Humphree and Dags race inside the ship. I start jumping around and waving my arms like I'm a hummingbird trying to take flight or something. **"HEY, GARGANTUID!!!"** I holler. "We're edible!!! And TASTY!!! **FOLLOW US!!!**"

The gargantuid's massive, snaky eyes look me over with disinterest. Fair enough ... He's got a whole smorgasbord of creatures to dine on like fifty yards away! What's one loser kid, his big buddy, an evil princess, and a hovering robot butler matter? That's probably like six calories for the gargantuid.

But Humphree starts the engine and fires up the jets, blowing a blast of heat directly into the gargantuid's face. The thing snarls, and its silvery eyes flash with displeasure.

I shriek, **"YEEP!"** and hotfoot it inside the *Wiener*.

My fingers are practically strangling the copilot's chair as the *Neon Wiener* skims above Alzion's jagged surface at max, max, max, triple top speed.

F.R.E.D. is doing everything possible to keep our damaged engine from pooping the hammock: flipping power switches, spinning the dynamic drive dial, and diverting energy to the rear jets. But it's not enough . . .

"That giant monster jerk is **CLOSING IN FAST!**" Dagger shouts.

Humphree throws the control stick forward, and I'm flattened against the seat like a pancake as the *Neon Wiener* plunges into a narrow canyon.

"Flying through a **FRAPPING RAVINE**, Humps?!" I scream. "One wrong move, and we'll all be Smithereens brand spaghetti sauce!"

Dagger glances in the rearview. "Guys? Um. The mouth is opening . . ."

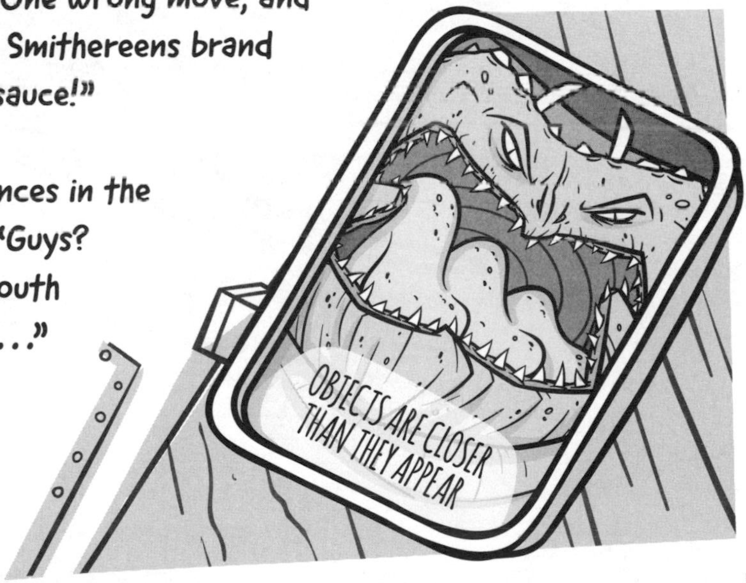
OBJECTS ARE CLOSER THAN THEY APPEAR

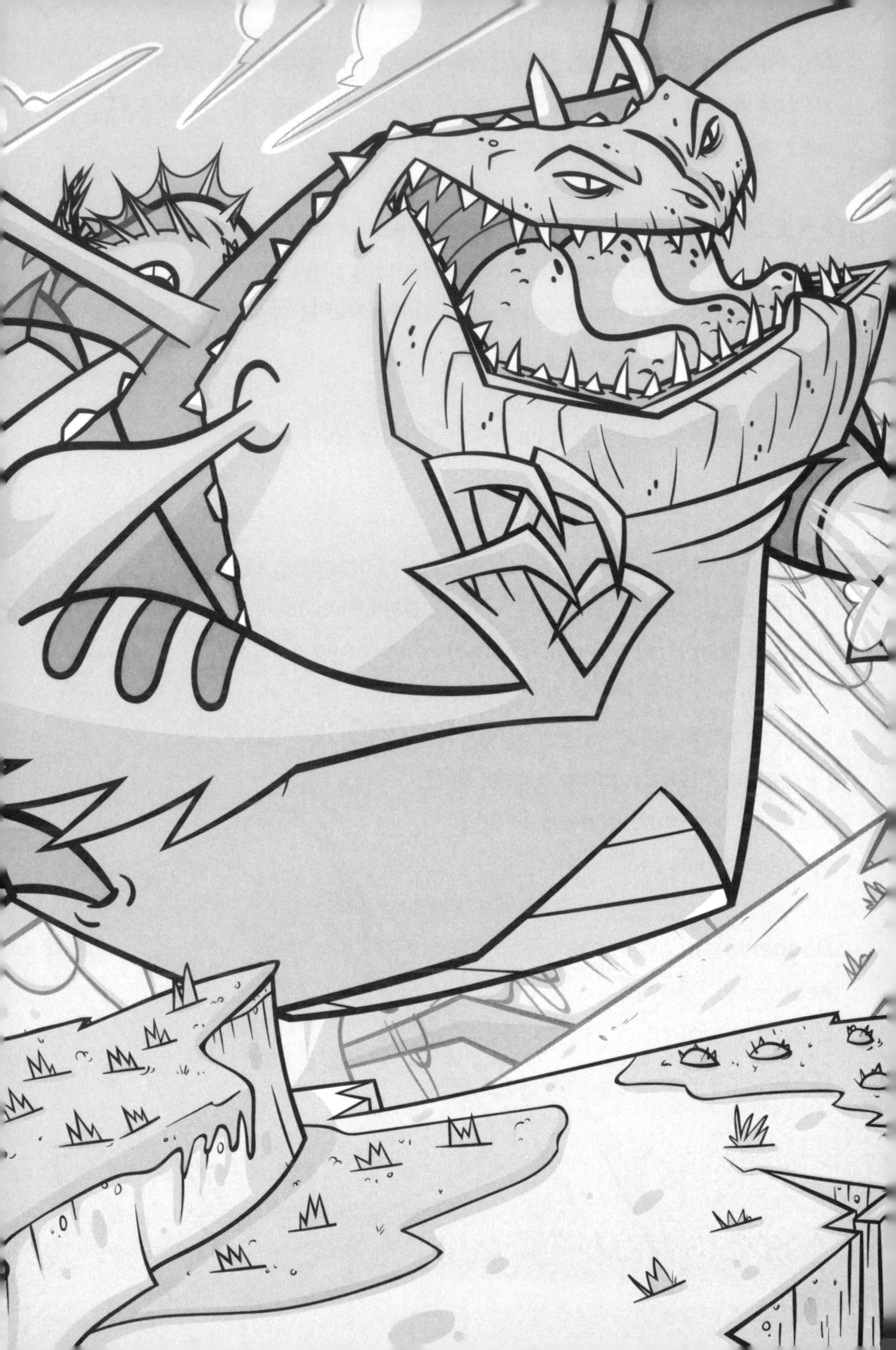

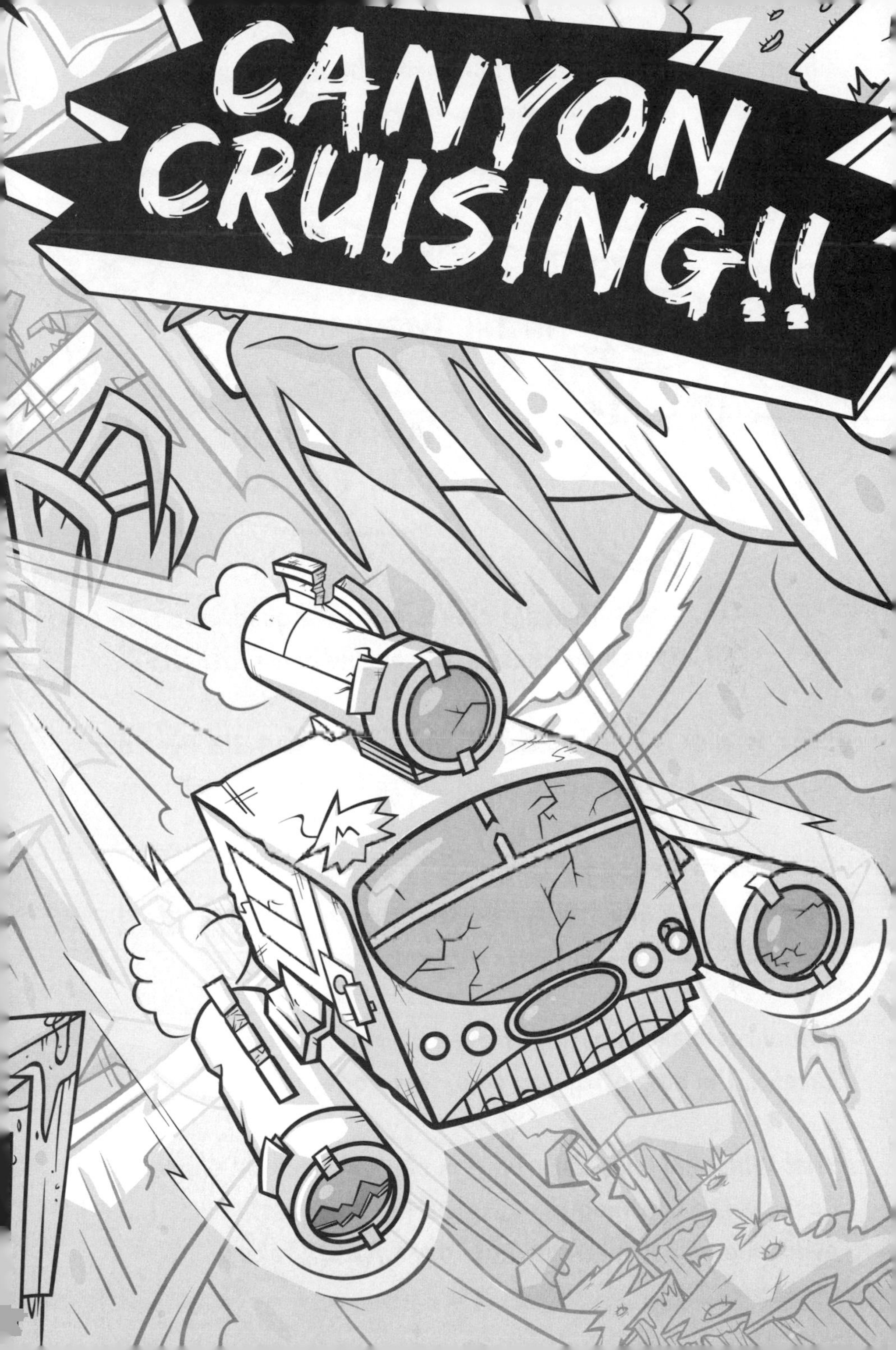
CANYON CRUISING!!

"Hang on to your butts!" Humphree shouts, as he sends the *Neon Wiener* into a vicious barrel roll . . .

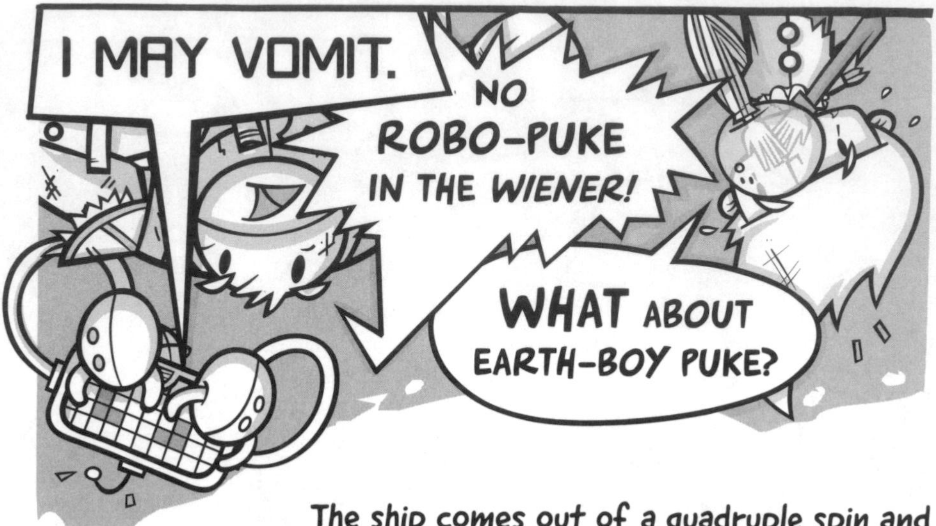
I MAY VOMIT.
NO ROBO-PUKE IN THE WIENER!
WHAT ABOUT EARTH-BOY PUKE?

The ship comes out of a quadruple spin and Humphree punches it. The engine only **COUGHS** . . .

"The *Wiener* is beat-up **BAD**," Humphree says. His eyes dart across the cockpits dials. "And we're leaking gas . . ."

We need to make a move, or we're all done for. I unbuckle my seat strap and stand. "Humphree, you just stay ahead of fang face back there. Dags, with me."

Humphree glances back. His eyes narrow. "You guys be careful. I'm not losing you two. Not today."

"Ha! When am I not careful? I'm captain careful! Captain Cosmoe the Continuously Careful! In fact, that's what I want everyone to call me from now on. F.R.E.D., take a note."

Two space minutes later, I'm being 100% not the least bit at all careful—about to do maybe the single most not-careful thing of my life. But it must be done. The life of every creature in the circus depends on it.

WE'RE GOING TO **JUMP** ON ITS BACK.

THEN WHAT?

"WE WING IT!" I say, shouting over the roar of the engine and the speed.

"Is that an earth pun?" Dagger shouts. "Because the gargantuid has wings?"

"No! But oh man, that's a good one. I wish I thought of that!"

Dagger rolls her eyes while I punch the radio button and call to Humphree. "Keep her steady, buddy!"

"Steady as she goes, short pants!" Humphree calls back.

I look to Dagger and grin. "Then it's time we . . ."

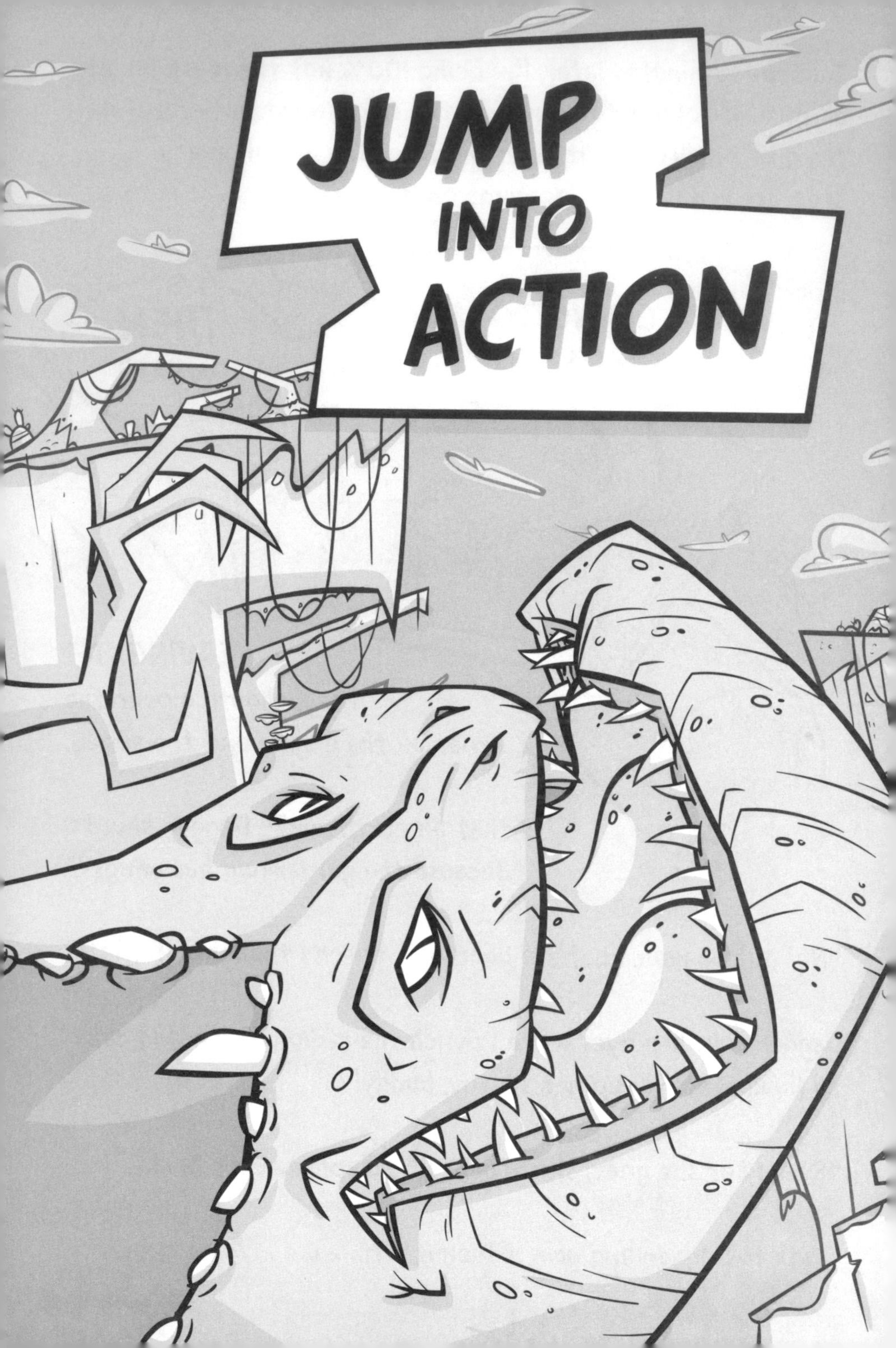
JUMP
INTO
ACTION

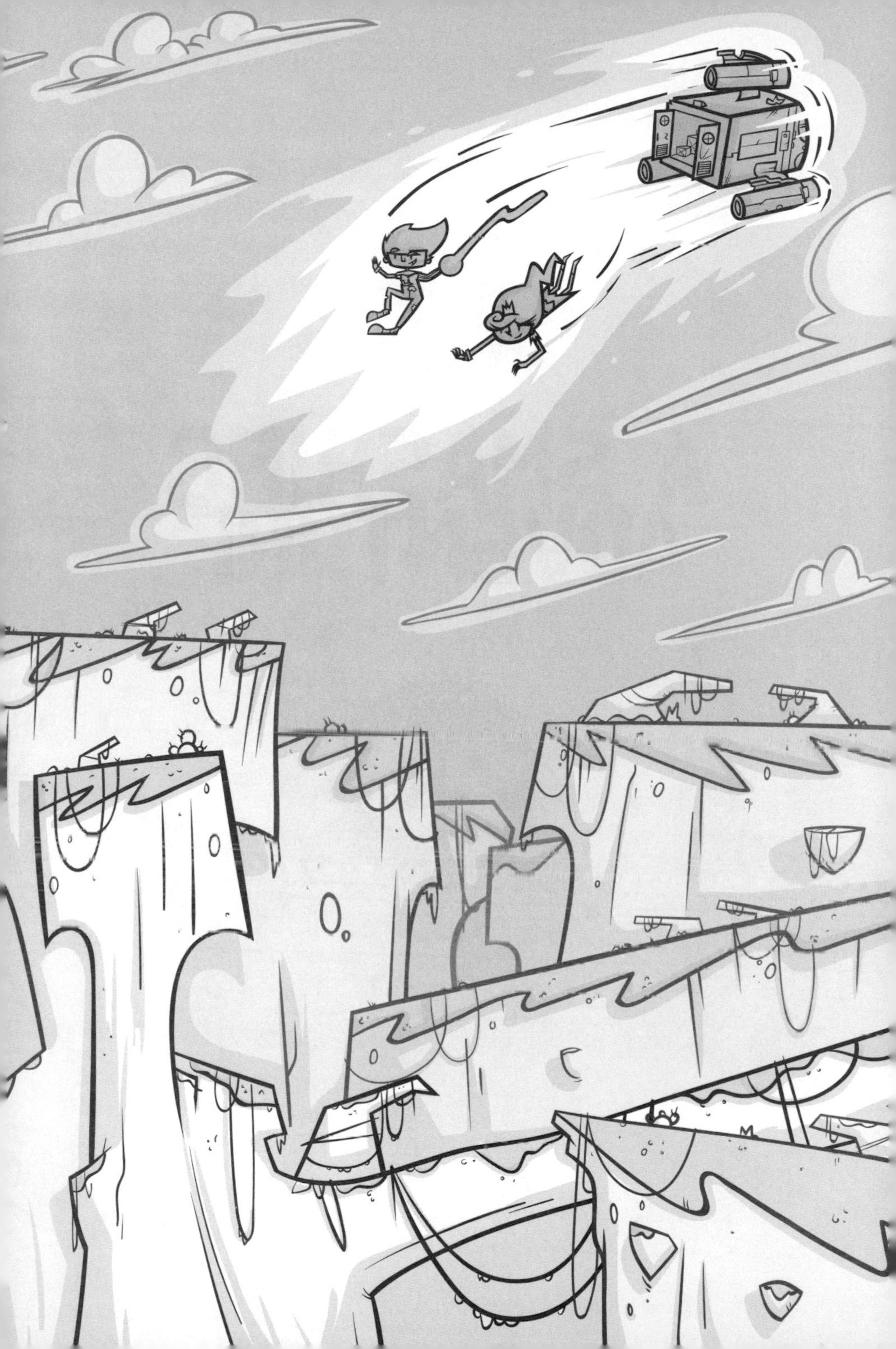

A SMASHING ADVENTURE

23

I *slam* into the gargantuid's rock-hard hide like a brick dropped from space. My face bounces, pain shoots through my nose, and then I'm tumbling, end over end . . .

Just before I plummet to my doom, Goober **SCHLURPS** to the creature's scales. I reach out—and I feel Dagger's hand clasp mine, just an instant before she plunges over the side.

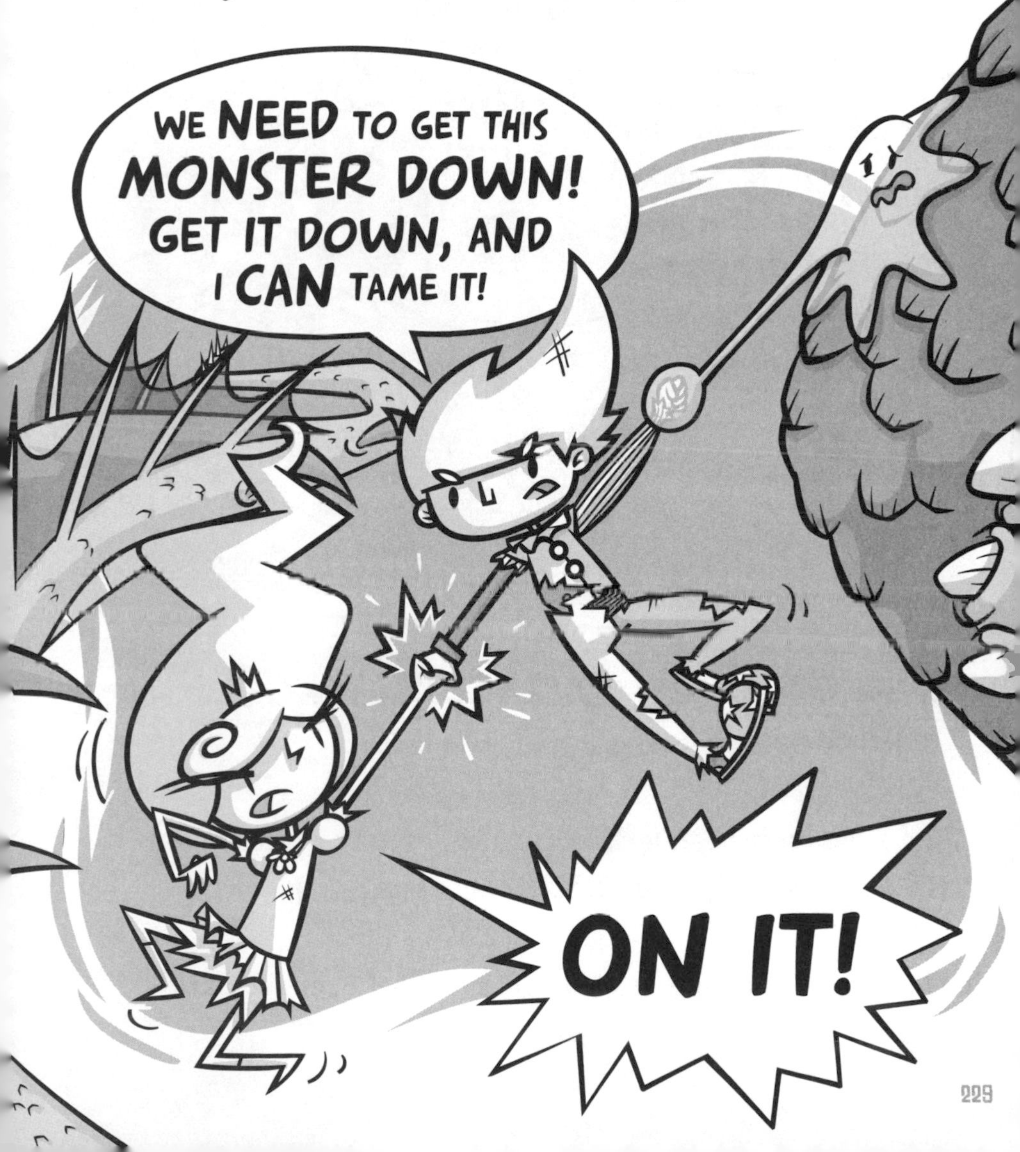
WE NEED TO GET THIS MONSTER DOWN! GET IT DOWN, AND I CAN TAME IT!
ON IT!

Dagger leaps over me like she's spring-loaded. Her hair whips around like a bunch of dancing snakes as her evil acrobatic abilities allow her to scale the gargantuid's back like Spider-Woman. BTW, is that a thing still, Spider-Woman?

Suddenly, Dagger's massively long scroll appears—and she hurls it over the monster's eyes—

HEY, GARGANTUID!
LET'S HAVE AN ADVENTURE!

Unbelievable: Dagger's **ADVENTURE SCROLL** is actually useful! The gargantuid is totally blinded!

The monster's head jerks and thrashes, but it can't tear through the evilly unbreakable Malfenzia parchment!

"He's getting beastly saliva spit stuff all over my list!" Dagger shouts. **"THAT'S RADICAL!"**

I'm flapping and flopping in the breeze like a kite as we careen through the canyon. I catch quick glimpses of the chasm and the sky, and then—**WHOOMP**—the gargantuid swoops up and my entire body slams into its spinal plating. "That's gonna hurt tomorrow," I groan.

"It's landing time!" Dagger shrieks as she squeezes her legs tight like a vise around the monster's neck and yanks on the indestructible scroll.

The gargantuid emits a final roar and then, clueless as to what's up and what's down, nosedives into the ground . . .

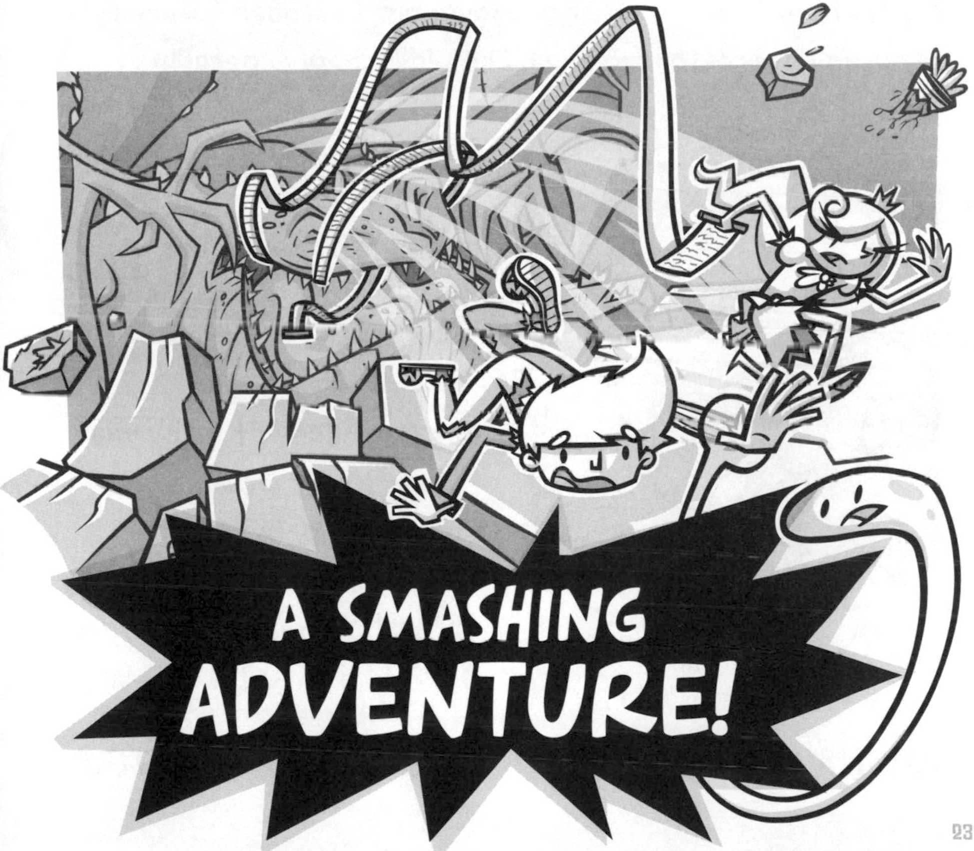
A SMASHING
ADVENTURE!

You ever get the wind knocked out of you? Well, I get the wind SHATTERED out of me. Exploded out of me. NUCLEAR DETONATED out of me!

I hit the ground and tumble about twenty-two times. Every inch of my body is pain. I heave and heave and struggle to get my breath back. At last, Dagger helps me to my feet.

At the same time, the gargantuid is rising.

DAZED. CONFUSED. <u>ANGERED.</u>

I swallow hard. My fingers are trembling. But it's time. My feet really don't want to move, but I stagger forward, catching my breath, and then, like old-school Superman . . .

RIP!

Dagger's beyond confused. "Uh, Cosmoe, why are you getting shirtless? This is definitely NOT the time for shirtlessness."

But Dags doesn't know that I wasn't only wearing my clown getup. Beneath my tattered clown clothes is my father's lion-tamer costume. **THAT'S RIGHT—**

I'M AN AWESOME TWO-COSTUME-WEARING HERO GUY!

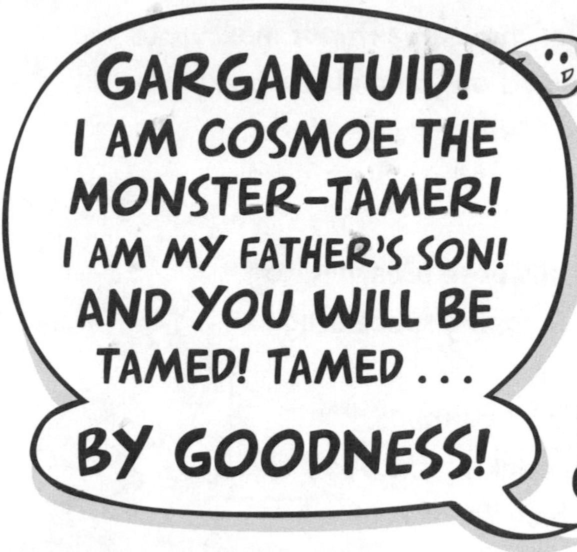
GARGANTUID!
I AM COSMOE THE
MONSTER-TAMER!
I AM MY FATHER'S SON!
AND YOU WILL BE
TAMED! TAMED . . .
BY GOODNESS!

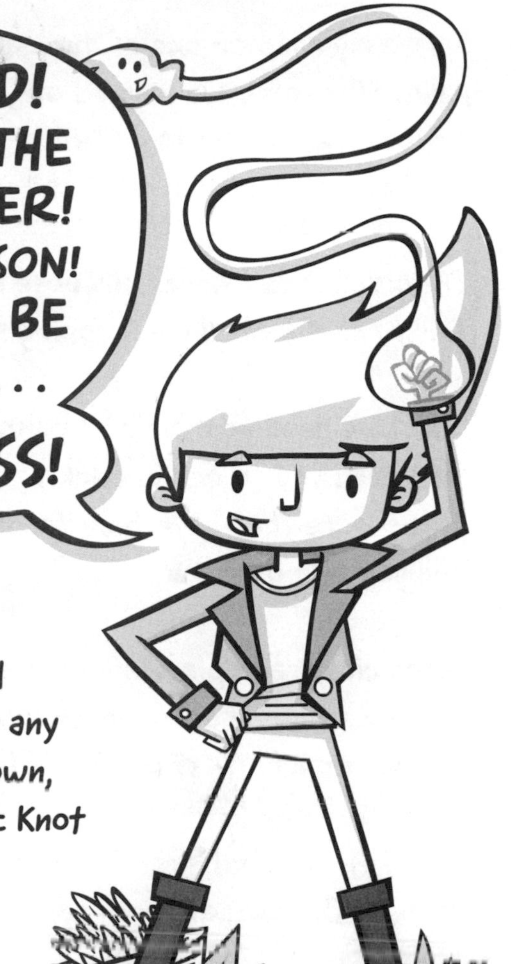

The gargantuid eyes me with a monstrous mixture of contempt, annoyance, and curiosity. He could eat me at any moment. Just swallow me down, one bite, like a Galactic Garlic Knot from Caprizi's Pizza Zone.

But I can't let that happen.

I think about my father always telling me that every creature deserves respect. I'm going to make my old man proud.

"Listen, gargantuid," I say slowly and softly. "I'm not going to hurt you. I promise. But there's a bad man named Crostini who **WILL** hurt you. He wants to lock you up and make you part of a big evil army."

I place my hand on one of the gargantuid's monstrous paws. "I'm sorry we jumped on you and crashed you. But you were going to eat all those creatures. And I couldn't let you do that."

The gargantuid exhales. His nose breath is hot. This thing is basically a frapping space dragon.

"Now we need your help," I continue. "We need you to get us back to the bad guys before they have time to regroup. Will you help us?"

I step closer and place my hand on the monster's side. He shivers. But he doesn't bite. He doesn't eat me. Go me! A+ start for not getting eaten.

"So, if it's cool," I say, "I'm just going to climb up here. On your, ah, neck sorta area."

Slowly, I climb his scales. So. Very. Slowly. Until I'm on top of the thing. I look down to Dags and give her a nod. She follows me up onto the gargantuid's back. A moment later, in a furious rush of speed, the gargantuid's wings flap, and we blast off into the sky . . .

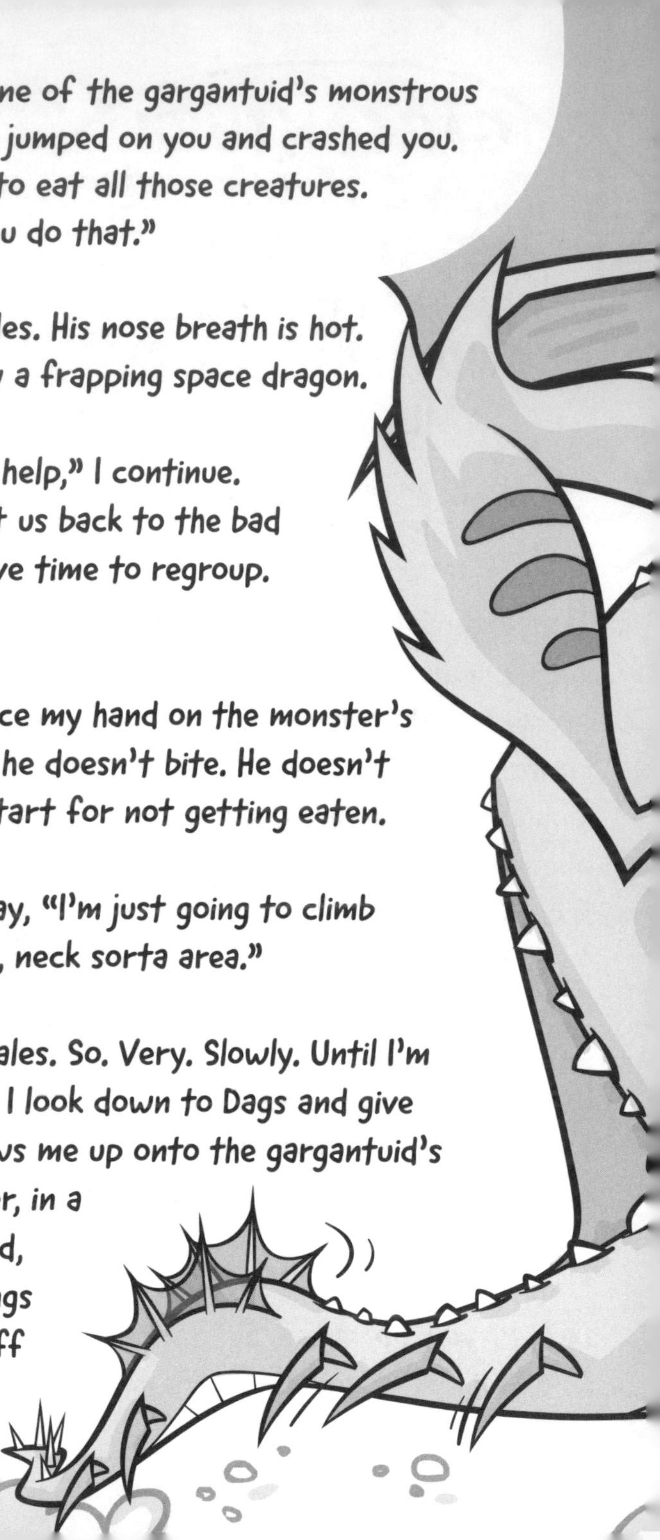

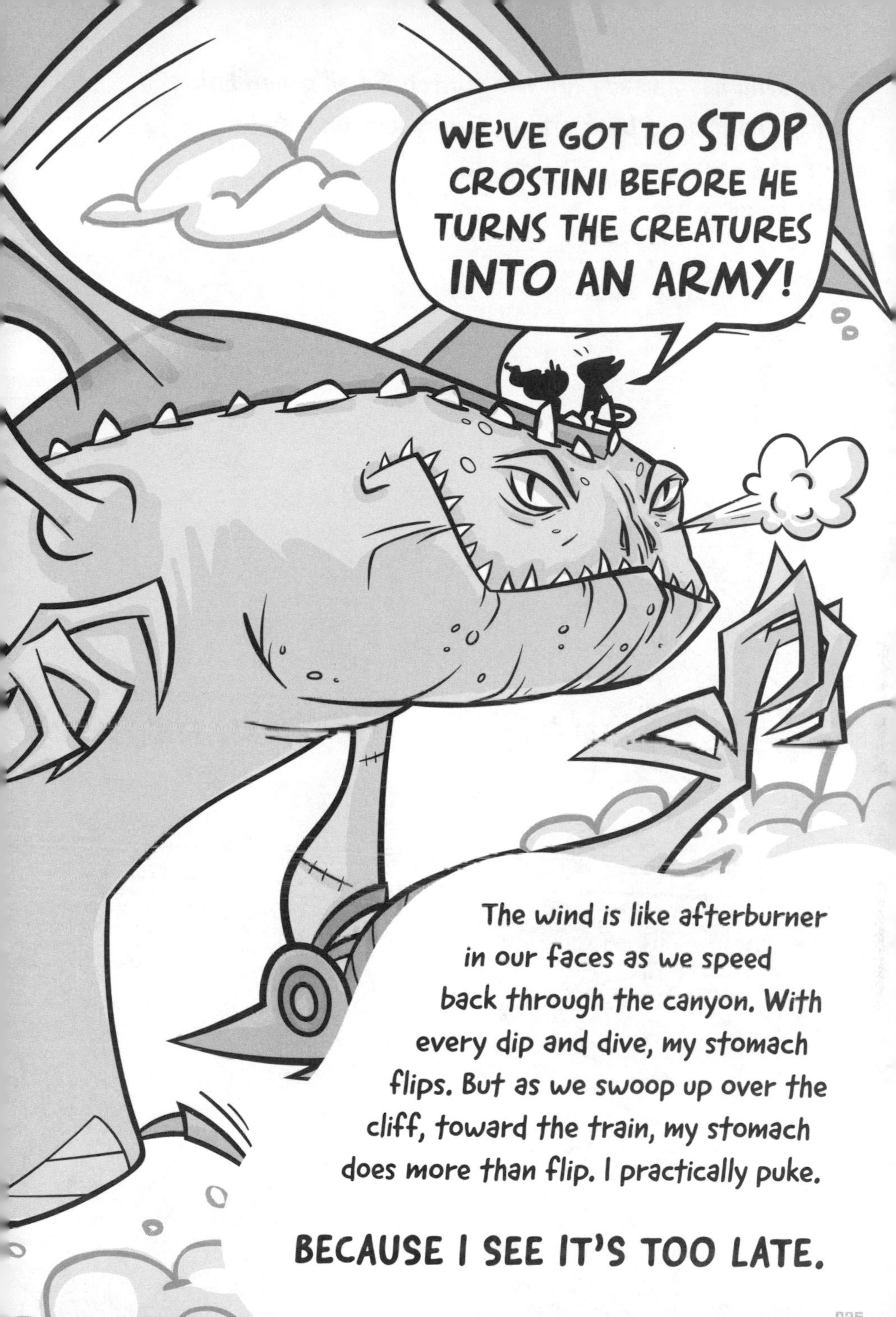
WE'VE GOT TO STOP CROSTINI BEFORE HE TURNS THE CREATURES INTO AN ARMY!

The wind is like afterburner in our faces as we speed back through the canyon. With every dip and dive, my stomach flips. But as we swoop up over the cliff, toward the train, my stomach does more than flip. I practically puke.

BECAUSE I SEE IT'S TOO LATE.

Crostini has already hit the switch. Small green lights dot the ground beneath us. Every last one of the creatures has mutated.
His army is ready . . .

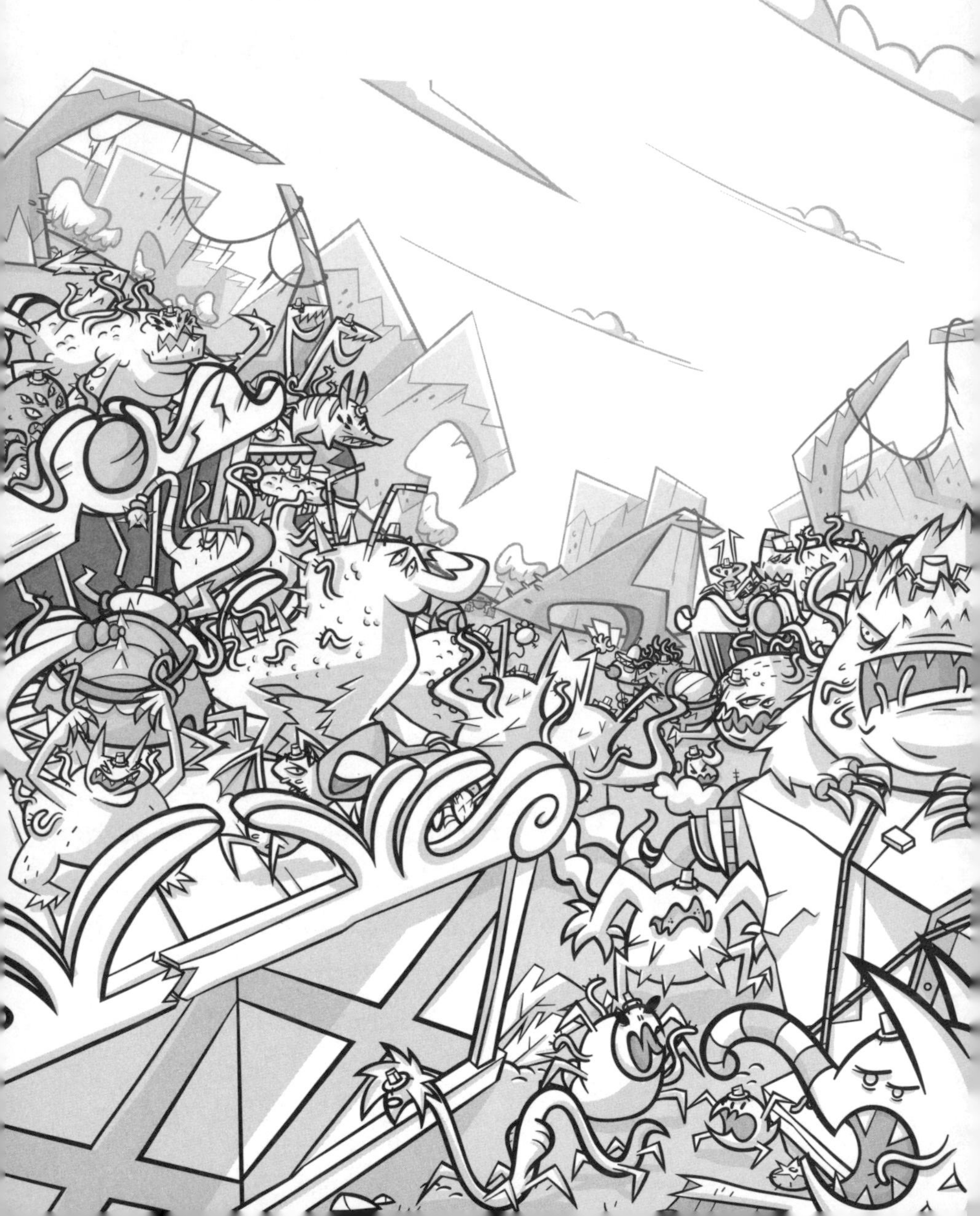

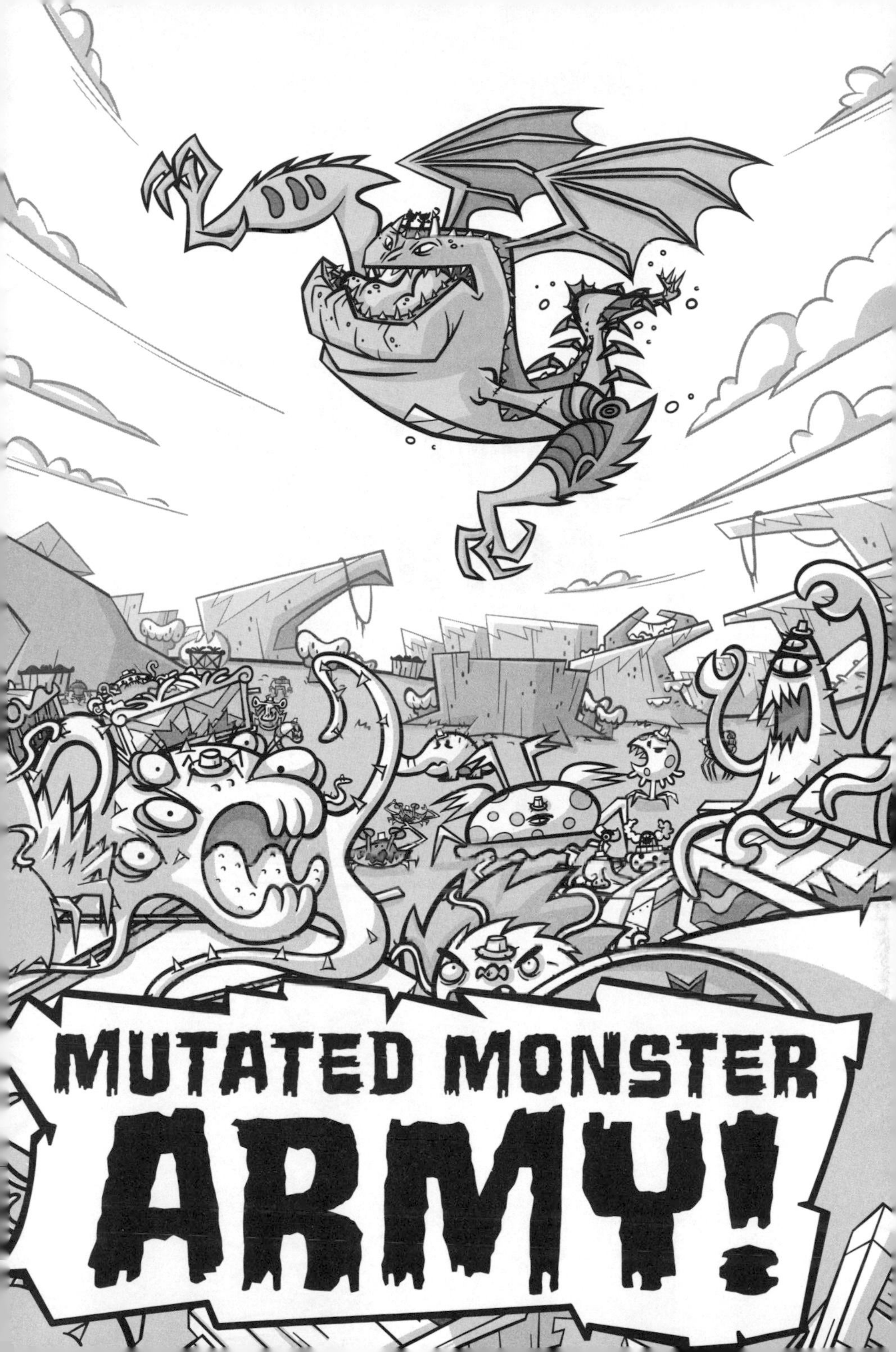
MUTATED MONSTER
ARMY!

FOOT FACE FLASH KICK ACTION!

ROUST-A-BOTS!

KNOCK THAT UGLY BEAST FROM THE SKY!

A busted-up bot heaves a massive chunk of plasty-steel. **"DAGS, DOWN!"** I holler just before the rubble batters the gargantuid.

The gargantuid releases an enraged roar. Guess that's a good life lesson, folks: don't heave massive chunks of plasty-steel at a gargantuid, 'cause that gargantuid will be **TICKED.**

The gargantuid plunges downward. His massive front talons grip the ground and his tremendous armored skull lowers as he charges toward the mutated monster creatures. These animals have no control over what they're doing—and it's all because of that dastardly Crostini ...

"Dags!" I call out. "I'll try to slow down this big guy. But you **NEED** to shut down the governator gizmos or else the creatures are done for!!!"

"On it!" Dagger says. Quicker than a shot from a flash blaster, she sprints up the monster's back and leaps.

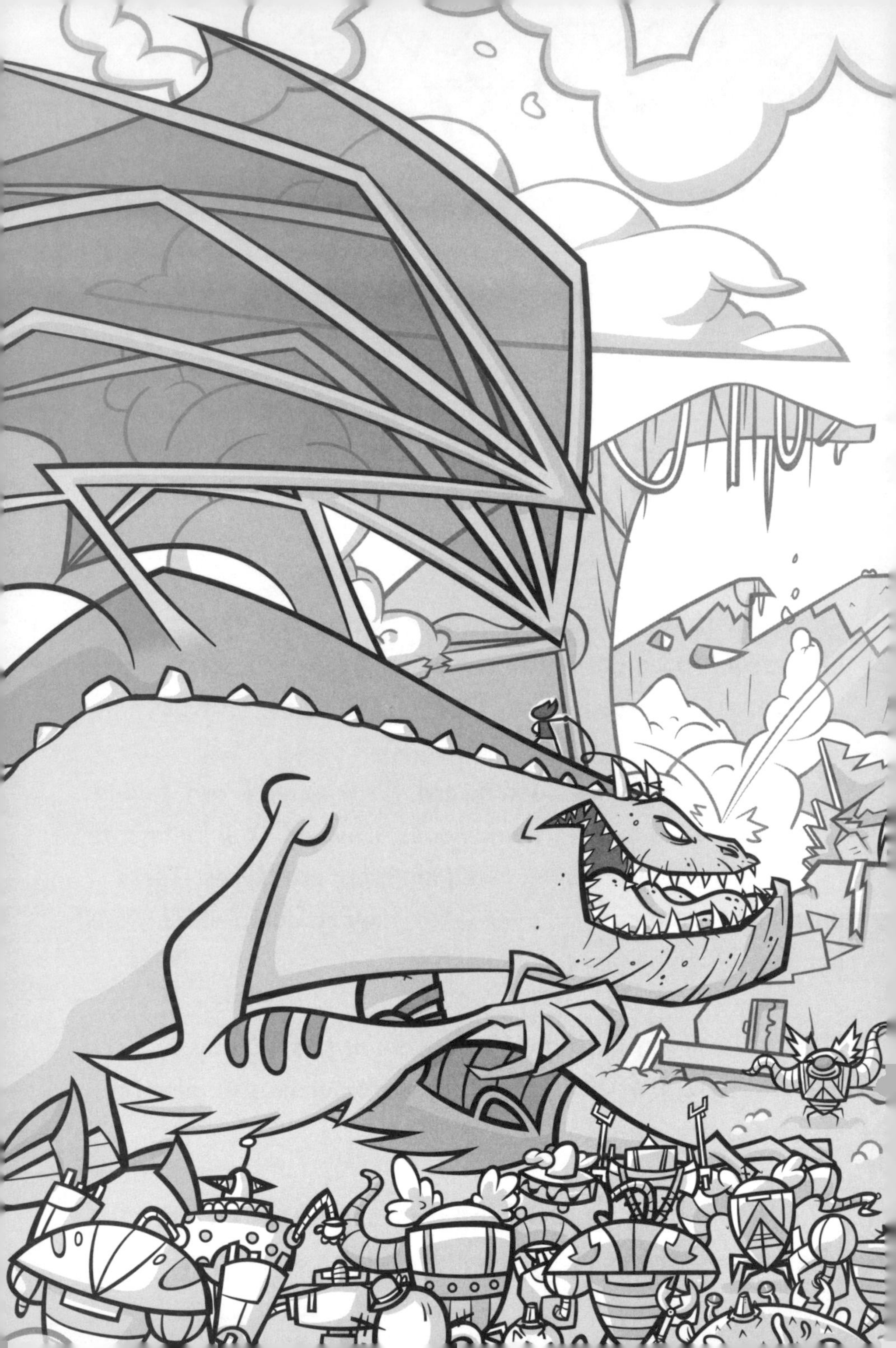

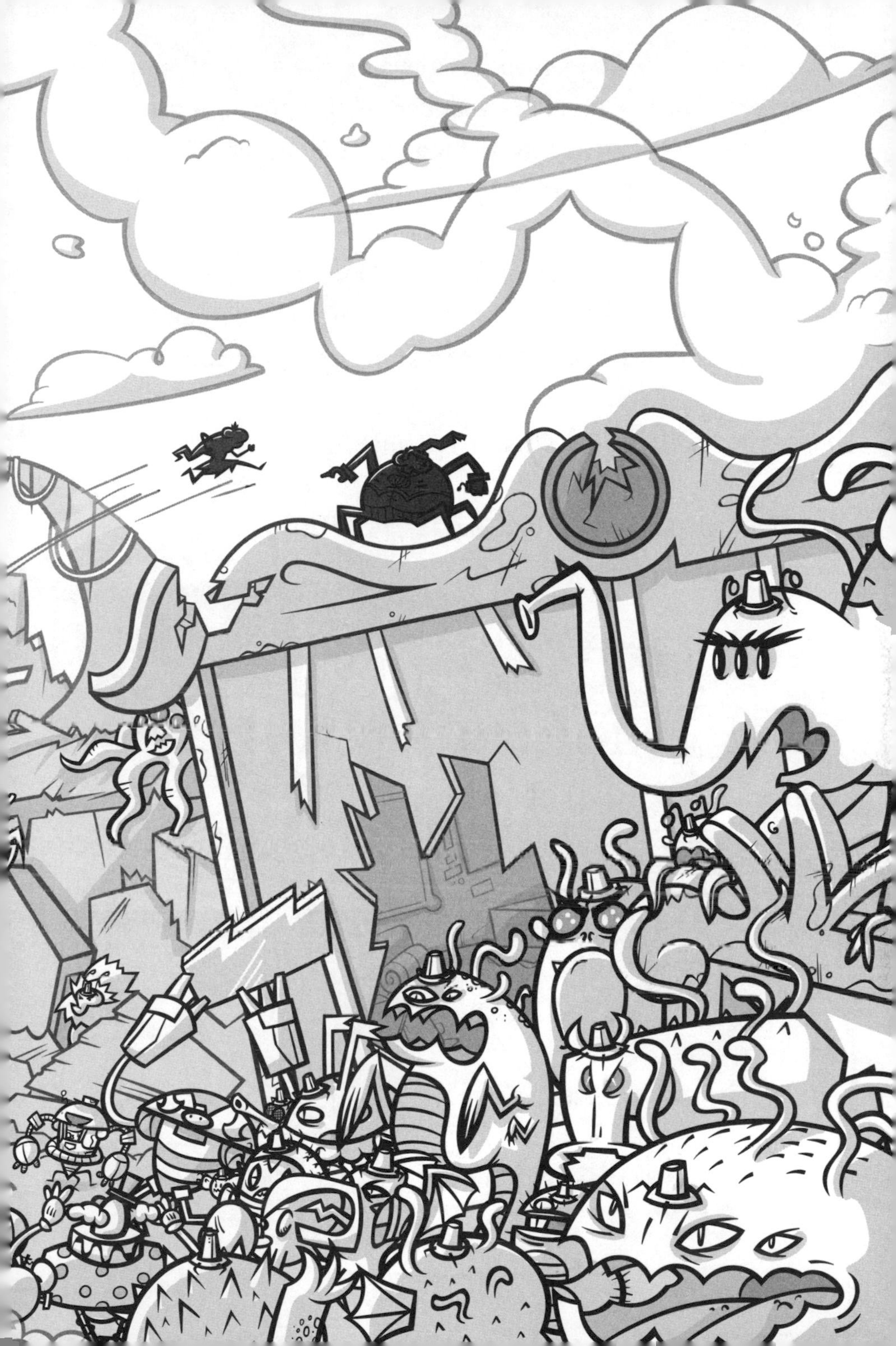

I keep one eye on Dagger and one eye on the army of mutated monsters ahead of me. I'm reminded of Humphree. A great dude who was momentarily turned into a monster! These are good creatures—and the gargantuid is about to run them down!

"Goober, rein us in!" I holler. Goober loops around one of the gargantuid's rounded spikes, and I tug. The gargantuid's tremendous front arms slow the stampede, just barely.

Impact is still **EXTREMELY** imminent . . .

But then, an instant before impact, I spot Dagger! And she's doing some . . .

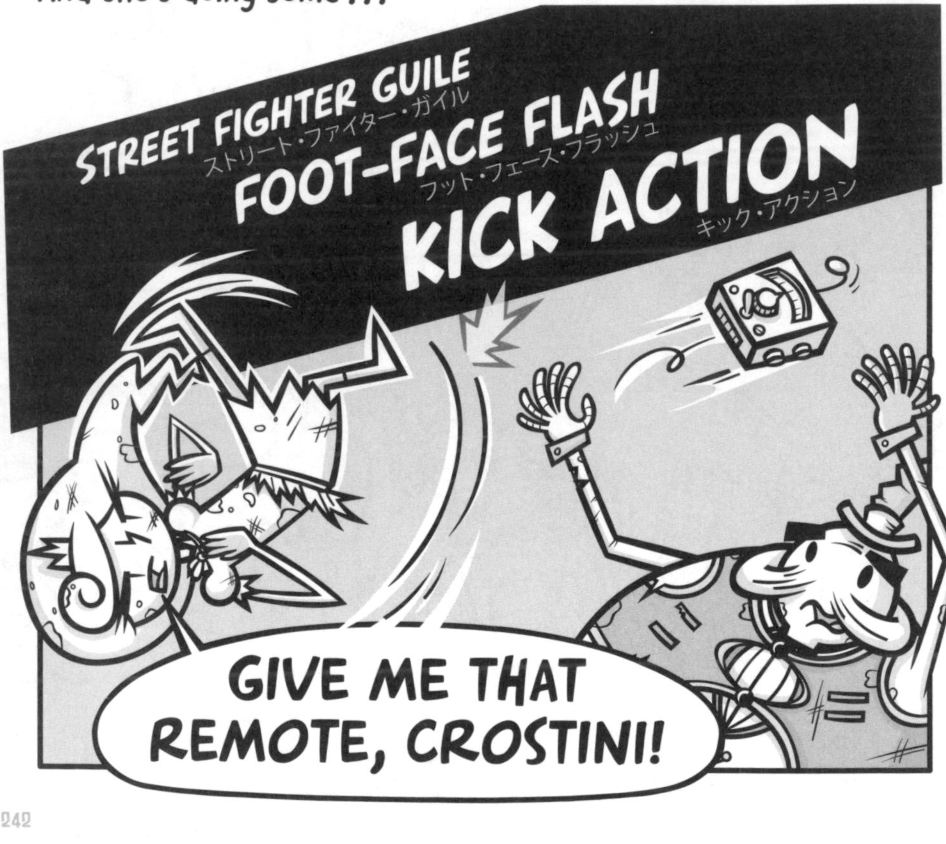
STREET FIGHTER GUILE
ストリート・ファイター・ガイル
FOOT-FACE FLASH
フット・フェース・フラッシュ
KICK ACTION
キック・アクション
GIVE ME THAT REMOTE, CROSTINI!

I watch in serious suspense as the remote doinks off a bot's head, clonks against the roof of the train, and spins ...

Leaping, jumping, whirling, Dagger manages to SNATCH the remote out of midair. And then—

I'M SHUTTING DOWN THE **BIG BAD GUY,** AND I'M KICKING ADVENTURE-SCROLL BUTT RIGHT NOW!

The instant Dagger flicks the switch, a hundred governator gizmos flash from green to red. The creatures shriek and howl and their bodies twist and bend as they transmogrify back to their true forms.

And then—all at once—their eyes go wide with fear as they see the gargantuid charging toward them! An earsplitting shriek of horror cuts across the planet.

The creatures scatter, suddenly very much NOT monsters, and suddenly VERY scared of the stampeding monstrosity. Crostini's bots aren't so lucky ...

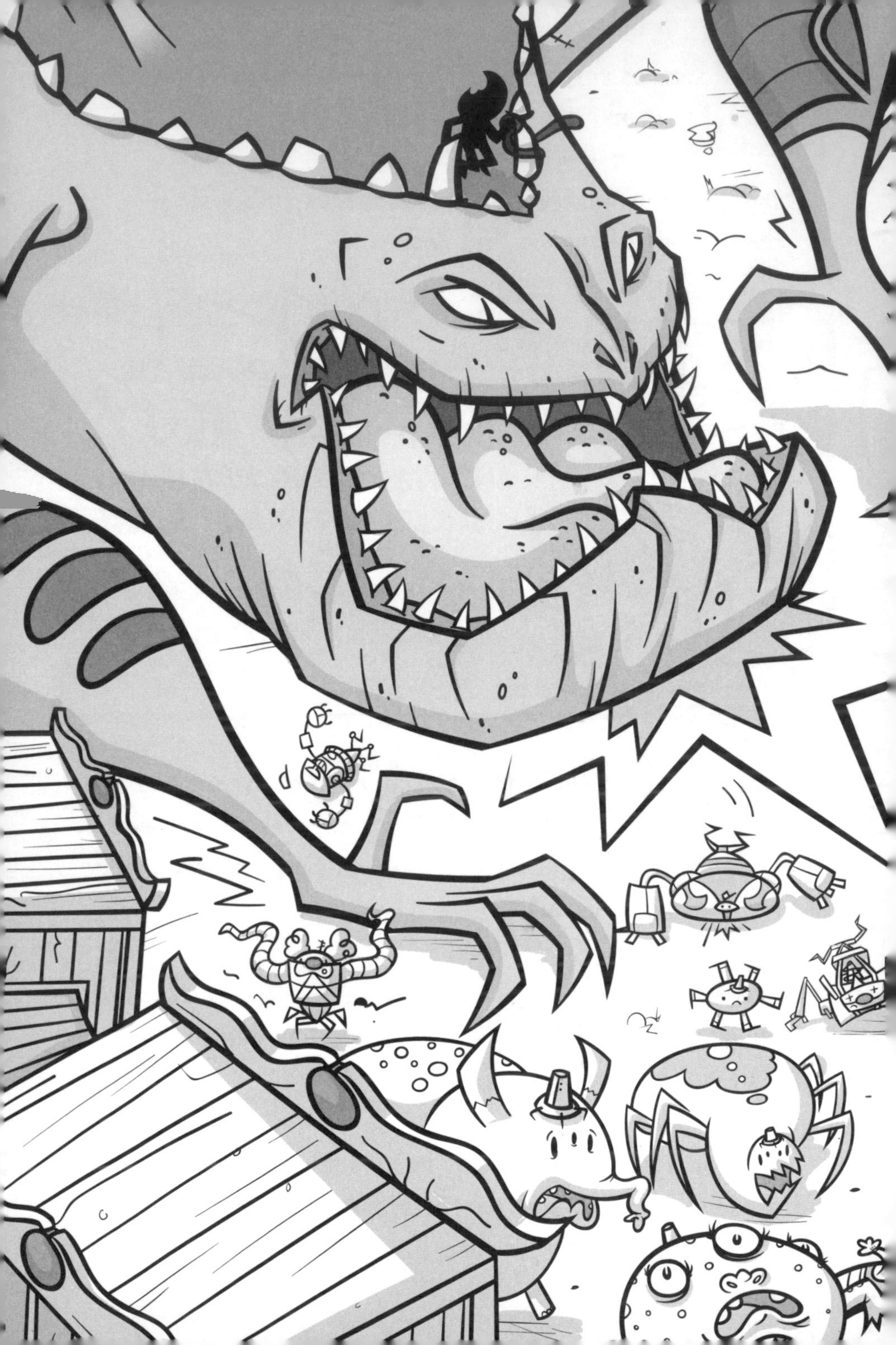

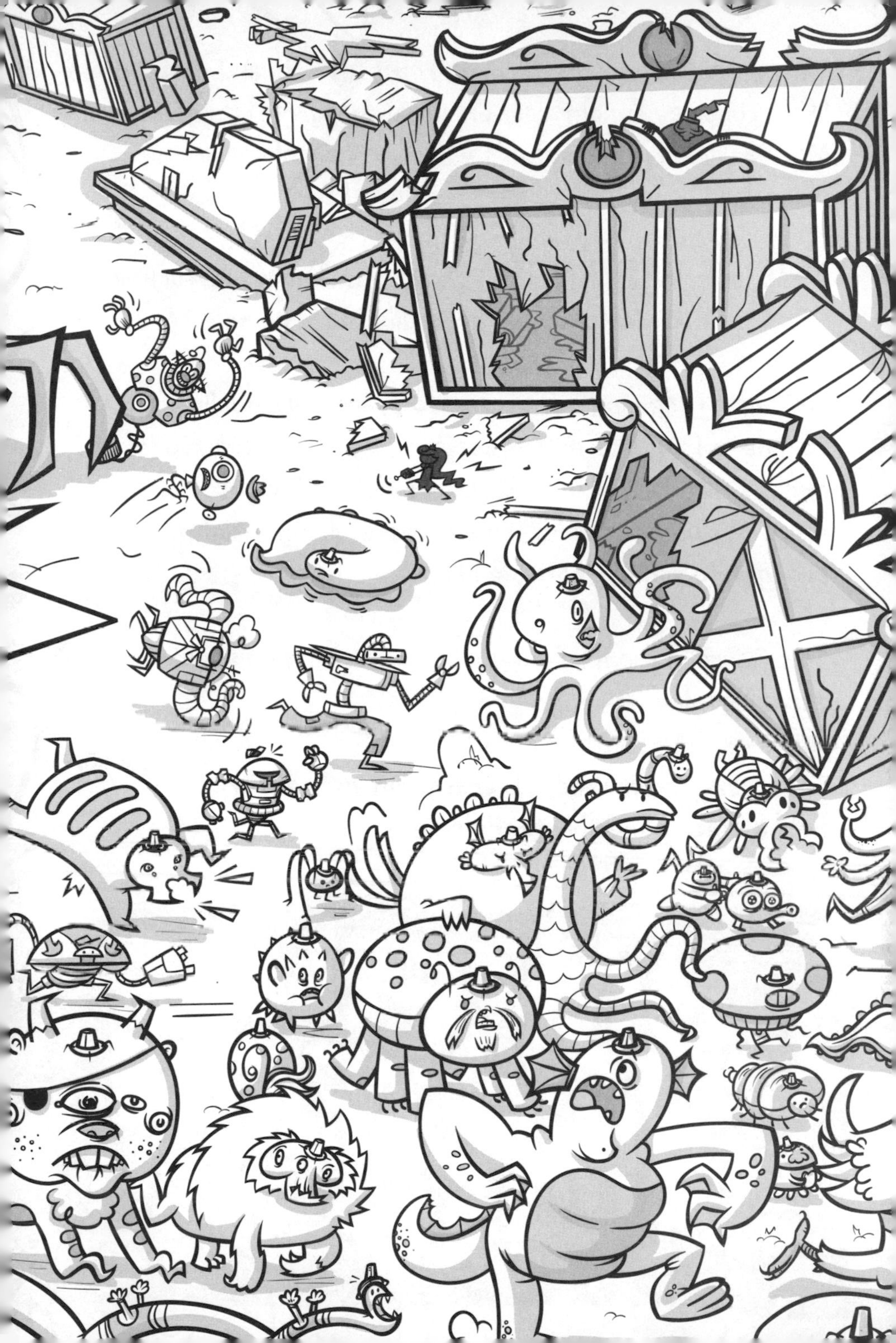

The gargantuid stomps through roust-a-bots and clown-bots like a runaway freight carrier. Steel snaps. Metal cracks. Machinery bursts. Crostini's villainous henchbots are pulverized beneath the beast's colossal feet.

"WE'RE WINNING!" I shout. "The tides are turning! I feel real wonderful about how things are going!"

But what I see next causes me to practically swallow my tongue in fear. Our advantage has just come to a sudden end ... Through the wreckage and flying steel, I see him. He steps out of the smoke like a monster from a nightmare, brought to sudden, horrible life.

This figure in front of me makes my limbs tingle and my throat go dry.

The wrangler survived the crash. But he's different. He's a steel-boned brute. He's ...

BROKEN.
SHATTERED.
FREAKISH.

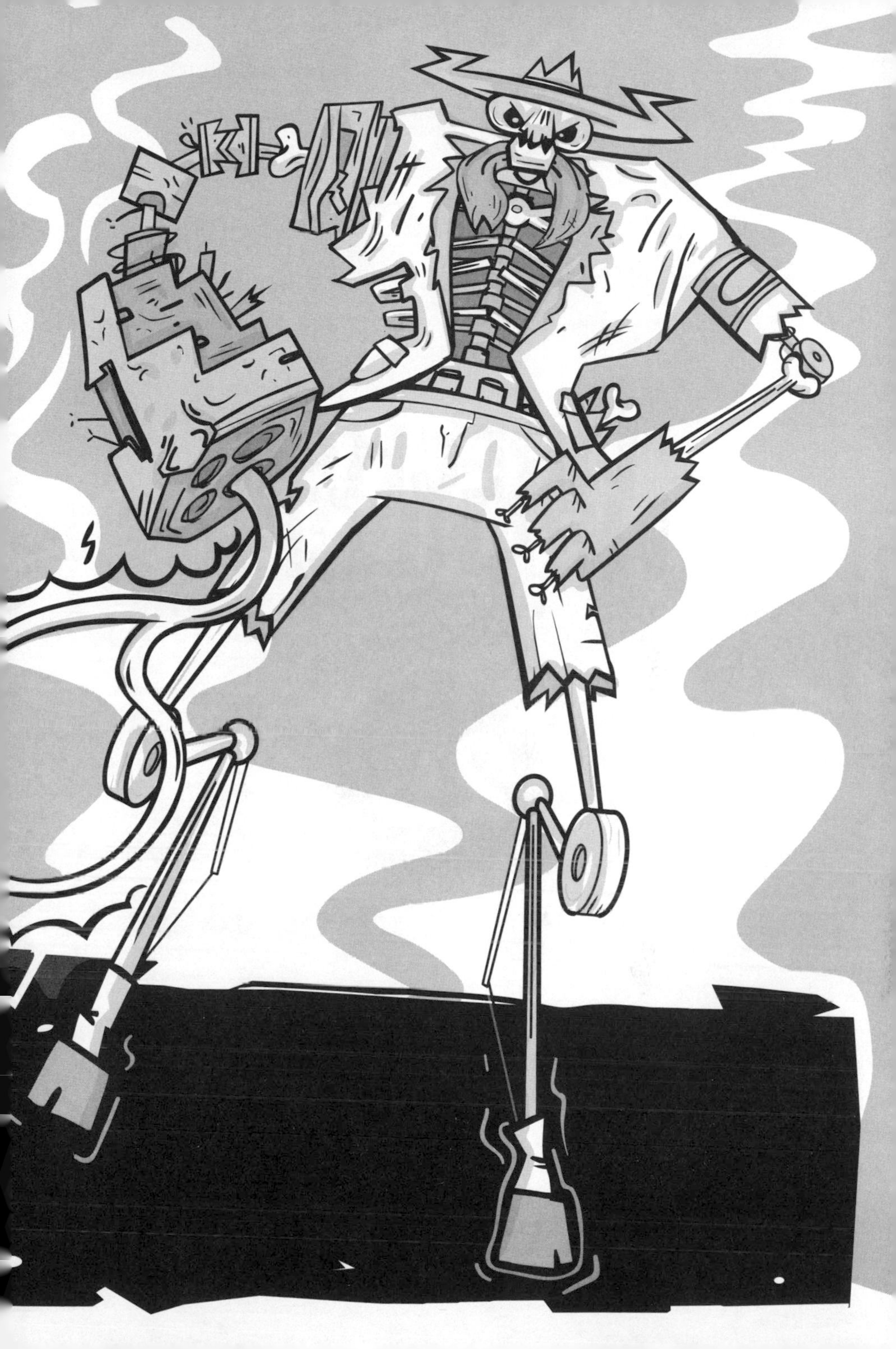

WRECKED WRANLGER

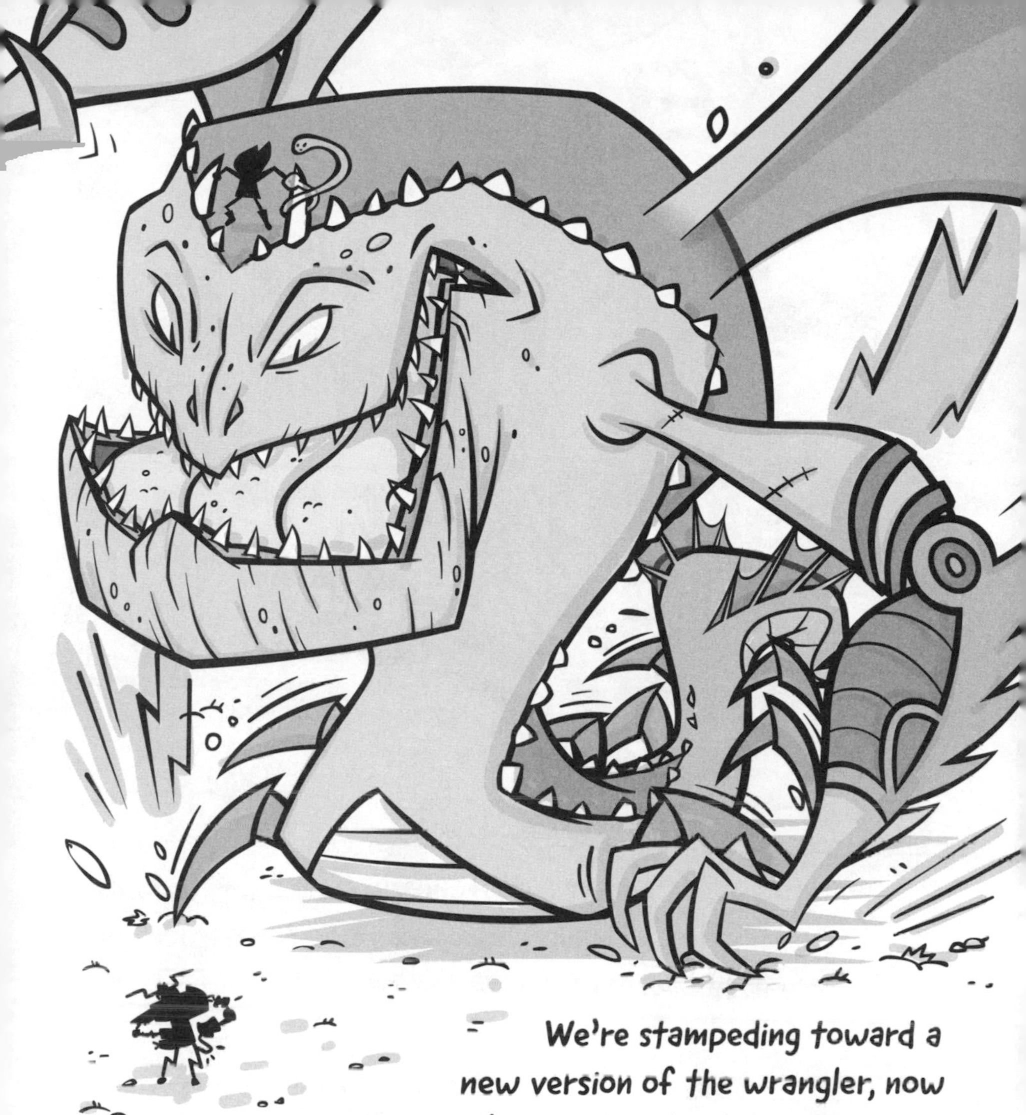

We're stampeding toward a new version of the wrangler, now with a wrecked-up bod. I dub him the . . .

WRECKED WRANGLER.

And this wrecked wrangler appears to possess no fear. He does not move. He does not flee. Instead, he simply raises his zappo-lasso and . . .

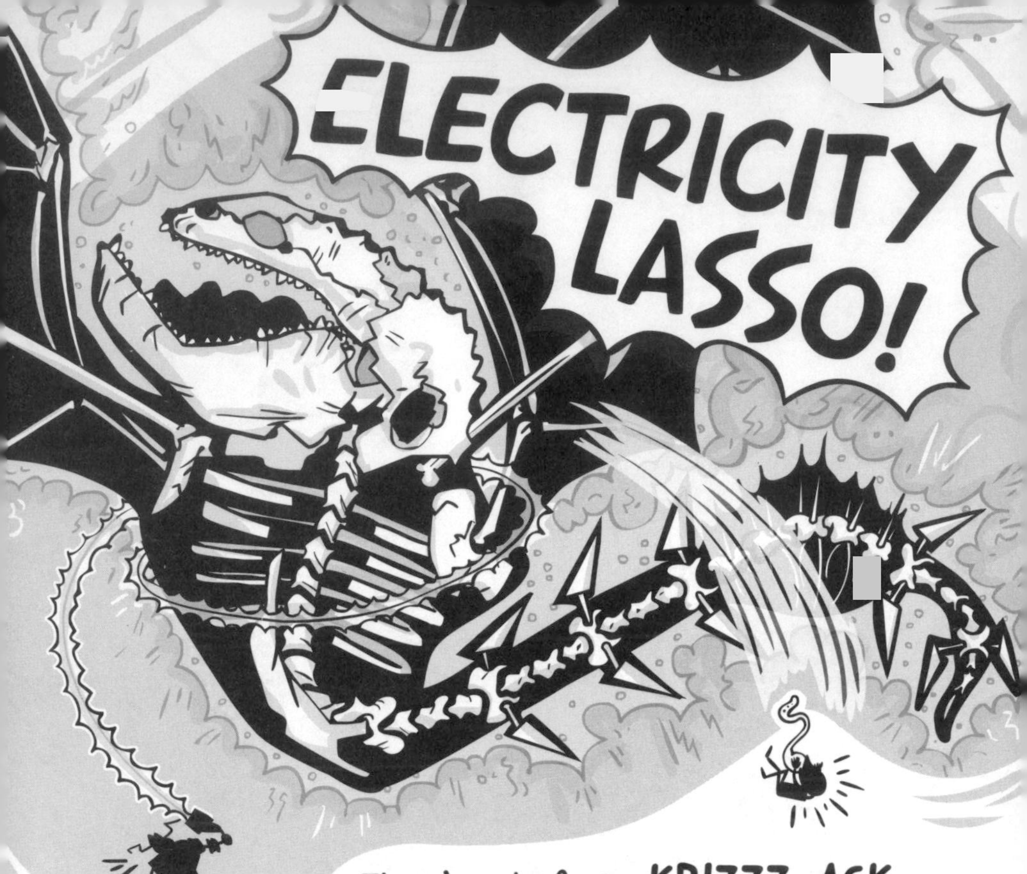
ELECTRICITY LASSO!

There's a deafening **KRIZZZ–ACK** as the electrified lasso encircles the gargantuid. Energy courses through the beast.

The surge launches me from the monster. I hit the ground like a sack of snord potatoes. My head is bowling-ball heavy as I lift it. I watch in horror . . .

The gargantuid twitches, spasms, convulses, and then goes nearly still. Its huge frame heaves with short, slow breaths. I can't believe it—the wrangler knocked it unconscious with a massive voltage blast!

Cracking, sizzling energy fills the air as the wrangler snaps the zappo-lasso back to his side. The villain surveys the destruction. Other circus creatures are still running for cover.

I wiggle my toes. They move. Okay. That means I'm still alive enough to make a final stand.

The wrangler slowly stomps through the rubble. He calls out my name almost playfully. "Cosmoe. Where are you?"

I jam my hand into the debris and force myself to my feet. I'm dog-tired. Zonked of all my action energy. But I see no other choice . . .

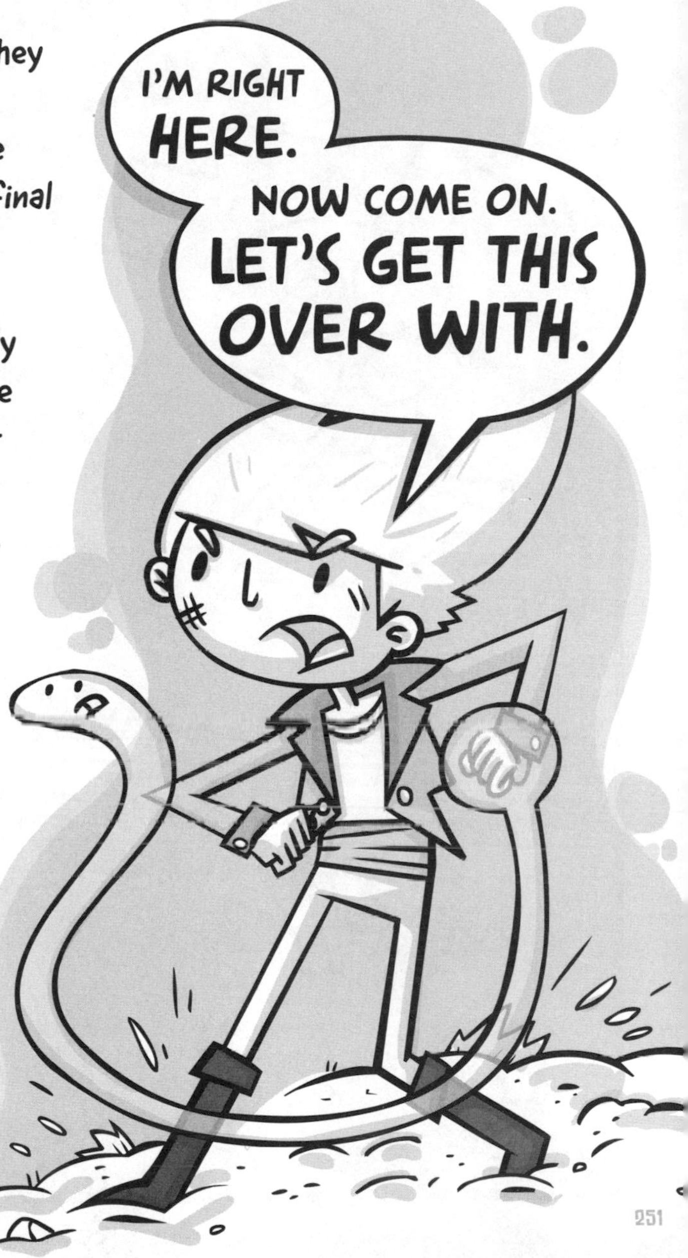
I'M RIGHT HERE.
NOW COME ON. LET'S GET THIS OVER WITH.

But just then, I hear the voice of a supremely radical and kinda-evil friend.

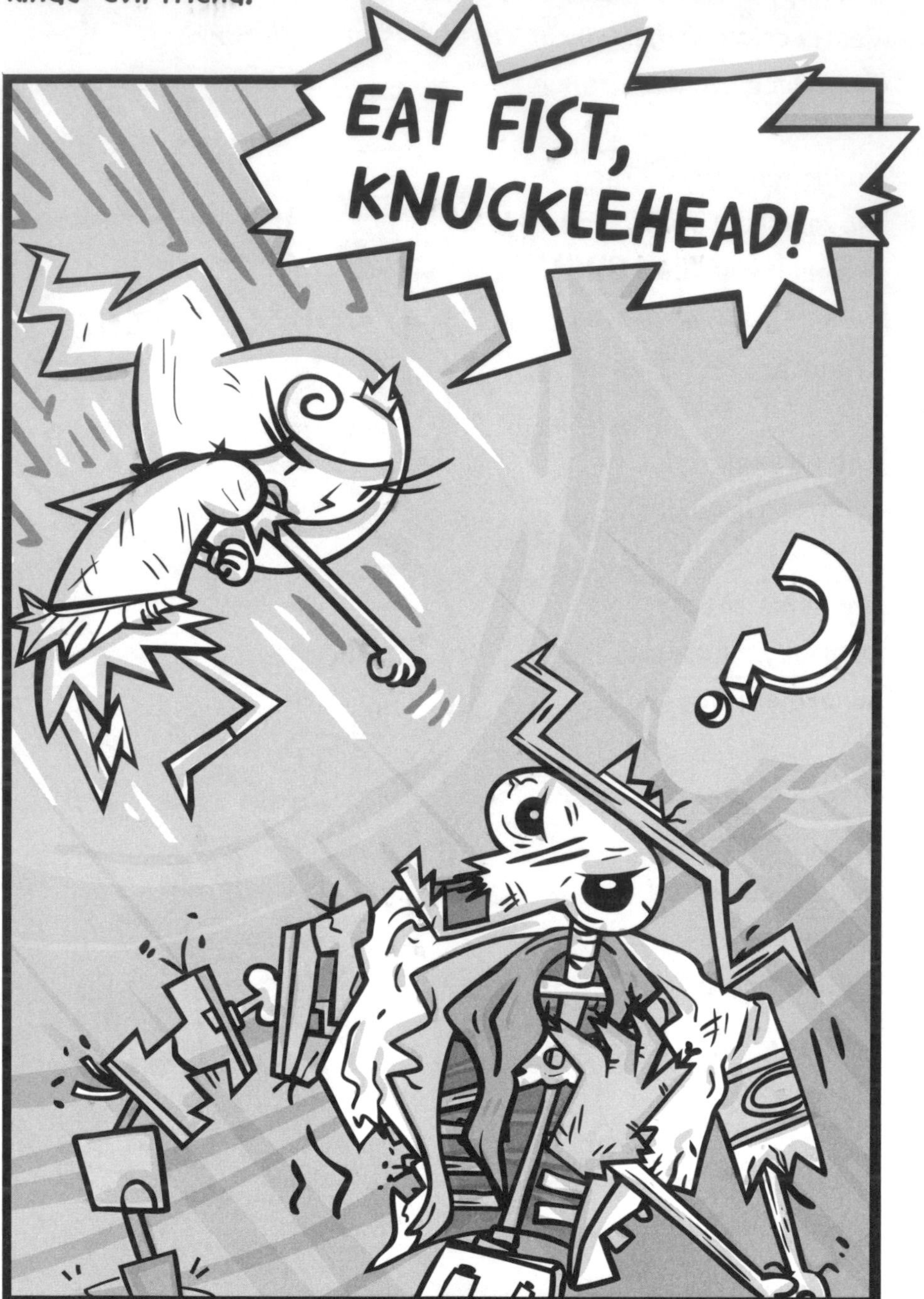
EAT FIST, KNUCKLEHEAD!

Holy smudge! Dagger's flying in from out of nowhere, looking to straight clock this villain in the chin.

But the wrecked wrangler isn't having it. He's too ferocious, too quick.

He emits a spooky, spine-tingling giggle—then cocks back his massive hand and SWINGS.

KA-KRAK!

The wrangler's swat is savage. Dagger spirals through the air. A puff of blue dust kicks up as she crashes to the ground.

He just swatted Dagger! NO ONE SWATS MY BUDDY DAGGER! "That's it!" I shout. "I'm knocking your block off, buddy! And I'm feeding you that blasted hat!"

Apparently, though, the wrangler isn't hungry . . .

In a flash, he's towering over me. His mechanical arm transforms into a massive metal fist. A fist so big he could arm wrestle a Muck Ogre—AND WIN.

His heavy metal foot lands squarely on my chest, driving me into the ground. I gasp for breath, but nothing's coming. Feels like his steel toes are going to crush my chest and liquefy my lungs.

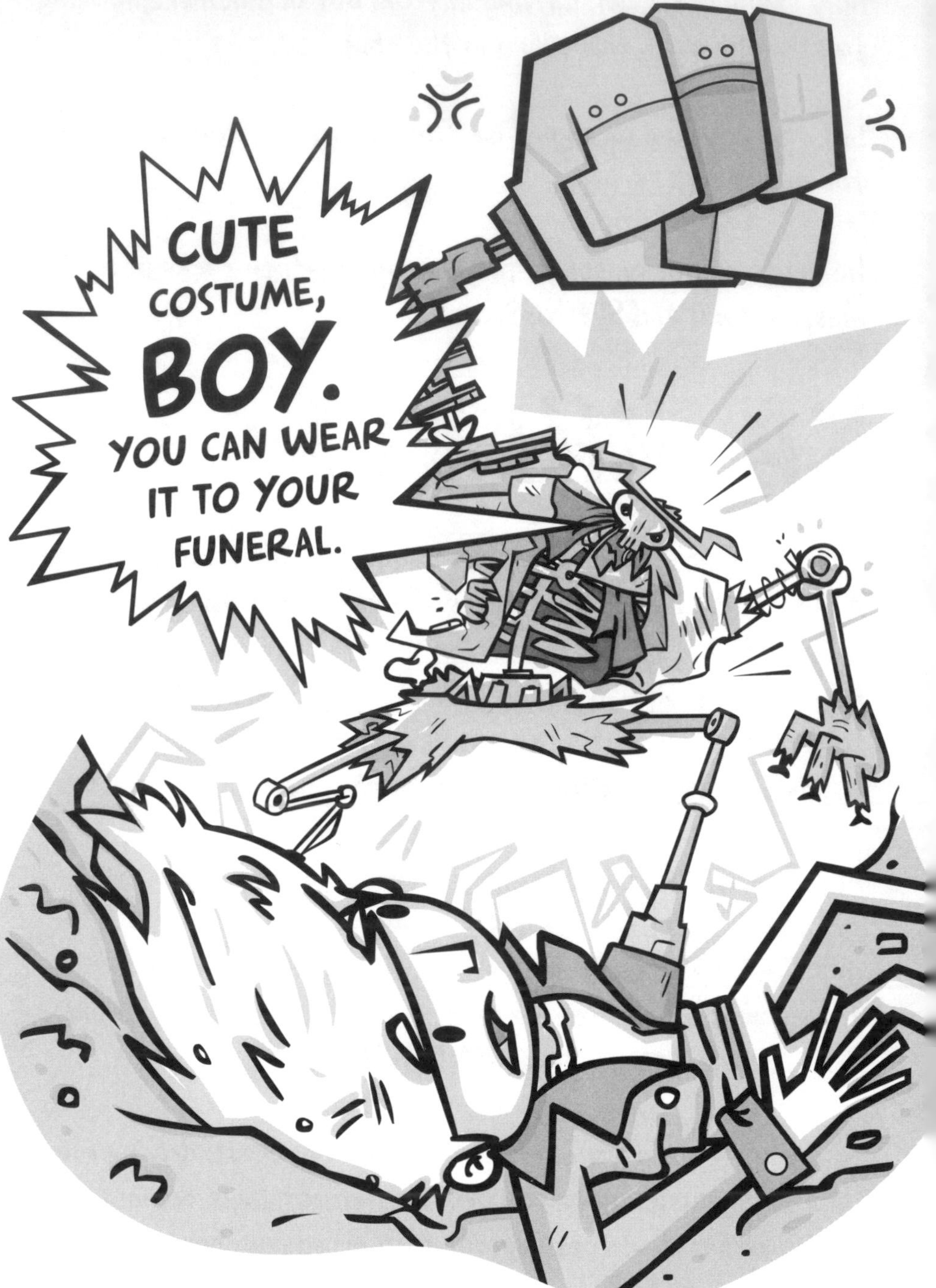
CUTE COSTUME, BOY. YOU CAN WEAR IT TO YOUR FUNERAL.

Then I hear it. Something loud. At first I think it's my rib cage cracking. But no . . .

Hooves. Stampeding. I glance back and I see the greatest sight ever: HUMPHREE riding atop the LYANUX!

He's gripping his Smash Hammer Derby bat like a massive mallet. **HUMPHREE + LYANUX + DERBY BAT** is a match made in space hero heaven.

"HEADS UP, WRANGLER!" Humphree barks, and then he unleashes a brutal Great Bambino swing . . .

KRAKA-A-POW!

With a thunderous **KRUNCH**, the wrangler crashes into a creature car.

Awkwardly and ungracefully, Humphree blunders down off the lyanux.

"We've got unfinished business," Humphree growls, stomping toward the dazed wrangler. "You electro-lassoed me. Nobody electro-lassoes Big Humphree, Bronkle space pirate (retired) and Head Chef of the hot dog truck the *Neon Wiener.*"

AND WITH THAT . . .

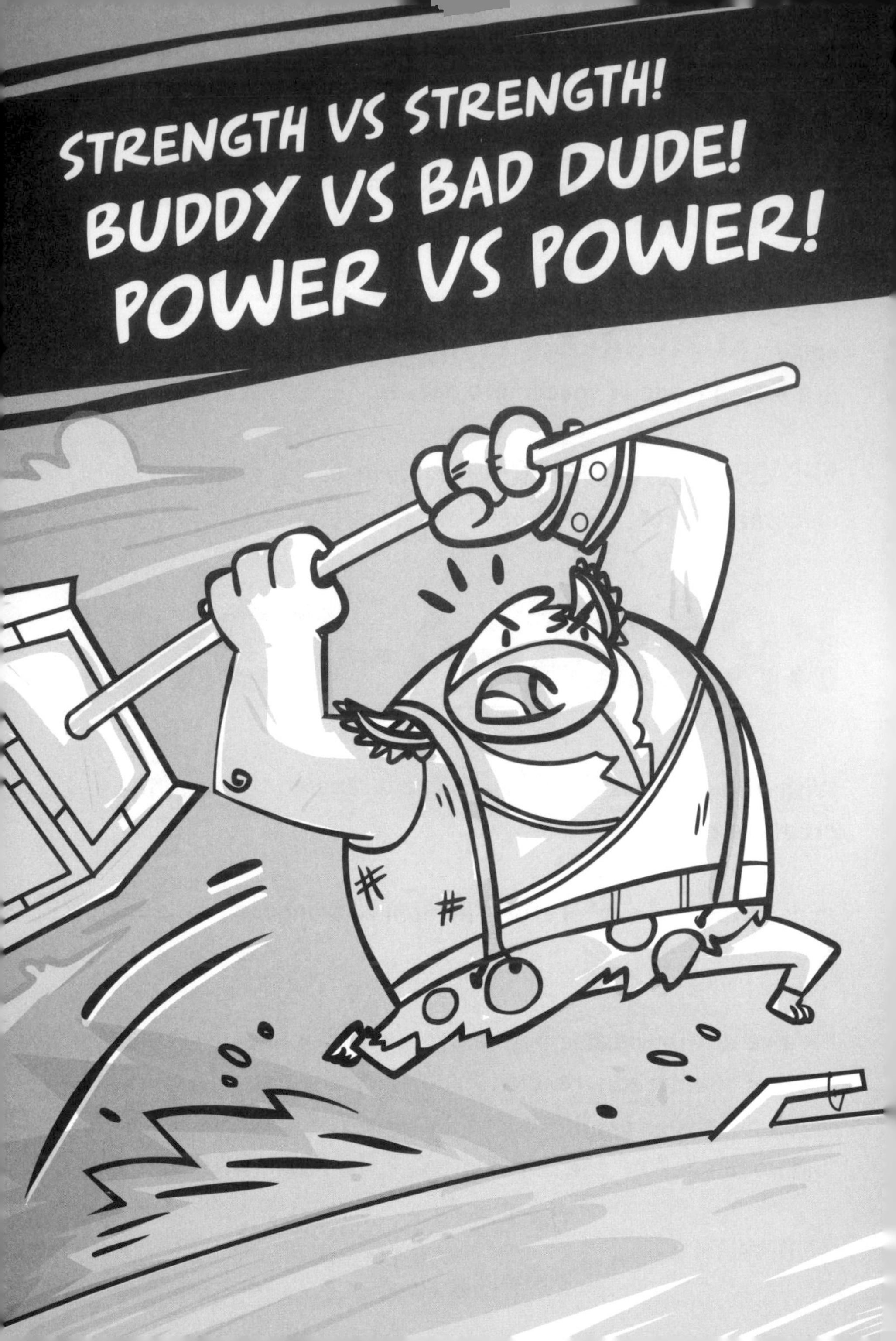
STRENGTH VS STRENGTH!
BUDDY VS BAD DUDE!
POWER VS POWER!

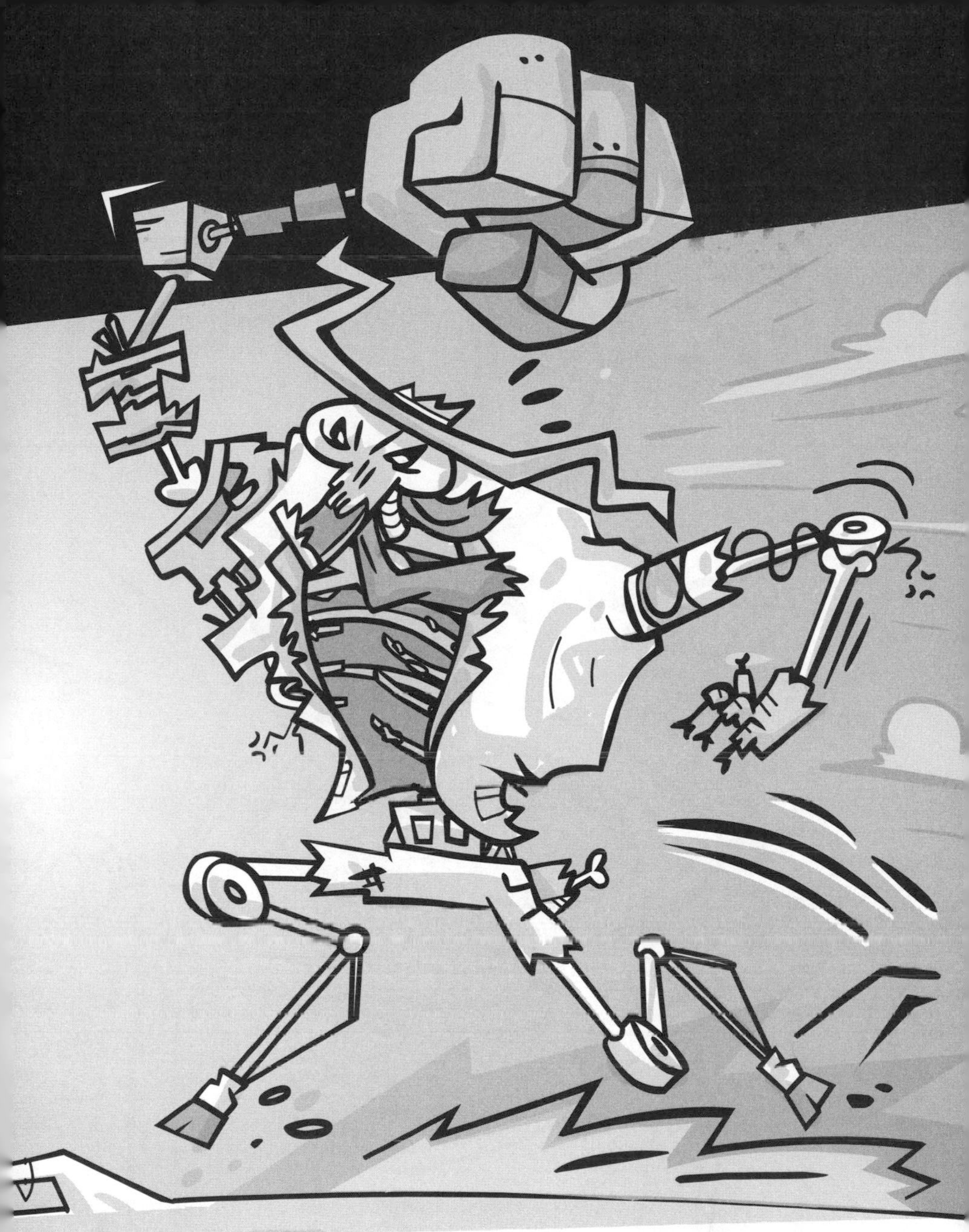

After the first blow, it's chaos!
The wrangler's massive mitt swats away
the derby hammer, leaving . . .

. . . Humphree wounded and on the brink of destruction!

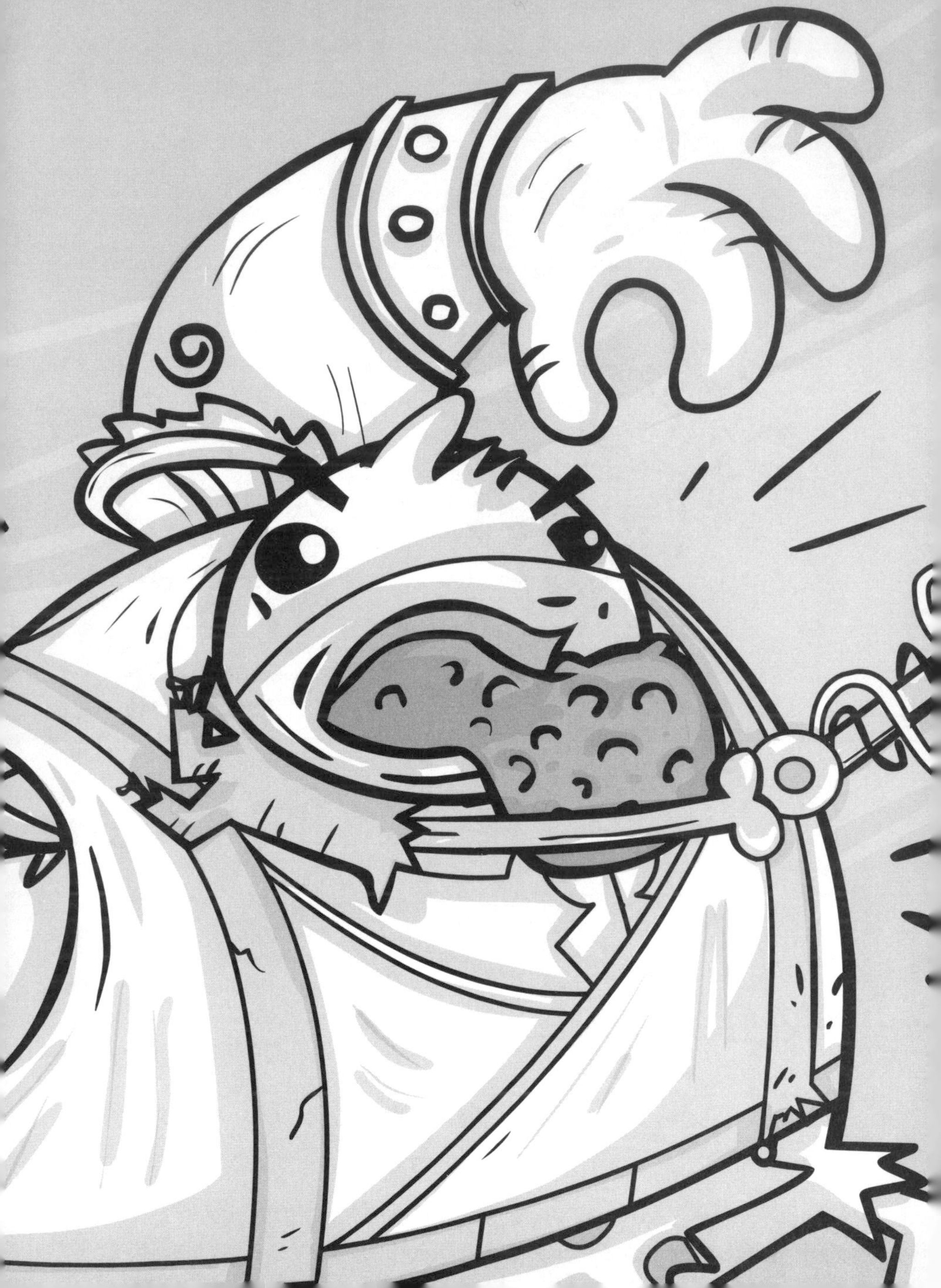

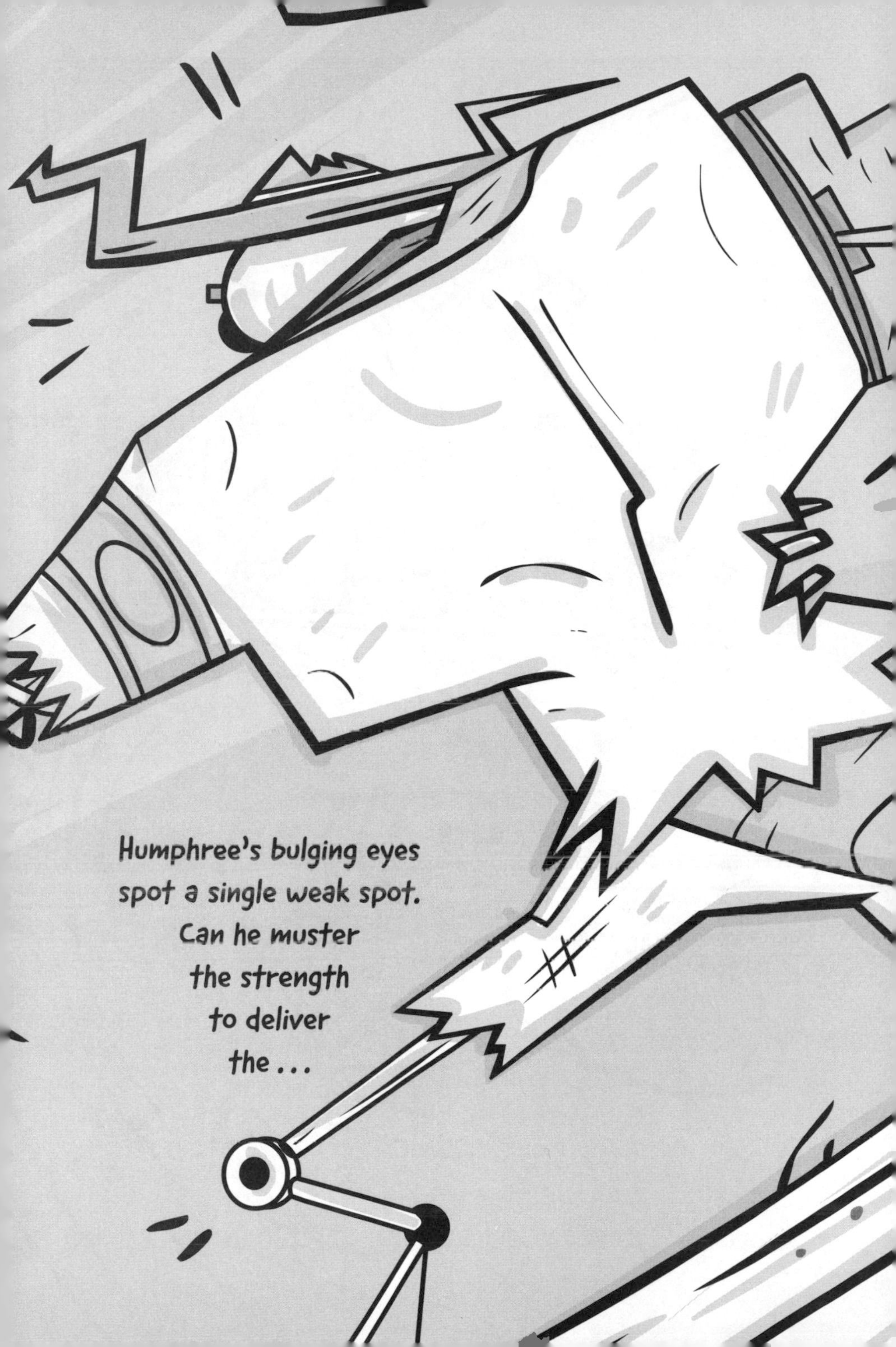
Humphree's bulging eyes
spot a single weak spot.
Can he muster
the strength
to deliver
the . . .

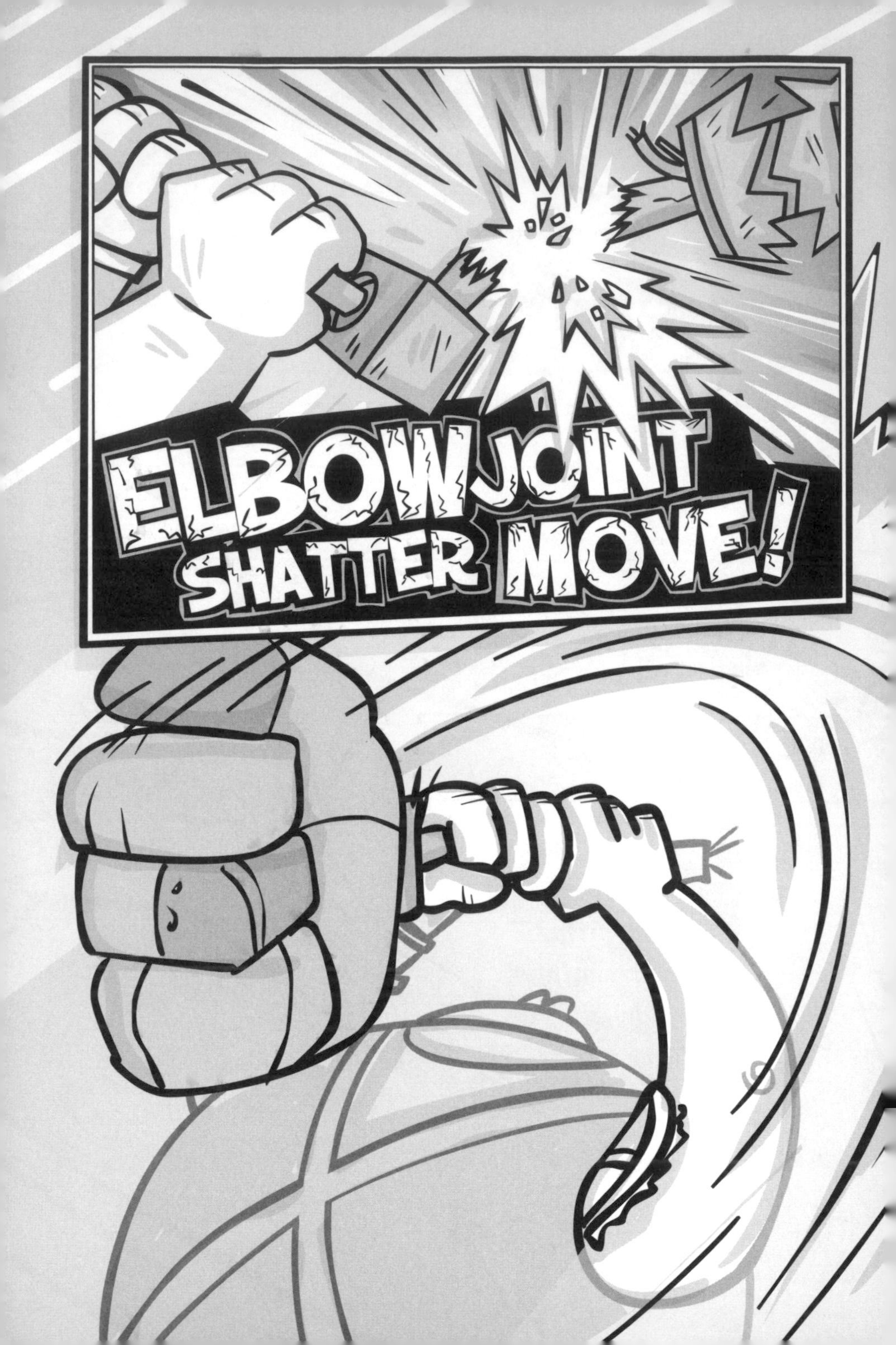
ELBOW JOINT SHATTER MOVE!

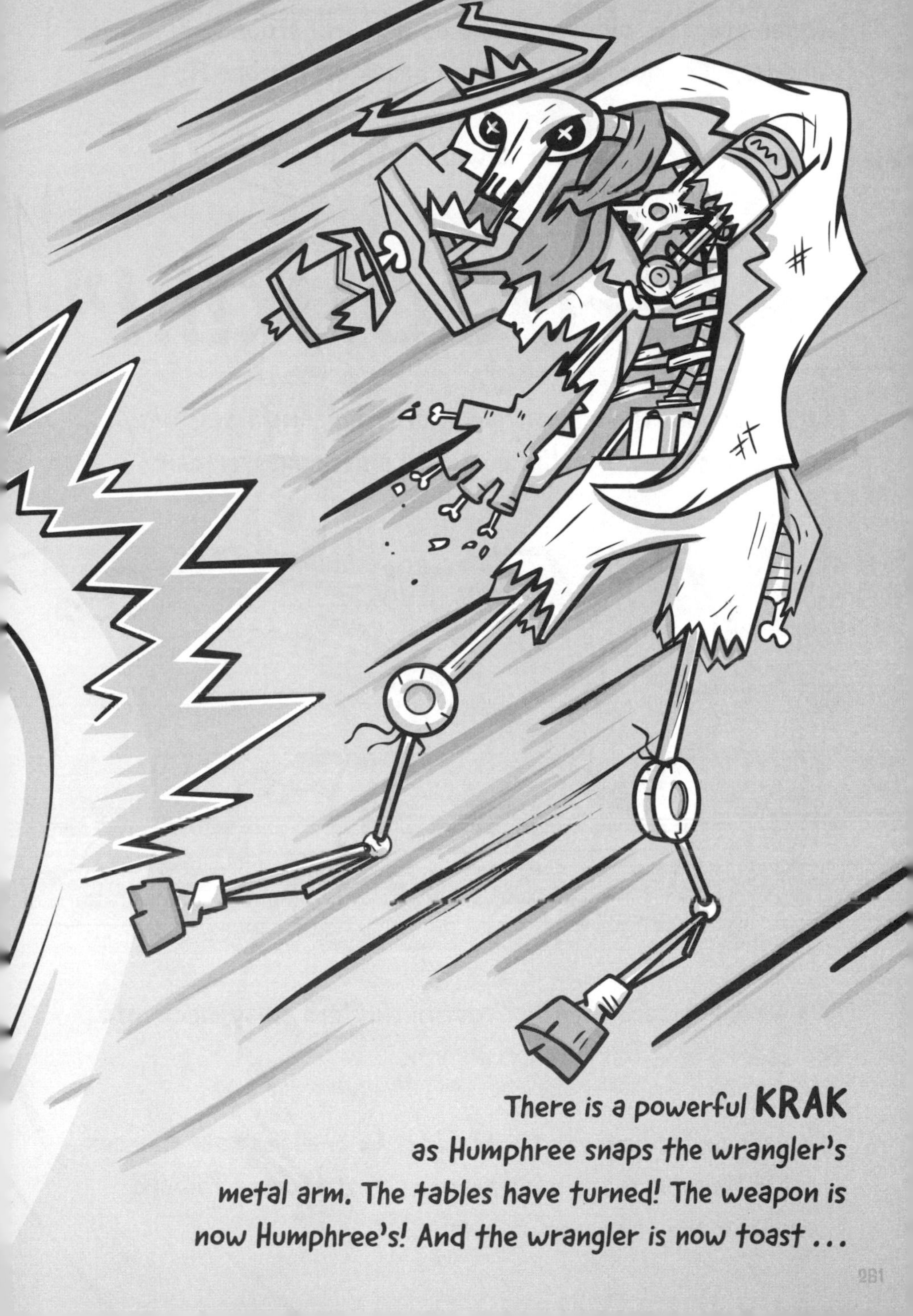

There is a powerful **KRAK** as Humphree snaps the wrangler's metal arm. The tables have turned! The weapon is now Humphree's! And the wrangler is now toast . . .

Dagger staggers over and throws her arm around my shoulder. "Cosmoe, should we go break up the brawl?"

I shake my head. "Humphree will never forgive me if I get in the way of his—"

"REEEOOONK!!!!"

I whirl around. The gargantuid is stirring! And I see why . . . Crostini is poking it in the eye with his ringmaster cane!

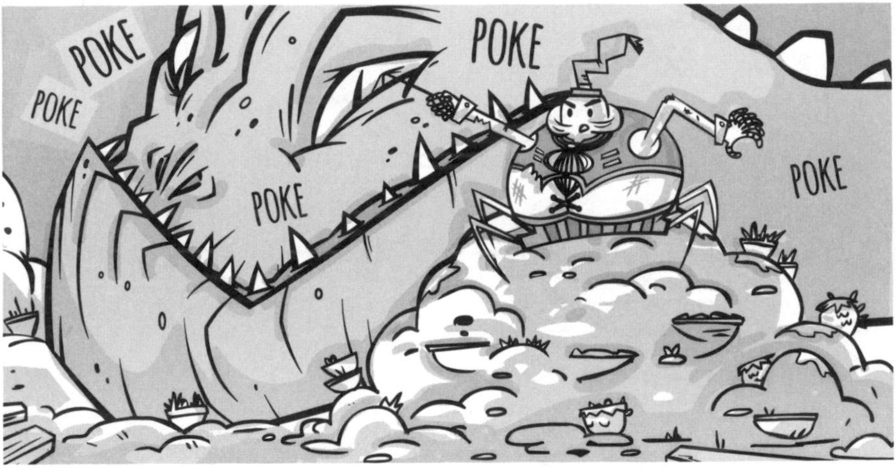
POKE
POKE
POKE
POKE
POKE

Like a real coward-pants, Crostini skitters away, back into the safety of a battered train car.

The gargantuid lumbers to its feet. An enraged roar pierces the air. Its monstrous mouth opens as it stomps toward Humphree and the wrecked wrangler . . .

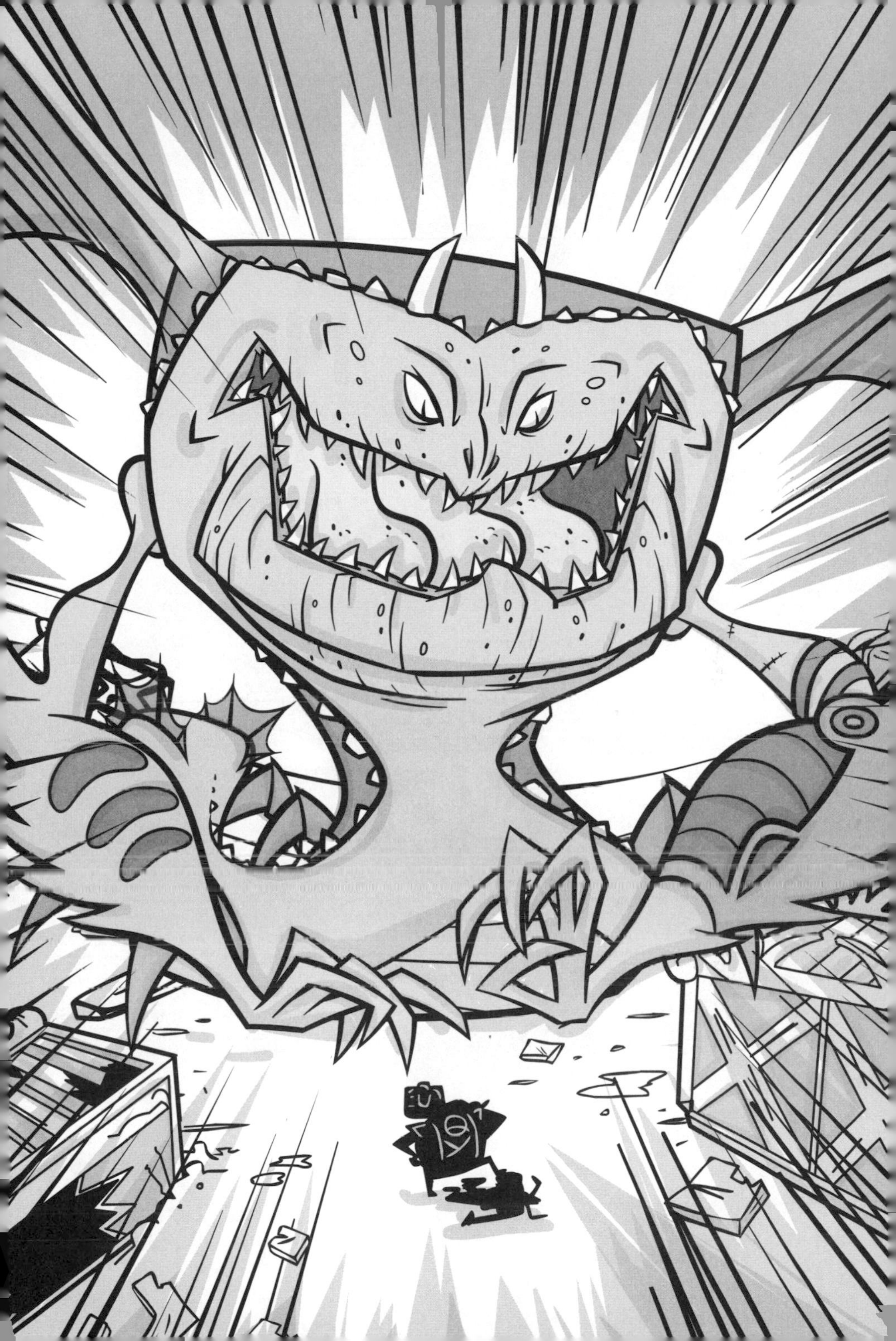

SNAP!

26

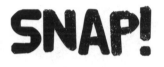

I cup my hands around my mouth and, with my every last ounce of energy, I scream, **"HUMPS! WATCH OUT!!!"**

But Humps isn't listening. He's about to deliver a Big Bertha blast to the wrecked wrangler's gut.

I grab hold of Dags and we speed toward our buddy. **"WHAT DO WE DO?"** Dagger shouts.

"We tackle! Like Humps, in a game of Agony Ball!"

An instant before Humphree can deliver the final blow, Dags and I **LEAP!**

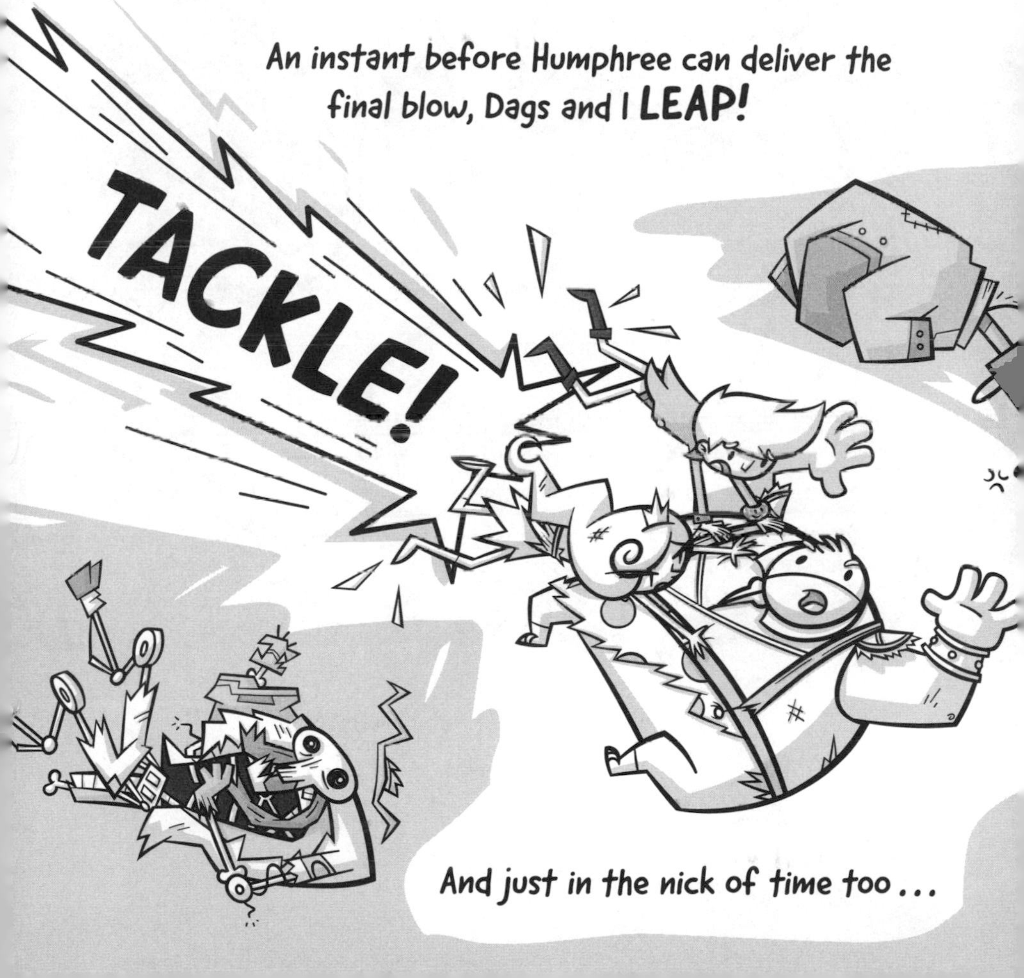
TACKLE!

And just in the nick of time too . . .

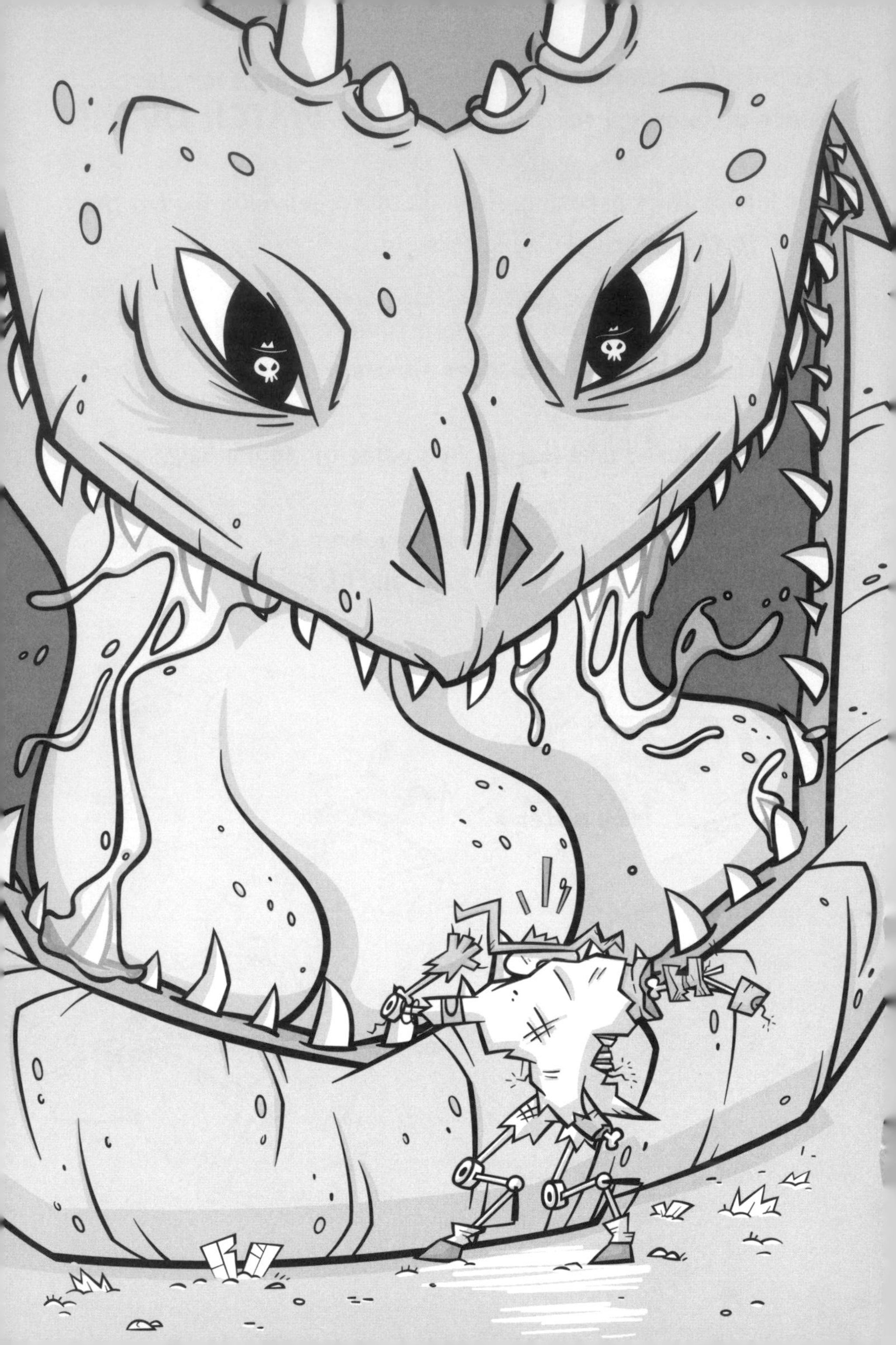

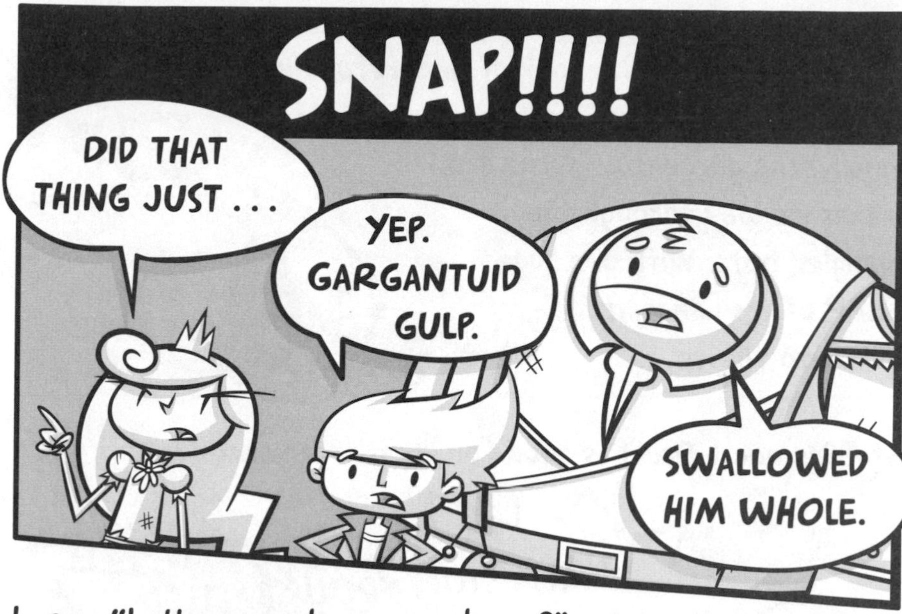
SNAP!!!!
DID THAT THING JUST . . .
YEP. GARGANTUID GULP.
SWALLOWED HIM WHOLE.

I gasp. "Is the wrangler . . . you know?"

Humphree shakes his head. "Nah. The gargantuid can't digest all that metal. The wrangler will get puked back up in a week or so. But we'll let him figure out how to get his keester off this rock . . ."

I picture that. And I can't help but grin . . .

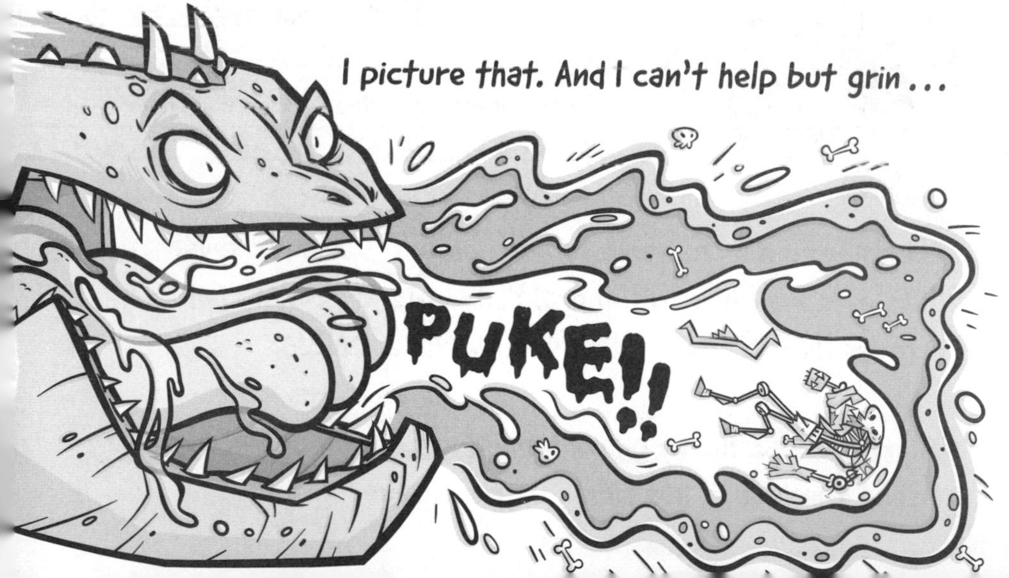
PUKE!!!

The gargantuid gives me a long look up and down. I return his stare—the look of understanding between monster and monster-tamer. Finally, the gargantuid turns and makes its way through the mangled bots. With one huge FLAP of its wings, it lifts into the air.

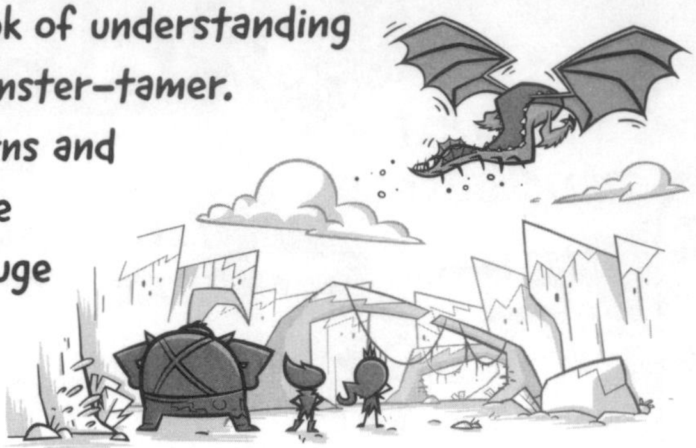

Stuff is good. Stuff is good for about two seconds, until . . .

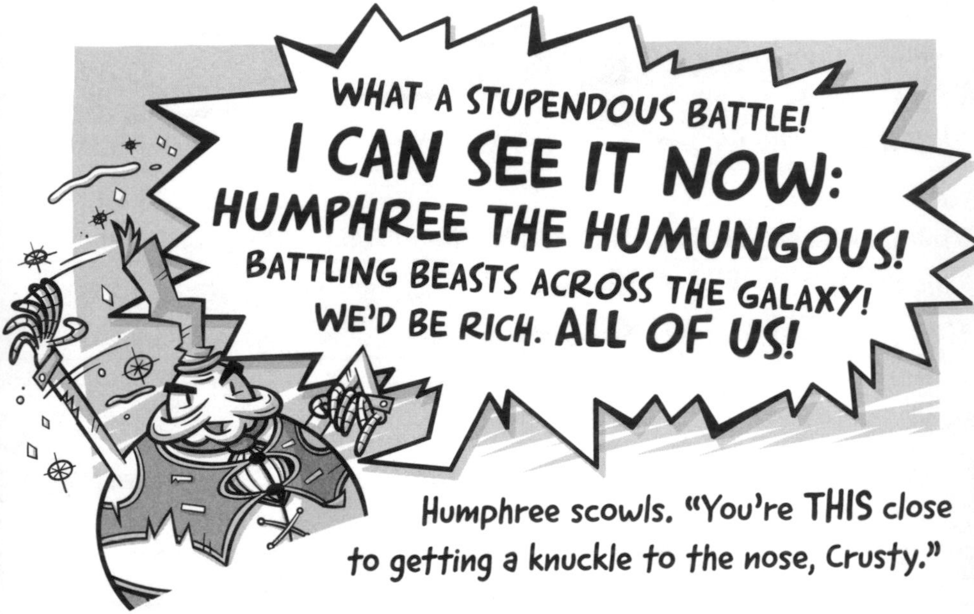

WHAT A STUPENDOUS BATTLE!
I CAN SEE IT NOW:
HUMPHREE THE HUMUNGOUS!
BATTLING BEASTS ACROSS THE GALAXY!
WE'D BE RICH. ALL OF US!

Humphree scowls. "You're THIS close to getting a knuckle to the nose, Crusty."

"Let's feed him to some super-spiders!" Dagger says. "Or let's mail him to General Krax, and Krax can drop him into his INTESTINE-INVERSION MACHINE!"

There's a low, heavy growl behind me. I look down. My furry friend the lyanux has sidled up beside me.

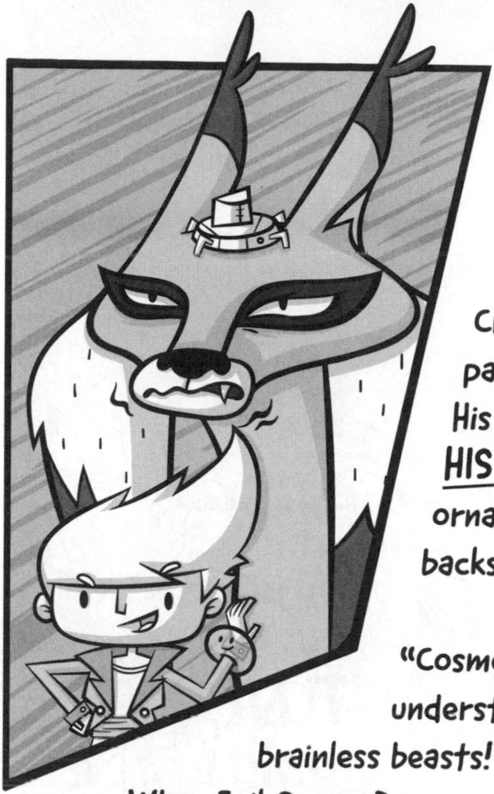

A dozen more growling creatures come forward, forming a half circle around Crostini.

Crostini's face suddenly goes pale. He skitters backward. His butt is against a train car. <u>HIS</u> train car. The luxurious, ornate home he built on the backs of these creatures.

"Cosmoe," he says, "you don't understand! Living with these brainless beasts! **IT'S AWFUL!** When Evil Queen Dagger offered me a chance to leave it behind—

SO MUCH MONEY

I had to take it! You would have done the same!"

"No," I say simply. "I **WOULDN'T** have."

More creatures are coming up behind me. More snarling and growling. I can smell the dripping saliva . . .

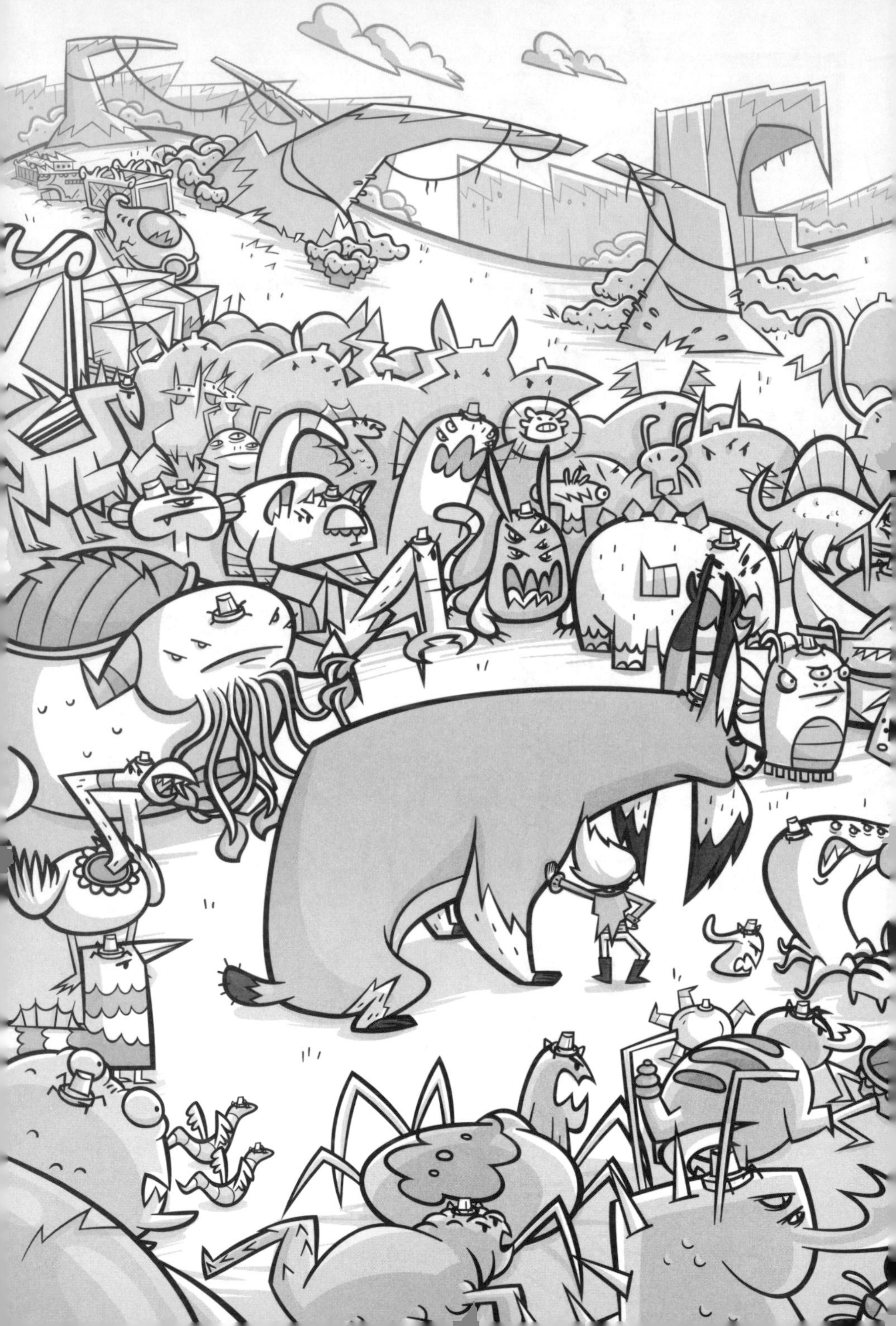

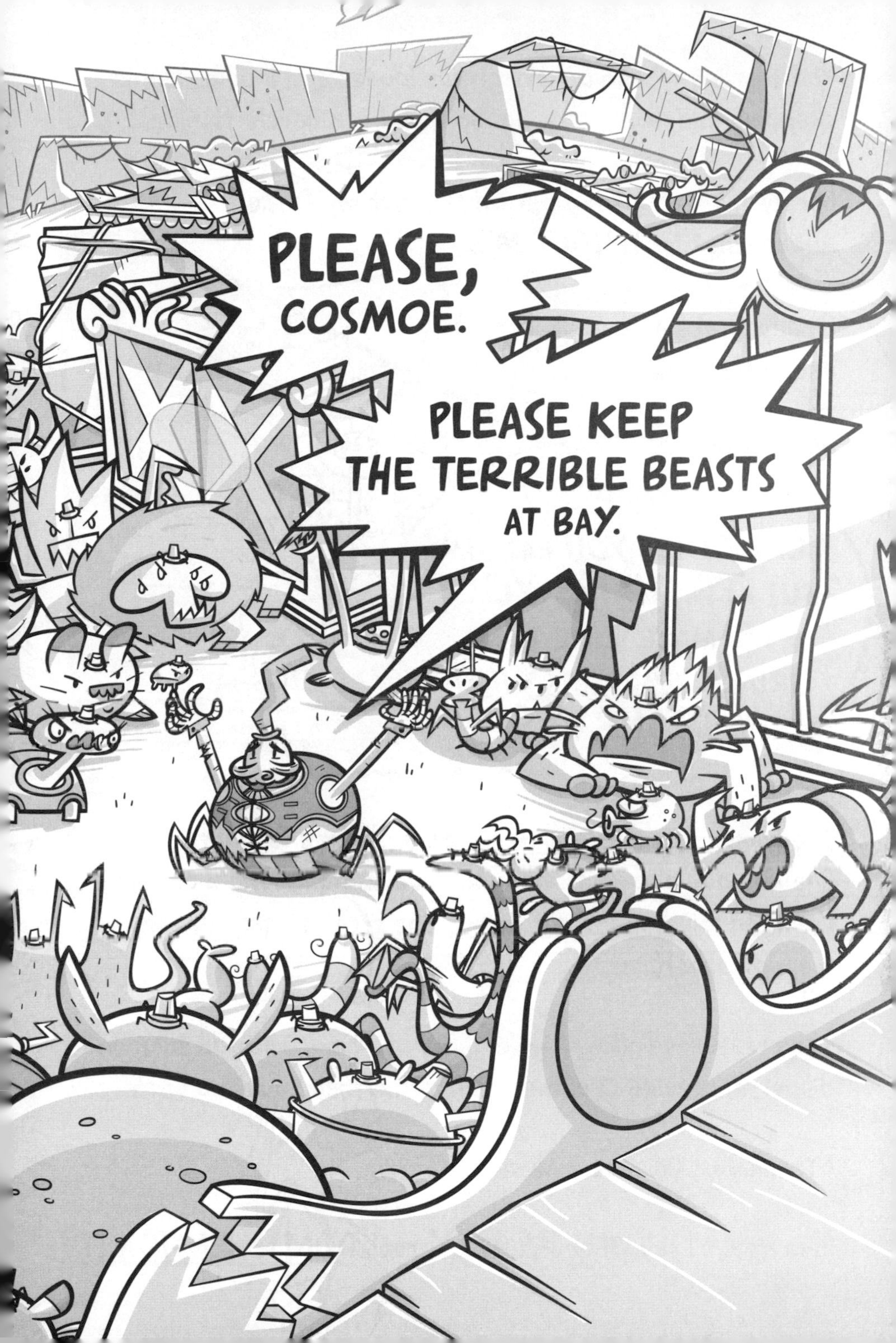
PLEASE, COSMOE.
PLEASE KEEP THE TERRIBLE BEASTS AT BAY.

The snarling of the beasts grows louder and louder. Fangs snapping and jaws clapping. So loud I can barely think...

Barely think about my parents. About my father. About what he TAUGHT ME.

Finally, I take a deep breath, and I step forward...

DUDES, I CAN'T LET YOU EAT HIM. BUT I PROMISE YOU, I'LL MAKE SURE THIS CRUMB HEAD GETS WHAT HE DESERVES.

The Iyanux watches me. Her eyes are thin and tight. She lets out a soft growl. And then, after a long moment, her head lowers, and she turns. She strides through the mass of creatures.

The creatures follow her lead. All of them. They all turn and disperse. Leaving Crostini against the train, quaking with fear.

"Thank you, Cosmoe," he says.

"For real," I say. "For REALLY real. DON'T MENTION IT."

Humphree is quick to yank Crostini to his gnarly little toes. "'Moe, you wanna load this bozo up into a blaze-cage?" Humphree says. "And make sure he isn't too comfortable. We'll drop him off at the nearest Galactic Roamer Outpost. They can deal with him."

Dagger frowns. "But the creatures were gonna tear him to bits," she says. "Would have been GREAT . . ."

"Goober, cuffs," I say, and Goober transforms into a pair of galactic spacecuffs. My rubbery buddy wraps around Crostini's wrists.

I pull him along toward the train like I'm Officer Awesome.

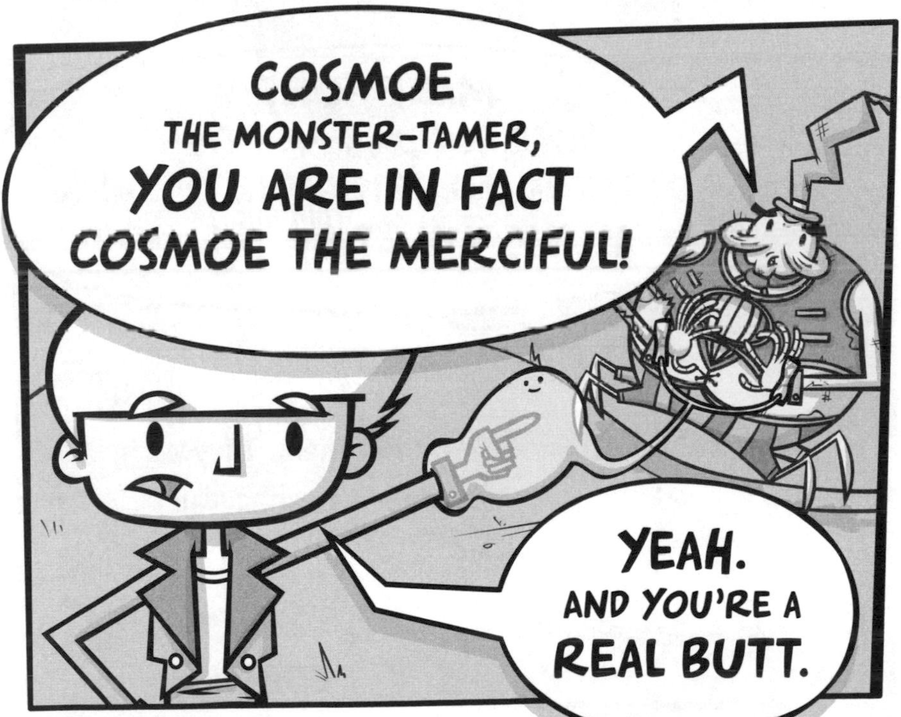
COSMOE THE MONSTER-TAMER, YOU ARE IN FACT COSMOE THE MERCIFUL!
YEAH. AND YOU'RE A REAL BUTT.

With Crostini taken care of, Humphree and F.R.E.D. get to futzing with the wiring on the roust-a-bots and clown-bots. Soon, there's a whole assembly line thing going, fixing their bad guy heads and making them into **NOT** bad guy heads.

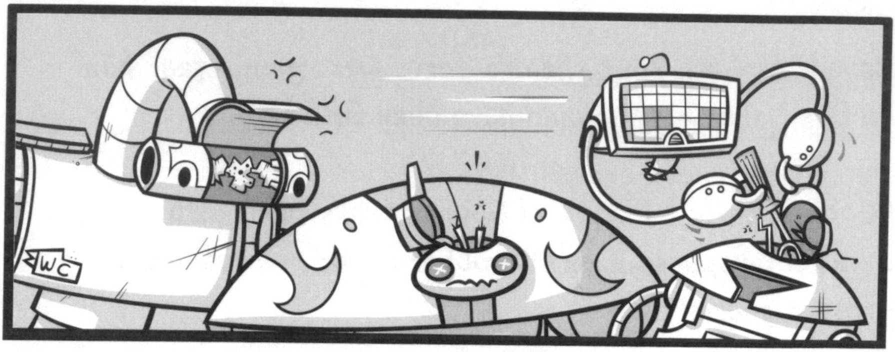

And the newly reformed bots are eager to work . . .

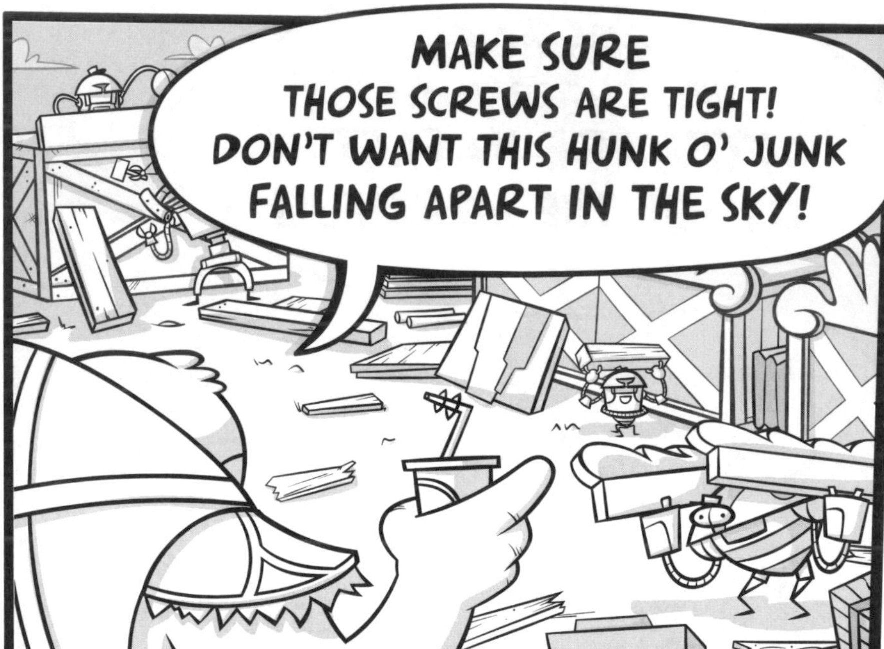
MAKE SURE THOSE SCREWS ARE TIGHT! DON'T WANT THIS HUNK O' JUNK FALLING APART IN THE SKY!

After a hot week's work, we get the train totally jam-packed full of creatures and bots. We're about to take off when I spot Dags off on her own, perched on a big blue shrub.

"Whatcha doing, Dags?" I ask, strolling over.

"Going over my Awesome Adventure Scroll," she says. "Ride a giant dragon monster thing? <u>CHECK</u>! Shut down an evil army? <u>CHECK</u>!"

"So it's coming along?" I ask.

UM. **BIG TIME.** I JUST FINALLY CHECKED OFF "**PUT THE KIBOSH ON ONE OF MY MOM'S ULTRA-EVIL** PLANS."

That's when I remember. "OH YEAH!!! The army was supposed to go to your mom."

Dagger grins. "Uh-huh. She's going to be ticked! I can almost see her now . . ."

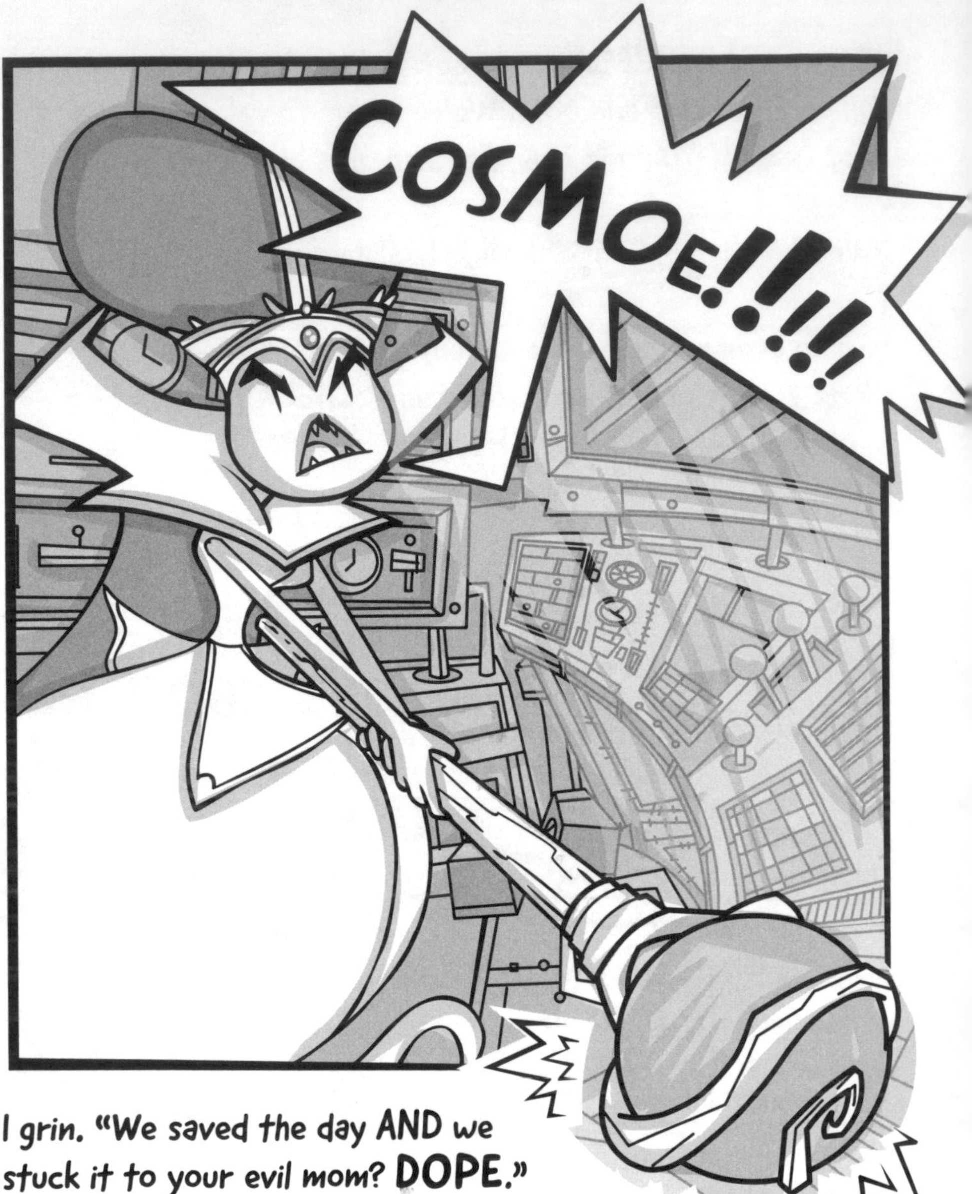
COSMOE!!!!!

I grin. "We saved the day AND we stuck it to your evil mom? **DOPE.**"

Dags smiles. "**DOUBLE DOPE**, boy!"

"C'mon, gang," Humphree calls, waving to us from the *Wiener.* "Time for us to get up off of this rock."

We pile back into the *Neon Wiener*. But as soon as I sit down at the wheel, I notice something—something that gets my lip trembling and my eyes producing salty H_2O.

But . . . I don't understand. My parents?
How could it? Where did it? And why is it on the rearview mirror?

Confused, I turn to Humphree. He grins. "Found it back on Earth. Thought you might like to have it. I put it up there on the rearview, so whenever you look back, you'll see 'em. A little bit of home, while you're flying the unfriendly skies."

I want to laugh and cry and drink a milk shake all at the same time. It's a weird feeling, and I'm not sure how to handle it. Luckily, someone interrupts me . . .

"HEY!" Dagger barks. "You two going to be a pair of **EMOTIONAL BUTT CHEEKS** all day, or are we gonna get this train into the sky?!"

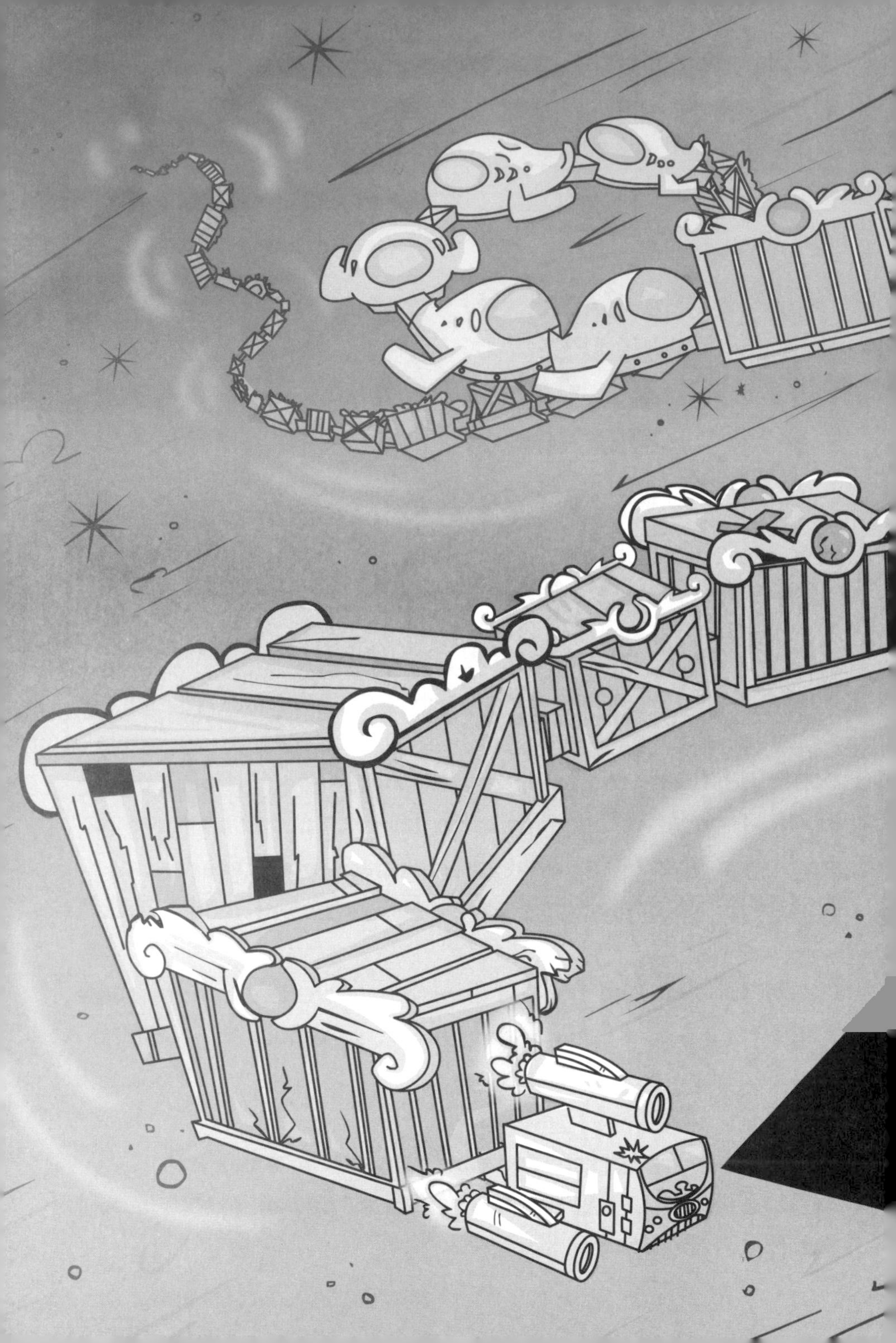

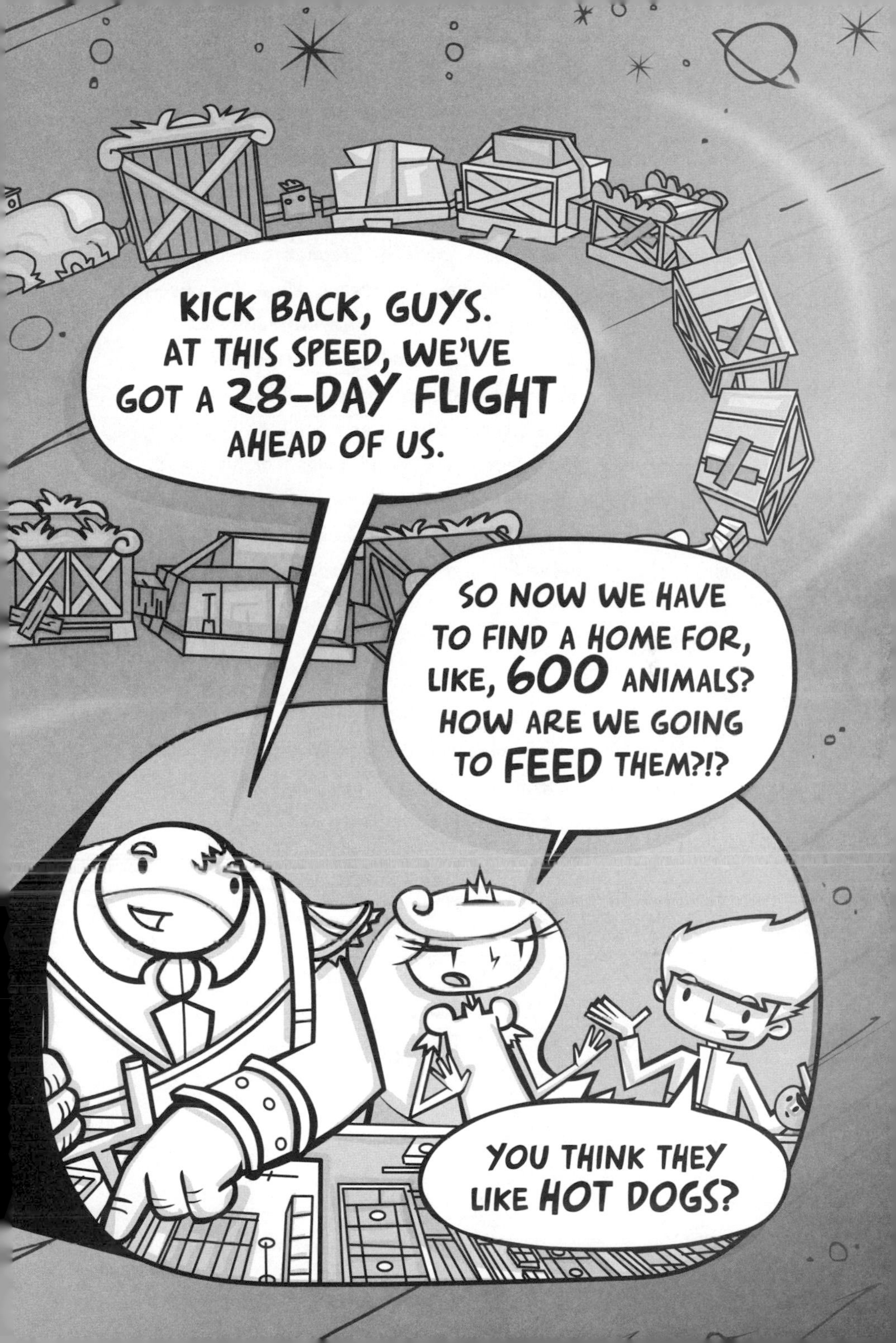
KICK BACK, GUYS. AT THIS SPEED, WE'VE GOT A 28-DAY FLIGHT AHEAD OF US.
SO NOW WE HAVE TO FIND A HOME FOR, LIKE, 600 ANIMALS? HOW ARE WE GOING TO FEED THEM?!?
YOU THINK THEY LIKE HOT DOGS?

Acknowledgments

Rachel, Nichole, and Mike—it's the killer illustrators that bring this story to life. Thank you! Jeff Faulconer, for everything—you make this job fun. Stephen Connolly and the entire FunBrain and Sandbox team. Liesa Abrams—I heart you. Dan Potash, for endless smarts. Mara Anastas, Mary Marotta, Lucille Rettino, Jodie Hockensmith, Carolyn Swerdloff, Jon Anderson, and all the other brilliant publishing minds at Simon & Schuster. Dan Lazar, Cecilia de la Campa, and everyone at Writers House. Bob Holmes, for his steady hand. My family, my friends, and my wonderful wife—thank you! And last but not least, the good folks at Think Coffee and Pushcart Coffee for letting me write, write, write.

—M. B.

The art for this illustrated novel came to exist on the shoulders of the following people: Max Brallier, Mike Rapa, Jeff Faulconer, Bob Holmes, Dan Potash, Liesa Abrams, the folks at Sandbox, and the crew at Simon & Schuster.

—R. M. & N. K.

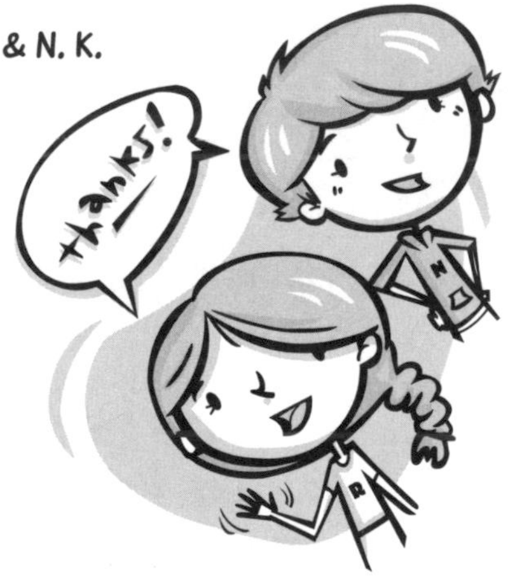
thanks!

About the Author

Max Brallier is the author of more than twenty books for children and adults, including *The Last Kids on Earth* and the Eerie Elementary series. He lives in New York City with his wife, Alyse, where he spends his time chasing fortune, glory, and the perfect hot dog.

About the Illustrators

In a realm south of Boston lives an artist armed with a whimsical drawing style and a Wacom pen. Her name is Rachel Maguire and she grew up ice-skating, frequenting libraries, and drawing from video game manuals. Previously she has designed characters, props, and backgrounds at Soup2Nuts Animation Studio on WordGirl and SciGirls, colored comics for KaBOOM!, and worked as an in-painter for The Oil Painting Conservation Studio. She currently teaches comics at the Eliot School in Boston.

Nichole Kelley does not like to define herself as any specific kind of artist. In the past she has worked professionally as an animator, illustrator, and designer. This combination has allowed her to work on a variety of awesome projects, including web animation, casual games, console games, board games, and children's illustration. In her free time she enjoys video games, board games, toys, crafting of all sorts, and sleeping. Her latest venture is learning to make glass beads and marbles.

READ MORE BOOKS BY MAX BRALLIER!

MAX BRALLIER
Author of Galactic Hot Dogs
THE LAST KIDS ON EARTH
Illustrated by
DOUGLAS HOLGATE

"TERRIFYINGLY FUN!

Max Brallier's *The Last Kids on Earth* delivers big thrills and even bigger laughs."

–JEFF KINNEY,
author of the
#1 *New York Times* bestseller
Diary of a Wimpy Kid

And check out:
THE LAST KIDS
ON EARTH
AND THE
ZOMBIE PARADE!

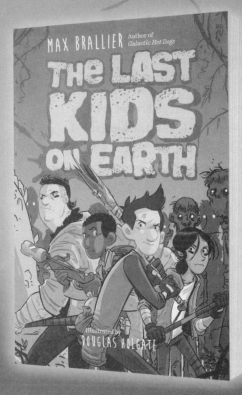

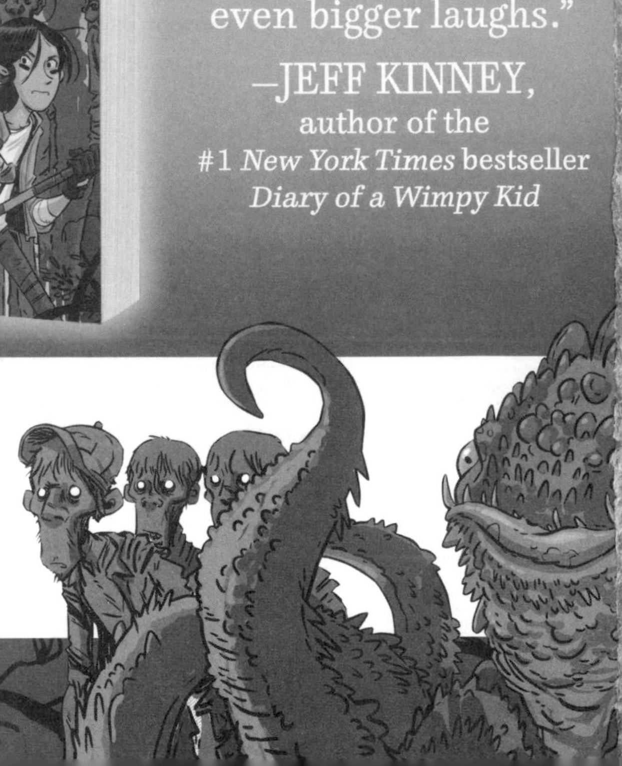